this book to and then we should do lunch! I love you to pieces! Aunt Mel

Snow White Sorrow

The Grimm Diaries Book 1

written by
Cameron Jace

Edited by Melody Benton

Copyright © 2013 Akmal Eldin Farouk Ali Shebl

ISBN-13: 978-1491292044

This book is a work of fiction. The names, characters, places, and incidents are products of the writer's imagination or have been used fictitiously and are not to be construed as real. Any resemblance to persons, living or dead, actual events, locales or organizations is entirely coincidental.

All historical facts about the Brothers Grimm, vampires, and timelines are true. Of course, the interpretations and fantasy elements aren't. They are the author's imagination.

'I guess you think you know this story.
You don't. The real one's much more gory.
The phony one, the one you know
Was cooked up years and years ago
And made to sound all soft and sappy
Just to keep the children happy'
-Ronald Dahl's Revolting Rhymes

'She'll sting you one day, Oh, ever so gently, so you hardly ever feel it. 'Til you
fall dead.'
— *Jacob Ludwig Karl Grimm*

'Have you ever been in love? Horrible isn't it?
It makes you so vulnerable'
-Neil Gaiman

Table of Contents

1
The Boy Who is a Shadow

The children of the town of Hamlin loved Charmwill Glimmer, famously known for being the greatest storyteller in the world. Unlike Santa Claus, Charmwill didn't walk around with a sack full of gifts and wonders. Instead, he arrived with a parrot on his shoulder. The children giggled because they knew that it wasn't an ordinary parrot. It was an enchanted book, which carried almost every fairy tale ever told.

Before Charmwill began reading, the parrot's green wings magically transformed into the book's cover, the yellow feathers turned into pages the color of old treasure maps, its backbone into the book's spine, and its claws laced together into an obsidian lock that guarded the tales between the pages.

Charmwill unlocked the book by knocking on the parrot's beak, which now stuck out of the middle of the book's front cover like a doorknob. He knocked five consecutive times on it: *tic-to-tic-tac-toc!*

Once opened, Charmwill rested the book on his lap. Then he pulled out a golden comb and smoothed his long silver hair and beard. The children enjoyed playing with his beard, pulling it slightly and feeling its cottony texture. Charmwill didn't mind. He joked that if he ever shaved it, he'd turn it into a marvelous pillow they could rest their heads upon while listening to his bedtime stories.

When the children had enough playing, Charmwill read them the most wonderful tales from his enchanted book, which he called the Book of Beautiful Lies.

The children's eyes gleamed and widened, listening to his stern yet sweet voice. Charmwill's wondrous tales had everything they were looking for: castles, dragons, villains, evil stepmothers, witches, enchanted frogs, unicorns, godmothers, pumpkins, coaches, candy, forests, mermaids, giants, dwarves, elves, breadcrumbs, princesses, princes, and of course true love kisses, which were Charmwill's favorite part.

But the tales also had other elements the children liked. They told of scary things like vampires, werewolves, demons, monsters, shape shifters, boogeymen, secret societies, and forbidden powers which they had never heard spoken of in fairy tales before. It was what made Charmwill's stories fantastic, fabulous, and their favorite.

Between chapters, Charmwill Glimmer smoked his pipe. It was a special pipe, filled with Dragonbreath, which gave him certain powers. Like wizards had their own powers to face their enemies, the world of storytellers was the same, if not more interesting and adventurous. There were dark forces that didn't want the world to know the truth about the fairy tales in Charmwill's book. These evil forces were looking for him so they could steal it, but the man was smart and hard to find. He'd even called it The Book of Beautiful Lies to elude them, for in reality, the book didn't tell lies, but only the untold truth about fairy tales.

"I love your fairy tales, Mr. Charmwill," a little boy said. "They're not like the stories my grandma told me."

"That's because your grandma leaves out the scary parts," Charmwill took a drag from his pipe, "which are the awesome parts."

The children giggled.

"Your stories are so much fun," a little girl said while sitting among the other kids around the fire. "They're like poisoned apples. Once you taste them, you will never think of fairy tales the same way again."

Sometimes, Charmwill picked one of the parrot's feathers and used it as a quill for writing in the book. He used a peculiar ink, which looked like blood. When the children asked him why the stories he collected were written in blood, Charmwill said it was an ancient tradition to remind the storyteller that fairy tale characters weren't fictional, but in fact were real enough to bleed.

"So why can't we meet them?" a boy asked, resting his head on his bent knees.

"Because they aren't awake yet," Charmwill said.

"How long will they stay asleep?" one of the kids asked.

"That's a long story. All you need to know is that the fairy tale characters were cursed into an eternal sleep centuries ago. They can only wake up for a little time every one hundred years, and that's when you can meet them."

"You mean the way Sleeping Beauty was cursed to sleep for a hundred years?" a girl asked.

"Yes, indeed," Charmwill chuckled. He loved smart children for they usually figured out things much faster than the adults. "It's called the Sleeping Death," Charmwill whispered, drawing a serious face.

"The Sleeping Death?" the children chimed in unison, exchanging worried looks.

Charmwill nodded.

"So how soon until they wake up again?" another boy asked.

"It's just about time," Charmwill glanced at his pocket watch, which showed a sun and a moon inside. "Very soon, they will all wake up again in our world. Not all of them will remember who they are, though."

"Can't we remind them?" a girl suggested.

"I wouldn't recommend that," Charmwill said. "There is a big war going on in the fairytale world. Besides, many of them have become wicked and dangerous. We might not want to wake those characters up."

"Like the Wicked Stepmother?" a girl said.

"Or the witch from Hansel and Gretel?" a boy asked.

"And many more," Charmwill said. He looked as if he remembered something that happened long ago but couldn't forget. "Actually, some of the fairy tales we think of as the loveliest have become the scariest, and the other way around."

After Charmwill finished reading, he locked the book and threw it in the air, watching the pages flutter like a bird's wings then transform into a parrot again. The children clapped their hands as if he were a magician showing them his latest trick.

Charmwill called his parrot Pickwick. It was mute.

The children were sad that Charmwill and Pickwick had to leave for another town.

"Do you really have to go, Mr. Charmwill?" a little girl asked him, pulling on his cloak.

"Yes, I have to," he said. "Old Charmwill Glimmer has to take care of other kids, too. I also have to seek and collect more tales so I can read them for you next Christmas."

"So you're going to visit us the same time Santa Claus does?" a girl with a lisp, asked. Charmwill liked the sound of the words *Thanta Clauth* on her lips.

"Maybe," Charmwill tilted his head. "I'd really like to talk to him about sneaking into people's houses without permission."

Some of the children snickered.

"We like you better," said a girl with a missing front tooth. "We never get to meet Santa in person, but you, we can see and talk to, which is much better."

"Can't you at least tell us where you're going? We could sneak out of this awful town and visit you wherever you are," a boy suggested.

Sighing, Charmwill tucked his hand-held reading glasses in his pocket, rubbed his puffy eyes, stood up using his cane, and lit his Dragonbreath pipe again. "I'm afraid you can't come with me because I am going to sail to a faraway place."

"Does it have an address?" the kids asked.

"But of course, it does. It's located East of the Sun, West of the Moon," Charmwill explained.

"East of the Sun, West of the Moon?" the children wondered. "How can we get there? You have a map?"

"It's really hard to find, and no map can get you there. Only a few special people, like fairy tale characters, know about it."

"Wow!" the children's eyes widened. "Are there other children like us there?"

"Yes, only a little older," Charmwill nodded. "I am going to look for a very special boy there."

"A boy?" they asked.

3

"Yes, the Boy Who is a Shadow," he whispered to the children. "But don't tell anyone, not even Santa. It's our secret."

The children cupped their hands over their mouths as if it was the only way they could keep such a secret. No one had ever shared secrets with them before, and they weren't sure they could keep one.

"Why is this boy so *thpethia?*" asked the lisping girl.

"Because he might be able to save the Fairyworld," Charmwill said.

"From whom?" they asked.

"From *her*, I prefer not to say her name," Charmwill puffed his pipe then coughed. He'd never been fond of talking about her, and it always got colder when her name came up. Even though he hadn't revealed her name, the children felt a sudden chill fill the air. A crow cawed somewhere while the trees rustled around them. The Children took a step away from Charmwill as if they'd sensed her vicious presence on his breath.

"Is she a witch?" asked the girl with the missing tooth. She was the bravest girl in the pack, standing in the front line, spreading her protective arms on both sides.

"I'm afraid if I talk more about her, you'd have nightmares," Charmwill said. "She has her way with dreams, feeding on the dreams of the young sometimes."

"Then will you tell us about The Boy Who is a Shadow before you go?" asked the lisping girl, "*Pleath?*"

"I can't, because the boy's story hasn't been written yet," Charmwill patted the child as she took a step back toward him. "The Boy Who is a Shadow is the only one who can write his story, depending on the choices he will make and the destiny he will choose."

"Choices?" the missing-tooth girl wondered.

"Destiny?" another boy scratched his head.

The children questioned each other to see if anyone knew about what 'choices' or 'destiny' meant. They were new words to them. In the town of Hamlin where they lived, they weren't allowed to ask their parents too many questions or oppose their way of thinking.

"Is this boy going to be famous? A hero, maybe?" a girl asked.

"Hmm…" Charmwill fiddled with his beard then coughed. Smoking Dragonbreath wasn't easy. "It's prophesized that the boy should be a hero, but it's up to him to choose. Prophecies don't come true unless we make them."

Before Charmwill left, he gave the children enchanted candy that would turn their dreams into fairy tales until he visited again. He also gave each one a Book of Sand, which was a small book that carried a single fairy tale. Once a child read a page, it dissolved into sand. Once they finished it the covers of the book turned to dust.

With Pickwick on his shoulder, Charmwill walked to the river Weser, climbed inside his small canoe—which sometimes transformed into a swan—and rowed toward the North Sea.

Charmwill watched Pickwick flutter freely in the skies above. It reminded him why he had created the book enchantment for the parrot long ago. If anything bad ever happened to Charmwill, Pickwick was the world's savior of true fairy tales; he'd be fluttering high in the sky, and as long as the tales were kept from being altered, they'd eventually find the children somehow so they could read them and retell them. Pickwick didn't realize that he carried the most treasured scripture known to mankind.

While rowing in the North Sea, a thick fog floated upon the water in the distance. Charmwill stopped smoking and tapped his pipe twice, then watched it turn into a magic willow pipe, which produced a sound like chirping birds that only Pickwick could hear. The parrot responded to the call and landed back on Charmwill's shoulder, sharing his stare at the fog that was spreading an eerie feeling over the sea like a dense layer of wavy ghosts. Pickwick looked worried.

"It's alright. Don't fear the fog, Pickwick," Charmwill tapped Pickwick's toenails gently then continued rowing into the fog. "I know this place. It's safe. It's only another dimension, not known to the people in the Ordinary World."

A big tide struck but Charmwill managed to ride it easily with his magical canoe. When it passed, Pickwick saw a black fish with two golden bottle caps for eyes, floating on the water. It had a signpost on its back which read:

Welcome to the Missing Mile
East of the Sun, West of the Moon

Charmwill pulled out his compass, which didn't point to directions known in the Ordinary World. It pointed to the unseen realm of fairy tales, which was hidden from humans. Charmwill liked to call it the Fairyworld.

Finally, the fog subsided and only then could they make out that the blue sea was filled with enormous dragons that people rode instead of ships. Others rowed in smaller swans and used them like Charmwill used his canoe—which had turned into a swan once they'd crossed.

There were also floating houses in the Missing Mile; they were small whales. When the residents entered the whale through its mouth, its jaws closed behind them. All whales sank deep into the water for privacy at night. Pickwick smiled when he heard the password for opening a whale's mouth was knocking on it five times: *tic-to-tic-to-toc*.

5

Pickwick had never seen such a place before. He wondered why Charmwill hadn't talked about it earlier, and why he decided to visit it today.

"The Missing Mile is a bit vacant now," Charmwill educated Pickwick. "It's because the fairy tale characters are still asleep. The few of them who are awake, are either lost or dealing with their own problems. You have no idea, Pickwick, how important this place is. It only comes alive for a small period of time every one hundred years."

Pickwick saw a train emerging out of the fog behind them. It seemed like it was coming from the Ordinary World. It was a huge train that ran on rails which floated on the water, passing through the Missing Mile without stopping, until it reached an island in the distance.

Pickwick saw that the island rested on the back of a huge whale that seemed forever asleep. The train disappeared into the island, and Pickwick saw turrets rising high out of a castle in the middle of it. The island itself was exactly in the middle of the Missing Mile, surrounded by water.

"Ah," Charmwill announced. "I see you're looking at the Island of Sorrow. Don't worry, the whale it rests on rarely wakes up."

Pickwick waited for Charmwill to tell him more about the island but it was clear that he wasn't going to, because he was there only for the boy.

The parrot watched the magical world with his eyes almost bulging out. Then Pickwick saw the mermaids in the Missing Mile. They were so beautiful they almost took his breath away; swimming gracefully between the ships, giggling, whispering, and splashing water at Charmwill. They jumped out of the water like dolphins, welcoming the old man and his parrot to the Missing Mile. Wishing he could play with them, Pickwick squawked instead. The mermaids giggled again, covering their mouths with their wet hands as if they weren't supposed to be in the presence of old man Charmwill.

"It would be better if you don't stare at the mermaids too long," Charmwill warned Pickwick. "I know they're beautiful, but they can read your mind if you let them stare into your eyes. They're curious about the secret stories you keep inside you, and eyes are windows to the soul."

Pickwick fluttered his wings with obedience and closed his eyes, straightened his back, and pulled his chin high, away from the mermaids.

"Good parrot," Charmwill said then wet his forefinger with his tongue and held it out to test the wind. "It's a beautiful day in the Fairyworld."

Charmwill continued rowing toward a Dragonship surrounded with floating glass coffins, which were half-filled with water. He stopped near a specific coffin and looked at a black, wavy shadow of a boy inside. The shadow had been chained as if it was capable of escaping, and the coffin was guarded by two mermaids. Pickwick shrugged. He had never seen such a thing before. The shadow seemed in pain, trying to free itself.

"The Boy Who is a Shadow," Charmwill muttered as he climbed the zigzagged dragon's tale up the ship's deck—which was the dragon's back. Sometimes, in the middle of sailing, dragons needed to take a nap, and that was when they came to a stop in the water. Pickwick wondered if they breathed fire when they snored.

Following Charmwill, Pickwick saw an old woman sitting on the deck. Her skin was tanned and her hair was a mesh of black-and-white. She had a weary look on her face, and it appeared as if she hadn't been properly introduced to a comb before. Pickwick thought Charmwill should lend her his golden comb, but couldn't tell him.

The woman on the deck was blindfolded, sitting in front of a scale that carried apples in one pan and snakes in the other. Although the apples outnumbered the thin snakes, the snakes were still heavier, pulling the scale down to their side.

"Charmwill, my dear," the woman welcomed them as a playful mermaid splashed more water, somersaulting from one side of the ship to the other. The woman shushed it away.

"Godmother Justina," Charmwill bowed his head, paying his respects.

"Who's your friend?" Justina asked, adding an apple to the scale, which still leaned toward the snakes. "Never saw you with a parrot before."

"That's because it's been a hundred years since we last met. I found him and enchanted him years ago," Charmwill chuckled. "I call him Pickwick."

"I am Pickwick," the parrot squawked. "And I am mute!"

"Interesting," Justina said. "A parrot that is mute, but actually isn't."

"It's the only phrase it can say," Charmwill explained. "Other than that, it is mute."

"And may I ask why you've bestowed such misery upon your parrot?"

"Because it's also my Book of Beautiful Lies," Charmwill said. "Parrots tend to talk too much, so I thought I'd enchant it with eternal silence."

Pickwick folded his wings like humans fold their arms in front of their chest. He looked away, displeased.

"Then you shouldn't have chosen a parrot in the first place," Justina mused. "But you're charming Charmwill. You always do things your way, and I won't argue with you. Nice to meet you, Pickwick," she nodded toward the parrot as if she could see. "I am the Justice Godmother of the Fairyworld, but as you see I've been blinded by the dark forces, trying to spread evil into our world," Justina sighed at the irony. "I'm blindfolded, and you're mute. We might be the perfect match."

The mermaids let out a sympathizing whistle.

"Any luck with balancing the good and evil in the Fairyworld?" Charmwill wondered. He knew the apples resembled the good, and the snakes represented evil.

Godmother Justina kept silent for a moment. She had been trying her best to balance good and evil, but the evil in the Fairyworld, however little, caused a lot of mischief.

"So tell me, Charmwill. What brings you to the Missing Mile?" Justina asked, rummaging in a basket next to her for a healthy apple to balance the scale.

Charmwill put his hand-held glasses back on, walked to the edge of the ship, and looked down at the coffin with the shadow of a boy in it. "I came to free the boy," he said.

"What boy?"

"The Boy Who is a Shadow," Charmwill looked back at her.

"Loki?"

"Yes, Godmother," Charmwill nodded. "I came to free him from being shadowed, and give him a second chance in life."

"And why would you want to do that?" she wondered. "You know this boy has great darkness in him. That's why he was banned from Fairy Heaven. He's been sentenced to be shadowed for eternity."

"Eternity?" Charmwill narrowed his eyebrows.

"When an immortal, particularly a half-angel, sins, his soul is turned into a shadow as punishment: forever. His shadow is very strong though; that's why it's chained."

"I can't believe you did that to a fifteen year old boy," Charmwill said.

"It was the right thing to do, or the darkness inside him would have taken over his soul, and the consequences would be irreversible."

"He is mentioned in the prophecy," Charmwill said. "This boy is going to help save the Fairyworld. How could the Council of Fairy Heaven do that to him?"

Pickwick had never seen his master so upset.

"It looks like the prophecy was false," Justina said, adding half an apple to the scale. Still, the snakes won. "The boy has proven that by defying the Council's orders. You know what he did, Charmwill."

"I don't care what he did," Charmwill said. Pickwick was curious as to what the boy did to be punished. "He was one of the best Dreamhunters ever. He killed many demons, defending the Fairyworld."

"That was before he fell in love with a demon girl," Justina said. "Disobeying the Council of Heaven is the worst thing a half-angel can do," Justina sighed. "In Loki's case, the phrase 'like father like son' proves to be true."

"Are you saying that because his father also fell for a demon girl?" Charmwill asked.

"Although his father was a pure angel, we both know that he defied the Council of Heaven, too, when he married Loki's mother, a demon girl as well," Justina said. "Can't you see it runs in the family?"

"I still have faith in the prophecy, Godmother. I still want to free the boy," Charmwill said.

"You don't understand," Justina said as she rummaged in the basket, desperately wanting to balance apples and snakes. She had picked the ripest, red apple from a basket to create a balance, but without success. The problem was that the snakes grew bigger and heavier whenever she added an apple to the scale. It made her mission impossible. She found a rotten apple in the basket with a worm climbing out of a hole in it. "This boy you're trying to save is like this rotten apple," she sighed, about to throw it away.

"Wait!" Charmwill said. "I see you've failed to balance the scale with the ripe apples. Would you accept a suggestion on my behalf, Godmother Justina?"

"And that would be?"

"Why don't you try using the apple in your hand?" Charmwill said.

"You mean this rotten apple?" Justina shook her head, "no way."

"Just trust me," Charmwill said. "You compared it to the boy, remember? What if it balances your scale? Would that change your mind about him?"

"Charmwill, Charmwill, Charmwill," Justina exhaled. "You're always trying to see the ripe in the world, even when it's rotten. I will do it, only to prove you wrong."

The Godmother added the rotten apple to the scale. It didn't work. But before she could comment, Charmwill shushed her and pointed at the worm climbing out of the apple, gliding over to the snakes. Surprisingly, the little, helpless worm freaked out a couple of snakes, scaring them out of the pan, balancing the scale in turn.

"Some worm," Justina said.

Pickwick really wished he could talk now, and scream that Justina could not be blind. How did she know about the worm? Instead, Pickwick occupied himself with the rotten apple healing itself afterwards.

"See? I told you," Charmwill said, and pulled out his pipe. He felt proud, puffing Dragonbreath in the air. The ship shook slightly when he did, and Pickwick wondered if the dragon waking up. "Like the apple, you should give the boy a chance. All the apple needed was to get that worm out of it. In fact, the darkness inside the boy could be the weapon he could use against evil if nurtured and taken care of, if you only let me show him the way."

"Alright," Justina gave up, waving her hands in the air, almost blushing. "I'll free the boy, but under the three conditions of the Council of Fairy Heaven."

"I'll do whatever it takes," Charmwill winked at Pickwick with a victorious smirk, still drawing on his pipe. Pickwick winked back.

"Rule number one is that the boy will be sent to the Ordinary World as a mortal, which means he could die like any other human," Justina said.

"Agreed," Charmwill said with the pipe in his mouth.

"Rule number two: the boy will be sent to the Ordinary World without previous memories. He will not remember anything about his past. You will have to tell him that he's a half-angel that used to live in Fairy Heaven, though."

"That's a bit contradictory," Charmwill commented. "Why would I torture him by telling him he was banned from Fairy Heaven if he is destined to live as an amnesiac mortal?"

"Because of rule number three, which is that he has a choice to continue living as a mortal in the Ordinary World or seek forgiveness and go back to Fairy Heaven." Justina said. "In that case, erasing his memories is for his own good, so he doesn't think about the girl that got him banned."

Charmwill rubbed his chin, "I thought that he was doomed not to be forgiven. What has changed?"

"Your desire to save him is what changed," Justina said. "If someone as prestigious as you has decided the boy should be saved, why not give him a chance to repent? As Justice, I believe in wrong and right, but I also believe in strong willed hearts."

"And what does he have to do exactly to be forgiven if he ever chooses to return to Fairy Heaven?" Charmwill said.

"He has to kill ninety-nine vampires in the Ordinary World," the Godmother raised a forefinger in the air.

"Ninety-nine vampires?" Charmwill's heart missed a beat. "That's an absurd amount to kill for a mortal without powers."

"These are the rules upon which I am allowed to unshadow him. You will have to teach him to be a mortal vampire hunter, and if he desires returning home, free and forgiven, he will have to do as I said."

Charmwill considered the offer for a moment, looking down at Loki's chained shadow. "Like I said, I accept," he nodded back at the Godmother who signaled to the mermaids to pull the coffin up to the ship.

The mermaids opened the glass coffin, hypnotized Loki by staring at his shadow a tad too long, and freed him from his chains. Charmwill knocked on Pickwick's beak, *tic-to-tic-tac-toc*, and it turned into a book, which he started drawing in. As he drew, Loki began to come back to life, taking the form of the human Charmwill designed in his book.

"You're not planning to change his looks in the Ordinary World, are you?" Justina asked.

"Not at all," Charmwill said, turning the book back into Pickwick. "I only gave him black hair, instead of blonde, as the prophecy reads."

One of the mermaids wrapped a thin necklace made of seashells around Loki's neck and kissed his mouth, murmuring something about the second life the boy was just given. It was part of the waking ritual. Everyone stared at the unconscious boy in the glass coffin because he looked like a male sleeping beauty.

Within minutes, the mermaid's kiss would wake Loki up for the second time in his life. He was going to be reborn, and have another chance in the Ordinary World. The mermaids couldn't stop staring at him. There was something mysterious about Loki that made them believe that he would save the Fairyworld from the imminent evil that was prophesized. Pickwick was sad that Loki would wake up in the Ordinary World oblivious to all of this.

"What are those black tattoos he has on each shoulder?" Charmwill asked.

"They are black stars," Justina said, "it's how the Council of Heaven brands banned angels—or half-angels in his case. It will stick with him until he kills the ninety-nine demons or dies as a Minikin."

Pickwick raised his eyebrows because he didn't know what a Minikin was.

"We call ordinary people who aren't related to the Fairyworld Minikins," Charmwill explained to Pickwick. "'Kin' means ordinary human in our fairy language, and 'mini' means small and helpless. So, why does he have two tattoos, and why are they on his shoulders?" Charmwill turned back to Justina.

"They're placed where he would have grown wings if he'd passed the age of sixteen without breaking the Council's rules, and would have been promoted to angel," Justina explained.

Charmwill didn't comment. He ordered the mermaids to move Loki to his canoe so he could sail him back through the fog to the Ordinary World.

He is also not allowed to use his last name," Justina said. "Will you choose a new one for him?"

"Blackstar," Charmwill smiled, looking at a sleeping Loki. "Loki Blackstar. I like it," he added as he turned around to walk away, "sounds badass."

"What did you just say, Charmwill?" Justina looked furious.

"It's just a word I learned in the Ordinary World," Charmwill blushed. He wasn't supposed to say such words in her presence. "It means...nobleman."

The mermaids and Pickwick snickered for they knew that the word meant otherwise.

"Yes, he's going to be badass," one of the mermaids agreed.

"Oh," Justina said. "One last thing, Charmwill," she said. "Can I ask you why you're doing this? Really? Saving a damned boy? There must be another reason than just believing in a prophecy."

"Of course, there is, Godmother Justina, and it's very simple,"

Charmwill said stepping down the zigzagged dragon's tail. "No one deserves to die before knowing who they really are."

Charmwill climbed into his canoe and rowed away with Pickwick and the Boy Who was a Shadow. Soon the boy would wake up and Charmwill would have to teach him a lot of things. He raised a finger again to test the wind and commented on how the day had gotten even better. A smile landed upon his face as he puffed on the pipe again.

"I hope Godmother doesn't find out that I enchanted the rotten apple. It's a little magic I learned," Charmwill told Pickwick. "She thinks she can balance the good and evil in the world by sitting on her lazy butt next to her scale. Little does she know that it needs courageous and dedicated people with strong hearts to outsmart evil in this world. I have a feeling only two kids in the world can do that. One of them is Loki Blackstar; the Boy Who *was* a Shadow."

Deadly Ever After

The masquerade party bustled with teens at the secluded Haunted House at 112 Ocean Avenue. The place was decorated like the setting of a cheap horror movie. Everyone was disguised as a fractured fairy tale character mixed with unusual vampires and other legendary monsters.

A screaming Cinderella ran up the stairs. She held the rim of her blood-spattered dress while the wooden steps creaked underneath her. Her predator, a Prince Charming with fangs, climbed after her with a chainsaw.

"I love you, and can't live without you. Kiss me or die. Mua, ha, ha!" Prince Charming proclaimed.

Cinderella threw him a flirty look over her shoulder before he caught her by her dress and pulled her a step down to him. He rolled her back into his arms theatrically and embraced her. Instead of killing her with the chainsaw, or kissing her, Prince Charming bit Cinderella on the neck, a true love's bite.

Everyone at the party cheered happily. Boys and girls saluted the couple on the stairs, raising their half-filled glasses in the air while pink silly-string poured from the second floor. The bass in the music throbbed like a mad frog, croaking from inside the walls, and everyone danced frantically. A girl's dress, smeared with blood-like red syrup, hung loose like a crescent moon from the ceiling. It had the party's theme written on it:

Deadly Ever After

And a little below, it read:

Dead is the new cool.

"Silly Minikins," Loki mumbled, gazing at the kissing couple up the stairs. They were making out now; biting was only an appetizer. Loki was leaning against the kitchen door with tensed up shoulders, hands in his pockets. He was trying his best to avoid the girl who'd spilled her drink on him minutes ago. "Why did they have to ban me here in a world where I don't belong?" he sighed, staring upward, which he often did when he had no one to talk to. The ceiling never replied.

Another girl bumped into Loki, spilling her drink on him, too. She wore pink bunny ears and had a moustache drawn on her face. Loki closed his eyes and pursed his lips, swallowing his anger like a bitter pill. "I'm *so* sorry," the girl said, poking her head out from under her boyfriend's armpit. "I hope I didn't ruin the party for you."

Loki opened his eyes and lowered his head, then gazed at her with a fake smile on his face. He wanted to show her how irritated he was, but Charmwill Glimmer, his guardian, had told him he wasn't allowed to express his anger toward the Minikins while he was in the Ordinary World or he wouldn't be allowed back into Fairy Heaven. Loki had to pretend he liked them.

"I couldn't be happier," Loki said; the smile still stamped on his face. In his mind, he imagined slapping her with frog legs across her cheeks until all she could say was *bbblllrrr*—Loki hated frogs, so he couldn't think of a better punishment.

The girl with bunny ears checked out Loki from top to bottom. "Yummy," she said, licking her strawberry-stained lips, unable to take her eyes off his outfit.

While everyone else was disguised as vampires, werewolves and fractured fairy tale characters, Loki wore a Scottish kilt, which made him look out of place. He didn't care.

"Why the kilt?" the latest girl inquired, shooing her boyfriend away. Loki took a step back. He wasn't fond of girls, especially curious ones; in his experience, they usually were demons in disguise. He was told he was banned from Heaven because he loved a demon girl, so was he always on high alert.

"I am a vampire hunter," Loki said, still plastering the fake smile on his lips.

"What do you hunt?" she asked again, eager to make conversation.

"Beetles," Loki tilted his head, wondering why she didn't laugh and leave him be. He'd been unshadowed for almost a year now, and if there was one thing he'd learned about Minikins it was that they hardly ever picked up on verbal signs.

"Ah, sorry, I drank too much tonight," the girl dressed as a bunny said. "But you're funny…and cute. I didn't know vampire hunters wore kilts."

"I hide my stake underneath it. It's my secret trick," he winked at her. *Now, please go.*

It was true. Loki had even told the bouncer at the door that he was hiding a stake underneath the kilt. The big man had laughed at what he thought was Loki's sarcastic joke. It frustrated Loki when he wasn't taken seriously, even if it had helped him fool the bouncer and enter the party with his hidden stake.

Loki wasn't there to celebrate true love kisses or document the Minikins' preposterous behaviors, lives, love, parties or otherwise. He had one thing on his mind; to stake the vampire he was hired to kill, grab some cash to pay for school, and get a bit closer to finishing off the ninety-nine vampires he had to kill before his sixteenth birthday. Today's vampire was going to be number thirty-eight.

"Stake? You got a stake under the kilt?" the girl's eyes shone brighter, taking a step closer.

"Hit the road, or I'll rip your ears off," another girl, wearing a latex devil costume interrupted. She sneered at the girl with bunny ears and pushed her away. It was Lucy Rumpelstein, the girl who hired Loki to kill the vampire tonight. "He's mine," Lucy grinned, pursing her heart shaped lips. The bunny girl showed displeasure at the interruption, but walked away immediately.

Somehow, Lucy had a messed up idea about fairy tales, which led to her wearing the devil costume. It was an expensive one, with horns, white fur and silver sequins around her neck. Loki thought she was as weird as the rest, but he didn't mind when it meant an opportunity to kill another vampire.

"You know it's never a good idea to tell a girl that you have a stake under your kilt," Lucy mocked Loki, handing him a drink. "Stake under the kilt? What were you thinking?" she rolled her eyes. "You sound like you're from another planet," Lucy laughed while Loki put the drink away.

"Whatever this drink is, it tastes weird," Loki said, "kinda salty."

"I've never tried it. The bartender said it's called Baby Tears. It sounded cool so I thought I'd grab you one."

"Thanks for pretending to be my date."

"It's unusual how a good looking guy like you isn't much into girls," Lucy said as she sipped strawberry juice. "Are you gay?"

"No. I'm a half—angel—"Loki stopped, almost biting his tongue. He wasn't supposed to tell anyone about his past. "I'm a vampire hunter," Loki said a little louder, hoping she didn't notice what he had just sad.

"Does that mean there are no gay vampire hunters?" Lucy teased him.

"Why are we having this conversation?"

"Why does anyone have a conversation? We're all talking monkeys in this world," Lucy suggested. "It's just that you look more like a…huntsman with this kilt than a vampire hunter."

"I love the huntsman," Loki said casually, gazing at the dancing crowd. "In fact, he is the only fairy tale character I respect. He spared Snow White's life when he could've just killed her."

"But he didn't kiss her," Lucy winked.

"I don't believe there's a true love's kiss."

"At least we agree on that part," Lucy raised her glass.

A guy disguised as Robin Hood approached Lucy, probably wanting to ask her to dance. Before he opened his mouth, she held her finger, with manicured fake fingernails, up to his nose, still sipping her drink. "Hit the road, loser," she quipped, waving him away like an annoying mosquito.

"So," Loki said, pointing at a different boy in the middle of the dance floor. "Is that the boy—I mean the vampire we're here to kill?"

The boy he pointed at was short, wearing a Count Dracula cloak and plastic fangs. He was looking for a partner to dance with, but girls ignored him repeatedly. A girl dressed like the Wicked Witch of the West made fun of his thick glasses and sprayed silly string on them.

"Yes, that's him," Lucy said, showing Loki a photo of the boy. She claimed the boy's parents had given it to her and asked her to hire a vampire hunter to kill him for a hefty price, so she hired Loki to split it. It didn't sound like a plausible story to Loki, but he didn't care as long as he had a chance to kill another vampire.

Loki took the picture and read the scribbled lines on the back:

Please get rid of my son, ASAP. He is terrorizing the family. I'll pay you when you finish the job.
P.S. Kill him, but be gentle.

"I still don't understand how this dork is a vampire," Lucy remarked. "He looks like a total loser. You see the way he's spinning around like a doll on a stick? I thought vampires were tall, dark, and handsome."

"He is not a dork," Loki explained. "He is trying to fool us so we don't stake him. This party is infested with vampires. They come here to feed every week. What better place than this where you can't distinguish real from fake blood? Unfortunately, there are many other vampire hunters in the house as well."

"I thought you were the only vampire hunter here."

"There are three others," Loki said. "It's a game we all play every weekend. If I was the only one, I'd have killed my ninety-nine already."

"Ninety-nine?"

"Don't bother," Loki waved his hand. "Look!" he pointed at three big boys wearing huge mice outfits, dark glasses, and holding long canes. They were disguised as the Three Blind Mice, and they were focusing their negative attention on a helpless girl dressed like a cat, teasing her relentlessly. "The canes in their hands are actually stakes. They are rival vampire hunters who always try to kill the same vampires I am after so they can take the money. They're called Beetlebuster, Cricketkiller, and Beebully. Donnie Cricketkiller is their leader."

"Horrible names," Lucy frowned.

"Here's what we're going to do," Loki said. "If I approach Dork Dracula, they'll know I'm chasing him and beat me to him. That's why I need you to help me lure Dork Dracula out of this party so I can kill him outside."

"What?" Lucy almost spilled her drink. "You want me, Lucette Rumpelstein, to seduce that nerd? He wouldn't even dream of talking to me."

"You're right, that's why you have to talk to him. Tell him you want to walk out in the fresh air and then drag him to my Cadillac parked behind the bushes outside."

"Cadillac?"

"It's a red 1955 Coupe Deville. Her name is Carmen. You'll take the boy to Carmen and sedate him."

"With what?"

"Magic Dust," Loki pulled her hand closer and poured a handful of golden sand into her open palm. "Throw some of it in his eyes; just make sure you don't inhale it."

"Yeah, yeah," Lucy said. "And I have a magic spindle that weaves beautiful prom dresses on its own."

"You're such a Minikin," Loki mumbled as he saw the girl dressed as the Wicked Witch of the West passing by. He puffed Magic Dust in her eyes from the palm of his hand without anyone noticing but Lucy. The girl stopped in her tracks, instantly falling asleep. Loki caught her before she made a huge thud on the floor. "See?" he grinned at Lucy. "Another drunk bites the dust!" Loki raised his voice against the loud music and pointed at the sedated girl. Her friends hurried toward him and pulled her back to what they called the 'rescue room.'

"We've just avenged Dorothy!" One of her friends, dressed as the Cowardly Lion, shouted with the Wicked Witch of the West piled onto his back.

"Any more questions?" Loki said, with a hint of cockiness.

"Who are you, Loki Blackstar?" Lucy's eyes shined. She eyed him from top to bottom like the other girl. "I can't believe I'm going to let this dork think I like him," Lucy scowled then took a deep breath and strolled toward him.

"There's a first dork for everything," Loki grinned.

Dork Dracula looked like he'd been struck by lightning when Lucy talked to him. In less than a minute, he was on his way out the door with Lucy. When he tried to touch her, she slapped him on the back of his hand like a naughty child.

Before Loki could follow them outside, someone bumped into him. It was Donnie Cricketkiller with his two vampire hunter friends.

"I brought you a drink," Donnie smirked. He was almost twice as big as Loki.

"I'm on a diet," Loki said, knowing all Donnie wanted was to get his hands on his vampire.

"Take a day off," Donnie sneered, squeezing Loki up against the wall.

"My only day off is Easter, so we're going to have to wait a while," Loki showed him his academy-award-winning fake smile. "You can occupy yourself with coloring some eggs until then."

Donnie spilled his drink over Loki's head. His friends laughed and a couple of girls who'd seemed interested in Loki walked away. Although Donnie was big, Loki was a tough hunter and had his own way to fight back.

"We're short on vampires for the night. So we thought we'd kill yours like we always do," Donnie chuckled, tapping his fleshy hand on Loki's cheek.

Loki made his hand into a fist, but avoided gritting his teeth. He was too proud to show his frustration to Donnie. There were times when Loki thought of staking Donnie like a vampire, and the hell with going back to Heaven. It took all of his willpower not to.

Charmwill had also told Loki about his past life and how dark and dangerous he had been. The darkness was the reason he wasn't allowed to fight back against guys like Donnie Cricketkiller. If he did, it could re-surface. He was puzzled by the kind of darkness Charmwill was talking about, how it played into his past life and why it made him so dangerous.

"If you don't cooperate, we're not going to beat you up, but we're going to beat your lovely Carmen," Donnie said.

Loki couldn't let that happen. Carmen was his best and only friend.

"Look, Donnie. The party is infested with vampires," Loki choked. "Pick someone else."

"But I heard yours had a large price on his head," Donnie said.

This was what bothered Loki the most. Donnie and his friends were merely normal vampire hunters, doing it for the money. Loki had to get rid of them. He was already behind schedule for meeting up with Lucy.

"This big boy here is a vampire hunter!" Loki shouted to the crowd, pointing at Donnie who instantly let go of him. If Loki wasn't allowed to defend himself against Donnie, at least he could outsmart him. "He's a real vampire hunter!" Loki yelled, still pointing at Donnie.

The music stopped abruptly, and every *real* vampire in the house turned their head with their *real* fangs out to face Donnie Cricketkiller, Beetlebuster, and Beebully. Girls started screaming as the vampires went rogue and began biting teens. Things got messy in the blink of an eye. Donnie and his friends abandoned the melee before they became victims to the bloodbath.

"And the party went *buh-bye.*" Instantly a great idea struck Loki like a light bulb above his head: escaping.

Usually, people would escape through the main doors, fire escapes, or the windows. Loki was fond of bathrooms, and he didn't know why. In his Ordinary World hometown, Snoring, he'd always found refuge in the school's bathroom. He hid there when he didn't feel like mingling with other students, when he wanted to avoid girls who could turn out to be demons, when he wanted to avoid bullies he wasn't allowed to retaliate against, and particularly when he was bored with classes. He ate in the bathroom, read comics, and tried to find the missing digits of God's cell phone number, which was partially written on the wall.

Locking the bathroom door behind him, a sudden storm lit up the night outside.

"And it was a dark and stormy night in the toilet," Loki proclaimed, looking for a way out. As the bathroom's door sprung open, Loki climbed out of the window, and in the true fashion of a Road Runner, he raced across the moonlit street toward the bushes.

Finally, Loki spotted his Cadillac shining red in the dark. He dove into the driver's seat through the window as if he were superman. Lucy was sitting in the passenger seat, listening to music on her phone, checking out her fingernails.

Loki didn't exactly land in the driver's seat. He landed in Lucy's...well...never mind.

"Get off me!" Lucy shrieked.

"I'm trying," Loki said, unable to sit up straight. "They're after me!"

"They who?"

Loki tilted his awkwardly-positioned head, amusing himself with Lucy's chin moving upside down. Her eyes were looking at an invisible something at her lower left, which Loki assumed was his upper left.

"Do you mean those boys and girls I see in the mirror?" she laughed.

Loki freaked out and adjusted himself in the driver's seat. "What's wrong with you?" he said to Lucy. The way she was adjusting her blouse would've led someone to believe they were making out ferociously in the car.

It took everything Loki had to take his eyes off sexy Lucy and her blouse. He started kicking Carmen with his foot. Keys weren't Carmen's thing. Although she was Loki's best friend, and worst car, she needed a real *kick-start* to operate.

Carmen's engine picked up. It sounded like an angry zombie calling for brrr...brrrr...brrrrraiins. The radio sprung to life with the melody of one of her favorite songs called 'Run for Your Life' performed by a band called the Piedpipers—Loki had googled the band before but found out they didn't exist. It was how Carmen played her music. She played, Loki listened, no questions asked.

"Nice girl, Carmen. Yeeeha!" Loki spit out proudly as the Cadillac gunned through the muddy road ahead.

In the rear-view mirror, he saw Donnie Cricketkiller talking friendly with the vampires who were watching him with angry red eyes and fangs. Donnie must have persuaded them that Loki was the real vampire hunter, and that he was out to kill one of them. It was a relief that vampires didn't fly. If they wanted to get him, they had to chase him in a car like everyone else.

Loki suddenly remembered Dork Dracula whom he noticed was tied up on the roof of his Cadillac while jumping in.

"How did you get the boy tied up on the roof of the Cadillac?" Loki asked Lucy, gripping the wheel while driving down a bumpy road with creepy, curving trees above.

"Which boy?" she said nonchalantly, her eyes looking dizzy, and then let out an unnecessary laugh.

"Dork Dracula!"

"Ah, that, hmm," she said, brushing her hair back.

"Ah, hmm, what?" Loki snapped. "Wait. Did you inhale some of the Magic Dust by accident?" Loki didn't expect her to answer. The Magic Dust was designed to affect the eyes. Some people were allergic to its smell, and it made them hallucinate for several minutes.

"I let the doorman tie him up to the roof of your car, like luggage," she laughed with big pupils, clapping her hands together. "Dork Dracula wanted to kiss me before I sedated him so I kicked him in the balls, and he fainted."

"You didn't sedate him?"

"He'd already passed out. Don't worry. It always works. I kicked all my ex-boyfriends," she was already hallucinating.

"This means Dork Dracula might wake up any moment now, and I can't stop the car because the vampires from the party are coming after us," Loki wanted to scream and pull his hair. "And why did the doorman agree to help you?"

"I seduced him," Lucy brushed her forefinger across Loki's nose, laughing still. "I showed him my…"

"You showed him your what?" Loki's eyes widened. This night was getting mad as a hatter by the minute.

Trying to remember, Lucy's face changed. She looked puzzled and vaguely serious.

At least you stopped laughing. That's a good sign. It'll only be a couple of minutes until the effect wears off," Loki said. All he needed was to reach the location where Lucy had parked her four-wheeler, stake Dork Dracula, add him to the list and get some money.

But suddenly, it started to rain and in Loki's short life it only seemed to rain when things went wrong. He turned the headlights on; a yellowing hue pierced into the night and split the darkness in half.

"With all this wind and rain, Dork Dracula will be waking up soon," Loki said. "I need to get on the roof and stake him, and you have to help me."

Lucy nodded wearily.

"Take the wheel," Loki said. It wasn't the greatest idea to let her drive, but he had no choice.

Loki pulled himself up to the edge of the window while Lucy shuffled to the driver's seat, gripping the wheel. She was trying her best to stay focused, although she was having another laughing fit.

"This is awesome," she squinted at the road. "Look at all those yellow……..things."

The weather outside was getting nastier, and the heavy torrent of rain blurred Loki's sight. He held onto the edge of the roof, preparing to pull himself up.

"Keep your hands tight on the wheel or I'll fall," he yelled at Lucy.

"Don't tell me how to drive," she yelled back, wiping rain from her cheek. Just do your job and be quiet, "you're spitting on me."

"You think *I'm* the one who's spitting. This sky is doing all the spitting," Loki said, climbing up. "No one ever told me that killing vampires required the skills of a stuntman."

Loki was now head to head with Dork Dracula, who was tied lying flat on his back, his hands and legs stretched out on the roof. Out of nowhere, Dork Dracula's head tilted to the side, staring at Loki with glaring red eyes. He was awake, although a little drowsy.

"Hi, my name is Loki Blackstar," Loki faked a smile. "And I'm going to kick your ass."

Loki managed to punch the kid in the face to buy a few seconds. Then he clung to Dork Dracula's body to pull himself up, while listening to the boy's drowsy growling. As soon as Loki had managed to climb onto the roof, the car hit another bump in the road. He lost balance and almost fell, but hugged Dork Dracula's body.

"*Spread the love,*" Loki wisecracked.

Finally, Loki managed to sit on Dork Dracula with his knees touching the roof. He raised his stake in the air and took aim at the boy's heart. "Finally, number thirty eight!" Loki chanted his victory, "sixty-one to go."

But something stopped Loki in his tracks. It was the squeaky sound of a squirrel, stuffed under Dork Dracula's costume, right above his heart. Loki knew it was a common trick vampires pulled. Every vampire knew Loki had a soft spot for squirrels.

"Seriously?" Loki ripped Dork Dracula's costume open and saw a squirrel duct-taped to his chest. "You bastard," Loki screamed at the drowsy vampire who was smirking happily at him. "Why would you do that to this tiny, helpless animal?"

Loki freed the squirrel carefully, closing his eyes to the sound of pain it made when he pulled the duct tape away. Loki held the squirrel in his hand tightly. "Please tell me you're OK? Talk to me!" Loki spattered rain onto its face.

The squirrel tried to pull Loki's hand away because he was unknowingly choking it. "I'm sorry," Loki said. "I'm really sorry. Are you OK now? The squirrel nodded, Loki set it free, and then it climbed up and plastered a kiss on his cheek then fled away.

"The vampires are coming after us!" Lucy shouted, sounding alert now.

Loki looked back, and he saw them in their Jeeps and Audies. He wondered why the Council of Heaven had given him an old Cadillac when everyone in this world had cool cars. Wasn't he the half-angel?

Turning back, Loki noticed Dork Dracula was fully awake and growling, fangs out, red eyes glowing in the dark.

"Are those your fangs or are you just happy to see me?" Loki splashed the words out against the rain, happily spitting on Dork Dracula's face. He didn't look insulted.

"Stupid, Loki," Dork Dracula grunted. "You'll always be a kind-hearted loser, just like your father," the vampire grasped Loki around his neck, ready to bite him.

"You knew my father? Loki asked, his stake slipping from his hand. "Every vampire knew your father, the most famous loser of all, who gave up on Heaven for the love of a demon woman," Dork Dracula smirked with crawling green veins in his face, waving like a mad snake. This was definitely not the nerdy dude from the party anymore. "If only you could remember who you really are. You used to be like us, one of us, Loki.

Suddenly, something hit Loki in the face. He thought this was the feeling of getting bitten, but it wasn't. It was a thick branch from one of the creepy trees bending over the road that punched him.

Loki had been hit hard. He wrapped his arms and legs around the branch like an amateur monkey in a lousy circus.

When he opened his eyes, the night looked blacker and blurrier. He dangled his feet but there was nothing underneath to reach. He wanted to bang his head against something, watching Carmen disappear into the dark of the road in front of his eyes. He was simply left behind, hanging on a tree in the middle of the night.

Behind him, he heard the vampires getting closer, so he crawled deeper into the thick arched branches and hid behind the leaves, watching them chase after Lucy.

Loki wondered if Lucy noticed his absence. It wasn't like you lose the guy on the roof of the car you're driving every day.

Sitting helpless on the branch in the dark, his phone vibrated in his pocket. He had never answered the phone while on a tree before, so he struggled pulling it out with one hand while keeping balance with the other. "Keep your balance, Loki. One hand on the tree, one hand on the phone," he said to himself teasingly. "That's the kind of skill they don't teach you in school."

Loki checked the caller's name. It was Lucy.

"Where the tic, tac, toc, are you?" Lucy shouted through the speaker, fully awake now.

"I'm on a tree," Loki said. He didn't feel exactly proud about it.

"How could you leave me alone with all those fang-gang vampires following me? This is no time for trees, Loki."

"Actually it's me who was left behind—" Loki fired back. His loud angry voice must have awoken some creatures of the night. Something was rattling in the nearby trees. "*Actually it's me who was left behind, not you,*" he repeated, now whispering and lowering his head to hide from any malevolent night creatures. A wolf howled in the distance, and Loki wished he was a lizard so he could change his color to match the tree.

"Why are you whispering?" Lucy yelled.

"You have to lose the vampires and come back to pick me up," he said.

"I can't believe you need my help again," Lucy sighed impatiently. "You're supposed to be the vampire hunter," she huffed and hung up.

"Goodbye to you to you, too," he said to an empty line.

Loki saw his shadow reflected by the moonlight on the road. It looked a lot taller and a little bent, which he was fine with. What troubled him was the other shadow next to him. It was of something short and chubby with what looked like spiky feathers. He wasn't alone on the tree.

Slowly, biting on the phone like a dog with a bone, Loki turned to his right. It was an owl; a friggin' white owl with yellowish eyes, standing firm and proud, looking like a happy stuffed pillow. It said nothing and only blinked occasionally.

Loki held the phone in one hand so he could shrug.

"Hi," Loki paid his respects.

Usually animals talked back to Loki when they were alone—or maybe he was only hallucinating—but this owl didn't respond. It didn't even nod back. They shared a long moment of silence. It seemed that Loki was of no interest to the owl, which made him feel even lonelier.

When Loki's phone vibrated again, the owl let out a sigh, and Loki held tighter to the tree branch so it wouldn't vibrate him to his death.

Loki apologized to the owl for the disturbance, hoping he could count on its continued silence as permission to pick up the phone. This time, he didn't know the caller's number.

"You think I should pick up?" Loki asked the owl. The owl blinked once, so Loki picked up the phone.

"Mr. Loki?" a man on the phone inquired. His voice struck Loki as foreign, probably German. "Loki Blackstar the vampire hunter?"

"Speaking," Loki furrowed his eyebrows, exchanging looks with the owl.

"My name is Igor the Magnificent," the man said in his old, archaic German accent.

"And I'm Loki the tree hugger."

"I'm calling to offer you a job, Mr. Loki."

Loki asked permission from the owl, clamping his hand over the speaker. He saw another owl-friend had joined their small party on the tree. "He's offering a job. Probably a *magnificent* job," Loki explained to the pair. "I need the money, you know. I need an education in case I can't kill ninety-nine demons and get back to heaven. It's either that or I will have to apply to American Idol, and sell my soul to the devil so he will gift me with the talent of singing."

The owls became three, still not uttering a word. To Loki, silence was a sign of approval.

"Sure," he said to Igor.

"I need you to come to visit me in Hell," Igor said.

"You're in Hell?" Loki thought that talking about selling his soul was a mistake, not to mention the grand irony in asking a half-angel to do Hell a favor.

"It's a *town* called Hell. Haven't you heard of it?" Igor said. "On behalf of our town, I am asking you to help us kill a vampire that has been threatening our families."

Although the offer reeked of weirdness, Loki was happy he could compensate for failing to kill Dork Dracula.

"The town's council will reward you with a year free of school fees in our town high school if you kill her." "Wait a minute," Loki shrugged. "Did you just say *her?*"

"The vampire is a girl, yes," Igor confirmed. His tone had changed, gone softer, as he preferred not to tell Loki she was a girl.

"I'm sorry Mr. Igor. I can't do it," Loki said without thinking. His heart pounded so fast it felt like it was going to burst out of his chest and his mouth went dry. "I don't kill demon girls."

"Please, Mr. Loki. We really need your help," Igor said. "She has been killing and scaring everyone in the city for the last one hundred years. People are afraid to speak her name. The town is terrified. Oh, and one more thing, she has killed every previous vampire hunter we've hired."

"A hundred years?" Although Loki should have worried about the fact that no other vampire hunter survived her, it was the least of his concerns.

"Yes, her name is…" Igor hesitated. Loki almost thought he'd hung up then Igor ended his sentence, as he tried to hide the name Snow White behind a fake cough.

"Snow White?" Loki wondered if he'd misheard the name. A crow cawed somewhere nearby, and a couple of doves fluttered out of the trees. "Snow White?" Loki repeated, raising his voice so the owls could hear him. One of them raised a single eyebrow, the other sneezed, and the last one winked at Loki.

Loki felt dizzy all of a sudden, as if he were going to faint and fall from the tree. It was a strange feeling he hadn't experienced before, but the headlights of his Cadillac flashing in the distance shook him out of it. Lucy arrived.

"Are you still there, Mr. Loki?" Igor wondered.

"Yes, but like I said, I'm sorry," Loki replied. "I can't do it. I don't do girls—I mean I don't kill demon girls."

"Is there anything that could change your mind?" Igor sounded sneaky.

"Not a thing," Loki said. "If she's Snow White like you claim, then she doesn't need a vampire hunter. She needs a true love's kiss," Loki mocked Igor. "Better find her a Prince Charming."

Loki's Cadillac was coming nearer.

"I have to go now," he told Igor. "I'm about to jump from a tree onto the roof of a 1955 Cadillac, and I haven't really practiced for this—"

"Could you just promise me you'll think about it," Igor the *Insistent* pleaded. "They say she is actually *the* Snow White from the fairy tales."

Loki simply hung up. After being told he had been banned from Fairy Heaven for falling in love with a demon girl he wasn't about to risk it again.

The Cadillac was almost underneath him. Lucy waved at Loki. He wasn't surprised that Dork Dracula wasn't on the roof anymore.

Loki blew the owl a kiss and prepared to jump. One of the owls blew him a kiss back. Lucy wasn't going to stop with all the cars tailing her.

"If Snow White is a vampire," he told the owl. "Then I am Prince Jumping," he said, hoping he'd successfully land on the roof of his Cadillac.

He landed on the muddy ground instead.

Lying on his back, he lifted his head up and saw the car following Lucy wasn't the vampire's. It was Donnie Cricketkiller's car. They drove by, laughing, splashing mud on him and throwing their trash at him.

Loki saw why they were cheering victoriously; they had Dork Dracula staked in the backseat.

Still stretched out on the ground, Loki's back ached from the fall, so he closed his eyes on the world.

"You think it's him? The One?" Loki thought he heard an owl on the tree talk to another.

"Nah, it can't be," the other owl replied.

Loki didn't bother checking if he was hallucinating. He heard Lucy come trotting up.

"Loki Blackstar," Lucy stood in her devil outfit, her hands on her hips "How can anyone be as unlucky as you?"

Loki said nothing. The last thing he needed was someone to remind him of the wasted evening.

"You know why I asked you to kill Dork Dracula?" Lucy said. "Because some people in my town think that you're the only one who can kill the Snow White vampire."

"You're from the same town Igor called from?" Loki frowned.

"Yes," Lucy said. "He is like our town's council representative. He insisted on calling you even when I told him that you failed the test of killing Dork Dracula."

"This was a test?" The hits kept on coming.

"Some ancestors in our town wrote a prophecy claiming that a fifteen year old vampire hunter would kill Snow White. Clearly, it couldn't be you," Lucy said. "If you want my advice, forget about vampire hunting. Stick to wearing that stupid kilt of yours."

Loki was speechless. Lucy knelt down and pulled a small card from her pocket. She wet it with her tongue and plastered it on Loki's forehead. "It's our town's address. Our town's council still thinks you should give us a visit," she held Loki's head between her hands and looked at him, "Loki Blackstar," she sighed. "Why don't you try to live up to that cool name?"

Lucy left and Loki didn't bother standing up. When Lucy's spit dried, the card fell and he picked it up. It read:

Welcome to the Island of Sorrow
East of the Sun West of the Moon

A Town Called Snoring

Loki didn't have the luxury to return to a house or a family like other teens. He spent nights sleeping in his Cadillac, one of the few gadgets the Council had provided for his journey in the Ordinary World.

In the beginning, Loki thought he'd be able to park his car in the suburbs and sleep in it, but he was wrong. House owners mistook him for a creep or intruder and woke him up in the middle of the night, prompting him to leave. A ninety-year-old woman accused him of being a peeping tom. She tried smashing his window with a frying pan as the rest of the neighborhood threw eggs at him. He had lost his money to a hole in his pocket that day so he didn't mind the raw eggs. They tasted good as long as he licked them from his face and not from the ground.

Loki couldn't afford parking lots for his Cadillac, and he didn't have friends who'd let him sleep over and park in their garages. For weeks, he ended up guarding his car at night instead of sleeping in it. Carmen was old, unregistered, had broken headlights, and out of the ordinary plates, which read:

H… is Where the Heart is.

The space after the letter 'h' was worn out, and Loki thought the missing letters would make the word: home.

Loki avoided the police. Almost sixteen, he hadn't applied for a driver's license yet, and the police usually suspected Carmen was a stolen car. Also, the police didn't believe vampire hunters existed, so Loki didn't know how to explain the stakes and hunting tools in the trunk of his Cadillac. To the police, everything about Loki had 'lunatic' written all over it, and he didn't want to end up in jail. His life was a bad joke already, and a night in jail was a night wasted without trying to kill a vampire.

At some point, he decided he'd sneak into the garages of abandoned houses. He thought he'd roll up the windows, lock the car from inside, and hide under a blanket until the morning sun came.

He was wrong again.

The houses were ghost carnivals, and they wouldn't let him sleep.

He ended up driving away and hiding his Cadillac in the thick bushes in the forest. It was a shaky ride, but he'd finally found a place where he could sleep. Well, only until the frogs started croaking.

Loki's biggest fear was frogs. When they croaked, he felt as if a giant monster was roaring at him. The croaking sound was the scariest thing Loki had ever heard, and he wasn't talking about the *ribbet, ribbet* part. He was scared of the other sounds frogs made: *crooock, crrrrooock.*

Sometimes he dreamed of frogs wanting to kiss him.

"Yucccckk! I'm not going to kiss a frog!" Loki woke up screaming and drove away from the bushes, his hands shaking on the wheel.

Eventually, Loki decided to use a fortune cookie the Council of Heaven had given him through Charmwill; it was to help him when he needed to make a tough decision. It was an enchanted fortune cookie. Whenever Loki asked it something and crushed it open, an answer appeared written on a small piece of gummy paper from inside it. It turned back into a fortune cookie on its own afterwards, so he could question it again later. Loki loved the taste of the gummy paper, chewing the answer away—it tasted accordingly of the answer itself; bitter answer, bitter taste, and vice versa. The fortune cookie was Charmwill's least favorite gadget, but Loki loved it. He named it Sesame.

When Loki asked Sesame where to park his Cadillac, he got the strangest answer. The small piece of gummy paper read: pet cemeteries.

Loki liked the idea; pet cemeteries were only occupied with dead animals. There were no humans, zombies, or sleepwalking dead girls to interrupt his sleep; just cats, dogs, and other pets. He'd heard about animals returning from their graves as zombies, but he knew he could deal with them. Loki hoped people didn't bury frogs in the pet cemetery.

His first night in the pet cemetery was the hardest. He didn't mind that the dead animals woke up and played drums on the roof of his Cadillac, or that they killed each other in a zombie dogs-and-cats fist fight. What he didn't expect was them to talk to him.

"Loki!" a cat meowed outside his car, scratching its nails on the window. "Open up!"

Loki opened one eye, still tucked under the blanket, thinking he was dreaming, but then he heard another sound.

Knock. Knock. Knock.

Loki lifted his neck from under the blanket and saw what was knocking. It was a squirrel.

"You'll be alright, Loco," the squirrel said. "Want a nut?"

"This isn't really happening, right?" Loki squinted "I'm not going *nuts*, am I?"

"You're not nuts," the squirrel said, looking at him with its big curious eyes. "I'm offering you a *nut* in exchange for letting me sleep in the car because it's really cold out here."

Loki tilted his head to the side and saw a black scruffy cat nodding its head.

"Please, don't speak," Loki begged it with sleepy eyes.

"OK, I won't…" the cat meowed. "Until you tell me to. But do you think it will be long? Can I sing you a song until I'm allowed to speak?"

"Oh, no," Loki crept back under the blanket and stuffed cotton into his ears. There was nothing he could do. It was the only place where he could sleep.

In the morning, Loki crushed Sesame open and asked it where he should go next; sometimes, it knew where the next vampire would be—he was only allowed to ask Sesame one question per day.

The paper read: *go to Snoring.*

Snoring was the town where Loki went to school, and where Charmwill Glimmer lived, disguised as his teacher in Boring High, named after Snoring's founding father Snoring Von Boring; it was a mystery if that was his name or an absurd joke.

Some people liked to call the town the Great Snoring as they thought the word *great* made it sound more important. Loki thought both names were horrible.

Charmwill had advised Loki to attend school and get good grades. He thought getting a proper education would be plan B for Loki in case he failed in his mission and couldn't go back to Heaven. There was one catch though; that Loki had to pay for his school. To do that, he had to keep killing vampires for money just like he had tried to do yesterday.

The sun was shining high when Loki entered Snoring, reading the welcome sign by the entrance:

Welcome to the Great Snoring.

A little lower, someone had paint-brushed the words:

Where dreams come true….LoL

A little lower, someone carved the letters with a knife:

Zzzzz!

"Yeah, right," Loki said, steering the wheel.

Snoring was so boring that students went back to school on weekends. School was just as *boring*, but it made them feel somewhat alive in this forgotten two-story town. Other students sought adventure outside the borders by attending the masquerade parties in abandoned houses on the weekends, but only a few came back.

Loki parked his Cadillac in the school's busy parking lot, and sighed.

"It's only one week before I turn sixteen, and I haven't killed half the vampires I need to go back," he talked to Carmen who played a song called 'We'll Make Heaven on a Place Called Earth' for him.

"Shut up, Carmen. What am I going to do?" Loki snapped. The Cadillac shook momentarily and grey foam spread out at the front. It was Carmen's way of shrugging her shoulders at Loki's question.

"Fix the stupid car!" Loki heard a student shout from the distance. The others laughed at him.

Loki reached for his backpack and got out, now dressed in a white shirt and blue jeans with holes in his pockets.

Charmwill forbade him from kicking the butt of any students' in the school, so he played nice most of the time, clinching his fist behind his back.

Although Charmwill Glimmer's history class was fun, Loki was late again. Charmwill didn't believe in history books; he claimed they had all been forged. So instead of teaching history, he read fairy tales to the students, and they loved it. It was only Loki who didn't believe in fairy tales.

No one knew Charmwill was Loki's guardian, disguised as a teacher to stay close and watch over him in his journey. But Charmwill wasn't always helpful. Sometimes, he was a little tough on Loki.

"Late again, Mr. Loki," Charmwill said without raising his head from the Book of Beautiful Lies he was reading from. Most of the girls in class had their chin rested on their hands as they listened to Charmwill's tales. Boys fidgeted or secretly flew paper planes at the daydreaming girls.

"I'm sorry, Mr. Glimmer," Loki said.

Girls turned their heads at him. Loki looked away. Although he liked many of them, it was better to treat them like the flu than to fall in love with one. 'Sorry' is the most pitiful word in history, and it's a lame excuse, Mr. Blackstar," Charmwill said. "Is that your final answer?"

"With all due respect, sir, you don't teach us history," Loki shrugged. "All you teach us is fairy tales. They're all clichéd and easy to predict."

"Is that so?" Charmwill turned to Loki, staring at him from behind his glasses. "Can you tell me then what the pigeons did to Cinderella's stepsisters in the end of the Brothers Grimm fairy tale?"

"There were pigeons in Cinderella's tale?" Loki's eyes widened. "Hmm...kissed her and turned into a Prince Charming?"

"I know the answer, sir," a noisy girl with bushy red hair raised her hand while looking at Loki. Her name was Pippi Luvbug. Loki knew she had a crush on him, and had tried to avoid her repeatedly. "I know the answer," she stretched her hand and waived it in the air as if wanting to go to the bathroom instead of answer a question.

"Please enlighten Mr. Blackstar for me, Miss Luvbug," Charmwill rubbed his beard, proud of his enthusiastic student.

Pippi stood up, fixed her dress a little, and brushed her teeth with her forefinger before talking. "The pigeons pecked out both of their eyes, sir," she said happily.

"Awesome answer," Charmwill said. "Thank you, Miss Luvbug. You can sit down now."

Pippi winked at Loki before sitting down. He found it rather creepy from a girl who was so happy with pigeons pecking out people's eyes. Deep inside, Loki felt funny about the strange fact he'd missed in the Cinderella story.

Charmwill allowed Loki inside, and continued reading. Loki sat next to Pippi who couldn't stop looking at him and was sitting too close for comfort. Sometimes, Loki didn't always think of Pippi as a bother, even if she was a little bit off her rocker. He could relate to that.

Loki avoided Pippi until the bell of freedom rang and class was over. He had to meet up with Charmwill to report his failed attempt at killing Dork Dracula, and he wanted to discuss the weird phone call from Igor the Magnificent.

Walking the empty corridor on the last floor, which led to Charmwill's office, the storage door opened suddenly and someone pulled him inside. Loki didn't have time to pull out his stake, but he eased up a bit when he saw it was Pippi. She closed the door, leaving them stuck among brooms and stinky cleaning buckets.

"Kiss me, Loki," Pippi pulled him close.

"What?" Loki panicked while detergents fell from the shelves.

"Kiss me," she closed her eyes, and pursed her lips, stretching them out like a duck's beak. "Let me know if you're the one for me."

"Get off me, Pippi," Loki said. She had wrapped her legs around him and he couldn't set himself free. Looking at her, he confessed, "I don't want to kiss you." He tried to push her away, but Pippi had limbs like an octopus and they were sticking to him.

Pippi opened her eyes, disappointed with Loki. She pulled him even closer and plunged her lips onto his. Loki felt like he was struck by lightning. He'd never kissed a girl in the Ordinary World before—and he couldn't remember if he had in his previous life. And even from Pippi, it felt so...so...good. Why hadn't he tried this before?

Suddenly, Loki forgot he was a vampire hunter. *The hell with going back home*, this kissing thing was awesome. It didn't really feel like true love, but it felt pleasant. He found himself giving in to Pippi and kissing her back, closing his eyes.

After she pulled away, he had a dreamy smile on his face, neglecting the stinky smell of brooms. He felt as if tiny lovebirds tweeted all around his head.

Happily, he opened his eyes, and that was when something crazy happened.

Pippi Luvbug, the quirky redhead wasn't herself anymore. She had morphed into a red eyed, pale skinned, vampire with fangs and yellow eyes. Something crawled under her skin that looked like tiny eels.

"Welcome to hell, Loki," she said in an awful voice.

The storage room was too narrow, and there wasn't enough time for Loki to reach for the stake in his backpack. He was about to get bitten by a vampire. It quickly occurred to him that he really didn't want to die in school.

Suddenly, the door sprung open and light shone through. It was Charmwill. He pulled Loki back and staked Pippi mercilessly in the chest, almost pinning her to the wall. Shocked, her body wriggled for a while before she gave in and died.

"Wait for me in my office," Charmwill said. "I will take care of the body."

Running back to the office, Loki thought about what would happen if someone saw Charmwill killing Pippi. They would persecute him for being a sadistic, mad teacher. Most of the town's people were looking for the person who murdered their children at parties, and if anyone saw him the story wouldn't have a happy ending. Loki entered the office and waited for Charmwill.

"I am sorry, sir," Loki said once Charmwill burst into the room and locked it from the inside.

"I don't think that I taught you to spend your life apologizing," Charmwill said as his Book of Beautiful Lies turned back into Pickwick the Parrot.

"I am Pickwick," the parrot said to Loki. "And I am mute."

"I'm Loki," Loki patted Pickwick. Charmwill eyed Loki for a moment. "I assume you killed your thirty-eighth vampire yesterday," he said.

"No, sir," Loki lowered his head a little.

"And what was it this time? Did Donnie Cricketkiller kill the vampire first?" Charmwill inquired, leaning back in his chair behind the desk.

"He did, eventually. But that wasn't why I failed," Loki shrugged. "The vampire had a squirrel taped over its heart, and I wanted to save the squirrel."

"Saved the squirrel, huh," Charmwill lit up his pipe, staring out his window.

Sometimes, Loki didn't understand Charmwill. He wished he could read his mind.

"Hmm..." Loki broke the silence. "I wanted to tell you something strange that happened to me yesterday."

"Oh?" Charmwill still stared out the window.

"This girl, Lucy Rumpelstein, who hired me to kill the vampire, had someone from her town call me at the end of the hunt and offer me a full year of schooling, free of charge if I kill a hundred year old vampire in their town."

"Go on," Charmwill puffed more smoke. It smelled really good, but Loki never asked what it was. "Sounds like a good job offer."

"The thing is the vampire is a—girl."

Pickwick flew away from Loki's shoulder to Charmwill's, as if it sensed Loki's weakness.

"I just saved you from a demon girl," Charmwill said. "She's been sitting in class next to you for a week. She's been playing games with you, and you couldn't figure out that she was a vampire. You wasted a good opportunity to kill another vampire, and when she tempted you, you gave in and were about to get killed," Charmwill spoke slowly, sounding considerate more than disappointed. "After all that I've mentioned, please explain to me how you're considering killing a vampire girl?"

"You're right," Loki clasped his hands behind his back. It seems I was banned for a good reason. I do have a weakness for demon girls—"

"—and squirrels," Charmwill added.

"Yes, demon girls and squirrels, sir," Loki quietly questioned how in the world liking both of those creatures could be considered a bad thing. "I just thought I'd tell you about the incident because the man also claimed the vampire's name is...well...Snow White," Loki rolled his eyes.

Charmwill turned to face Loki, and Pickwick's eyes widened. "What did you just say?" Charmwill asked. "Snow White?"

"Yes. Can you believe that? He even said she was the *real* Snow White," Loki tried to sound casual.

"What did the man say the town's name was?"

"I am a little confused about that," Loki waved a hand. "The man said the town's name is Hell. Then Lucy gave me a card that said its name is Sorrow. I guess Sorrow is a smaller town in Hell or something. I know it all sounds ridiculous."

Charmwill didn't find any of this funny. Loki hadn't seen him look so serious before, brushing his beard again and looking a bit dazed.

"Sit down, Loki," Charmwill said firmly. "It's time I tell you about something."

"OK?" Loki sat down reluctantly. He hated when people made introductions to their speeches. It usually meant bad news.

"You know it's your sixteenth birthday next week, and you've only killed thirty six vampires so far." Charmwill placed his hands over the desk and leaned forward.

"Thirty seven, sir," Loki corrected him.

"No. The one in Forks, Seattle, was resurrected. Someone dug him up from his grave, and pulled the stake out of his chest."

Loki gritted his teeth. How was he supposed to kill vampires that were so easily resurrected? You just pull the stake out, and they came back.

"At this point, it would be foolish to pretend that you'll kill ninety-nine vampires before next week," Charmwill followed. "You have to know that when I unshadowed you, I only told you about the rules because the Council of Heaven wouldn't release you unless I did."

"I will always be grateful, sir," Loki felt obliged to say.

"The truth is that I didn't really care if the Council of Heaven forgave you," Charmwill said. "I really cared about you for reasons I wish not to discuss now," he avoided Loki's eyes, saying the last sentence, and then looked back. "And part of my caring was that you get a second chance in life, whether here in the Ordinary World or back home. Frankly, I was hoping you'd like it here in the Ordinary World, and maybe spend the rest of your life here."

"But, sir, I hate it here," Loki gripped the edge of the desk. "Besides, why would I want to be mortal when I could live forever?" Loki wondered, and Pickwick nodded for it seemed a plausible argument.

"I can understand your reasoning, Loki," Charmwill said. "On the contrary, I like those Minikins. I find them amusing. I like their mortality, occasional stupidity, and flaws."

"But I don't, sir," Loki said. "I want to go back home. I know they don't like me there because I made a mistake, but I'll do anything to get them to forgive me."

"Anything?" Charmwill leaned forward.

"Anything, sir," Loki stressed. "If not for the sake of going home, then to know who my dad is, what I did wrong, and who that girl I fell in love with was. How do you expect me to move forward when I don't know my past?"

"As your guardian, it's my duty to teach you and help you fulfill the destiny you choose," Charmwill leaned back in his chair. "And now that you've decided, you should know that everything the man on the phone told you is true," Charmwill stopped Loki from interrupting so he could explain further. "There is a sixteen year old vampire called Snow White. She is a troubled girl with a mysterious past, who lives in a castle in a town called Sorrow. It's more of an island than town, and it can only be reached by passing through another town called Hell."

"So there is actually a town called Hell?" Loki wondered.

"There are many towns called Hell in America. You can easily spot them on the map," Charmwill said. "There is Hell in Michigan, in the Cayman Islands, in Cleveland, Ohio, in California, in Arizona, and in Kentucky. All of these towns serve as portals to the island of Sorrow—its residents like to call it a town, but it's actually an island. Snow White lives in that town. We're talking about things few people know about."

"But Lucy looked like a Minikin," Loki considered.

"Sorrow is a special place with special secrets," Charmwill interrupted him. "You shouldn't bother yourself knowing much about people like Lucy."

"So what should I bother with, sir?"

Charmwill stared directly into Loki's eyes, "That killing Snow White is worth ninety-nine vampires in the eyes of the Council of Heaven," he said.

"What?" Loki snapped.

"Like I said, if you kill this Snow White vampire in Sorrow, you will be forgiven and allowed to go home."

"Why didn't you tell me that a year ago?"

"Isn't it obvious?" Charmwill raised an eyebrow. "You're scared of girls, Loki. How did you expect me to tell you about her a year ago? I thought you might either like this Ordinary World or kill ninety-nine vampires, or even overcome your fear of girls. You didn't do any of that. Now, you're left with the only chance to fulfill your destiny."

"By killing the kind of vampire I am scared of the most," Loki shrugged his shoulders.

"Nothing comes easy. If you want to go back, you will need to face your fears. Going to Sorrow will be your greatest challenge because it will not only tell you who you are, but what you are capable of, and that's the one thing that is most important to me," Charmwill took a casual drag from his pipe.

"So all I have to do is go to Sorrow through a portal in a town called Hell, kill Snow White and it will be over?"

Charmwill nodded.

"But what if I kill her and someone pulls the stake out later like the dude in Forks? I am afraid they'll ban me again," he replied eagerly.

"That's why you will need this," Charmwill handed him a thick, but small notebook.

Loki picked it up. It was old with yellowish pages and hundreds of hand-written drawings and instructions. He flipped through it once without reading anything specifically. The notebook's title read: The Dreamhunter's Guide.

"Dreamhunter?" Loki said.

"You wanted to know about your past, and one of the things you need to know is that you were a Dreamhunter like your father, a very good one, too."

"I am? And what does a Dreamhunter do?"

"A Dreamhunter is the only hunter that has the ability to kill Demortals, which is the name we call a certain kind of immortal demon including vampires. Demortal demons don't die, no matter how many times you stake them. Like the vampire in Forks, once you pull the stake out of them they will come to life again. However, only a skilled Dreamhunter can get rid of them," Charmwill leaned forward again.

"How so?"

"A Dreamhunter stakes a vampire in their dreams while they're asleep so they can never wake up again. The Demortal's mind can't comprehend the idea of being killed in their dreams and it paralyzes their brains so they can't wake up again in the real world."

"Even when someone pulls the stake out?" Loki had to ask again.

Charmwill nodded. "The only way to kill the vampire girl in Sorrow is to kill her in her dreams, which is really not killing her, but putting her to sleep forever."

"Is that why they were looking for me?" Loki wondered. "Lucy said there was some kind of prophecy about only one person being able to kill the vampire."

"I don't know about that, but I know that if you learn what is in this notebook, you can do it," Charmwill said.

Loki flipped through the tiny pages and saw a picture of a vampire lying on her back with a stake in her heart. A circle of candles surrounded the vampire, and two mirrors stood opposite to each other on both sides, tangent to the circle. A boy who was Loki's age lay stretched on his back next to the vampire girl. The few lines written underneath the picture explained that the boy recited a spell to enter the vampire's dreams to kill her. It didn't make much sense, but the notebook was thick and Loki was excited that he had a lot to read concerning what he did before he was shadowed.

But when Loki finished reading the page, something strange happened. The page dissolved as if it had turned into sand, and was simply gone. Loki couldn't believe what he just saw and gazed back at Charmwill for answers.

"The Dreamhunters Guide is a special kind of notebook that's called a Book of Sand," Charmwill explained. "Books of Sand have magical pages that once read dissolve into sand and never appear again."

"Why?"

"To let you know how precious every word you read is," Charmwill said, "and to prevent enemies from learning the skill. Any Book of Sand is only readable once every one hundred years, when the pages reappear I see you've wasted a page already. I hope you remembered what you've read and seen."

"Wow," Loki said. "This is magic happening to me," he tucked his book safely in his pocket and intended to read it thoroughly later. Loki smiled, staring at the daylight outside the window. "I'm a Dreamhunter. You hear that, Pickwick?" The parrot fluttered its wings enthusiastically. In that moment Loki wished Pickwick could talk.

"And here is another little gift from me," Charmwill pulled a backpack from under his desk and placed it on the table.

"You got me a backpack?"

"This one is different. It's called a Wondersack," Charmwill said. "It's better if you don't open it now. When you read the Dreamhunter's guide, you will know exactly what tools you'll need from it and under what circumstances you will need them. Now, it's time for you to start your journey, Loki," Charmwill stood up and stretched out his hand. Loki stood up and shook his hand respectfully. He felt honored shaking Charmwill's hand. "I hope you find what you're looking for," Charmwill squeezed Loki's hand a bit too tight. "There are a few last words I feel like I need to tell you. It's just a small piece of advice that I have learned through the years."

"Please, do tell me."

"Follow your bliss," Charmwill smiled.

"I will," Loki said, although he didn't understand what it meant. "Aren't you coming along with me?" Loki asked, feeling lost for a moment. He'd never been anywhere without Charmwill nearby. "I'm afraid not," Charmwill said. "It's your journey, Loki. Not mine. But I'll always be in here," he pointed at Loki's heart.

"But—"

"Don't say anything now, not even goodbye. 'Goodbye' is a word even worse than 'sorry', although it's sometimes inevitable."

Loki suddenly realized how much he loved Charmwill, even with all that crap he told about fairy tales.

"I should also tell you that you're not prohibited from protecting yourself from bullies or getting in trouble once you enter Sorrow," Charmwill said.

"I'm not?"

"Sorrow is a place where you should find what your heart desires, and to do so, you'll have to be whoever you choose to be. You'll be facing your greatest fear by trying to kill a demon girl already."

Loki liked the idea passionately. Finally, he'd be able to stand up for what he believed in.

"Now, go," Charmwill said. "You have only a week to find what you're looking for."

Loki respected the fact that Charmwill didn't want to say goodbye, and turned around, walking to the door. He did it abruptly before Charmwill noticed his eyes tearing up. He didn't like anyone seeing him cry.

"One more thing," Charmwill said before Loki left, having sat down at his desk, writing again.

"Yes, sir?" Loki had gripped the door, preferring not to turn around.

"Is the squirrel safe now?" Charmwill asked unexpectedly.

"Excuse me?" Loki said.

"You said you couldn't kill Dork Dracula because you had to save a squirrel," Charmwill said.

"Yes, sir, I saved it, and set it free. It should be safe and sound somewhere," Loki answered.

"Good," Charmwill said. "Heroes always save the squirrel."

A wide smile took shape in Loki's heart as he opened the door and stepped out to begin his journey without Charmwill for the first time.

4

Babushka's Alicorn

Leaving Snoring behind was like escaping a closet Loki had been trapped in for a very long time; yanking the door open and starting a new life was way past due. Even Carmen felt good about it. Being a clunky, almost shattered Cadillac didn't deter her from helping Loki to reach his destination. She rattled and chugged on the bumpy highway while Loki tapped his fingers on the wheel, singing along with the radio. Today, Carmen played a song called 'Highway to Hell' by another deceased band called the Sweet Pickleheads.

Loki had what looked like a cigarette between his lips. Although he didn't smoke, and despised smokers, he thought the act made him look older, and seemed to make people take him seriously. The trick had worked before when clients doubted his ability to kill vampires due to his young age.

But that was in the past. What excited Loki was the Dreamhunter's notebook on his dashboard. He was curious about all the things he had to learn, and he planned to read it as soon as he got the chance. For now, he patted it while driving. He was a Dreamhunter. Although he didn't know how a Dreamhunter killed Demortals exactly, it still felt amazing to be important.

Driving under the waning moonlight, Loki gazed into the mirror to check a pimple on his cheek.

"Aaahhh!" Loki screamed as he almost hit the brakes with his foot. His eyes nearly popped out of his skull, and his jaw dropped while the cigarette clung loosely to the drool on his lower lip. There was a ghost in a white hood sitting in his backseat.

The ghost had long, black hair waving from underneath the hood as if floating in water. Its face was hollow and had two glowing-red spots where the eyes should be. For a moment, Loki's scream startled the ghost; unexpectedly, it bounced against the windows like a ball in a pinball machine—Loki had assumed ghosts walked through walls, but there was no time to argue.

When the ghost finally settled in the middle of the backseat, Loki watched it reach for him. It had skeleton fingers that shimmered like a wraith out of a movie projector, and when it reached for his face, Loki tried not to wet himself.

The ghost snatched the unlit cigarette from Loki's drooling lips then disappeared underneath the hood again. Loki heard a flicker of a match followed by the sound of the ghost drawing on the cigarette, finally puffing out spirals of curly smoke into the car.

"How many times have I warned you about cigarettes?" the ghost complained, talking in a heavy Russian accent, staring at him in the mirror. Loki watched the ghost's face slowly turn corporeal.

Wait. I know that ghost!

Loki let out a long sigh. It was all right. The ghost was just his—

"Mom?" he squinted in the mirror.

"Who else scares you like I do?" she said, looking happy while smoking her stolen cigarette.

"You look...awful," Loki said. "And scary," he meant it as compliment. Ghosts love to look scary.

"Behave, Loki," she pouted in her own monstrous way. "I don't look awful. I'm only aging. I was the prom queen when I was your age."

Yeah, yeah, everyone's mom was the prom queen.

Although she was turning corporeal, Loki had always wondered why his mom was different from other ghosts. She didn't have the ability to venture through walls, and she looked more like a zombie than a ghost.

"Naughty boy," she slapped him on the cheek. "Didn't I ask you not to call me 'mom'? It makes me feel old."

"You *are* old, mom—I mean Babushka," Loki hated calling her by that name. His earliest memory of her was from just a year ago after Charmwill had unshadowed him. While Charmwill took care of him, she was rarely around. She only appeared when she felt like it, criticizing his sleeping habits, reminding him to brush his teeth before sleep, urging him to clean his car, patching the holes in his trousers and socks, and pestering him about meeting an earthly girl he could fall in love with and marry. Calling her Babushka was silly; he needed to taste the word *mom* on his lips more often.

"I was just kidding," Babushka killed the cigarette in the palm of her hand. It produced a funny odor that made Carmen cough a little. "You can call me mom all you want. After all, *I am* your mom, and you're my little Loco."

"Please don't call me Loco. And by the way, what made you remember you actually had a son, *Babushka*?" Loki asked her, but she disappeared suddenly from the backseat and popped up next to him in the passenger seat.

He didn't know why, but she freaked him out.

"Wombles!" Loki banged his hands against the wheel. He didn't know why, but *wombles* was the only word he used when he wanted to swear in his mom's presence. "You can't freakin' sneak up on me like that, mom."

Babushka teased him, tickling him under his chin before she disappeared into the backseat again.

"Did I scare you, Loki?" she leaned forward, looking happy.

Loki didn't blame her. He knew that scaring him was an act of affection, more like cuddling to her. Even if it freaked him out, he knew she loved him dearly, and it wasn't her fault she died and became a ghost. He had asked her once how she'd became one, and she told him she died trying to save a kid who was about to be hit by a truck while crossing the street. She saved the kid who crossed the street safely, and the truck ran her over instead, so she crossed a little too far to the *other side*.

"Not at all" Loki tightened his lips and pretended she didn't scare him.

"Really? I didn't?" Babushka frowned, leaning back. "I'm a terrible ghost," she said. "I don't know what happened to me. I used to scare the bubblegums out of people. Now, I can't even scare the residents of the haunted house I live in," Babushka started sobbing. "I'm such a terrible ghost. I can't even walk through walls."

Loki felt sad for her, but he didn't know what to do.

"Come, on, mom," Loki said. "Don't be like that. You're an awesome ghost. You're very scary. I get nightmares when I think of you," it wasn't true. "Really?" Babushka leaned forward. "You do? Tell me how much I scare you? Does this scare you?" she turned her face into a gruesome monster that resembled Cerberus, guard dog of Hades. Loki thought she looked laughable. However, he screamed, pretending he was scared. He felt silly lying, but if it pleased his mom, he didn't mind.

"See?" Loki said. "You're very scary."

"That's such great news," Babushka said. "I'm going to leave now so I can go scare the residents of the house I live in."

"Wait," Loki waved his hand, looking at her in the mirror. "Did you just visit me to see if you're scary? What was that all about?"

"Oh, I forgot," Babushka reached for something that looked like a stake. It had a surface that resembled thin snakes spiraling around it. "Take this."

Loki took the mysterious item and looked at it. "What's this?"

"It's an Alicorn," Babushka said.

"What's an Alicorn?"

"A unicorn's horn," Babushka said. "There are very few of them in the world."

"Is it from a real unicorn?" Loki didn't know they really existed.

"Very real," she said.

Loki wanted to keep his eyes on the road but couldn't take his eyes off the white Alicorn. "Seriously, a unicorn's horn? Does that mean someone cut if off a unicorn? That's horrible."

"You're asking the wrong questions, Loki. If I were you I'd wonder why I gave it to you."

"OK. Why did you give it to me?" Loki hated beating around the bush.

"It's a stake, and it's one of a kind," Babushka said. "You see that spiral surface around it? It helps you drill into a vampire's heart; it turns into a snake, a whip, and sometimes a sword. This Alicorn has been enchanted so it can kill the strongest of demons, Loki. Don't ever let it out of your sight. Keep it within reach at all times."

"So you know that I am going to Sorrow to kill that Snow White vampire," Loki said. "How do you know that?"

"I'm your mother," she slapped him on the back of his hand and he almost dropped the Alicorn. "Mom's know everything."

"Ouch, mom," Loki arched his back.

"Focus, Loki," she said. "I'm giving you a precious weapon that chooses its master, and I am hoping you can make it choose you."

"What do you mean?"

"It chooses the master who deserves its powers."

"That's kinda lame, mom," Loki said. "I admit it looks awesome, and I want to believe that it's actually a unicorn's horn, but all that mumbo jumbo about choosing its master is ludicrous."

"Then give it back," she reached for it.

"Wait," Loki pulled the Alicorn away from her. "OK. I get it. I have to be worthy of the unicorn it came from to use it to kill the vampire in Sorrow. Truth is; I need anything that will help me overcome my fears, especially this one. What do I have to do to get the Alicorn to choose me?"

"First, there is spell that makes it work," Babushka said. "You gaze at it with determination, and say, 'Ora Pedora'."

It was a mystery to Loki why the things had to be so complicated.

"Ora Pedora—"Loki started saying.

"The spell won't work unless you fulfill the second condition," Babushka said.

"Which is?"

"You have to believe in the Chanta," said Babushka sternly.

"Chanta?"

"The Chanta, Loki," she reached with her skeleton hand over his heart. "It used to be called the Enchanta but it was shortened to Chanta."

"The Chanta is the unseen power of hearts that enchants us all. It's the secret of wills and the conjurer of miracles," Babushka elaborated, reminding him of the way Charmwill used to talk to him. "It's the human power that science can't explain. No one can prove it exists, but we all know it's there."

"English, please?"

Babushka leaned forward again. She neared his right ear then whispered, "If you believe, I mean truly believe and desire something with a true heart, the Chanta coaxes the whole universe to conspire with you and help you get what you want."

"The whole world is on your side, Loki," she whispered in his ear. "All you need is to follow your bliss and the world will walk in your footsteps."

"Have you talked to Charmwill lately?"

"How am I supposed to follow this bliss you're talking about?"

"When you learn to care for others the way you care for yourself," Babushka sounded serious for a ghost who scared *others*.

Why should I care for any of those Minikins?"

"I don't know, Loki, but I think you keep saying these things despite what you truly feel in your heart. I can't imagine you walking away from helping someone in need."

"None of those Minikins deserve my help. This is not my world. It's only temporary."

"It's your life, son. You will choose what's right for you. I'm telling you what I think is best for you," Babushka said. "Just promise me you'll always remember this conversation."

"I promise you I will."

"That's my Loco. Now close your eyes, breathe deeply, and desire what you want," she demanded. "Make sure it is what you really want before you say it."

"I'm kinda driving, mom. I can't close my eyes."

"If you believe in the Chanta, you can."

When Loki looked back in the mirror, his mother was gone. Sometimes, when Babushka disappeared like that, Loki began to think that he didn't really have a mother. But if he was hallucinating, what was the Alicorn doing next to him in the passenger seat? He reached for it to make sure it was real.

Loki kept staring at the Alicorn, wondering how he'd make it choose him—and if all that hocus pocus was true.

"Ora Pedora," Loki whispered to it as if trying to wake someone up.

Nothing happened; it was just a dead unicorn's horn lying in the seat.

"Ora Pedora," Loki raised his voice a little, the way you do when someone you are trying to wake doesn't hear you the first time.

Still, nothing happened.

"Ora Pedora," he straightened up his back and talked as if he were a wizard master in the sixteenth century.

Nothing.

"Crap," Loki stopped messing with the Alicorn and began focusing on the dark road ahead.

Carmen had stopped playing music. He drummed the radio with the palm of his hand, but still no tunes came vibrating from the radio. It was as if the few people he talked to in this world, didn't want to talk to him anymore, and he felt an eerie loneliness creeping up his spine.

Out of boredom, Loki pulled out Sesame, the fortune cookie. He put it on the dashboard and asked it where to go. He knew where he was going, but he needed Sesame to encourage him even more.

"Wait," he said to Sesame. "That's not the right question. My question is: Should I kill the vampire Snow White? Is that really what I need to do to go back home?" Loki asked and crushed Sesame open.

The gummy paper read: *Kill Snow White.*

Loki took the paper and started chewing it. It tasted of vanilla. A bit sour, though.

Suddenly, Carmen's radio came back to life. The presenter in the radio introduced a band called the Pumpkin Warriors. They sang a tune called 'Nothing's going to stop us now.' The lyrics went something like this:

We will hit the road together,
Together and forever,
Nothing's going to stop us now.

And that was it. The same three sentences over and over again. The music was uplifting and cheerful. Loki thought the Pumpkin Warriors were much better than the Sweet Pickleheads or the Piedpipers. He started tapping his fingers on the wheel again and singing along.

A few miles later, a cold chill filled the air outside, and a fog began crawling like sneaky ghosts above the ground. The fog was thickening, covering the Cadillac and the road ahead.

Loki saw a wooden sign on the right side of the road. He straightened his back and squinted at it, afraid to miss it due to the thick-as-pea-soup fog. The sign read:

Welcome to Hell
Only a few more miles to Sorrow

5

The Train of Consequences

Loki rolled down the windows and locked the doors as the Pumpkin Warriors announced they'd stop playing for the night. They said it was becoming too cold and foggy for their liking, but that they'd come back later when it warmed up a bit.

"See ya later, Loki," one of them said from the radio.

Loki wasn't surprised. It wasn't the first time a member of one of the bands that played on Carmen's radio had talked to him. He just wanted to focus on the road ahead.

The foggy surroundings oozed with creepy anticipation like a dark ride in an abandoned amusement park. Loki expected something to pop out of the fog at any moment.

"If you think you should go back, now would be the time," one of the Pumpkin Warriors' members told Loki. "It looks like there is no turning back from here."

Loki slammed the on/off button of the radio with the palm of his hand. "The last thing I need is advice from the dead," he mumbled.

"Ouch," the band members said before the radio's light dimmed into darkness.

A minute later, something glittered in the fog.

It was huge gate, blocking the road. Loki stopped the Cadillac, wiping the sultry fog off the window with his hand. The gate was the shape of a whale's mouth with what looked like vampire fangs drawn out.

Loki supposed it was the way to cross over to Sorrow. He wondered how such an expensive looking gate existed in the middle of nowhere.

A figure shrouded in the shadows appeared from behind the gate, as if it had just passed through like a ghost. It was approaching Loki.

The figure was of a hunched man in a black tuxedo, wearing what looked like a magician's hat. He looked like a twisted version of a circus ringmaster, as he stopped in front of the Cadillac.

Although Loki couldn't see the hunchback's face clearly through the fog, he noticed a silver tooth, gleaming in the dark. Loki supposed the dwarf-like man was smiling at him, but he wondered which kind of smile it was. There were smiles, and then there were *smiles*—the latter were the worst. Loki tucked his Alicorn in the back of his jeans and walked out to meet the bizarre, hunchbacked man.

"Excuse me, is this the way to Sorrow?" he pointed at the gate.

"It depends," the hunchback said, resting with his hands on his cane.

"Depends on what?" Loki asked politely.

"On how much you desire going there," the hunchback said.

"Very much," Loki plastered his two-time-academy-award-winning-smile on his face.

"How *much* is very much?" the hunchback said, his sound implying mockery.

Loki wasn't going to answer that. Things were getting bizarre. "I haven't caught your name," he offered, diverting from the silly conversation.

"My name is Magnificent," his silver tooth gleamed, "Igor, the Magnificent."

"Oh," Loki said. "You're the one who called me to come to Sorrow—"

"I know who I am," Igor snickered. "The question, is do you know who you are?"

Loki said nothing. "You don't have to answer that," Igor said. "What you need to know is that if it's your first time coming to Sorrow, then this whale's mouth is the only way in."

"Is that some kind of a special treatment for those who enter for the first time?"

"Something like that."

"Sounds *magnificent*," Loki said. "So could you open it then?"

"I could, but there's a slight problem," Igor said. "The gate doesn't lead straight to Sorrow. It leads to the Missing Mile, which then leads to Sorrow."

"The Missing Mile?" Loki wondered. "Interesting name, is there a reason for it?"

"Many, actually," Igor said. "One of them is that it *is* really a Missing Mile that few people know about," Igor snickered again. "Another reason is that everyone who finds the Missing Mile usually goes *missing*."

"Are you saying that in order to enter Sorrow, I have to cross the Missing Mile, which sounds like it's impossible to cross?"

"Not impossible, only dangerous," Igor lifted a finger in the air. His hand was crooked enough that Loki wasn't sure if it was a forefinger, middle finger, or even a thumb. "The only way to cross the Missing Mile is to ride the Train of Consequences," Igor pointed his cane at the gate like a magician showing kids into a candy store. A tray of flashy lights shone behind the gate which had just opened on its own. Spirals of green smoke formed plumes under a sparkling train. It looked like a huge diamond. The scene with the creepy man, gate and the train with its flashy lights and green smoke reminded Loki of a ridiculous Broadway show he'd seen on TV.

The whale's mouth was actually a train station. The train's windows were all foggy, and Loki wondered if there were any passengers inside.

"The Train of Consequences," Loki rubbed his chin.

"If I were you, I'd get on the train right away before you change your mind," Igor said. "The Train of Consequences runs with the power of *your* intentions, and I'm getting a hesitant vibe about yours."

"So what happens if my intentions weaken halfway to Sorrow?" Loki asked.

"The train slows down or even stops," Igor said. "And trust me when I tell you that you don't want to be stuck in the Missing Mile."

"What about my Cadillac? How will it cross over with me?"

"Do you have to have your Cadillac with you?"

"We're kinda dating," Loki patted Carmen's roof gently.

"There is a ramp you can use at the end of the train. You can drive it in with the rest of the cargo."

"Sounds good," Loki said. He got in his Cadillac and drove through the gate then up the ramp at the end of the train, and parked Carmen inside.

Entering the train, he saw it was empty inside. It had an eighteenth century vibe to it; dim lighting, brown colored motifs, and old decorations. Loki walked the aisle to take a seat, noticing that he couldn't see outside because of the condensation on the windows. He didn't bother wiping one off; all he wanted was for the train to depart from this freaky sideshow and take him to Sorrow.

Igor appeared again inside the train.

Standing closer now, Loki saw that Igor was blind. He used his cane to find his way through the aisle. Loki took a better look at him and saw that he had three eyes; two were in the normal places and one in the middle of his forehead. Igor had been blessed with a third eye, one more eye than most people, but cursed because they were all blind, which made him worse off than most people. Charmwill had told him that Sorrow was a special place, but he'd never mentioned anything about it being like a freak show.

"Tickets please," Igor said to Loki.

"What tickets? You didn't say anything about tickets. Didn't you say the train moves forward with the power of intention?"

"Yes, I did, but I never said that it was free. Have you ever taken a ride without paying a price?" Igor said. "Everything in Sorrow comes with a price."

"Tell me about it," Loki said, remembering how he'd struggled paying for his schooling, and the price he'd paid for falling in love with a demon girl. The problem was that Loki was penniless—he was counting on the town's council, or Lucy, giving him a down payment.

"I see you don't have money," Igor said, and his three blind eyes twinkled.

"You *see* right," Loki nodded.

"That's fine," Igor said. "The price of the Train of Consequences isn't paid with green bills and silver coins anyway. You pay with *consequences*," Igor said. "It's the Train of Consequences. Isn't it?"

Loki said nothing. Things were getting weirder and weirder.

"You just have to agree that by riding the train, you will accept the consequences that'll follow," Igor explained proudly.

With all this nuttiness, everything Igor said rang a bell. Eventually, Loki would have to the pay the consequences of entering Sorrow. Either he would succeed in killing the vampire princess and go home, or fail and stay here.

"I accept," Loki nodded.

"Then it's a deal," Igor turned around.

Reluctantly, Loki closed his eyes to use his power of intention to move the train forward. His heart skipped a beat when the train started moving.

"See? I told you," Igor said, standing next to another seat on the left, whispering to someone Loki couldn't see.

"Who are you talking to, Igor?" Loki asked curiously as the train took off in full speed.

"Just collecting tickets from another passenger," Igor said, still not looking back, "a first comer like you."

"But there are no passengers on this train but me," Loki said, turning around to see if he'd missed a passenger.

"Oh, there are," Igor stared back at Loki. His irksome silver tooth flashed, sending shivers through Loki's spine.

It occurred to Loki to wipe the fog away from the window to look outside at the Missing Mile. Although he was curious, he didn't do it. He laid his head back and closed his eyes, wishing this ride would be over quickly.

Half an hour later, the Train of Consequences halted to a stop. Loki walked back to his Cadillac and drove it down the ramp.

"Almost there," Igor appeared again with that annoying grin on his face.

"Almost?" Loki hung his head out the window. Something about the air Loki was breathing told him he'd already left the Ordinary World behind and it felt good in a wicked way.

"All you have to do now is follow the Snow Red Road," Igor said, resting his chin on his cane then winking at the road ahead.

Following Igor's blind eyes, Loki saw a road covered in thick white snow.

"Why is it called the Snow Red Road?" Loki said.

The answer came even sooner than he'd expected. Red snow started falling from the sky, snowflakes splashed against his Cadillac's windshield, leaving traces of oily liquid on the glass, trailing down slowly and leaving thin threads of reddish stains that shaped a message on his windshield. It said:

Loki rubbed his eyes to make sure he wasn't imagining this, but the words were gone, leaving trails of undecipherable curvy lines on the windshield.

Snowflakes fell onto his Cadillac's roof, sounding like a woodpecker pecking on a tree. The snowflakes fell slower, almost hanging in the air like angel dust you see floating in the air on a sunny day.

Looking back at Igor, Loki saw him tilt his head back and let the snowflakes fall into his mouth.

"Yummy," Igor grunted, licking his reddish lips. "This one tastes of strawberries."

Loki raised an eyebrow. The red snow looked like drops of blood that spattered on Igor's face, but maybe that was what strawberries tasted like to Igor the Magnificent.

"Oh, this one tastes of cherry," Igor stretched his hand out to Loki as if inviting him to sample one. "Do you have any idea what it means when it snows red?" Igor looked a bit worried now. "It means she is busy...shall we say... entertaining herself."

"Whose she?"

"She who lives in the castle," Igor said. "When Snow White feeds, it snows red in Sorrow."

"How does she do that?" Loki wondered. "That's where the mystery lies," Igor said. "Maybe she is sending us a warning to keep us in line and remind us all that we could be her next victim. Didn't I mention on the phone that it wasn't going to be an easy job? Follow the Snow Red Road to Sorrow," Igor pointed ahead.

"The Snow Red Road it is," Loki sighed, looking at the road. "I know it's been short, but I think I'll miss you, Igor. Don't forget to write," Loki said, adjusting the rear-view-mirror and checking out his hair. He gunned the Cadillac into the night as he mentally prepared himself to kill the vampire princess.

It was past midnight when Loki drove through the streets of Sorrow, which looked surprisingly like a normal town. It was so quiet that Loki could hear a fly as it buzzed to its death at the hands of a purple-lit insect-o-cuter.

The red snow had stopped.

"I guess she's finished her meal already," Loki said, tapping the wheel, "bon appetite, vampire princess."

Deeper into the town, most of the streets were curvy, rising up and down like steep hills in a way Loki had rarely seen before. Still, with all the ups and downs, Loki saw the tips of two high turrets from behind the hills. The turrets were incredibly high, almost reaching for the midnight clouds. Loki thought they must belong to the castle where the princess lived, but no matter how many streets he crossed, they still seemed far away, as if they moved. The curving streets made him fell as if he were driving in a maze.

A flying newspaper spiraled in the air and landed on the Cadillac's windshield. It fixed to the glass with its edges fluttering like a small bird. Loki was able to read the headline written in big read letters:

Welcome to Sorrow.

"Welcome me too much and I start worrying," Loki muttered, leaning forward to read the paper's date. It read July 26th, 1812; which didn't make sense. He didn't have enough time to make sure he read it correctly because the paper flew away as if it was a bird, flapping its wings in the air.

"It's alright, Loki. It's just a flying newspaper," he said reassuringly to himself. There's nothing to worry about. Remind yourself to tell Pickwick about it later.

Loki noticed Carmen hadn't played any music yet, which meant she was still scared.

He wondered if he should call Lucy so she could tell him how to reach the castle, and maybe ask her if there was a pet cemetery he could sleep in, but he decided it was too late in the evening. He checked the card Lucy had given him once more. It had an address of a school scribbled on the back: Rumpelstein High. He couldn't help but wonder if Lucy's family owned the school.

The address read 1812, Straw Street Nefilheim, but there was no one awake Loki could ask for directions. He assumed people in Sorrow went to sleep early, and decided to drive around, hoping he'd find the school so he could get some sleep in its parking lot.

Loki heard faint humming voices in the empty streets, but no one was visible anywhere. There was something irresistible about the unseen voices, peaking Loki's curiosity. Listening carefully, he heard children singing somewhere in the distance.

Loki hunched over the wheel, trying to make out the words to the faint song. They were definitely children, young girls, he thought, but he didn't recognize the song.

He tried to distract himself by reading the names of the scattered shops here and there. A restaurant's sign caught his eye. It was called The Belly and the Beast.

"I feel hungry already," he said as the singing voices returned.

He wondered why the children were out in the streets when everyone else was asleep. The singing was accompanied by the sound of clicking shoes.

The singing came from the narrower side streets, which were dimmer with a few flickering lamp-stands. It didn't seem like a smart idea to investigate them.

What scared Loki the most were the things he couldn't see. They frightened him, although he knew they were usually just a figment of his imagination.

After a time the voices grew louder. He couldn't make out the words, but it sounded something like:

One two,
Blah, blah, blah
Three four,
Tat, tat, ta

Loki's curiosity got the best of him. He started looking for kids jumping rope and chanting. Why would children be jumping rope in the middle of the night?

Three four,
Taps on the floor
Five six,
Clicks, clicks, clicks

Instead of locating the children, Loki found himself in front of Rumpelstein High's parking lot. It was a weird coincidence, but he parked Carmen nonetheless, forgetting about the singing girls. He needed to sleep so he rolled up the windows, locked the doors, leaned his seat back, and hugged his Alicorn ready to dream the night away.

***

An hour later, Loki's eyes flipped open to the voices outside his Cadillac. He thought it was the squirrels and cats trying to talk to him again, but it wasn't. He was too tired to sit up and look outside—and a little bit worried as well.

51

It was the singing children.

They sounded close enough they could knock on his window and if he looked outside and didn't find them, he was going to freak out and keep searching for them all night, so he decided to try to block the singers out. He already had his share of goose bumps for one night.

Loki started counting sheep in the moonlit sky, preparing to sleep and snore the night away. He imagined sheep playing in a green field in Heaven, making their happy sounds: *baa, baa ever after*. It was a lovely image, and he wished it were true. As he drowsed off, he spotted two black sheep, which the other sheep avoided. Closer, he discovered he was one of the two sheep.

While snoring in his sleep, the song the children were singing slipped into his dream. He could finally hear the words while the kids clicked their feet to the beat:

Snow White one, Snow White two,
Sorrow was coming out for you.
Snow White three, Snow White four,
Black as night, go lock your door.
Snow White five, Snow White six,
Blood red lips and crucifix
Snow White seven, Snow White eight,
White as snow, don't stay out late.
Snow White Nine, Snow White ten,
Snow White now killed Snow White then.

6

Rumpelstein High

In the morning, Loki woke up to a knocking on his Cadillac's window.

"Are you singing in your sleep?" Lucy asked with her nose pressing to the window, her face blocking the sun.

Loki straightened up in his seat with drowsy eyes, shooing her nose away from behind the glass. Lucy backed up as he rolled down the squeaky window.

"Good morning to you, too," Loki said, sticking his neck out to look at the parking lot. It was blooming with cars and students, and seemed utterly normal in daylight. "I was singing? What was I singing?" he wondered with one eye closed, his other eye trying to make peace with the glaring sun. "What is with the changing weather here in Sorrow?" he whispered to himself sleepily.

"Some silly rhyme," Lucy remarked. Her face glowed with energy, and her blonde hair was marvelously waist-long. Even now, Lucy didn't look like she was dressed for school. She looked as if she were going out to another party. Loki wondered if the demon girl he'd been in love with was as pretty as her. "You were singing something like: *One-two-I-love-you*. Like a nursery rhyme, you know? And you were also snoring. I detest boys who snore," Lucy added.

I was singing a song I learned from little girls who I couldn't see?

"Who said I want you to love me?" Loki rubbed his eyes with both hands. "Besides, don't blame a guy who comes from a place called Snoring when he's *snoring*. It's like our national anthem."

"Do all people in Snoring look so scared in their sleep? Nightmares much?" she folded her hands before her.

"I'm a Dreamhunter. I eat nightmares for dinner," Loki said, running his hand through his hair while looking into the rear view mirror.

"A day ago I would've lent you my comb, just to try to impress your pretty green eyes," Lucy said.

Loki didn't reply. He knew Lucy was a spoiled kid, and was disappointed with him after failing to kill Dork Dracula. He was occupied with one big hole in his sock, trying to put on his shoes.

"Is that a hole in your sock?" Lucy shrieked as if she'd seen a cockroach worming out of it.

"Relax, it's just my toe, saying 'good morning' to you," Loki said, wiggling it.

Lucy bent over and whispered in his ear, "We both know you're the lousiest vampire hunter in the world, so save your comebacks. And if you're not good to me while you're here visiting my father's school, I swear I'll—"

"Wow," Loki stood up, forcing her to take a step back. "I think we've started off on the wrong foot. Let's forget about that night at the party and start all over again, shall we?" Loki smiled and held out his hand. "My name is Loki Blackstar, and I'm here to save your town. Thank you very much."

Lucy didn't shake his hand so Loki brushed her away and started stretching his arms and legs in the parking lot. A couple of girls walking by, holding books to their chests, giggled at him over their shoulders.

"Morning aerobics anyone?" Loki inquired, not staring back.

"So you don't happen to know anything about little girls singing creepy songs late at night in Sorrow, I assume," Loki asked Lucy.

"What girls?"

"I thought so. Never mind. Do you have any knowledge about a Train of Consequences that brings newcomers to Sorrow?" Loki supposed she wouldn't have heard of it either and he doubted others knew about the crazy things he'd seen last night as well.

"A train of what en-ces?" Lucy replied quizzically.

Before he could explain, the earth underfoot started rumbling. It started with a faint drone as if there was a giant burping underground and then the drone turned to a rattle. Loki's eyes widened. He saw the cars in the parking lot shaking. Teens stopped in their places but none of them looked surprised. It felt like an earthquake that was about to start but changed its mind.

When it stopped, everyone went back to business, as if this was normal.

"Phew," Loki blew out a sigh, noticing Lucy had been amusing herself with the scared look on his face.

"Why am I the only one worried about the earthquake that just happened?"

"Because it happens all the time," Lucy said. "We're on an island. It does that almost every day, anytime of the day. Now, follow me," she signaled for him as if he were her private butler. "My dad left you something in his office."

"Left me something? I'm not going to meet him?"

"He is very busy; so busy I almost never see him," Lucy said without turning back.

Loki kicked the door of his car to close it, and followed her into Rumpelstein High.

Lucy was incredibly popular, waving to friends and high-fiving others while she strolled down the hallway. It occurred to Loki that he was the one who was saving the town from the vampire, yet Lucy got all the fame.

The school looked different from what Loki had imagined a school in

Hell would be like. He'd imagined it full of wizards, witches, vampires, werewolves, ghosts, and the whole nine yards. He'd imagined cobwebs on the windows; blood spattered on the walls, teachers with horns and large forks, and girls drinking their ex-boyfriend's blood and wearing it as lipstick for fun.

Rumpelstein High was far from it. This was just the normal American high school like in Snoring, only it seemed far from boring.

"So do you always go to school dressed as if you're going out on a date?" Loki was making conversation while they walked to her father's office.

"Not always, but today I am going out on a date after I give you the package my father told me to."

"You have a boyfriend?" Loki asked.

"Permanent boyfriend? Not a chance. Boyfriends are temporary, but I like this new one. He's better than the one from last month."

"Last month? I know people who don't change their underwear that much."

"And he's not one of the football team hunks," Lucy bragged. "I don't date boys from school. They're boring and there's too much drama when we break up. I like my boys to be outsiders in every sense of the word, and older."

Lucy stopped at the office and opened the door. Loki stood at the threshold as she entered and picked up an envelope from the desk.

"Here," she handed Loki the envelope. "That's your down payment."

"Wombles! Thank you," Loki took the envelope without opening it. He didn't want to look eager and broke. Still, the envelope was thick and tempting, and made him think of renting a room just so he could sleep on an actual bed. "I'm starting to like your father."

"I doubt you would if you met him," Lucy said. "Anyway, I have to go meet up with my boyfriend."

"Wait," Loki said. "Is that all? Aren't you going to tell me more about the vampire princess, where she lives, and how I could find her?"

"There is nothing to tell, Loki," Lucy said. "She lives in a castle in the Black Forest, the one whose turrets you see rising high wherever you go in Sorrow. You go there and kill her, that's if you're up to the job. Good luck, handsome. You're going to need plenty of it."

Lucy left Loki speechless in the middle of the hallway. He thought it was a bit weird that none of the town's council members had come to greet him.

"Oh, one more thing," Lucy turned around halfway down the hallway. "You have only six days to get the job done."

"One week?" Loki said. Loki wondered if this was pure coincidence. It was impossible for Lucy to know the deadline placed on him by the

Council of Heaven.

"That's when our new principal arrives," Lucy said. "I heard she's a woman of discipline, and the town's council is looking forward to working with her.

"What does the new principal have to do with the vampire princess?" Loki tiptoed to look at Lucy behind the growing crowd in the hallway. Mentioning the vampire princess had turned a lot of faces toward him.

"She's the one who demanded the princess be killed before she arrived and begins work," Lucy said, and then he couldn't hear her anymore as she disappeared behind the crowd.

Loki avoided the staring eyes, wondering why the students were so interested in him when he mentioned the vampire princess. He walked the hallway slowly, and thought he'd inspect it for a while.

There was a drawing on a bulletin board of a nasty young vampire princess with blood drooling from her lips. She had red eyes, tattooed arms, black hair, and was very pale. It looked like cleverly imagined fan art of the unseen Snow White. This wasn't the Disney Snow White girls loved when they were kids. It was a nasty one with fangs and blood. The drawing was creative and creepy and ecstatically dreadful. It amused Loki how this version of Snow White was interesting; lips red as blood, skin pale as snow; the description made the idea of her being a vampire seem not so far-fetched.

But Loki also thought that the idea was plain silly. He always had contradicting thoughts.

A couple of steps farther, Loki noticed there were numerous other pictures, drawings, photo-shopped and fabricated portraits of the vampire princess and her castle. There were ads about forums on the internet that required memberships to discuss the Snow White vampire—a notable forum called 'Harum Scarum' seemed to be the students' favorite. There were phone numbers of bogus vampire hunters who claimed they knew how to kill her. There were kids selling magic garlic, silver crosses, and charms to keep the vampire princess away and handwritten maps on the bulletin board of people who claimed they had been to the castle. It seemed that the Black Forest was some kind of a cerebral maze, where people got lost and never returned. The town of Sorrow was obviously obsessed with the vampire princess. That must have been why the students were looking at Loki.

"Those she lays her eyes upon," a voice said from behind Loki. "Don't live long enough to tell about it."

Loki turned around. He saw a boy hiding his face in a purple hood. He was munching on a sandwich and staring at the bulletin board.

"Excuse me?" Loki said.

"It's a famous saying in Sorrow," the boy said. "That whomever the princess lays her eyes upon is cursed instantly, and no matter what they do, they won't be able to escape death."

"Oh," Loki shrugged.

"No wonder every other vampire hunter has failed to kill her. The only way to do it is without her laying her eyes upon them. They must've not known that little tidbit."

"How do you know that, if you don't mind me asking?" Loki said.

"I have my secret sources," the boy said while Loki thought about looking under his hood to see his face. Even though the boy talked like he was something, Loki sensed he was faking it from the quality of his voice. "Did you hear what I said, Loki Blackstar?" the boy said, still hiding under his hood, and looking at the bulletin board.

"How do you know my name?" Loki said.

"We know everything, and we know you're here to kill her," the boy said with a mouthful. "We wish you luck," the boy moaned to the taste of his sandwich. It was as if he couldn't stop eating. He pulled on Loki's hand and stuck the rest of the sandwich in it. "Donkeyskin Burger, the best in town."

The boy left, leaving Loki speechless with a greasy sandwich in his hand. It smelled good. Loki couldn't resist bringing it closer to his nose.

"Donkeyskin Burger?" Loki mused. "What a freak," he dropped the sandwich in the garbage can next to him.

When he turned around, he saw that the corridor was empty. Apparently everyone had gone to class and he hadn't noticed. Loki decided he had seen enough of the school and walked out. His plan was to rent the best room he could get with the biggest and most comfortable bed just like he'd always dreamed of, conjure up some sleep, and then ask around to learn the way to the Black Forest.

Loki walked out to his Cadillac, unable to push the image of a comfy bed in a five-star hotel away—he even imagined eating delicious food and taking a hot shower. He wondered if Sorrow had five-star hotels, if any— and if the creepy singing girls would follow him there.

As Loki neared his Cadillac he heard a squeaky voice calling his name from the parking lot. Had he become famous already?

Loki turned around, looking for the person calling for him. He saw a couple of huge boys bullying a student in the middle of the parking lot. No one did anything about it. In fact, most of the students were watching and laughing at the undersized freak from the hallway squirming between two whopping boys. The scene reminded Loki of Donnie Cricketkiller, Beebully, and Beetlebuster back in the Ordinary World.

You're not here to save anyone, even if some stranger is calling your name. Save yourself first.

But Babushka's words crept into his ears again. He remembered his conversation with her on his way to Sorrow when she told him that she couldn't imagine him walking away from someone in need.

I don't like Minikins. Why should I even bother?

An imaginary slap from Babushka's hand landed on Loki's face, but it didn't faze him and he turned around to open the door to his Cadillac.

"I'm not a hero. I'm just a 15 and 3/4 year old, looking for a way back home and a comfy bed to sleep on," Loki climbed into his car, and rolled the squeaky window up so he wouldn't hear the voice calling his name. Still, each squeak pierced guilt into his conscience.

Before kick-starting Carmen, Loki felt something in his back pocket. It was the notebook Charmwill had given to him. Holding it in his hand, he suddenly doubted Dreamhunters gave up on people who needed help. It was true that Dreamhunters killed Demortals in their sleep, but something told him that they were heroic people that helped those in need and he was one of *them*. His thought was interrupted by Carmen's radio singing back to life. It was the Pumpkin Warriors again. One of them was playing a simple acoustic song on a guitar. It went like this:

Loki, Loki is such a big lie,
Left the boy and let him cry.
When the boy called out his name,
Loki said I'm not to blame.
Loki, Loki is such a big lie,
Left the boy and said goodbye.

"OK," Loki smacked the dashboard. "I get it!"

He opened the window and took one last look at the two big beastly teens, which were twice his size. He shrugged and opened the door, walking toward them.

"What are you doing?" the two girls with books held to their chests hissed at Loki. "No one messes with Big Bad and Paw Paw."

"Who are Big Bad and Paw Paw?" Loki stopped.

"Paw Paw is the stud with earrings, Big Bad is the one with the huge chest," one of the girls said. "They call themselves the Bullyvards. No one messes with them."

"They're playing 'Pig and Sheep' with the poor boy," the other girl elaborated. "They'll keep bullying him until he confesses he's either a pig or a sheep. If he confesses to being a pig they'll put him in a garbage can and huff and puff it away. If he confesses to being a sheep, they'll hunt him down and bite him as punishment."

"Loki! Help!" the boy screamed as he stretched an arm out from under

Paw Paw's armpit, looking his direction. Big Bad and Paw Paw turned their heads towards Loki. It was too late to chicken out.

"Who do you think I should take down first?" Loki said to the girls, his eyes fixed on Big Bad's titanic chest. It looked like it had someone else stuffed inside it, "the Big or the Bad?"

The girls giggled as Loki reluctantly approached the Bullyvards who were staring at him disdainfully. The closer he got to them, the shorter and skinnier he felt; in contrast the brute's smirks widened. He'd never seen a meaner expression on someone's face, not even Donnie Cricketkiller's.

"Hi," Loki waved his hand casually, pretending he was taking a walk in the park. He remembered Charmwill telling him that he could be whoever he wanted to be in Sorrow. Images of Donnie Cricketkiller and the other vampire hunters stealing his vampires flashed before his eyes. For a boy who'd been prohibited from fighting with bullies who picked on him and others, this was going to be a great opportunity to change. The Bullyvards were only feet away, but the walk felt like miles.

Closer now, Loki saw the boy, and figured out he was the one with the purple hoodie and the Donkeyskin Burger. His purple hoodie lay crumpled on the ground, covered in dirt and footprints.

"Looking for something?" Paw Paw growled, squeezing the boy's neck with his giant Popeye-arm. He looked almost twenty, heavily tattooed and too old for school.

"Actually, it's that funny smell that brought me here," Loki covered his nose with his hand, hiding some of his Magic Dust in it. "Phew, what did you guys eat today?"

The onlookers laughed then stopped immediately when Paw Paw looked back at them.

"Are you making fun of me," Paw Paw grinned, squeezing harder on the boy's neck whose face was turning blue as his tongue dangled from his open mouth.

"God forbid," Loki said. "I was making fun of him," Loki pointed at Big Bad.

Everyone in the parking lot held their breath. Loki doubted his attitude for a second, but hell, it felt good to make fun of the bullies, even if it meant he'd end up a Pig or Sheep. Instantly, Big Bad reached for Loki's shirt with one hand and lifted him up from the ground.

"How could you be so stupid to even think about insulting us?" Big Bad chuckled. He was about eighteen with long seventies side burns and a ridiculous Elvis style haircut.

"Stupid enough to do it, but smart enough to do it right," Loki said choking in the air.

A couple of students laughed, hiding in the crowd.

Paw Paw dropped the boy to the ground and kicked him away before grabbing Loki's legs and holding him upside down.

Loki thought it would be a terrible way to die, squeezed like a greasy fast food sandwich between these two.

"Wow," Loki said. "I'm sorry guys. I have to admit that it wasn't right to offend you. I'm really sorry. If you just let me down, I will make it up to you."

Big Bad and Paw Paw let him down, laughing out loud in the middle of the parking lot. Their voices were so intimidating that the students took a step back.

"I don't know man," Big Bad said to Paw Paw, laughing again at how cowardly Loki turned out to be. When he laughed, the muscles in his chest went up and down, down and up, like a heavy ripple in a swamp. "This one is neither a Pig nor a Sheep. He's a squashed beetle already."

"I think we started off on the wrong foot," Loki adjusted his shirt. "Let's play nice and start all over again. I'm sorry I haven't introduced myself properly," he held out his hand.

"So, introduce yourself," Big Bad said.

"I'm Loki Blackstar," Loki smiled. "And I'm here to kick your asses."

Loki took a step forward and got up close and personal with Big Bad, faster than a pussycat he blew Magic Dust into his face.

Big Bad got dizzy. Loki punched him in the face before he dropped to the ground like a heavy bag of groceries. Loki's fist hurt, but he turned around and blew Magic Dust in Paw Paw's face, punched him, and watched as the kid crumpled to the floor.

Everyone in the parking lot went whoooo! All they saw was Loki hitting the boys; it didn't quite register what he'd actually done. They didn't know a thing like Magic Dust even existed.

The boy grabbed Loki's fists and examined them, looking for the secret of his superpowers while the girls clapped and cheered.

It felt good being the parking lot's hero and Loki walked proudly back to his car.

"Wait!" the boy said. "Can you give me a ride home?"

"I ride alone," Loki said without looking back.

"Please?" the boy reached for Loki's hand. "If the rest of the Bullyvards see what happened to Big Bad and Paw Paw, they'll hurt me. I need to get out of here."

"OK. I get it. Hop in. I'll give you a ride."

The boy got in the passenger's seat and stretched out his hand. "I'm Axel," he said. "And I'm not here to kick your ass," he joked.

Loki shook Axel's hand, and thought he looked like a decent boy without the hood; cute features, natural spiky hair, and freckles on his face, a nerdier version of Macaulay Culkin, only a bit chubby.

Loki kick started his Cadillac. The radio played another fast-paced song by the Pumpkin Warriors that was about heroes saving the world.

Lucy walked up waving at Loki, her long hair fluttering in the breeze. *Damn that long, beautiful hair.* She must've heard the commotion in the parking lot and wondered what was happening.

Sitting in the passenger seat, jaw-dropped Axel couldn't stop staring at Lucy whose smile was beyond belief, just like the happy cute girls dancing in a Japanese Manga or Anime.

Lucy wasn't alone. A muscular figure with another outdated Elvis haircut, long sideburns, and a black leather jacket, was with her.

Axel stopped drooling like a puppy. Loki was chewing on envy as Lucy held the boy's hand.

"Hey," Lucy said, peeking through the window.

"Hey yourself," Axel, interrupted, tilting his head.

"You made friends already?" she asked Loki, bestowing an infuriating stare at Axel, as if he was some funny looking and unappreciated Gremlin. Axel swallowed an invisible fireball and stayed silent.

"Why are you still at school?" she wondered. "Shouldn't you be getting some sleep and buying yourself a new pair of socks? By the way, this is Ulfric Moonclaw," she introduced her boyfriend.

"Pleasure," Ulfric said, squeezing Lucy closer to him, and whispering something in her ear then kissing her on the cheek. Her eyes glowed, and Loki couldn't help but wonder what he'd told her. Ulfric didn't even acknowledge Axel who was officially invisible to most people in school, so he buried himself into the passenger seat.

"So what's the buzz about up there?" Ulfric wondered, pointing at the horde of girls trying to wake up Big Bad and Paw Paw. Loki gripped the wheel. If those two polar bears woke up, he wasn't prepared to face them again. It was time to go.

"Is that Big Bad and Paw Paw on the ground?" Lucy wondered.

"What?" Ulfric's face went red. "Who did that to them?" he looked back at Loki. "You know who did that to them?" he stared into Loki's eyes intensely. Loki felt as though he'd been punched in the face already.

"I'm the new dude, I don't know many students yet," Loki shrugged his shoulders, ignoring Axel pulling at his sleeves.

"I'm going to punish whoever did that to my friends," Ulfric said. Then he did something that struck Loki as odd. Ulfric titled his head up and yelled, 'Awooo!'

It was only seconds before others replied back, 'Awooo!" Loki assumed this was the rest of the Bullyvards' pack as Ulfric hurried toward them.

"Easy, Ulfric," Lucy pleaded after him. "He's reckless when he gets mad," Lucy said proudly. "And I love it."

But Loki wasn't there. He'd already sped away in his Cadillac, Axel still trying to bury himself under the passenger seat.

Closer to main street, Loki gazed in the rear view mirror and saw Ulfric Moonclaw chasing him on foot. He'd figured out it was him who had rendered Big Bad and Paw Paw unconscious.

Ulfric eventually gave up, swearing and panting in the middle of the parking lot. Loki couldn't hear what Ulfric was saying, but he assumed that he promised he'd soon teach Loki and Axel a lesson they would not forget.

Loki quietly speculated how much money he'd have made if he had a dollar for every time he looked in the rear view mirror and saw someone trying to chase him down.

"If you really want me to give you a ride home, you'll have to tell me how you know my name." Loki said while driving.

"Harum Scarum," Axel said. "It's an online forum. It's devoted to everything about the vampire princess. Someone mentioned that you'd be the next vampire hunter coming to town."

"What's with this obsession with the princess?"

"No one's ever killed her," Axel said. "I am a member of the forum, proud member in fact; I'm only twenty seven posts away from being an admin. I can help you since you're new to town."

"Like I said, I roll alone."

"Come on," Axel said. "You need an assistant. I bet you don't even know how to get to the castle, or about all the obstacles you'll have to overcome to get there."

"I can handle myself."

"Yeah, it showed when the earth was shaking and you were the only one in the parking lot who was scared. I saw you."

"You know what shook the earth in the parking lot?" Loki was curious.

"See?" Axel grinned. "You need me," he pointed proudly to himself.

Loki let out a short sigh. He didn't think there would be any harm using the help of someone who knew the town well. He was running out of time anyway.

"OK," Loki said. "You could show me the way to the castle, but that'll be it."

"Awesome!" Axel wanted to high five Loki, but Loki let him down.

"So what's shaking the earth in Sorrow?" Loki asked.

"The whale," Axel answered. "This island is built on the back of a whale, and sometimes it shakes a little after having a big meal."

"That's outrageous," Loki said with disbelief. "Not at all," Axel said. "I know they lied to you at school and called it an earthquake. Trust me, it's a whale."

7

Candy House

"Come on in!" Axel ushered Loki through the door. It was a lonely house atop the highest hill in Sorrow, a perfect spot to observe the rest of the street-curving town. "If you ever get lost, trying to get here," Axel explained, "ask for the Candy House on Breadcrumb Street. It's practically the last house separating the town from the woods beyond that leads to the water surrounding Sorrow."

Loki assumed Axel meant the Missing Mile, but he doubted Axel knew about it or the Train of Consequences. He had a feeling the things he'd experienced entering the town were tailored for him somehow; and he remembered Igor telling him that only those who entered Sorrow for the first time rode the Train of Consequences. Still, Loki didn't desire knowing more about all of this weirdness, as long as he was on the right track in his mission. Instead, he occupied himself with watching Axel's mysterious house.

Candy House was a peculiar piece of wicked art. It was constructed of wood and stone, and it had a sod-roof that curved like a magic carpet with two layers of green grass over chocolate-brown mud. Loki thought the house could easily go unnoticed because of how it was dug into the hillside. Only the irregularly-shaped, huge windows with hazel sticks suggested someone lived inside. It looked like a crafted woodcutter with chainsaws, hammers, and chisels built it. It was a perfect, primitive hiding place between the edge of town and the beginning of the labyrinthine woodland behind it.

"Nice house," Loki said, and took a step back to get a wider view.

The cornerstones looked like chunks of dark and vanilla-white chocolate, and the cement between the stones looked like bloody-red trails of sticky candy. The wood looked like the surface of hazelnut granola bars; crunchy, sweet, and edible. Loki licked his lips briefly, and felt an unexplained urge to touch the house to make sure it wasn't really candy, but he didn't want to embarrass himself in front of Axel.

The lantern above the porch was the shape of a pumpkin with smiling eyes and fang-like teeth; the yellow shimmering from inside complimented the ember shade of candles shimmering from behind the windows of the house. Candy House was spooky in a Halloween sort of way. Loki was confused because he felt good about it. He almost felt at home for the first time in the Ordinary World—if he could actually count Sorrow as part of the Ordinary World.

Axel tried to open the door with a key that was the shape of a gingerbread man, but he couldn't because of a spider web that was covering the keyhole. It seemed a bit odd to Loki that the house Axel lived in looked as if it had been abandoned for years.

"Something wrong?" Loki asked worriedly.

"Nah, it's just my sister's spiders. They love to play games with me so I can't get into the house," Axel said nonchalantly. "They don't like me too much."

"Sister? Spiders?" Loki countered with bewilderment, wondering why everyone treated poor Axel like a second-class citizen, even the spiders.

Axel didn't reply. He kicked the door with his boot as if he were a Kung-Fu master. The frame crackled and the door flung wide open.

Axel spread his hospitable arms, "Welcome to the Crumblewoods!"

"Crumblewoods?"

"I'm a Crumblewood," Axel said proudly. "Axel Crumblewood," he stretched out a hand to Loki. "And I'm going to kick your butt," Axel laughed, imitating Loki at the parking lot. "Nice line by the way—shame on Batman for not using it. But here we are, the Crumblewood's House, also known as Candy House, located at Seven, Breadcrumb Street, the last house at the edge of the world—that's how the mailman likes to describe it," Axel whispered.

Aside from silly names, dust, and creepiness, Loki still had a good feeling about the house. It felt insta-comfy, as if he'd been here before, but it was probably the fact that he'd been sleeping in his Cadillac for almost a year. It crossed his mind to ask Axel if they had an extra room he could rent later.

Inside, the house dumbfounded Loki with a different vibe. It was like a teenager's wonderland, devoid of any parental control. There was a big living room overlooking an open kitchen up front. The walls were also the color of chocolate, and there was a huge rug in the middle; its colors swirled like a mixture of vanilla, strawberry, and mango. There was also a huge TV, a comfortable red couch the shape of a liver, and a hammock hanging between two trees, which supported the structure as columns protruded out of the earth. Loki was impressed, and decided he would make a house like this when he returned to Fairy Heaven.

The Candy House was heated with a fireplace that looked like a huge oven, and it was lit with candles and chandeliers. The inner walls were made of bales of straw that were stacked on stones and staked with hazel sticks. Loki spotted another unused big, black, oven in the kitchen, which was either really old or a decorative antique. The house was definitely weird but looked like fun. Loki wondered about Axel's parents but decided not to ask.

All of a sudden, the fun vanished like the moon at daybreak…

The front door slammed shut on its own behind Loki, and a spiraling breeze swirled against the windows, blowing the white curtains inwardly into ghostly waves as if there was an invisible big bad wolf puffing the house from the outside.

"You have demons in your house?" Loki flinched, flashing his Alicorn.

"Well," Axel shrugged. "It's my sister," he started breathing heavily and his eyes rolled to the top of their sockets as if his sister was plastered to the ceiling.

"Your sister is a demon, too?"

"Of course, not," Axel said, fidgeting. "She's a witch; a wannabe witch."

"Stop it, Fable!" Axel shouted at the swinging chandelier dangling from the ceiling. Books started falling from the shelves and the tree-column swayed slightly. The house seemed to crumble and rumble as if they were standing in the belly of a whale that'd just had a heavy meal. Loki ducked to avoid a couple of flying dishes.

A skinny, cute girl, with pink-framed glasses and braided pigtails, stepped out from another room. She looked about fifteen, and she was holding a heavy vellum book of spells with her small nimble hands.

"Sorry!" Fable raised her voice against the flying objects, sounding overly apologetic as if she'd overcooked a meal with a bad recipe from the internet. "Wrong Spell!" she wiggled her nose then adjusted her glasses, trying to keep her balance as she looked back into the book. Although Loki wanted to escape this madness, he couldn't escape Fable's cuteness. He thought she needed to unbraid her hair and lose the glasses, though. Never had Loki felt so charmed by a girl he wished was his sister.

Loki noticed that the cover of the book she was holding read:

Magick and Voddoo for Dummies and the Unfortunate

Voddoo was written with two Ds and was missing an O. No wonder her spells had gone bad.

"Just a sec," Fable raised a forefinger and hollered over the noise. "If I can get the page turned; the solution is only one page away, but most of the pages are stuck together with grime, so it's going to take a minute."

"Wet your finger with your tongue and flip the page!" Axel shrieked, holding onto a tree, five feet up in the air.

Fable wet her finger and flipped through the next large page, which was the color of an old treasure map.

As the muddy roof rumbled louder, Axel hugged the tree tighter with his hands and legs like a monkey on a circus pole.

"I hate this," Loki announced, his legs fixed to the floor. His arms were stretched as if surfing on angry waters.

Axel's face looked like it was being sucked on by an angry, invisible vacuum cleaner.

"I found it," Fable shouted finally. "*Mumble, jumble, stop your rumble,*" she chanted, reading from the book, but nothing happened. "*Tumble, crumble, stop your mumble,*" she followed.

"What kind of spell is that?" Axel protested. "How many times did I tell you to try out spells before you actually *use* them?"

"Wait a sec," Fable flipped more pages. "Here it is. *One, twice, thrice and done. Wind of madness, just be gone. I command you from higher ground. Stop it now, no spellbound. Whoosh. Whoosh. Whoosh, and Whoosh,*" she stomped her feet with every *whoosh.*

It was incredible how the room suddenly seized, and relaxed from its grumpy tantrum. The curtains stopped fluttering, nothing fell from the shelves anymore, and whatever seemed to be sucking on Axel's face was gone.

"Are you guys alright?" Fable let the book fall, thudding against the wooden floor. She looked genuinely worried behind her embarrassed, grey eyes.

"I think so," Loki said, panting.

"Great. I'm Fable," she stretched out a hand toward Loki, and he shook it gently. "I'm Axel's older sister," she said.

Loki raised an eyebrow because he thought she looked younger than Axel.

"No. No. I'm just messing with you. I'm younger," Fable laughed with dimpled cheek.

"Fable, is such a lovely name," Loki said.

"It's short for Fabulous," she said proudly. "And I'm not messing with you this time. I was named Fabulous."

"Pretty neat," Loki said. "And Axel is short for what?"

"Why would Axel be short for anything? I'm Fabulous, he isn't," she stuck her tongue out at her brother who was still panting. "I don't think my parents knew what to call him so they just named him Axel."

"What kind of logic is that?" Axel protested. "There must be a great guy I'm named after, like Axelus the Great. He was a Greek god."

"There's no such thing," Fable said.

"Maybe I was going to be named Excellent, only our parents didn't know how to spell it."

"Whatever," Fable waved her hand. "Sorry about that madness, Loki. Axel doesn't usually bring friends back to the house. If I'd known, I wouldn't have messed around with the spell. Want some Pookies?" Fable offered. I finally learned how to cook!

"What are Pookies?" "Cookies made from pigs," Fable enlightened him. "They're sweet, pink, and have pig's noses that make funny sounds when you squeeze them."

"Cookies made with a recipe from the *Voddoo* book?" Loki questioned.

"You noticed? It's misspelled," she grinned. "That's why I got it cheaper. Almost for free," she whispered and nodded her head at Loki as if both of them shared a genuine secret. Although Fable's beauty wasn't as obvious as Lucy's, Loki couldn't resist her charms.

"Enough Fable," Axel interrupted. "Go back to your room to study. Loki and I have business to take care of. Besides, I ate all the Pookies this morning," Axel played older brother then headed to the refrigerator, ate chips from a bag that looked like they were two days old, and gulped from an open can on the way. He opened the refrigerator, pulled out a plate of red jelly and placed it on the counter. The jelly shook nervously on the plate. "Don't be afraid. I'm not going to hurt you," he talked to it, reaching for a spoon. "I'm just going to eat you. Yum, Yum."

Loki exchanged looks with Fable. She seemed like she wanted to scream and pull her pigtails out. Somehow, this was enough to prove to Loki that the house wasn't made of candy, or Axel would've eaten it long ago.

"Do we have any Coffincakes left?" Axel asked Fable with a mouthful of jelly.

"Coffincakes?" Loki wondered.

"Yeah, those little coffin-shaped cakes that you can open and eat the carrot-corpse then eat the cake, I mean, the coffin as dessert," Axel explained. "You never heard about them? Where are you from, man? They're just like Coffinmuffins."

It was official; food in Sorrow was peculiar, eccentric and bordered on madness.

"Can't you ever stop eating?" Fable growled at Axel. "You ate all my food."

"Because you ate my Sticky Cinnamon Frogs yesterday," Axel fired back, swallowing. "Besides, all you ever eat is bread."

"I don't eat bread all the time. I use it to find my way back from when I go to the market and back. Don't worry about Axel eating everything," Fable said to Loki, picking up her book of spells. "I have apples in my room, if you feel hungry; Bad Apples, Mad Apples, and Poisoned Apples."

"They're not really poisoned apples, are they?"

"Of course not," Fable laughed. It was a mesmerizing laugh; the laugh of a girl who rarely left the house or faced the dangers of life. Still, Loki adored her perkiness. "You just faint for a couple of minutes after eating them. It's like taking a nap after a heavy meal. Everyone loves Poisoned Apples in Sorrow," she elaborated.

Loki saw a small spider crawling on Fable's shoulder. When he tried to swoosh it away, she stopped him.

"Don't hurt him. It's Itsy," she patted it as it tickled her neck.

"I told you my sister is a wanna-be witch. What I didn't tell you is that she is also very weird," Axel laughed.

"And this is Bitsy," Fable pointed at a motionless tarantula, lying on the floor next to the couch.

"He looks ummmm-" Loki said.

"Dead—"Axel suggested, thrilled at making fun of his sister.

"No, he isn't," Fable explained to Loki. "He is just depressed. He broke up with his girlfriend."

"He's depressed because you charmed him with the wrong mood-lifter spell last week," Axel said, throwing the spoon into the sink. "Now seriously, go back to your room. Let the big boys do their work, and don't forget to do my homework, too."

"I don't want to go to my room, and you're not dad, you know," Fable insisted, hugging the heavy book to her chest. "Can I please join you in whatever you're doing? I'm bored," she complained, adjusting her glasses.

"No you can't," Axel insisted. "Girls should listen to their big brothers, be polite and not ask too many questions."

"That's a bit sexist," Loki tried to interrupt.

"Shhh," Axel eyed Loki. "Don't talk about sex in front of my little sister."

"Axel," Fable barked, "you're the dumbest brother in the world," she mumbled something else and waved goodbye to Loki who felt for her, and then went back to her room.

"So how come she is into magic?" Loki asked Axel.

"She wouldn't be if our mother hadn't been."

"Your mother is a witch?"

"Was, she and dad died when I was like three. I don't really remember them."

"Oh. Sorry about that."

"They're the ones who're dead. You should be sorry for them. My dad was a woodcutter. Mom was a witch; at least that's what I was told. All I know is that she was a lousy witch. Isn't it funny that my mom failed at being an evil witch? Maybe that's why the Bullyvards pick on me so much. I mean if you're going to be a witch, then be a freakin' kick-ass, spell casting, ingenious witch. What happened to raw, evil, villainous role models?"

"You wish your mother was evil?"

"Why not? She could've taught me what to do with Ulfric Moonclaw when I see him again," Axel made a claw of his right hand and made a goofy evil face. "I mean, listen to his name, Moonclaw. It oozes with evil. He should worship his parents."

"Don't you think it's bizarre you hate the guy but like his name?"

"Not at all; I like your name, too, by the way. Loki Blackstar. It sounds like a fictional hero's name.

Flawed logic aside, it was still hard to think of a villain with the last name Crumblewood, or even a hero for that matter.

"So who takes care of you and your sister?" Loki slumped back on the comfy red couch. He couldn't remember the last time he felt comfortable with the company of a teen he'd just met. It was a strange feeling, but a good one.

"We have a foster parent who picked us up two years ago from the Orphanage of Sorrow," Axel said. Loki thought this explained why Axel and Fable didn't have friends. "Her name is Mircalla. Strange name, I know, but she is a fantastic woman. She pays for everything and takes care of us although she doesn't spend much time with us. She's kind of like our fairy godmother, and she is awesome."

"Why isn't she here now?"

"She visits every week or so. She has other orphans to take care of all around the world, so we practically have the house to ourselves."

"Interesting," Loki thought Mircalla reminded him of the way Charmwill took care of him, only Charmwill never paid the bills or bought him a house. "I would love to meet her," Loki said, although he didn't mean it. By the time Mircalla came to visit again, he should have killed the vampire princess and left.

"She'll be back in a couple of days, which means we'll have to clean the house before that."

Loki thought he clicked with Axel and Fable because they were orphans like him. Aside from his lost memories, Loki hadn't had the chance to even know his father's name, and his mother refused to tell him. All he knew from Charmwill was that he was a great Dreamhunter who'd been shadowed after falling in love with his mother who gave birth to Loki.

Loki touched his pocket where he kept the Dreamhunter's notebook. He hadn't had time to read it to figure out how he'd kill Snow White in her dreams. He planned to stake her first then take her somewhere safe where he could learn the process of killing a demon. Loki suddenly realized he was wasting time. He needed Axel to tell him about the obstacles he had to pass to get to the castle.

"I'm logging into the Snow White forum, Harum Scarum, so we can acquire all the info we need," Axel brought his laptop over to where Loki sat. He picked up Bitsy, the silent tarantula, from the floor and threw him at the window. The spider stuck on the glass without complaint as if it were a big hairy magnet. "Useless dead spider," Axel mumbled. "If only Fable didn't love you so much."

"What about this forum?" Loki asked.

"I know you won't believe me, but teens are secretly infatuated with the Snow White vampire princess," Axel said. "Here, you'll find all the secrets, speculations, and conspiracy theories about Snow White, and what really happened to her."

"Assuming she is the real Snow White," Loki rolled his eyes.

"Well, that's what the boys and girls say," Axel said. "On this forum, you'll find the names of the teens she killed, those who've tried to visit the castle recently, and those who claim they have seen her and came back. They are liars by the way."

"So enough with all that; get the info we need and let's go to the Black Forest."

"Easy, Loki, if we eat, wash, and rest for a while, we'll be ready to go out a little before midnight. That's when the boys and girls go there."

"Why do we have to wait until midnight?"

"Because she's a vampire, and wouldn't come out in the sun? Gosh. What kind of vampire hunter are you?"

Loki tapped his fingers impatiently, not commenting about Axel still wanting to eat again. If Axel were a demon, he'd have eaten him and Fable already.

"But first," Axel flopped back on the couch next to Loki, licking jelly off his fingers. "We kill us some Zombies," he said with a fiendish grin.

"Kill Zombies?" Loki wondered, noticing Bitsy had disappeared from the window, leaving a web with one word written into it: 'dork', probably addressing Axel.

Axel turned on the TV and started a game. Hordes of ugly Zombies walked toward them on the screen. Axel threw a wireless controller into Loki's lap. "No one leaves Candy House without brain-blasting some Zombies. It'll be a good adrenaline rush before killing your princess."

Loki sighed, picked up the device, and started hitting buttons. It was much easier killing zombies than killing vampires in real life. The game controller was more of a magic weapon that did the job easily. Loki wondered if his Alicorn would turn out to be as effective and help him kill the pale princess.

8

Buried Moon Cemetery

A little before midnight, Loki drove with Axel toward the Black Forest. Axel insisted on stopping at The Belly and the Beast, which he described as the best hangout for teens in Sorrow.

"Seriously? Do you really feel like eating again?" Loki sighed, parking in front of the venue.

Cute girls on rollerblades, wearing short skirts, served customers who sat in their cars outside The Belly and the Beast. Axel didn't want to eat inside because there was a chance they'd run into the Bullyvards. Loki didn't mind the drive in and dine method as long as it was fast; he wasn't here to schmooze and make friends.

The Belly and the Beast's neon logo sign blinked pink then blue, pink, then blue, right above the entrance's glass door. The logo featured a princess screaming for help from inside the *belly* of a beast who was munching on a triple-layered saucy sandwich and a pickle. Loki determined the beast looked like a fatter, scarier version of Axel.

"Tonight we're killing Snow White, the most vicious vampire in town," Axel said, faking an evil grin. "I need something to munch on to ease my fears," he flashed a tiny cross at Loki.

"Just make it fast, please. And you can forget about that cross. They don't work," Loki tapped the wheel.

"What do you mean they don't work? My backpack is stuffed with crosses, holy water, and garlic. I even brought a Harry Potter wand, in case the princess needs a little 'avada kedavra.' I suppose you're going to tell me they don't work either."

"Garlic? That's why it stinks in here," Loki looked away, tapping the wheel. "Sorry Carmen."

Carmen shook a little, and winked the windshield once. Axel didn't comment.

"You call garlic 'stinky'?" Axel leaned forward, still flashing his cross, sniffing Loki. "Maybe you're a vampire, Loki Blackstar. That's why you can't take the smell of garlic."

"Would you back off, please," Loki pushed Axel, noticing a cute girl on rollerblades winking at him from outside.

Although Axel's window was open, the girl approached Loki with a wide smile on her lips, knocking on his window.

"That's why I munch," Axel muttered, staring at her. "It's my substitute for the sex I will never have."

Loki rolled down his window.

"So what can I get you handsome?" the girl on rollerblades asked Loki.

"You have Sticky Sweet Bones?" Axel interrupted, turning his head awkwardly and leaning down a little to look at her.

"Yup," she said, still looking at Loki whose hand had slid down to his Alicorn. "You want your bones caramel-flavored or hazelnut?"

"You are *awesome-flavored*, sweetheart," Axel thought to himself.

"Bring me two bags of caramel flavored Sticky Sweet Bones, please, plus a pack of Tragic Beans," Axel said.

"Yummy, Tragic Beans" the girl blinked at Loki. "Don't you think two packs are too much? They'll make you cry."

Loki looked anxiously at Axel.

"Tragic Beans make you cry like when you peel an onion," Axel explained. "But they make you feel funny at the same time. Could we get some Nervous Sausages, the chili flavored ones, for my *handsome* friend here," Axel patted Loki's chest, talking to the girl. "He is kinda shy with girls."

"Aw, a shy guy, just my type," the girl said as something flashed in her eyes briefly. Loki wasn't sure if he'd just imagined it, but he gripped his Alicorn tighter. He thought the girl was cute.

Pippi Luvbug was cute, too. Remember?

"Okey dokey, then," the girl said, rolling away.

A couple of minutes later, the girl came rolling back with Axel's food. Loki reminded Axel that they weren't there for a picnic, and eagerly drove away.

It was pointless telling Axel about the girl, or he would have spent the rest of the night freaking out. Loki needed Axel to be comfortable enough to lead the way to the mysterious castle.

"So how far is it to the Black Forest?" Loki said as he held on tightly to the steering wheel.

"We're heading to Buried Moon Cemetery first. It's at the Southern entrance to the Black Forest," Axel stretched an arm out of the window in a naïve attempt at trying to stop the wind with the palm of his hand.

"Buried Moon Cemetery?"

"Rumor has it that the moon was buried there in ancient times," Axel explained. "It's a mysterious but interesting story that claims the moon was actually a girl. An Evil Queen captured the moon with the help of a wolf called Managarm who was obsessed with it, and hunted it every night with a flying carriage. Then, when he finally caught the moon, the queen buried the moon in this cemetery, and the world went dark for a while. Demons roamed the moonless nights until—"

"—a Prince Charming kissed her awake and brought her back from the grave," Loki speculated.

"Don't you believe in happy endings?" Axel teased him, munching on the Sticky Sweet Bones that made crunchy sounds. "The only happy ending

I can think of is when you finish what you're eating," Loki said.

"You don't like Sticky Sweet Bones? These aren't real by the way—although this piece replicates a cat's spine. Think of the Sticky Sweet Bones as biscuits; the idea is that the bones won't break until you lick the sweet stuff from the surface. I don't know how they do it, but it's delicious," Axel licked one and shoved it down his throat without chewing, reminding Loki of frogs. "I believe in happy endings, and especially in a true love's kiss that saves the day," he said, swallowing.

Loki said nothing and watched the road. The houses on both sides disappeared into the dark as if consumed by the vale of blackness. The moon was shining full and bright, though, leading Loki to dismiss Axel's story.

"So after we cross the Buried Moon Cemetery, we find the Black Forest on the other side?" Loki said.

"You wish it was that easy," Axel said, putting the bag of Sweet Sticky Bones aside. He picked up his phone and started reading from the posts on the internet forum. "According to the Harum Scarum forum, Snow White resides in a mysterious castle called the Schloss."

"The Schloss?"

"It means *castle* in German," Axel said. "The Schloss is somewhere in the Black Forest. It's said that it takes on many different shapes and changes locations. It also says that it's been there since the beginning of time—whatever that means. No two people ever agreed on what it looks like. But the few who claim they've been there, say that it feels as if it's alive. People even say it has its own soul and seduces its victims, attracting them like a moth to a flame."

"Nonsense," Loki shook his head. "All that gothic propaganda, as if it's Dracula's castle."

"You just took the words out of my phone," Axel said. "It says here that it is actually as scary as Dracula's castle and that if you dare enter his domain, he'll snarl at you with his *pale as snow* face and feed on you."

"Could you please skip to the important facts? How do we cross from Buried Moon Cemetery to the Black Forest?"

"The Black Forest itself is a large circular island, surrounded by the Swamp of Sorrow, a magical swamp that separates it from the town."

"So the Black Forest is an island within an island, separated from Buried Moon Cemetery by the Swamp of Sorrow, right?"

"That's what it says in the forum," Axel said. "It's told that there used to be bridges to cross the Swamp of Sorrow, but trolls ate them some time ago."

"Trolls?"

"Yeah, you know those guys; ugly, obnoxious, dudes—sometimes big, sometimes little—who are good for nothing?"

"I've heard of them. So how then, do we cross the Swamp of Sorrow?"

"First, we have to go to Buried Moon Cemetery," Axel said. "It's the safest area to cross the Swamp of Sorrow. The guys in the forum say that no one has ever been able to cross from anywhere else. It's also close to my house in case we need to hightail it out of the castle and hide."

"And then what? You still didn't tell me how to cross the Swamp of Sorrow."

"In a canoe," Axel said.

"Sounds good, whose canoe is it?" Axel squirmed, looking worriedly at Loki, "the ferryman's."

"What ferryman?" Loki gripped the wheel.

"Skeliman, the Ferryman," Axel said. "It's all in here," he pointed at his phone. "Skeliman the Ferryman is a skeleton who once served as a ferryman on the river Styx, sailing people across Hell. Somehow, he ended up guarding the Swamp of Sorrow. In order to cross the swamp, you will need to ride with him in his canoe."

"This stuff just gets better and better."

"If I were you, I'd listen to the people in the forum," Axel said. "Half of them had someone in their family killed by your vampire princess. Besides, if you think that's insane, you need to hear the rest of it."

"I'm listening," Loki sighed. "It's said that, unlike the castle, Skeliman the Ferryman doesn't like anyone to cross over," Axel said.

"That's confusing," Loki said. "If the castle seduces teens for the vampire princess to feed on, why would Skeliman do otherwise?"

"I have no idea," Axel started munching on something. "But it gets even weirder. Skeliman is a skeleton; he doesn't have eyes, only sockets. Therefore, he can't see," Axel chuckled, having relaxed now after eating. Loki wondered if that was why he was eating all the time.

"Read on," Loki said impatiently.

"It's advised to take advantage of Skeliman's blindness and get on his canoe, but only if you can hold your breath most of the ride."

"Why should we do that?" Loki said.

"Skeliman can recognize the living by their breath. Usually, his passengers are dead, and he is alright with that."

"But that doesn't make sense," Loki said. "How did all the other teenagers cross the Swamp of Sorrow?"

"This brings us to the other option," Axel said, scrolling down his phone's screen. "According to a post by another contributor in the forum, some teens figured a way around it. They've invented a secret way to cross without the ferryman detecting them. It's a *secret*, so the only way to find out is to wait for some of the teenagers and follow them to see how they do it."

"I don't have time for this. What if we don't find teens trying to cross over tonight?"

"I think we will. Boys and girls enter the Black Forest every night. They come to have fun, drink, party, and fool around."

Loki let out a long breath, looking into the dark of the road ahead. Now that they were close to the cemetery, the weather turned chilly. Loki refrained from asking Axel about the weather, because he knew Axel wouldn't stop babbling and he needed him to focus. He kept silent, and caught a glimpse of Axel munching on the Sweet Sticky Bones out of the corner of his eye. The closer they got to the cemetery, the slower Axel munched, and the bigger his pupils turned.

"Do you fear the dark, Loki?" Axel broke the silence, staring at the road as if waiting for something to pop out from the ditch.

"At the dark too long stare and you'll end up seeing what isn't there," Loki replied.

"Wise words, Yoda, wise words," Axel nodded hypnotically then snapped out of it. "We're almost there," he said, pointing at grey tombstones, appearing out of the mist like spirits welcoming them from their graves. Behind it, Loki could only see silhouettes of dark upon silhouettes of darker.

They finally arrived at a desolate dirt road. Carmen complained, grumbling and rattling. Loki noticed the trees bending down and curving slowly, their branches tangling together in the dark, curving like snakes above them. A couple of them appeared to have a single eye on the end of their branches to spy with.

"You see this?" Loki said.

"I—"Axel almost choked on his food, trying to bury himself in the passenger seat. "I read about those trees in the forum. They're called Juniper Trees. It's best to avoid them if possible. They're spies for the vampire princess."

"I'm a bit skeptical about who posts on the forum," Loki said, slowing down his Cadillac.

"Genius Goblin," Axel whispered.

"Who?"

"Genius Goblin, he is the forum's creator and its most prestigious contributor."

"Did you ever meet this Genius Goblin?"

"Never had the honor, really," Axel said. "But I'd like to."

Loki watched the trees as they started to crawl away and silently wondered if they were going back to the vampire princess to tell her she had company tonight.

"When I was a kid, my mind used to play tricks on me," Axel began. "I used to wake up in the middle of the night with the boogeyman standing over me with my bowl of cereal, gorging on it, laughing and pointing at me.

Whenever I blinked, he was gone. Blinking solved a lot of problems when I was a kid. You know what's really strange about it? The boogeyman didn't look like a boogeyman. He looked like a pirate."

Loki struggled to find a safe parking place for his Cadillac. He wasn't even going to bother to comment that no one had ever seen a boogeyman, therefore Axel could not realize the one he saw didn't look like one.

As annoying as Axel was, Loki related to his unstoppable need for talking—after all, Loki mumbled to himself all the time. Axel talked incessantly because he didn't have friends to talk to. Loki was probably the first friend he'd ever made, and he decided that later he'd have to tell Axel that he wasn't staying in this town.

"I wonder why you never snuck in to see the princess yourself." Loki probed as he stopped Carmen behind a mammoth bristly bush, just wide enough to conceal her from front to back.

"I'm too chicken, which basically means I'm smart," Axel said. "I only come to Buried Moon Cemetery when I am lonely and want to watch the teens having fun, making out and stuff. But that's it."

"So you're a Peeping Tom?" Loki laughed. "How about Fable, do you ever bring her along?"

"Of course, not," Axel's face went red. "She's too young to watch teens make out."

"You know you suck at showing her that you love her, don't you?"

"I know. I've always been terrible at showing how I feel, but I'm all the family she has. I have to be strict with her, and make sure she's doing what she needs to do."

Axel got out of the Cadillac and walked to a tombstone and sat on it. He pulled out another bag of food, dangling his feet from the tombstone. To Axel, this seemed like a little family picnic. Loki didn't mind as long as Axel stayed calm enough to be his guide.

"Tragic Beans?" he offered Loki.

"No thanks. I'm not in the mood for crying and laughing at the same time," Loki sat next to him.

"It doesn't happen very fast," Axel explained. "You need to eat half a bag before the effect takes place."

A black cat with green eyes approached Loki after circling a couple of times around the tombstone. Loki worried it would talk to him like usual, but he remembered animals only talked to him when he was alone. The cat brushed its ears against Loki's jeans and meowed. Loki patted it reluctantly.

"I wonder why animals don't love me the way they do you and Fable." Axel said, dropping Tragic Beans into his mouth, one by one. "You know that when I walk with Fable in the forest behind the house, butterflies rest on her arms?"

"She is Fabulous, remember?" Loki replied, winking at the cat. It winked back, and even bit its lip and nodded.

"I still don't get what my name was supposed to mean. If she's Fabulous, then who am I?" Axel wondered.

"Hungry," Loki mumbled. The cat buried a laugh behind a sneeze, and crept away.

Somehow, Axel wasn't offended. In fact, he laughed whole-heartedly, swinging his dangling legs, munching and crunching.

"You're good company, Loki," Axel said. "I like you, and I might make you my friend."

"I like me, too," Loki said.

Loki reached over Axel's bag of beans and pulled out a single Tragic Bean. Although chatty and a bit trying at times, Loki thought Axel was good company, too, but he wasn't going to tell him.

The Tragic Beans were salty, and Loki wondered why they didn't make him cry or laugh.

Loki grabbed himself another bean; it was just food with a silly name, he thought. Munching turned out to be a good idea. It took his mind off the crawling branches overhead, and the strange noises in the dark.

9

The Swamp of Sorrow

With a full stomach, Axel lay sacked out on the tombstone while Loki read the Dreamhunter's notebook under the moonlight. There were many things he had to learn about the process of entering a vampire's dream, but he was beginning to understand the theories and ideas of doing it. He used his phone to write the information in the pages he was reading before they dissolved into sand. This way he had a copy of the notebook's material, except the drawings, which he used his phone's camera to capture.

Loki also noticed there were some missing pages, which he assumed someone had read before him—he wondered if Charmwill had read parts of the notebook.

"You know, I think it's a good idea we're waiting for other teenagers to arrive," Axel said. "Not only will they show us the way to cross the swamp, but we can also use them as a shield since Snow White will waste them first."

"That's mean," Loki raised his head from reading.

"Live mean or die trying," Axel crouched suddenly behind the tombstone, and motioned at an approaching car. Loki saw a Jeep's headlights shimmering in the distance, and heard loud rock music roaring from a radio. "Here we go," Axel rubbed his hands with enthusiasm.

The headlights flashed against the lower base of the tombs, illuminating the peeling grey of the stones with carved names and dates and insects crawling over them. Some of the tombstones were overrun by grass and weeds and others were broken in half. One had the following phrase written on it: *Happily buried since 1857. Don't leave flowers, leave a dime.*

The light penetrated through the cold mist as the Jeep stopped abruptly over the muddy earth before the swamp.

Buried Moon Cemetery!" a girl cheered, jumping out of the Jeep and landing in the mud while the others laughed along. There were two girls and two boys. The girl in the mud was a redhead, and wore long leather boots and strangely enough, a skirt, in the cold weather.

One of the boys threw a cooler filled with drinks on the ground. Axel swallowed so loud Loki thought he was saying something.

"It's Big Bad, and some of his friends," Axel said, almost choking on his words.

"That's strange," Loki squinted, making sure he wasn't imagining what he'd seen. Big Bad wasn't the only one with the girls.

The other boy next to Big Bad was...

"Donnie Cricketkiller?" Loki said. "What's he doing here?"

"You know this Cricketkiller?" Axel inquired.

"He's a ruthless rival vampire hunter," Loki said. "I wonder how he got to Sorrow." Loki's heart beat slightly faster. He couldn't imagine that Donnie was going to kill the vampire princess first and deprive him of going back home.

"I guess this means that once they show us the way to cross the swamp, you'll have to be beat Donnie to the princess if you want to get the job done."

"I think not. The best he can do is stake. I doubt he knows anything about Dreamhunting," Loki said. "This just makes no sense, why Big Bad and Cricketkiller?"

"Bad seeds end up in the same basket. What about Tweedledum, you know her?"

"Who's Tweedledum?"

"She's one of the girls. I call all pairs of girls Tweedledum and Tweedledee, Dum and Dee for short."

"Dum and Dee?"

"Just go with it," Axel insisted. "I have to name things, or I get...confused—I once named my microwave Samantha."

"Why?"

"You name your car Carmen, and frown at me for naming my microwave Samantha?"

"I mean why Samantha? It's a microwave."

"Samantha was sexy; she melted frozen food, because she was hot. Get it? I used it to dry my cat's hair, too—that was before it exploded in the microwave."

"And you wonder why animals don't like you?"

Axel looked like he'd been hit by a speeding train. "OK, OK," he said, snapping. "So here is how we'll name them. The redhead is Dee, blonde is Dum," Axel giggled. "Get it? *The blonde is Dum?* Funny stuff, huh?"

Loki saw Dum pull out a mirror from her purse, to check if the mud had hit her face. Big Bad jumped near her, making silly zombie faces, with stiff hands and legs. He snatched the mirror from Dum's hand and ran away with it toward the middle of the tombstones.

"Let's try this," Big Bad sneered, holding the mirror with one hand and a beer can that was foaming over in the other. He looked tipsy, glaring at the mirror and saying, "Snow White, Snow White, Snow White."

"It doesn't work like that," Dum laughed. "It's not Snow White. It's Bloody Mary, you fool. If you say her name three times while alone in the bathroom in the dark, she will come out of the mirror and do bad things to you."

"No one does *bad* things to Big Bad," he said, hugging Dum and tickling her.

"Even the thought of Bloody Mary is creepy," Axel whispered to Loki.

"When I was a kid—"

"Could you stop commenting on everything as if this is a movie you've seen before?" Loki gritted his teeth. "Munch on something."

"What's that?" Dum asked Big Bad, pointing at the bag on his back.

"It's my ghost-hunting-vampire-busting tool bag," he snorted like King Kong.

Donnie Cricketkiller laughed mockingly at Big Bad, "You don't need all that; a stake like mine will do."

"You're not going to try to kill her, right?" Dum looked worried at the serious Donnie. "We said we'd have fun in the castle. I have to be back before two or my mom will notice my absence."

"Donnie is a vampire hunter, baby," Big Bad told Dum. "And there is a big reward for him if he kills her."

"If I see that bratty vampire princess, I'll stake her," Donnie snorted. "Huzza!" he clicked cans with Dee.

"This group is wicked," Axel whispered. "The kind you want to die first in horror movies."

Loki grinned at Axel again.

"B-horror movies?" Axel shrugged his shoulders. Loki was too serious for him sometimes.

Loki didn't reply, staring at him with intensity.

"Slasher movies?" Axel guessed. "Alright, I'll zip it."

"Poor Donnie," Loki turned back to watch the boys and girls. "He doesn't know that she can only be killed in her dreams."

"What's all this stuff you keep saying about Dreamhunters and dreams?" Axel questioned, and then acted like his mouth had a zipper and pretended to zip it shut.

"Hey," Dum said to Donnie. "We're just having a little Amityville Horror fun where everyone survives the scary house and returns home tonight right?"

"Who said killing her wouldn't be fun?" Donnie smirked.

Big Bad laughed. "You're right. Killing her would be fun. After all, she has been causing our town problems. I like that," he gulped his beer. Glock. Glock. Glock. Then he threw it in Axel's direction. Axel ducked as the can whizzed over his head and landed in an open grave full of other beer cans.

"May you beers rest in peace," Axel mumbled. "I think if this was a movie, Big Bad would die first. What do you think, Loki?"

Loki pretended Axel was only a figment of his imagination for the moment, and kept his eyes on the boys and girls.

"Let's do it," Donnie tossed Big Bad another beer then crushed a beetle on the ground with a big nasty grin from ear to ear, as if doing the world a favor.

Big Bad led the way to the swamp using his flashlight. Dee, Dum, and Donnie followed him after throwing a suspecting gaze in Loki and Axel's direction. Tucked away in their hiding place, there was no way he could have noticed them. He looked back ahead into the thickening mist.

"How are we going to avoid the Ferryman?" Big Bad asked Donnie.

"Just walk in that direction," Donnie pointed. "I have a friend who's a witch. She designed a log boat which Skeliman can't detect."

"Now what?" Loki said to Axel. "They have their own enchanted log boat. We can't exactly hop in it with them."

Axel shrugged his shoulders, looking at them disappearing in the mist.

"Great," Loki said with disgust. "We can't even see them unless we use our flashlights."

"No can do. They will notice us," Axel said.

All Loki could see was swirling silhouettes moving in the mist. He relied on their voices for direction.

"We should move slowly so they don't hear us," he said to Axel. "Maybe there is another enchanted log boat they use for backup. If not, we'll have to ride with Skeliman."

Loki heard Big Bad announce that he'd found their enchanted canoe. They were still laughing when Loki heard the squishing sounds of their feet in the thick swamp.

"What now?" Axel whispered. Loki could barely see him in the mist.

"Follow me. I'll find something," Loki said, walking into the mist with Axel gripping his shirt until Loki took a cautious step into the swamp.

"Stay cool Loki, pretend it's just thick, dirty green pudding soup," Loki reassured himself as he saw the wavy smoke hovering over the swamp's surface. It looked like hot steam erupting from a kettle that was boiling the green brain of an extraterrestrial being. Loki felt a sudden chill in his spine when he heard the others rowing nearby in the swamp.

The girls in the canoe were singing as they rowed. It was a rather peculiar song, and it went like this:

Row, row, row your boat.

Big Bad countered with a husky voice:

Gently down the swamp.

The girls finished and clapped:

Deadly, deadily, deadily…

"Ha ha," they all laughed and clapped their hands.

"*Life is but a dream,*" Loki silently joined in, actually enjoying their take on the song. The phrase 'life is but a dream' reminded him that he was supposed to be one of the greatest Dreamhunters in the world.

"They sound like drunken pirates," Axel said, his teeth chattering from the cold. "I think you can use the flashlight now. They can't see us in the mist, and they're already ahead of us."

Unexpectedly, Loki bumped into a canoe in the swamp.

"Why did you stop?" Axel shivered.

"I found it," Loki said, inspecting the canoe, looking for the ferryman. The canoe was empty.

Loki aimed the flashlight back at Axel to tell him. Axel let out a silent shriek, followed up by the chattering of his teeth.

"If there is a canoe, then it belongs to Skeliman," Axel whimpered.

"Man up," Loki said. "It's empty. Now get in it."

"I think—"Axel stuttered. "I think I am going to wait here."

"If you keep stalling, I'll have to leave you here alone in the dark," Loki said, ready to row.

"No, I will come with you. But can I ask you something first?" Axel said.

"What?"

"You killed vampires before, right?" Axel asked. "Can I count on that?"

"You can count on me," Loki said, not really sure he was able to kill the vampire princess. Loki was using a fake-it-until-you-make-it approach. He dragged Axel into the canoe. "I'm not going to fail this time, you hear me?" Loki gritted his teeth.

"Now you're scaring me, Loki," Axel said.

Noticing he was losing it, Loki let go of Axel, and started rowing. He couldn't hear the boys' and girls' voices anymore. Rowing across the swamp, he pretended he didn't hear the many voices of nightly creatures all around. He just rowed, hoping to reach the other side safely. Axel crouched next to him, burying his head under his hood. The cold was increasing substantially.

"This weather is just crazy," Loki said. "There must be an explanation to it."

"It's *her,*" Axel said in a muffled voice. "It's Snow White. She can manipulate the weather."

"Are you sure?"

"Everyone knows that vampires can manipulate the weather, making it colder to suit their environment. Snow White likes it cold and snowy around her until she feeds. It makes it harder for her enemies to attack her. After she's fed it starts to snow red. It's some sort of ritual for her."

"How do you know more about vampires than I do?"

"If you've ever read Bram Stoker's Dracula, you'll know that vampires have the ability to manipulate the weather, especially those from the 18th century."

"She's from the 18th century?"

"That's what I read in the forum. I'll tell you more about her. If. We. live."

Loki watched the vapor coming out of Axel's mouth shaping into letters on the surface of the misty night in front of him. 'If. We. Live.'

"You saw that? The letters?" Loki said.

"I did," Axel had already closed his eyes. "Blink, Loki, blink, and it will be gone."

He blinked once, and the letters were gone. But now there was this sound that scared him. Loki flung his eyes open. The girls were singing again. Those girls he'd first heard when he arrived in Sorrow. He listened to them singing faintly, somewhere in the dark:

Snow White one, Snow White two,
Sorrow was coming out for you.
Snow White three, Snow White four,
Black as night, go lock your door.
Snow White five, Snow White six,
Blood red lips and crucifix
Snow White seven, Snow White eight,
Row your boat, before it's late,
Snow White Nine, Snow White ten,
The Schloss will get you and what then?

"Can you hear that?" Loki asked Axel.

"Yup," Axel clutched his lips together, stressing on the letter 'p' so hard Loki worried Axel wasn't going to open up again. His cheeks bubbled up like a balloon, and his face went blue. Loki poked one cheek with his finger. Axel let out a breath with one long *pfoof*.

The mist started to clear, and Loki could see the Black Forest in the distance.

"We're almost there. Ease up," Loki said.

"Can you see Big Bad and his friends?" Axel said.

"No," Loki saw a dense orchard of Juniper Trees blocking the entrance to the forest. "But I can see their empty log boat."

"They must've found the Schloss by now."

"Maybe," Loki took a deep breath and dragged Axel behind him into the dark of the forest.

Tingling goose bumps grew on Loki's skin, and hair prickled on his back. The forest had a presence of its own, an aura of chilling cold and muddy ground that smelled like the crushed bones of the dead buried underneath. It was both fascinating and frightening. Suddenly Loki saw flashes of things that happened here hundreds of years ago: a vision of a princess running away from something—or someone. Then the vision vanished.

"Are you alright?" Axel worried.

"*Fangtastic*," Loki replied, as always, too proud to show his fears.

The crawling Juniper Trees blocked the view of the night sky above them. It felt like they were entering a cave made of arching trees.

"Hey, I just remembered something I once read about," Axel said.

"What now?"

"Those Juniper Trees were mentioned in a Brothers Grimm fairy tale."

"I bet it was a bright and happy Christmas-like tree," Loki used his Alicorn to make his way through the dense bushes.

"Not at all," Axel said. "You probably don't know much about the Brothers Grimm fairy tales. They are full of gore and killings. In this specific fairy tale, the tree was an incarnation of a boy who was murdered by his stepmother and buried in the ground."

"Really?" Loki noticed that whenever someone told him something about fairy tales lately, they didn't seem as giddy and happy like he'd always thought of them. He continued walking in silence for a while.

"Hey," Axel whispered as if not to disturb the trees. "I think something tapped me on my back."

"Shhh," Loki said, trying to find his way through the dense trees. His flashlight was hardly lighting the way.

"I am serious," Axel insisted. "Something touched me."

"Once we find the castle, we'll look into this thing that tapped you," Loki sighed.

"It just happened again," Axel shivered. "It's as if a bunch of tiny cold hands are tapping on my head and my back."

"OK, OK, just stop tapping *me*," Loki said.

"What?" Axel asked. "I didn't touch you."

Loki froze in place. He questioned why ghosts would tap him on his back instead of just coming out of their hiding places and scaring him.

Loki turned around. Axel was gazing upward at an unseen sky blocked by the curling branches. Small white snowflakes were dropping all around, passing through the voids between the trees.

"This is a divine warning," Axel said, "wrath from the sky."

"What?"

"Can't you see that it only snows behind us, never in front of us? It's as if the snow is hunting us."

"Crap."

"I can't believe you're a vampire hunter when you say things like that," Axel complained. "You sound like someone's parent, saying there is no boogeyman in the closet. They're always the first to die for not believing the kids."

Loki saw eyes staring back at him from behind Axel. He knew they were eyes because they blinked. They were mostly golden; a pair here and there, always pairs.

"Listen," Axel said, tiptoeing. "I can hear them."

Loki heard Dee singing with the boys nearby. They sounded officially drunk. Big Bad was singing again:

Snow white sucks the blood. La O la la la
And when she sucks you will die La O la la

"Creative, I must say," Loki raised an eyebrow, exchanging looks with Axel.

"I got a better one," Axel said. "*Princess Snow White sucks the blood, ee-i-ee-i-o. She's gonna waste them all like rats ee-i-ee-i-o.*"

Loki covered Axel's mouth with his hand, "You're singing is too loud. They'll hear us."

"Ten dollars, Big Bad is the first to die," Axel said, pulling Loki's hand away.

Unexpectedly, Axel walked past Loki, fueled with sudden bravery. "You know what?" he said. "If they're not scared, then I'm not scared."

Both of them reached the end of the forest and peeked through the last line of trees into an open snowy area.

Dee and her friends trotted farther ahead in the heavy snow, singing, telling jokes, and occasionally swearing about Snow White.

"Loooook!" Axel pointed ahead. "Holy Lord-"Axel shrieked. "Of the rings."

Loki looked. It was the castle, the Schloss, far ahead beyond the boys and girls. It shined through the night like an enormous jewel, bigger than the biggest five-star hotel he'd ever seen. It was an immense golden structure, a bit too curvy with too much glass, standing proud in the snow, imposing its presence and causing Loki to take an unconscious step back.

What the tic tac toe is that thing?

The Schloss looked like a fairy tale castle, out of this world, like the Taj Mahal, only the architecture was European and a bit gothic.

Loki brushed his eyes to look again at the immense beauty. From a distance, it seemed like it was painted gold. The truth was that it was *made* of gold and glass, and the windows were made of transparent pearls. The windows were huge, staring down at him like dead rectangular eyes. The white curtains behind the windows fluttered like ghosts dancing and waving at the intruders. Loki had to blink again to make sure he wasn't imagining this.

The main entrance had a great door, the shape of what looked like a whale's mouth—Loki remembered the gate to the Train of Consequences. The double door looked like it needed an army to pull it open. Although it was shiny, an aura of gloom surrounded it, as if the castle was telepathic, passing on its thoughts to Loki's brain. In short, Loki was almost sure the castle was alive.

"What the—" Dee stood with an open mouth, amazed by the castle's appearance. She must've seen a detailed version since she was only strides away from it.

From Loki's point of view, the boys and girls seemed tiny compared with the castle's size. They looked like Alice in a snowy Wonderland, ready for a magical journey with their hands down at their sides, looking up at the incredibly beautiful façade walking toward it hypnotically.

"That explains why the town's council wants to use it as a tourist attraction," Axel said.

"A tourist attraction?"

"I heard that new principal wants to get rid of the vampire princess to turn the castle into a tourist attraction and make the town rich," Axel said. "If there is no vampire princess inside, this could be the best tourist attraction in the world. It's the most amazing thing I've ever seen. I wonder why no one has photographed it and uploaded it on the forum."

"To tell you the truth," Loki said, "I imagined it'd be a dark, scary, abandoned mansion with dirty, blood-spattered walls."

Dum threw her beer can away and rubbed her eyes, skeptically amazed by the Schloss's appearance. Dee danced around like a little kid who'd just found Santa Claus's cabinet of curiosities. Big Bad was eagerly trotting toward the main entrance. Only Donnie was unimpressed. Loki thought that he'd sensed the same dread he felt, that killing the vampire princess was far from easy, and this castle was in no way ordinary.

"Come out, you evil monster," Donnie shouted provocatively. "She is playing games with us," he told his friends, then abruptly countered with "I say that's it for tonight. Let's go back."

"What kind of vampire hunter are you?" Dee laughed at Donnie. "You wanted to kill her seconds ago."

"I still want to," Donnie said. "But something here isn't right."

"What's with Donnie?" Axel wondered. "How come he's so scared now?"

"He's a vampire hunter, and he senses that something is very wrong with this castle," Loki said. "I can feel it too."

Loki wondered if he should summon Donnie and his friends and convince them to turn back. But why would he do that? He didn't care about anyone, let alone Donnie. He was here to find his way home, and it meant that he had to detach himself emotionally from everyone else.

But I do like Axel, even if he's annoying. And boy, I like Fable so much I'd adopt her.

Loki fidgeted at the voice in his head.

As Loki's head was about to explode from the conflicting thoughts, he tilted his head casually to the castle's second floor, looking at the waving ghosts behind the windows.

This time, there were no ghosts.

No curtains.

There was something even scarier. He let out a short squeal.

It was her, Snow White.

He saw the vampire princess up there, behind the pearl-framed glass on the second floor, standing in the middle of the window as if she was the Mona Lisa sitting in her framed portrait, watching her intruders tentatively with a slight smile on her face. She was watching them, surveying their weakness, and sewing their dreadful fate like a spider's web, seducing them with the power of the Schloss. Except she was much younger than Mona Lisa, not to mention much scarier, and she was looking right at Loki, straight into his half-angel eyes.

10

Scariest of Them All

Snow White was looking down upon the intruders of the castle in her white dress, a shade darker than her pale skin. Loki couldn't make out the details of her face, but her hair was as black as the dark night surrounding him. Still, it was a different kind of black; the root of everything dark. There was a red ribbon placed in her hair, making her look like an innocent child.

He stood speechless. No words dared to leave his throat. His heartbeat slowed down like a train avoiding a catastrophic crash. Time stood still, and flashes came before his eyes again; flashes of her running in the Black Forest. A wild urge ran through Loki, making him want to take a closer look at her. She was like the Schloss, shining beautiful but deadly, like forbidden candy.

Axel woke Loki from his trance, tugging at his arm. Loki breathed steadily, and gazed at Dum and her friends, wanting to stop them, but he was too late. They were already inside the Schloss.

Loki looked up again for Snow White, she was gone.

He pulled out his Alicorn, gazing at the front door of the castle, now slightly open. Walking through the thick snow that started falling in front of him slowed him down. Axel panted behind him.

Donnie and his friend's flashlights shone from inside the Schloss, sending thin beams of light toward the walls and windows. Their shadows looked tall and scary behind the curtains. Some of them were on the second floor already.

A cold breeze whirled into the pants legs of Loki's jeans, spiraling right through his underwear. It felt ticklish and was extremely cold. Loki uttered a painful chuckle.

"Why are you chuckling?" Axel wondered.

"Funny how pain and laughter sometime sounds the same," Loki said, adjusting his jeans.

"Keep mocking me like that, and we both die tonight."

Loki saw Big Bad's silhouette, pulling Dee into a room and kissing her while forcing his body against hers, causing her to draw back.

"Is that Dee?" Axel asked.

Loki nodded.

"Isn't Dum Big Bad's girlfriend?"

"What do we care?" Loki responded.

A denser mist orbited slowly around the Schloss. It started whirling upward, picking up speed as the midnight-sky above faded to a dark-purple that looked like a bruise meshed with a faint brush of yellow and orange. The mist dwelled up high enough for Loki and Axel to lose sight of the castle.

"Hey," Axel said. "I just remembered I forgot to lock the house," he was trying to avoid the mist by standing in Loki's shadow. "I'll go back and make sure it's locked."

"Be brave," Loki said.

"I'm *brave* enough to admit that I'm chicken."

Loki stepped through the mist, pulling Axel along, now seeing the castle again. Big Bad and Dee were still making out. Dum showed up a couple of windows away, fiddling with her hair and staring at something inside.

"Let's go back, Loki," Axel said. "If we look at her eye to eye, we will die."

"I already did. I saw her in the window," Loki said, wondering if she'd done it on purpose. Was she playing Loki, daring him to see if he had the guts to come closer and try to kill her? Did she know about Loki's weakness for demon girls? "Count me cursed already. Besides, I need to do this. *I need to*," Loki held Axel by the shoulder.

"I don't think you'll get cursed," Axel said. "You're the handsome dude. In the movies the good looking guy always lives. On the other hand, I am the nerd. I can't afford to let her look at me. I have *'first victim to go'* written all over my forehead."

"Does that mean you're going to chicken out now?"

"No, I'm coming with you," Axel shouted against the increasing wind. "Because even if I'm not a handsome dude, I have another power that you don't have," Axel placed his hand on Loki's shoulder. "I have nothing…to lose!" he said as if he'd just discovered peanut butter.

One of the Tweedle girls screamed suddenly behind the mist. The unspeakable was already happening.

"Listen to me, Axel," Loki shook him, feeling guilty about bringing him along. "You don't want to go in with me. This is *my* thing. I have to do this. You have a sister who needs you. She doesn't have anyone else but you. You're stupid thinking you have nothing to lose. You're *stupid*, Axel. Do you hear me? You have *a lot* to lose. You have a family and a home. If Fable were my sister, I'd slay dragons for her. Go back now!" Loki pushed Axel away then turned back to the castle, taking a deep breath as the lights in the castle all went out.

"It's true that I want to take care of Fable, but she never thought of me as a hero, so now there's a possibility I could be her hero," Axel said. "If I die, tell her I was a hero. Tell her good things about me, Loki. Tell her that I died fighting a nine-headed lion, not a fifteen year old vampire. I could be Fable's role model. In fact, if I die and she thinks of me as a role model, I'd like it."

"Just go, or I'm going to punch you in the face!" Loki pushed Axel away.

Axel took a moment, trying to figure out if he had the guts to stay, but Loki's stare was strong and Axel thought he'd better go back to his sister. "Can you at least spare me a flashlight I can use on my way back?" Axel said.

Loki grabbed a spare flashlight from his bag and handed it to Axel. *Tick Tock. Tick Tock.* Axel turned the flashlight on and off. "Just checking," he looked embarrassed as he stared into Loki's blaming eyes. "Rule number seven in surviving a horror movie: Always check your flashlight's batteries before you use it because they usually don't work when you need them."

Loki was about to smile. If he didn't make it today, if he died trying to kill the vampire princess, he thought he might miss Axel, even though they'd spent so little time together.

"I found her!" Donnie's voice echoed from inside the castle.

Loki turned around and heard the sound of separate movements. Big Bad and Dee must have still been alone. He heard Dum accusing Donnie of being like the boy who cried wolf, pulling pranks on them.

"I'm not joking," Donnie shouted nervously. "She is—"his voice echoed like he was in an empty room. "I can't believe my eyes!" he yelled hysterically.

Alert, Loki stood with his Alicorn ten feet shy of the castle's entrance, trying to figure out what was happening inside. He turned to see if Axel had changed his mind and decided to stay, but he was gone.

"What is it?" Big Bad yelled at Donnie from somewhere in the castle. "Where are you? I can't see anything."

It was obvious that most of them had split up in the castle, and that Donnie was alone somewhere. Loki was unable to locate each of them.

"I'm coming, too!" Dum cried out. "I can't find my flashlight. Wait!"

Loki was still watching, fixed in place, confused about who was who. It was all happening very fast, and death was inevitable. Something bad was going to happen. If Big Bad was climbing up the stairs, why couldn't Loki see his flashlight shining against the windows?

"Oh my God!" Dee shrieked. Her tone implied fascination rather than fear. "I found her glass coffin just like in the fairy tale. It's so beautiful."

"Found the damn flashlight," Dum cried out. Light showed through the window on the first floor. "I'm on my way. Where are you Donnie?"

Loki saw her climb up the stairs, jumping two steps at a time. Before she reached the second floor, her flashlight spotted Big Bad, standing frozen atop the stairs.

"Here you are, baby," Big Bad said.

Loki knew that if Axel was still here, he'd want to expose Big Bad for cheating on her.

"What coffin?" Donnie cried out.

"We're coming," Dum said, panting next to Big Bad. "Where are you?"

"I don't know but I see a faint light coming out of one of the rooms in the corridor," Dee said. "Is that you guys?"

"What damn light?" Donnie asked. His sound was a bit muffled. Loki wondered where he was, too. Didn't he just say he saw her?

"It's our flashlight," Big Bad said. "Where are you guys?"

"The coffin is empty," Dee said.

"Of course it is—" Donnie shouted.

"Where are you guys?" Big Bad and Dum were furious.

Loki understood now that Dum and Big Bad thought Dee and Donnie were in the same room, while they apparently weren't. Loki knew from their voices.

"—it's after midnight. Why would she be in her coffin?" Donnie said with a trembling voice. "She is right in front of me. That's what I've been trying to say from the beginning."

"*Where are you?*" Big Bad pleaded for the last time.

"I'm in the cellar!" Donnie screamed in pain.

Big Bad and Dum hurried back down the stairs. Dee dashed out of the coffin room, which Loki saw was on the second floor now.

"Stay put," Big Bad yelled. "We're coming for you. I have my stake."

"Don't bother," Donnie said. "You can't save me."

"Hang on," Dum yelled.

"She is so beautiful," Donnie said and let out a final moan.

This last sentence made Loki curious.

Loki rushed into the castle with his Alicorn in his hand. Inside, he bumped into the three of them in the hall.

"Who the heck are you?" Big Bad groaned at Loki with a stake in his hand. It was a plastic stake, meant for kids. Loki couldn't believe his eyes; a light saber from Star Wars would have been better.

Big Bad decided that waiting for an answer might not be a good idea, so he raised his plastic stake to kill Loki.

"I'm not the vampire," Loki screamed at him. "Do I look like Snow White to you?"

"You're the boy from the parking lot, Loki Blackstar," Big Bad growled in the dim light. "Guess what? My name is Big Bad, and I'm going to kick your ass!"

"Seriously?" Loki frowned. "You're stealing my line now?"

Before they got into a fight, and before the girls finished climbing down the stairs, something white appeared out of the cellar as if floating in an aquarium.

The vampire princess glided like a ghost in the air, her white dress swirling around her body, reminding Loki of his mother.

Bite me! Why does she have to remind me of my mother? Do I need more reasons to make killing her such an impossible task?

The Tweedle girls screamed, dropping their flashlights. Their squeaky voices confused Loki, and he dropped his flashlight, too. Listening to it crashing to pieces against the marble floor almost took his breath away. Loki remembered how Axel had said that flashlights conveniently stopped working just when needed in horror movies. The whole place faded to darkness, except for the pale princess's skin and dress.

Dum's flashlight still flickered infrequently on the floor. It had fallen on Big Bad's tool bag, ending in an awkward position that sent its round beam toward the stairs.

Flash on. Flash off. As if they needed more scare factors in the situation.

The impact of the moment left Loki paralyzed, scared to go pick up the flashlight from the floor. The vampire princess levitated an inch or two above the third step of the staircase while the light blinked on and off at her.

Tick. Tock. Tick. Tock.

Snow White's dress was spattered with Donnie Cricketkiller's blood— Loki wondered if he should've been thanking her for getting the world rid of bullies like him. She continued floating above the stairs like a marionette, swinging loosely on the invisible threads that controlled her. Loki thought she was examining them, her prey, having had an appetizer in the cellar.

The mixing shadows in the castle prevented Loki from seeing the vampire princess's face. He hadn't seen her face clear enough when he was outside, and he was dying to see it now. He wondered what the sixteen-year-old goddess of scare looked like up close and personal.

The Tweedle girls shielded their faces from looking at her, knowing that meeting her eyes meant their inevitable death. Having already done that, Loki knew that if he wanted to go home, he'd have to look death in the eyes again tonight. He had to stake her to stay alive.

This annoying, blinking flashlight, now I see her, now I don't.

Loki noticed her hair was combed neatly, looking as fine as nurtured silk cascading down her shoulders. Was she really a princess?

It was obvious that she was around sixteen year old. The fairy tale twisted demon princess was so young it was impossible to believe that she had been scaring this town for a hundred years. Based on her beauty, it was equally impossible to believe she was a vicious vampire. Seeing her, made Loki want to argue with his eyes. Something about her was beautiful in a wicked way.

Stop it, Loki. You know demon girls are your weakness. She uses her looks to kill the likes of you, the way she did Donnie Cricketkiller.

Loki had never analyzed a vampire he was about to kill, but he couldn't help it. Her white dress looked royal, 18th or 19th century style; it was expensive, canvassing her body like angry ocean waves longing for peace, longing for a shore, and showing her bare slim arms. Her small figure added to her wicked innocence, and led one to believe she'd been a normal girl before she turned into a vampire, maybe centuries ago?

She was also wearing a pendant, the shape of a red, partially bitten, apple.

"Stay put," Loki whispered to the others, not taking his eyes off the observing princess as she floated down a couple of steps. Finally, he could see the lower part of her face, from her nose down to her chin.

Blood was dripping from the corner of her lips, onto her dress, all the way down to her bare feet, finally landing on the stairs. It trickled down farther to the floor like red mercury. The flickering of the flashlight made everything look like a slow motion movie. Loki felt as if he were in a cheap vampire discothèque, dancing for his life.

"Stay away, monster!" Dee screamed, flashing a digital cross she had on her phone app at her. "You horrible looking brat!"

"Seriously?" Loki gritted his teeth. "Stupid Minikins," he wanted to advise her against being rude to the vampire princess, let alone flashing the cross-app.

But he was too late.

Snow White attacked Dum on the spot.

Boy. The vampire princess moves fast.

Dum was executed as fast lightning from the sky could ashen a poor soul.

It was hard to see what Snow White did to her in the dark, but Dum let out a short scream before she supposedly rested in peace, and stopped talking forever.

Every one held their breath while the princess disappeared in the dark. It amazed Loki that no one ran for their lives. Fear did that to the people, paralyzing their thoughts and blinding them to the available solution.

Loki saw Big Bad stupidly approaching Snow White with his plastic stake. The vampire princess backhanded him and sent him flying. Loki saw it happen, but it appeared as if she hadn't even touched Big Bad, as if she had the power to move things with the stroke of her hand. The scene was laughable; Big Bad was at least twice as big as she was, and she still managed to send him flying through the air like a huge cannonball. He ended up slamming against the wall like the frog in the fairy tale the Princess and the Frog— Charmwill had told Loki that in the original version the princess had thrown the frog violently against the wall.

"Who's the fairest of them all now?" Loki couldn't help himself, talking to the unconscious Big Bad. He was also calming himself down, knowing he had no clue how he would stake her if she attacked him.

I came last, so I guess she will finish me last. There is a pecking order, right?

Loki noticed that he was standing in a perfectly darkened spot now, and supposed that if he didn't move she wouldn't see him. If he survived this, he would go back and research how to kill the vampire princess. It was obvious that he wasn't going to be able to kill her tonight.

"What is going on in there?" Axel yelled from outside the castle. "Answer me, Loki!"

It was a good and bad thing that Axel had returned. The good thing was that Axel *was out there*. The bad thing was that Snow White had turned her attention to Loki.

Thank you very much, Axel Crumblewood!

Dum's corpse smacked against the floor, falling onto the bag with the flashlight, causing the light to alter its direction, highlighting the Snow White princess.

"Some flashlight," Loki spoke to it as if it could hear him.

Snow White floated in front of Loki, her dress and black hair waving awkwardly and horizontally to the left as if the castle had turned on its side. She let out a soft sound as if saying *ahhh* after a great vein-filling meal. She stretched her arms sideways and tilted her chin slightly up. Her eyes turned demonic black and she levitated another inch higher.

Her villainous eyes blocked whatever soul hid beyond her monstrous persona—if there was any soul left in the undead princess. A golden glint flashed in her eyes for a fraction of a second, so intense that it lit up the aura around her as if she were a firefly lost in the dark of night. The glint was short lived, but enough to see that she looked diabolically enchanting.

Something about her was spellbinding. Loki froze in the moment, looking at her. He could see nothing else but her face. She had consumed his mind and soul, and he was resisting the feeling of wanting to know her story, her real one.

He understood why Donnie stood staring at her and called her beautiful instead of running away. There was something about her that was indescribable. It was like having butterflies in your stomach when you fall in love, a feeling that could only be expressed with a brush in paintings, a beautiful song that could make you cry, a rhyme in a poem, or the delicate choreography in a dance. Loki wanted to shake his soul free from her, but he knew he was too late.

Those she lays her eyes upon, don't live long enough to tell about it.

They were right. Loki was taking his last breaths in his mortal life as she finally decided to come closer.

The vampire princess approached him slowly, soaring over the breathless air in the castle, like karma that came calling after years of waiting. Elegantly yet beastly, carefully yet deadly, she came down to him.

Loki felt that both of them had a lot in common. He could see it in those black eyes. Looking at her was like looking into a mirror that only reflected the darkness he possessed; the darkness Charmwill had told him about.

They shared a certain pain, and it struck Loki as ironic that they both wanted to kill each other. It was inevitable, though, one of them had to die and one had to live. Only Loki was the weaker of the two.

Loki held his pose, hoping she wouldn't sense his fear. Mesmerized by her presence, he waited for her to come even closer. He thought that when she was close enough, he'd give it a shot and stab her with the Alicorn. He tried to whisper 'Ora Pedora' to it, but nothing happened.

It's my only chance. It's my job, and for all I know she is tricking me into liking her like she did Donnie.

He was eye to eye with his tormentor.

Snow White stretched out a hand and touched his face with the back of her smooth hand, sliding it across his cheek. She did it slowly, almost tentatively, yet it made Loki's skin crawl. How was she capable of stirring all these contradicting feelings in him?

When she pulled her hands away, he felt undone. Why did he feel like he wanted her soft hand back on his cheek?

Focus, Loki!

Loki let her run her fingers across his other cheek. It was a feeling of pleasure and pain. He stared at her, held his breath, persuading himself that she wasn't close enough to stake her.

Who are you fooling, Loki? Do it! Just do it!

Once it showed on his face that he was about to stake her, she choked him with the same hand that caressed his face, pressing hard against the veins in his neck, her fingers marking the flesh as if it was clay. Her reflexes were too fast.

Loki missed her heart, and staked her in the stomach, which was a careless mistake.

Loki cried out. She didn't.

It was an intense moment, Loki still gripping the Alicorn that was half-buried in her stomach while Snow White was still gripping his neck. They could have both died right then, him staking her, and her asphyxiating him.

She pressed her thumb against his Adam's apple so hard it forced him to twist his head in pain, unable to readjust his body to stab her again.

How could this tiny girl do that?

She lifted him off the floor with her hand as her black eyes turned bloody red. Loki wrapped his arm around hers, trying to defend against her attack.

She pulled the Alicorn out of her bleeding stomach and threw it into the darkness, and like a skilled knife thrower, she hit Dee square in the head.

On the other hand, Snow White's wound didn't cause any real damage. It would heal in a matter of minutes. Loki had seen it before. For the moment, Loki had to concentrate on the fact that the vampire princess was choking him to death, and there was very little he could do about it.

A sudden ray of light came from behind and hit her in the face.

"Leave him a-al-alone," Axel stuttered. Loki was surprised Axel had the courage to venture into the castle, trying to save him—or die with him.

Snow White didn't flinch, and disregarded Axel's presence, but shied away from the white light aimed at her eyes as they turned from red to black again. Nobody seemed to acknowledge Axel's presence, even demons.

Instead, Snow White continued staring at Loki in a way that made him feel guilty, as if he were the one grasping her by the neck.

Then something amazing happened.

The fine tender skin of her face loosened up. Although she was undead, Loki saw some of her life force coming back into her pale face.

It was true. Her face was white as snow. Her lips, curved in the shape of a broken heart, red as blood. Her hair was as black as if it were cut from the fabric of the mysterious souls of night. Her eyelashes were like ancient Roman feather fans, majestically waving like a ship's sails flying in the stratosphere.

There was even a slight touch of golden-green mascara over her eyelashes, reminding Loki of ancient Egyptian goddesses.

She *was* a goddess.

Slowly she let him down, loosening her grip. She did it with grace and care. It made him feel like the woman in King Kong's huge palm, awkward.

Standing on the same ground now, she was an inch shorter than him—not that it gave him any credibility.

She looked up into his eyes as hers turned slowly from black into ocean blue with a hue of gold.

"What the h—" Axel said, still holding his flashlight with both hands as if it were his magic wand.

Loki let out a sigh. Snow White's blue eyes had that fabulous shine he didn't see in most Minikins' eyes. It was the type of shining there was no name for, but implied that the person was full of life—and that they had a great story to tell.

With the blood dripping from her lips, and with her pale skin, she was just an excruciatingly attractive sixteen-year-old girl living in a castle of her own hell. There's nothing wrong with that, right? Loki thought. He'd been living in this hell called Earth for a year now.

In her new state, she looked so lovely she could sneak up and kill you without you even noticing it, a girl who knew when to kiss and when to kill.

Loki understood why no vampire hunter could ever kill her. It wasn't her strength or superpowers. It was her hypnotic and charming magnetism.

Big Bad moaned behind Loki on the floor.

"You're still alive, monster!" Big Bad roared at her. "Monster!" his voice seemed different as if he were a monster himself. Loki couldn't see Big Bad in the dark, although he thought he'd heard his bones breaking or something without anyone touching him.

The vampire princess twitched at his words as if she was about to turn into something more sinister than what she was minutes ago. Instantly, her eyes turned black again.

Loki sensed her anger. It was as if she was humiliated by Big Bad calling her a *monster*.

Axel followed her with his flashlight, acting as if he were the lighting supervisor on the Broadway play: Wicked. Snow White was certainly turning nastier than the Wicked Witch of the West, and it was all because of Big Bad's foolishness.

Her head twisted around on her shoulders as the chandeliers above her flickered and swung violently over their heads. Loki didn't bother looking back at Axel, the light supervisor. He heard the sound of his knees clanking together like the chains around the neck of the ghost of Christmas past.

A swirling wind of chilling snowflakes filled the room. Loki didn't think she needed to kill them. She could just leave them to freeze in here. She stretched her arms sideways like a witch casting a spell, her arms showing purplish veins curling like tiny snakes all over her body, all the way down to her bare feet. Her head rotated back into normal position, and she looked down at them with her mouth wide open, snarling with her white fangs.

Loki couldn't explain how he felt exactly. Her angry eyes were fixated on him. He continued to feel guilty without understanding why. Whenever she looked pleadingly at him like that, he thought she wanted to tell him something, which made him question why she never talked.

She shifted her eyes to Big Bad who was still invisible in the dark, and Loki could still hear him growling and his bones breaking.

What was going on with Big Bad?

There was no time to figure it out now. The vampire princess rushed down, as if upon an invisible transveyor belt, faster than the speed of light toward him, and finished Big Bad in the dark.

Axel was too scared to follow her with the flashlight, keeping it on Loki as if he were the star of the show.

"Mirror, Mirror on the wall, who's the scariest of them all?" Loki chanted.

Axel and Loki exchanged reluctant gazes. Loki wondered how fast, and far, they could run. He thought he'd save himself tonight, so he could think of an effective way to come back and kill her later.

Snow White turned back to Loki. She wiped her lips with the tip of her white dress then grunted at him. She took a step closer, smelled his neck, and inhaled the odor of his body. She breathed over his neck slowly like cold wind upon the water and then she brushed her tongue softly above his earlobe. The chilling touch caused the veins on his neck to show like a singer singing his highest note. Her edgy teeth touched his veins slightly. It felt like the tip of a needle flirting with his skin.

She stood like that for a while, not biting him. Then she finally talked, and it wasn't like anything Loki had expected to hear.

Whatever she whispered in his ear, he thought he was imagining it.

It couldn't be. She didn't say that. Did she?

Her voice was musical and deliciously feminine. She rested her cold hand on Loki's chest, detecting the pulse of his racing heartbeat.

"*Save me,*" she whispered one more time.

When she said the words, her voice was low, even fainter than a whisper, as if she was scared someone would hear her. But who would that be? The castle was empty.

"What did she say?" Axel whimpered from his hiding spot.

Loki said nothing. The surprise was overwhelming. Somehow, he knew that this moment was going to change his whole life.

Snow White disappeared back into the dark, leaving him undone, just like that. The scent of apples lingered in the air, and Loki inhaled it as flashes of blurred memories passed before his eyes again.

What's happening to me?

He inhaled her *appleicious* scent unconsciously as if wanting to take something of her back with him, as if wanting to let some of her naturally deadly perfume run through his veins.

But he had to leave. She had spared his life, and he didn't know why. He was beyond confused.

He turned around, grabbed his Alicorn, then Axel's hand and sprinted out of the castle. As they hurried back through the Black Forest, red snow began to fall from above.

11

Bedtime Stoories

All the way back to town, Axel sat with his knees on the passenger seat, looking back at the empty road, and making sure the vampire princess wasn't after them.

When Loki stopped the Cadillac in front of Candy House, Axel didn't bother to invite him in. He slithered out of the car, almost hypnotized, forgetting about his backpack of crosses and food, and entered his house with a slouched posture. He snorted with anger when he found Bitsy had sewn his web on the key lock again. It presented a good opportunity to release himself from the chains of fear by kicking the door open with his boot.

Loki drove away, back to the parking lot, which would be his sleeping place until his sixteenth birthday. He wasn't angry at Axel for not inviting him in. He understood. Axel had seen more than enough, and Loki felt slightly guilty for dragging him into this. Vampires were Loki's everyday business. None of them had been a beautiful girl though. Certainly none had asked him to save them before.

The parking lot was empty, and Loki needed the sleep. He locked his car, and tried to see if the Pumpkin Warriors were playing music, but they were snoring in their sleep. Scared and lonely, Loki decided he'd keep the radio channel open and let their snoring keep him company.

"Turn off the car's light!" A band member whimpered.

Loki turned off the dashboards light, slipped under his blanket, and hugged his Alicorn. One of the things he wanted to go back home for was the possibility he'd end up hugging a girl he loved at night instead of an Alicorn.

He started counting sheep again. After sinking into sleep, he saw two black sheep. All the other sheep were *baaaa, baaaing* at the two outcasts. He knew he was one of the two black sheep, and wondered who the other one was. Was it his dark shadow from the past, the one Charmwill had told him about, or maybe Snow White, the vampire princess herself?

Loki stopped dreaming and slept soundly to the melody.

Zzzz. Zaa. Zoomm.

It was very early morning the next time Loki opened his eyes. Tucked under his blanket, eyes heavy, he noticed the Pumpkin Warriors had stopped snoring. The darkness was silent as the dead.

Loki wasn't ready to wake up, so he decided to roll over on his other side and continue sleeping.

Then he heard something.

"Row, row, row your boat," a girl with a sweet voice was singing outside his car.

Loki's eyes sprang open. It wasn't the little girls singing this time. He knew the girl's voice. It was the same sweet voice he'd heard earlier. He doubted he'd ever forget it as long as he lived. It was Snow White's voice.

"Gently down the stream," she sang.

Loki was afraid to look through his window and find her waiting for him outside. Had she followed him?

He held his Alicorn ready, wondering how close she was.

"Horribly, horribly, horribly," she hummed happily. "Now it's time to scream."

Loki straightened up slowly, wiping the tacky fog from his window. As he moved, he noticed Carmen was shaky as if not standing on stable ground. He looked outside the window and the situation became all too clear. The parking lot had turned into the Swamp of Sorrow, and his Cadillac was floating in the middle like a lily pad.

A shriek argued its way out of him. The swamp stretched as far he could see. There were no street lamps, no school, and no parking lot.

"Don't forget to scream," Snow White repeated the last part again, but she still sounded angelic, not scary.

Loki saw her rowing what appeared to be a white swan. She was in her normal, beautiful girl form, dressed in white with that same red ribbon in her hair. There was no blood spattered on her face, and she wasn't flashing her fangs. She was just a pretty girl, rowing away in a dirty swamp.

Turning her head, she saw Loki, and seemed surprised.

"Loki?" she asked. "What are you doing here?"

Loki shrugged.

What's going on?

"How did the parking lot turn into a swamp?" he said.

"What are you talking about?" she asked. "Did you come here to help me? Are you going to *save me?*"

Her voice was ripping Loki's heart out. It was smooth and vulnerable, pleading for help. She reminded him of the squirrel he'd saved; a small helpless being, just looking for a nut, but forced to live among Minikins, monsters, and vampires. Every moment of every day, it had to escape the danger of the monsters that overshadowed it so it could live in peace.

"What a ridiculous metaphor," Loki knocked on his head as if it were a nut he wanted to break open and fix.

"Did you say something?" Snow White blinked, her cheeks blushing red. She had eager doe eyes that made one want to sacrifice themselves just to protect her-but only when she was normal like now.

"No," Loki shook his head. "I'm in the mumbling business. I mumble to myself all the time."

"I noticed," she laughed.

Her laugh made Loki want to throw away his Alicorn and dance on the water of the swamp while rain poured on him.

"I mumble to myself a lot, too," she said. "I am lonely you know—"

This isn't right, Loki. This just isn't right. Think of a way to cross over and kill her now. She's sparing your life so she can make fun of you. She's a bratty princess who wants to have some fun with her next victim. She knows your weakness.

"But I prefer to sing instead of talking to myself," she continued. "I know a lot of songs."

"Enough," Loki shouted, waving his hands nervously in the air. He was silencing her, and silencing the annoying voice in his head that compelled him to doubt his eyes and kill her. "Back in the castle, you said you want me to save you."

Snow White's face changed. She looked worried, but nodded her head reluctantly.

"Who do you need me to save you from?" Loki asked.

Snow White didn't reply. She looked appalled as if something was going to jump out of the water and pull her down. She only shook her head 'no.'

Loki understood that she wasn't going to answer him. "If I come closer, will you be able to whisper it to me?" Loki said as he lowered his voice, too.

No, don't come closer. It's a trap!

Loki squeezed his eyes shut momentarily, until the annoying inner voice passed.

Snow White nodded, lacing her hands together.

"I'll swim over," he said.

"You don't have to," she said. "You can walk on water."

"What are you talking about?"

"If you take a deep breath and don't think about the water underneath you, you can walk on its surface as if it's land," she said. "I do it all the time."

"If you say so," Loki decided to try, and didn't mind if it didn't work since he had planned to swim over anyways.

He opened the Cadillac's door, and stretched out one foot. He let it touch the surface of the water, closed his eyes and pretended it was land. Surprisingly, it worked. Loki found himself stepping on something, a little bit soft and spongy, but rigid enough he could walk on it.

Opening his eyes, he let out a laugh. This was amazing. He was standing on water, walking toward Snow's swan canoe.

"This is magic," he said.

Snow White nodded, and spread her welcoming arms.

Suddenly, a frog croaked nearby.

Loki stopped in his tracks.

"What's wrong?" she said.

"No frogs, please," he mumbled. "I hate frogs."

"You mean you're afraid of frogs," she squinted, almost laughing at him.

Another frog croaked, and another. Tons of them were nearby, jumping happily on the surface of the water.

Loki lost his concentration; the spongy earth underneath him turned back into liquid and he sank.

As he was drowning, he saw Snow White laughing at him above the surface of the rippling water, pointing a finger, fangs drawn, thousands of frogs surrounding her. "Loki. Loki. Loki," she said. Strangely enough he could hear her plainly under the water. "How many times can a person be fooled? No wonder they banned you."

Snaky plants, like octopus arms, clung to his legs and arms, pulling him deeper. A sudden rescue didn't look promising.

Suddenly, Loki jolted awake in the Cadillac, sweating and panting, while waving his Alicorn in the air. The Pumpkin Warriors were still snoring in the radio. Outside his window, he saw the parking lot. There was no swamp.

"Bad dreams?" one of the Pumpkin Warriors moaned. "Happens to me all the time when I sleep on my stomach."

It was a dream, a horrible dream.

Loki yanked the door open and stepped outside. The yellow street light was faintly glowing. He was glad it was a dream, and he pinched himself to make sure he was awake. What if all of his life was just a bad dream?

"Hey, Loco," a voice called him.

It was a tiny voice, and he wasn't scared of it. Besides, he knew who called him 'Loco' in this world. It was either his mom or an animal. Loki looked down at a black cat with green eyes rubbing against his jeans.

"What do you want?" Loki grunted. "Leave me alone."

"You know what I want," it said. "It's cold out here, Loco. I need a place to sleep."

"Shouldn't you be in the pet cemetery?"

"I followed you here so I can sleep in your car," the cat said, sweeping its tale back and forth. "I hear you have an amazing backseat." It spat on its paw and rubbed it with the other. "I promise I won't tell any of the other animals that you let me in."

"OK, OK," Loki said, "but no meowing early in the morning, deal?"

"But of course," the cat nodded.

"And no snoring."

"Cats don't snore, dogs do," the cat said proudly.

When I wake up, you wake up, and don't you dare ask me to feed you, deal?"

"Deal," the cat said, looking up at him. "Want to shake paws on it?"

"No thanks. You just spat on yours," Loki replied, going back to the Cadillac.

"My name is Nine by the way," the cat followed him.

"So why do you only talk to me when I'm alone, *Nine*?" Loki rolled his eyes.

"It's a gift only you have," Nine said, shuffling next to him. "We pets love to talk to you, but we really hate Axel. He treats Bitsy so bad. We won't bother wasting our time talking to someone who treats other animals and insects so poorly. "Stop babbling and hop in," Loki said, and closed the door.

Since Nine was going to sleep in the backseat, Loki wasn't going to need the radio's company, so he turned it off.

"You need a blanket or something?" Loki asked.

"I'm fine," Nine said. "I tucked myself in your warm backpack, hope you don't mind."

"Good for you," Loki said. "Aren't you going to tell me why you're really talking to me?"

"Like I said it's a gift," the cat yawned. "One day, when you remember your past, you'll know why."

"If I ever do remember," Loki mumbled.

Loki was close to asking Nine about his past, but he was too proud—and maybe too sane—to do so.

The earth rumbled suddenly, conjuring that soft earthquake he'd experienced before in the same parking lot. It was much shorter this time. The car shook a couple of times and then it stopped.

"You know anything about that whale thing?" Loki asked.

"I'm sleeping," Nine said. "I can't talk while I'm asleep."

Loki pulled the blanket tighter around him before he found himself in a fistfight with a cat.

"But I think the whale had a big meal," Nine continued, even though he had confessed to trying to sleep. "That's why its stomach grumbles sometimes. I always wonder what will happen if the whale decides to roll over. You think that is how Atlantis was wiped off the face of the map?"

"I'm sleeping," Loki moaned playfully.

"Oh, sorry, nighty, Loco," Nine said. "You'll be alright. Just follow your bliss."

An hour later, Loki woke up to find the cat tucked underneath his blanket, sleeping comfortably on his chest. When he lifted the blanket a little, he saw a squirrel had sneaked in, too, and slept beside it.

"Sneaky devils," Loki smiled.

They were both snoring. Loki didn't mind. He needed the company of safe creatures.

***

In the morning, Loki showed Nine and the squirrel the way out, then he noticed he'd received a message on his phone. It was from Axel:

Meet me in Bedtime Stoories, Rumpelstein High's library. I found evidence she is the real Snow White, and that she's always been a vampire. Someone forged the original stories and replaced them with pancake fairy tales.
P.S. Burn after reading

***

Rumpelstein High's library, Bedtime Stoories, was bigger from the inside than it measured from the outside. It was humongous. Loki speculated it was even bigger than the school itself, which didn't make sense, like almost everything else in this town.

Axel showed Loki into the library, explaining to him how no one attending or working at Rumpelstein High cared about it or its books.

"Every commercial book you need, you can find on the internet. You can download.it with a click of a button and a drop of blood from your credit card," Axel said. "It's that simple. Only the real books, the ones that haven't been forged or re-edited are found somewhere inside Bedtime Stoories. Those are the old, dusty, handwritten books with yellow pages, and the smell of age on them. They are the books people think aren't needed anymore. We're smarter, because those are exactly the books we need to solve our mystery."

The library was dimly lit, and it became darker with every step. Hundreds of books were stacked on the shelves on both sides, buried under thick layers of dust and spider webs. The floor underneath Loki creaked as if no one had been there for ages. He wished he'd find someone reading a book, but nobody was there. The library was suspiciously vacant. It was like a haunted house, only with thousands of books. It seemed that Axel was right when he said that no one used it anymore.

A spiral staircase in the middle led to a second pitch-dark floor. Loki tried to catch up with Axel who walked silently but fast, hurrying between the tables and shelves like a rat on rollerblades. Loki thought he saw him turn right between the shelves somewhere.

While looking for Axel, Loki finally saw someone sitting by a dusty table, burying his head behind a large book. He couldn't see his face, but white silvery hair was showing from above the book's cover. Scanning lower under the table, Loki saw that someone was tapping an impatient foot against the floor. Scanning upward again, he saw two holes in the book the library patron was holding. Two pairs of eyes stared back at him from behind the holes. Loki looked away, and followed Axel.

"Hey," Axel whispered from behind the shelves. Loki saw two grey eyes looking at him from between the books. "In here," Axel said.

Silently, Loki walked around the shelves into a darker area. "Where are you, Axel?"

"Right here," Axel ordered him to follow him deeper into the dark.

"I think I saw someone reading a book with holes in it," Loki said.

"Yeah, yeah," Axel said, not looking back. "It's Skeliman the Ferryman." Axel said, the light from his phone shining in the dark. "I read something interesting about him this morning. It turned out he stopped working as a ferryman in the Swamp of Sorrow. That's why we didn't come across him yesterday. He guards Bedtime Stoories now. His new name is Skeliman the *Libraryman*."

"Seriously?"

"Yes. I think they pay him more in the library. That's why he likes it in here. They say you just have to act like he isn't there when you see him, and he won't harm you. It's rumored that he's fascinated with children's books about wizards and witches. He reads them all the time and forgot about his job as Libraryman. That's why the library is a mess."

"You said he was blind," Loki said. "That he had empty sockets because he was a skeleton, so how can he read?"

"Maybe he pecked eyes out of someone like the pigeons in the Cinderella tale," Axel said. "You know that story, right?"

Loki nodded, missing Charmwill glimmer—but not missing Pippi Luvbug so much. "I'll have to ask Genius Goblin about that, later," Axel said.

"If you say so," Loki brushed a spider web out of the way. "Why are these corridors so dark?"

"That's the way libraries are everywhere," Axel whispered, not turning around. "Each library is camouflaged, hiding the *real* library inside it somewhere, which can only be reached if you walk the darkest aisle until the end."

"Are you saying the darkened aisles are made to keep normal people away?"

"Indeed. No one walks a dark aisle in a library to its end, especially when it gets pitch-dark. People are scared of these dark aisles but they don't talk about it. It's very scary if you ask me, but there is a reason for it; the dark leads to the real library. "And why is there a real and unreal library?" Loki whispered, following Axel.

"The unreal library encompasses the forged books everyone is reading nowadays. The real library contains the most important historical books written about fairy tales before they were forged," Axel said.

"I don't buy this crap," Loki said.

"I do," Axel insisted. "I read a theory about it in the forum, and I believe it. The history of the world has been forged to conceal the truth from us. I read that every nursery rhyme, song, lullaby, and silly fairy tale has clues between their lines, but we have to decipher them to discover the truth."

Loki didn't comment. Axel was too enthusiastic about his nutcase theories, so he let him talk. Maybe he'd end up telling him something useful to help him reveal the vampire princess' mystery.

"I heard there is a war between storytellers in the world; between those who forged the tales and those who want the truth known," Axel kept walking. "The original texts are buried somewhere in the darkness of libraries all over the world, only for those who want to know the truth. Not all of the truth has been documented, though."

Axel's wild theory reminded him of Charmwill who had always talked about the fact that fairy tale characters were real enough they could bleed. The fact that he kept the fairy tales he knew locked inside a book that turned into a parrot was enough evidence to support Axel's idea.

"The more we delve into the library, the more we'll breathe the dust of books that haven't been used for centuries," Axel said. "Don't resist inhaling the dust," he stopped and turned to face Loki who was about to laugh hysterically at Axel and the ridiculous goggles he was wearing. "The dust in the darkest part of the library contains the magic spell that will lead us to what I want to show you."

"Listen," Loki said. "I don't mind your nonsense, but I can only take so much. You're crossing the line of rationality."

"And entering a haunted castle to kill a Snow White vampire princess was rational to you?" Axel mocked him, adjusting his goggles. "Trust me. It's Fable's idea. She's the one who told me about the secret library. She found out about it in one of her mysterious books, the ones full of spelling mistakes."

Loki couldn't argue now; he trusted Fable, even if she was a bit off her rocker like her brother. "Why are you wearing goggles?" he said.

"I'm prepared to inhale the dust, but I don't want it to hurt my eyes."

"And you think the dust won't hurt *my* eyes?"

"How many times do I have to tell you that you're not a nerd? Only nerds wear goggles. You're a good looking vampire hunter. Nothing bad should happen to you. It's only miserable guys like me who are always running into a series of unfortunate events," Axel said and started walking again.

Loki coughed slightly, inhaling the dust, but kept walking. They reached a point where it felt as if they weren't in the library anymore, as if they had walked through a portal of darkness into another dimension. Loki hated dark aisles in libraries; he'd always thought they were creepy and ghost infested.

When it became too dark for even cats to see, Loki flicked on his Zippo lighter.

"Not now," Axel turned around, and clicked the Zippo lid back down.

"You don't like my windproof Zippo pocket lighter?" Loki frowned.

"It's not the Zippo. It's your brain that I don't like."

"It's a *Don't Fear the Reaper* Zippo. I love it," Loki flicked it on again, messing with Axel.

Axel blew the flicker of fire dead then clicked it shut again. "Not yet. Stop talking, and follow me."

"Whatever you say, Holmes," Loki rolled his eyes, and followed him into the dark. The floor felt as if it could barely hold their weight.

"Stop," Axel said, striking his own Zippo to life.

"Oh—so this is a war of Zippos," Loki grinned in the dancing fire. "I light up mine and you don't like it because you think that yours is better. And where did you get that Zippo; a Darth Vader Zippo? Are you kidding me? You don't even smoke."

"Shut up." Axel's face blurred behind the fire. Loki thought Axel's little Snow White adventure yesterday helped boost the feistiness in him.

"Don't you ever tell a vampire killer to shut up," Loki raised his voice from a soft whisper to a thick angry whisper, spitting all over the fire.

"I haven't seen you kill cockroaches. The vampire princess could've torn you to pieces yesterday. God only knows why she spared you."

Loki lowered his eyes. Axel was right. There was no explanation why she'd spared their lives yesterday, but he doubted she did it for Axel. Why was Loki different from the others and how was he still alive after she'd laid her eyes on him?

He wondered if he should tell Axel about his dream in the parking lot, but he thought Axel would read too much into it.

"Look here," Axel said. He pointed at a small door, the height of a chair. It was a wooden door with strange engravings on it. It had a doorknob the shape of a rabbit's nose.

"Axel?" Loki pointed a finger at the door. "What is this?—and don't say it's a door."

"It's not a door," Axel took off his goggles and leaned forward. "It's a *secret* door."

Instead of stomping his feet and screaming, Loki leaned forward, so that their noses almost touched. "For your information, a door that looks like a *door* can't be a *secret* door. If it were a fireplace that actually turned into a door it would be a secret door."

Axel thought it over, scratching his temples. "It's a magical, short door. Are you satisfied?"

Loki sighed, breathing out warm air that stuck on Axel's face like steam from a boiling kettle.

"So why is it short?" Loki said.

"I think it's made for dwarves," Axel giggled. "You know Snow White and the Seven Dwarves, and now a short doo—"

"Yeah, yeah, I get it. What's behind this door?"

"All the secrets we need to know about your vampire princess," Axel reached for the nose-shaped doorknob and began twisting to open it. The nose looked too real. Loki twitched a little.

"Peep," Axel squealed, "just kidding. You know that doors don't have noses, don't you?" he said as he opened it. Golden light showed through from inside.

Loki knelt down to peek in. He saw a huge room, the secret library with the un-forged books, he presumed. Axel squeezed himself through, crawling on all fours. Loki followed him like a rat after cheese.

"Close the door behind you," Axel demanded, standing up, wiping the dust off his jeans.

"Are you sure no one can lock the door from outside and trap us inside?" Loki asked.

"Stop worrying so much. Live a little," Axel said, standing behind a big round table with a single lamplight the shape of an apple next to numerous books. "Why is it that you always have to have a plan? We've just entered an amazing secret library. Enjoy it, and loosen up."

Loki wasn't going to argue now. Axel had no idea who Loki was and why he wanted to kill the vampire princess. To Axel, this was the best adventure he'd ever had, and Loki envied him slightly. It would be amazing to enjoy every moment of your adolescence without being on a mission.

Loki examined the multi-leveled shelves stacked up high. The secret library was circular, with a ceiling that was tapered to a point, suggesting they were inside some sort of a tower—he'd never seen a tower sticking up out of Rumpelstein High. The walls were lined with bookshelves so high Loki didn't think that the tall ladders set on casters could reach the top. The books were bound in leather and velvet, clasped with locks made of obsidian. The spines were decorated with glowing gold scripts and waving calligraphy that he couldn't read. Some shelves were labeled as incomplete; some were empty and labeled with mysterious languages. The floor underneath was inlaid with chips of glass and precious stones woven together, forming some kind of pattern, like a secret message. Loki circled around it, trying to unlock the logic of it. He sensed that the pattern held readable letters designed to look like a crawling snake on half a circle.

"Is that a letter j?" Loki asked Axel.

"Yep," Axel raised his head from the book he was inspecting.

"J," Loki tried to read. "a," he circled around it. "Is that a w?"

"The whole word reads: Jawigi." Axel said. "Fable told me she heard it's a secret and powerful word that not many people know about. It's a kind of a spell or doorway to something."

Loki looked at it again and Axel was right. It read:

J A W I G I

Loki swallowed, looking back at Axel.

"What's wrong?" Axel asked.

"I think I've read this word somewhere before," Loki tried to remember. He wondered if it was a suppressed memory from the days before he was shadowed.

"How so, have you ever been here before?" Axel raised an eyebrow.

"Of course, not," Loki rubbed his forehead.

"Don't sweat it. No one even knows what it means. It could be a new hamburger in Sorrow for all I care," Axel said. "Come over here. I want to show you why I brought you to Bedtime Stoories in the first place."

"I'm listening," Loki said.

"Yes. I've found evidence that the princess we encountered yesterday is, in fact, the real Snow White, and that she's always been a vampire," Axel repeated proudly. He climbed up the ladder then dropped thick volumes of ancient books, thudding onto the table.

"I don't care what she is," Loki said. "I just want to find a way to kill her," he tried to neglect the guilt he felt inside saying this.

How could you still want to kill a girl who spared your life, and needs you to save her?

"Look, I don't know why you're so keen on killing her, but if you really want to, knowing who she really is should help you find her weakness. Yesterday, when she had you in the grip of her hands, I thought you were really going to die."

"You actually have a point," Loki nodded.

Axel climbed down the ladder then stood next to Loki, facing the table with a set of books. "Let me see," he said, searching through them. "You know this library has some intriguing books that I have never heard of," he started reading titles. "Listen to this: *The Books of Always and Never. I skimmed through it and it's crazy. It's full of lines like these, 'Always brush your teeth, never sleep without brushing them.' And 'Always be brave, never fear anything.' And 'Always love, never hate.' It goes on like this, forever.*"

"*Can you please show me the important book?*" Loki tapped his foot.

"*I'm looking for it – and here, listen to this title,*" Axel said. "*'The Secret History of Nursery Rhymes' See? I told you there's something wrong with them. And here's another one, 'The Book of the Purpose of*

Good and Evil,'" Axel read, and flipped to another book. "'The Unlawful Laws of Evil' I like that one," he said. "It goes on like this: "'And Then They Were Gone,' written by 'One of Them,'" Axel laughed. "'Think and Go Witch,'" I have to save this one for Fable. "'The Common-sense of Nonsense,' 'To Kill a Ladybird,' 'Gone with the Wand,' 'The Snow in the Sorrows: An Incomplete and Unreliable History of the Town of Sorrow,' and finally the strangest title of all, 'How to Win Friends Even When they are Minikins.'"

"Let me see that," Loki grabbed the book.

"You know what a Minikin is?" Axel wondered.

Loki didn't know what to say. He didn't understand what this library really was, but very few people called humans Minikins, mostly half-angels and Dreamhunters. "Let's just get to your book," Loki said, unable to confront Axel with the truth about being a Minikin himself.

"Here it is," Axel said, "'The Complete Fairy Tales of the Brothers Grimm.'"

"Are you going to read me a bedtime story?" Loki wondered.

Axel dusted the book off with his palms. "This book is a treasure. You couldn't find this out in the main library. It has most of the Brothers Grimm *original* fairy tales," Axel tried to sneer at Loki for an effect on his words, but he had dust plastered all over his face.

"Again, what exactly do you mean by original?"

"Since you're not a superhuman nerd like me, and you hate comics and fairy tales, I assume I have to repeat myself and tell you that all the fairy tales we read about today were forged," Axel ranted, wiping his face clean.

"Well, I always hated the true love's kiss that solved everything in the end," Loki said. Charmwill had been feeding his brain with fairy tales from the Book of Beautiful Lies; stories that didn't interest Loki.

"You will like the real fairy tales in the Brothers Grimm un-published version. They are full of blood spattering, eye-shattering gore, and unhappily ever after's."

"Sounds awesome."

"And you think *I'm* weird," Axel chewed on the words. "Anyway, here is what you need to know. Whoever created this secret library did it to preserve some of the town's many secrets—it should be obvious by now that this isn't a regular town."

"I noticed."

"Fable only knew about this secret library because she's into witchcraft, and read about how to get to it through secret scriptures in books. It means we don't know who we're dealing with here. What matters is what I discovered reading some of these books."

"And?" Loki was getting impatient.

"There's also another original edition of a Brothers Grimm book called 'Children's and Household Tales.' It's handwritten, and it contains original versions of the tales before the book was published. After the crazy night we had at the castle yesterday, I have no doubt this tiny girl that kicked your butt and killed Big Bad and Cricketkiller is Snow White herself. I mean, did you take a good look at her? Like really take a good look? In spite all of the blood and gore; she fits the profile exactly; lips red as blood, skin pale as snow, and hair black as night. So I asked myself one single question: how come she is a vampire? "

Axel's long speech was interrupted by someone outside the secret door. Moments later, Fable came crawling inside.

12

The Brothers Grimm

"Miss me?" she said with an irresistible smile on her face.

"What are you doing here?" Axel's face knotted. "Didn't I tell you that Loki and I are on a secret mission, and that it's dangerous?"

"I love danger," she said. "And I'm the one who told you about the secret library. I deserve to get involved. I finished my homework—and yours. I washed the dishes, fed the spiders, and now I'm bored. You have no idea what a girl can contribute to your quest. Try me."

"She has a point," Loki said, even if he wasn't comfortable with too many people getting involved.

"Alright," Axel muttered. "As long as you don't do anything stupid, and listen to what your bigger bro has to say."

"Alrighty, bro," Fable stomped her feet on the floor and raised her hand sharply, saluting him like a soldier. "He thinks because he is older than me, that he's smarter," she winked at Loki. "So I have to pay my respects."

"So," Axel coughed, pretending he didn't hear her, now posing as if he were a professor in a lecture hall. "Like I said, all you need to know about the real Snow White is here," he rapped his knuckles upon the book, and dust flew in his face again.

"Come on, spit it out, Axel," Loki mocked him. It was fun having Fable around.

"Yeah," Fable giggled. "Spit. It. Out."

"Stop swearing in front of my sister. She is only fifteen."

"'Spit it out' is swearing?" Loki said.

"I am fifteen and a half," Fable ranted, hands on her waist.

Loki disliked that Axel thought his sister needed to be treated like she was still a child. She was smart, cute and had great energy oozing out of her.

"One day, all of you will know what kind of genius I am," Axel said. "Here is why I think that the vampire princess is really Snow White. First of all, you have to know that the real story of Snow White in the un-forged books was considerably different than the famous story we all know. Snow White was not portrayed as innocent, shallow, giddy, or useless."

"Snow White isn't useless," Fable insisted. "She is awesome, and Prince Charming is possum," Axel stuck his tongue out like an annoyed lizard.

Loki couldn't escape the feeling that he was in kindergarten all over again—although he didn't remember one, but it wasn't hard to imagine it.

Axel and Fable's childish behavior showed how little interaction they had with others their own age, and why they had no friends. Loki shrugged, reminding himself that when it came to loneliness, he wasn't that different from them. He just owned a car, traveled around, and met a lot of Minikins. Even though Axel and Fable acted younger than their age, it puzzled him why he liked them so much, even when they were Minikins. He felt good around them. It was a great feeling that his inner voice resisted, because he was going to leave this town in the end.

"After reading the original stories and commentaries on the history of fairy tales," Axel elaborated, "I found that certain aspects of the original story, written by the Brothers Grimm, hinted to the fact that Snow White could have been a vampire. It's all in the original texts, if you read between the lines. It's as if the story was some kind of a hidden message, or as if they wanted to hide the truth, making it sound fairy tailish and suitable for children."

"She wasn't a vampire!" Fable protested.

Loki advised her they should give Axel a chance and listen to what he had to say.

"Before you claim she wasn't a vampire, you need to ask yourself some questions. For instance, why would a fairy tale for children start with a mother pricking her finger and dropping blood on the snow?" Axel wondered, "Gory stuff, right?"

"I once heard students in Snoring saying that the tales by the Brothers Grimm weren't actually meant for children in the beginning," Loki said.

"That's right," Axel said. "When they first collected the tales, they didn't have children in mind. But later, when they noticed that elders liked to recite them as bedtime stories, they toned them down and made them suitable for children. Still, mentioning blood in the beginning of the Snow White story, strikes me as weird. It's strange that the story starts with a mother seeing blood on the snow and fantasizing about having a baby with red lips—"

"Red as blood," Fable interrupted as if she felt the need to defend Snow White, "hair black as the window-frame, skin white as snow."

"Yeah, thanks," Axel said. "See?" he turned back to Loki. "I can't think of a single mother in this world who would relate seeing blood to wanting to have a girl with lips red as blood. What kind of wish is that? Besides, two of these descriptions perfectly fit the attributes of a vampire: *lips red as blood and skin white as snow*. All vampires have pale skin and their lips are covered with the blood of their victims they have bitten," Axel dropped the book and picked another to show to them. "And look at this pretty picture," Axel mused, pointing at the picture of a man with white fangs, wearing a black and red cloak.

"Dracula?" Loki furrowed his brows.

"Count Dracula himself," Axel pointed a forefinger in the air. "A man whose name has always been synonymous with the same three colors Snow White's mother wished her daughter's looks would replicate. He wears a black cloak that is red on the inside, and his skin is always as pale as snow. Red, Black, and White."

"That's absurd," Loki said.

"Look who's talking," Axel remarked. "You're a vampire hunter, aren't you? Half of the people in the world don't believe in vampires."

"Yes, but I never said fairy tale characters were vampires," Loki shrugged his shoulder.

"Fairy tale characters aren't supposed to be real," Fable said.

"Yeah, and when I asked my history teacher about vampires, she told me they weren't real either," Axel shot Loki a cruel eye. "And I'm sure I saw one yesterday."

Loki shrugged. If Charmwill were here, he would have argued otherwise.

"Look," Loki started. "I understand that the earlier versions of fairy tales were full of gore, blood, and twisted morals; nothing new here. The fact that there are common color motifs between Dracula and Snow White doesn't prove anything, so where is this going?"

"Alright, let's skip the color part," Axel said. "Here is something else you should consider. In the end of Snow White's story, the dwarves preserve her in a coffin—"

"A glass coffin," Fable corrected him. "Because she was so beautiful, that they couldn't imagine not looking at her after she died."

Axel ignored her and turned to Loki.

"I see what you're getting at," Loki said. "Vampires sleep in coffins, so it's reasonable to question why the authors wrote that Snow White ended up sleeping in a coffin. I get it. Still, this sounds coincidental to me. It's not solid evidence."

"Don't you get it?" Axel said. "She was kept in a coffin until the prince came and woke her up after the dwarves thought she was *dead*, which means that when he kissed her she became undead," he stopped for the effect and looked at Loki and Fable. "The same thing that happens to the vampires you kill. They're not dead but they're not alive either after you stake them. You put them in a coffin, but if someone else pulls the stake out, they wake up again. It's almost the same scenario, only told in riddles for those who can read between the lines. To me, this means that the kiss in the fairy tale equals pulling the stake from a vampire's heart. And I'm not even questioning why Prince Charming was there in the first place, or how he knew about her whereabouts, or why he kissed a dead girl. Yuck."

"So what? The prince kissed her awake from a long sleep that was induced by her being poisoned with an apple," Fable said, acting as if she were Snow White's lawyer.

"Aha," Axel seemed to have an Einstein moment, his eyes shone with victory. "You only say this because it's what you've been told in school. The truth is that the magic kiss never happened. It's not even true," Axel explained.

"What do you mean it's not true," Fable said. "Everyone knows that Prince Charming kissed Snow White awake."

"Total nonsense," Axel said proudly. "In the original Brothers Grimm text written in 1812 and then republished in 1857, the prince never kissed her. It's a Walt Disney fabrication."

"He didn't?" Loki wondered.

"Prince Charming wanted to take her away in her glass coffin, back to his castle," Axel said. "It didn't even cross his mind to kiss her. When her coffin slipped off the carriage, the chunk of poisonous apple in her throat, which she had been poisoned with by the Wicked Stepmother, popped out and she woke up."

"Really," Loki said. "So there was no true love's kiss?"

"Not even a peck on the cheek," Axel assured them. "Or a blown kiss from a hand."

"So the apple wasn't poisoned? She was choking and they thought she was dead?" Loki said.

"That's what is written in the original text. In my opinion, the chunk of apple is a metaphor for saying she was staked. Remember that in 1812, when the story was first published, the world was horrified by what they called the Vampire Craze. You know what that is, right?" Axel said.

"Yes," Loki nodded. "It was the first time people reported seeing vampires, and they were hunting them viciously all over Europe."

"See?" Axel said. "So it makes sense to try to hide that Snow White was a vampire, and write the tales in riddles that only the open-eyed, like me of course, can figure out."

"You're a horrible liar, Axel," Fable stomped her feet again. "There must have been a kiss."

"I'm not. Look for yourself," Axel handed her the book, and pointed at the paragraph in the story where the kiss should have happened. Loki and Fable read it. Axel was right.

"So why did the prince want to take her away from the forest? Did he know her from before?" Loki said.

"Yes, when she was younger," Fable said. "He talked to her at the well because she was beautiful, but she ran away because she was shy. Didn't you ever watch the movie?"

"Again, this was the Disney version. This was never mentioned in the original story," Axel said. "Neither did they explain why he wanted to take her away with him. You know the deal with charming princes in fairy tales.

They never do anything to deserve the girl but they get her anyway."

"Easy on the prince, don't hold grudges because he got the girl," Loki smiled. "So Snow White was just a vampire asleep in a glass coffin?"

Axel nodded.

"Wow. That's not the story my mother told me," Loki said. He hadn't told them about his ghost mother, but it was true. Sometimes, when he was asleep in his car, she crept in and read fairy tales to him when he was asleep before she pulled the blanket tighter around him. Small things like that let him know that she cared about him. He never told her that he knew because he thought it was embarrassing that his mother still read bedtime stories to him when he was fifteen.

"I know, it's very different from the tale we were told as kids," Axel said. "For some unknown reason, someone sold the world different fairy tales."

"I still can't see how this could help me kill her?" Loki said.

"Because that's not all I have to say; I have tons of surprises for you, guys."

"What else?" Fable folded her arms. She was devastated. Axel had just shattered her entire childhood into pieces of a puzzle she didn't have a clue how to put back together. Loki looked at her and wondered what it was like having childhood memories. He didn't mind Axel messing his up as long as he actually remembered them someday.

"In the Brothers Grimm version, the reason why Snow White slept in the coffin was because of the apple, of course. But it was never implied that she was dead. Instead, the Brothers Grimm had a name for what happened to her after she'd taken a bite from the apple. They called it the Sleeping Death."

"What?" Loki's face knotted. The Sleeping Death sounded like it had to do something with vampires more than fairy tales.

"This is actually written in the text, *the Sleeping Death*, which is another strange expression," Axel said, "It implies that she wasn't dead, but sleeping like she was dead. This stuff is mind boggling."

Loki found himself feeling the Dreamhunters notebook Charmwill had given him. He remembered reading that some scholars in the Dreamworld Arts called the state of a staked demon the Sleeping Death. In fact, the only way to enter a demon's dream was when it was in a state of Sleeping Death. The name was derived from the fact that the demons could still be awakened by removing the stake, so it wasn't considered dead, but sleeping like the dead.

"So there was blood, gore, glass coffins, and the Sleeping Death," Loki counted on his fingers, giving it a thought—he wasn't going to discuss anything about Dreamhunting with them now.

"What about the wicked witch who gave her the apple?" Loki asked.

"It wasn't a wicked witch who gave her the apple," Fable explained. "It was her stepmother, using witchcraft to appear like a peddler or a hag who gave her the poisoned apple."

"Which brings us to the scariest part of Snow White's story," Axel said. Loki sighed impatiently, exchanging looks with Fable. "We all know that the wicked stepmother sent her huntsman after Snow White to kill her, right?"

"The huntsman couldn't kill her," Fable said. "Because she was beautiful and he couldn't bring himself to do it."

Axel looked like he wanted to hit Fable with a feather pillow; hard. Loki almost laughed, thinking it was a good thing Fable was the wanna-be-witch, and not Axel, or this could've been how the world ended in sixty seconds.

"Now, listen to me because this will blow your mind," Axel said. "In the original story, the wicked stepmother asked the huntsman to bring her Snow White's heart and liver after he killed her."

"Interesting," Loki said.

"Are you serious?" Fable leaned forward. The poor girl had given up after everything she knew about fairy tales had been shattered in a span of minutes.

"Not just that. Although it's true that the huntsman didn't kill Snow White, he brought the stepmother a boar's heart and liver to convince her he'd killed her," Axel said.

"Gross," Fable said. "Is this really written in the original Brothers Grimm text? Why didn't they just turn fairy tales into cheap penny dreadfuls?"

"I'm beginning to wonder why I didn't read those awesome fairy tales long ago," Loki grinned. It made him wonder if what Charmwill had said about the darkness inside him was true.

"Are you guys starting to get my point?" Axel said. "I don't know how much more proof you need to see that she was a vampire."

"I'm still skeptical about if she is the real Snow White," Loki said. "Tell me, why did the evil stepmother want Snow White's heart and liver?" Loki asked.

"She thought that by consuming Snow White's heart she could be the fairest of them all," Fable answered voluntarily.

"I don't think so," Axel objected. "In my opinion, the heart was evidence that the huntsman had actually staked Snow White, the vampire. Or why would she ask for the heart. She could've simply asked for the princess' blood-spattered dress as evidence."

Loki scratched his head. He liked that explanation. "In a very weird way, all this makes sense," he said. "As far as I know, people believed staking a vampire in the heart killed it once and for all in those days. It makes sense if I ask you to bring me the heart of a vampire as proof of killing it. It was a plausible way for the huntsman to prove he killed her. Even nowadays, it still applies. So this explains the heart, but why the liver?"

"That one took me some time to figure out, but I finally found the answer, not in fairy tale books, but in history books," Axel said. "Remember when we talked about the Vampire Craze in the 18th and 19th century?"

"Yes," Loki nodded. "It was the first time historians ever mentioned, or suspected, the existence of vampires."

"Exactly," Axel clicked his fingers. "People reported that their relatives came back from the grave after they had buried them. They returned as vampires and bit their loved ones, turning them into vampires."

"Where did that vampire craze start?" Fable inquired.

"In Europe," Axel replied. "That's why the Dracula story originated from Transylvania. People in Europe went crazy, watching their loved ones come back from the grave with an urge for blood and the inability to tolerate the sun."

"That's interesting," Fable remarked.

"Yes," Loki confirmed. "Only these weren't vampires. It was a disease—not that vampires didn't exist, but the disease's symptoms were similar to the needs and actions of vampires," Loki said.

"I don't understand," Fable shrugged her shoulders. "This is confusing."

"It was a disease that spread in the 18th century," Axel said. "It was called Porphyria back in the day," Axel read from a history book like a mad scientist. "'Porphyria was a genetic *liver* affliction that affected the biosynthesis of blood creating severe reactions to sunlight and causing gums and lips to recede creating a fang-like effect and pale skin.'"

"In English, please?" Fable said.

"The disease caused people to have pale skin, grow slight fangs, and its only cure was to get injected with blood through the liver," Loki explained. "Of course, it was an old fashioned cure in a time when medicine was still primitive."

"Really?" Fable said with an open mouth. "Sounds exactly like vampire symptoms."

"So what does this have to do with the liver the evil witch wanted to cook for dinner?" Loki asked Axel, clapping his hands together.

"Don't you get it?" Axel said. "The disease caused failure of one's liver. The only possible way of relieving the problem back then was the ingestion of large amounts of blood, which can be absorbed into the bloodstream through the stomach wall and then on to the liver."

"So? You still didn't' answer the question," Fable asked.

"When the rumor spread that the infected people were vampires, people began exchanging advice on how to kill them. It was obvious that you had to stake them in the heart first because this was how you killed vampires. Ripping the heart out was probably even better; to make sure the vampire didn't wake up from the grave. But then people noticed that when the liver stopped functioning, the vampire died as well—"

"And of course this wasn't the vampire; it was the dude with the disease that made him look like a vampire," Fable clicked her fingers together.

"Ahh—" Loki struck his forehead. "They thought this was a manner of killing vampires, so they spread the idea that to kill a vampire you had to stake them in the heart or stake the liver?"

"Stake it, eat it, whatever. As long as the liver was destroyed, no one could infuse it with blood again to resurrect the vampire," Axel said, his face shining bright. "If this was what was thought of vampires in the beginning of the 19th century, then this was what the evil stepmother thought of Snow White, because Snow was a vampire."

"But you base all of this on the assumption that Snow White was born in the 18th or 19th century," Fable said. "I thought Snow White's story was much older than that."

"It must've happened in that time because the Brothers Grimm wrote the first version of Snow White in 1812," Axel said. "The Brothers Grimm collected the story from the locals, who must've witnessed the stories themselves. I'd say the real story happened ten to fifty years prior to that date, sometime at the height of the vampire craze.

Don't forget that Snow White was a princess, so maybe her father, the king, didn't want anyone to know that she was a vampire, because then she would have been killed."

"I still can't believe Snow White is a vampire," Fable said, considering the facts.

"That's some twisted logic, Axel. All I know is that I'm sure I saw a vampire yesterday, and your evidence, especially the liver thing, is considerable. Does that mean that her liver is a weak point? Should I stake her in the liver? I don't understand," Loki remarked, although he knew Charmwill had told him the only way to kill her was in her sleep, but he never told him if she should be staked in a special way, different from other vampires. Loki let out a laugh of mockery, remembering that he couldn't even stake her in the first place.

"She is not a vampire!" Fable stomped a foot.

"She is," Axel insisted. "You know what I also think? I think it's a damn scary family she came from. You know what the queen did with the heart and liver that she thought were Snow White's? She ate them," Axel's head lunged forward, as he chomped his like Jaws. "Yum, yum."

"Thank you for destroying my childhood, Axel," Fable howled. "I hope you can do your homework from now on, because I quit."

"It all makes perfect sense," Axel totally neglected his sister. If he really cared for her like he'd told Loki, then he had a poor way of showing it. "All vampires were super beautiful and gorgeous. I saw her yesterday in the castle, so lovely, posing innocently when she wanted to, and acting vicious when she wanted to. This is the perfect description of vampires."

There was no doubt that the girl in the castle was a vampire, Loki thought. She was super powerful, super scary, super lovely, and super manipulative. But was she the real Snow White? The idea made Loki feel like there was something he should remember but couldn't. Were fairy tales true? Does she even know who she is?

Loki let out a sigh. "Even though all you just said would make a perfect book, I don't see how this could help me kill her."

"This is what I wanted to talk to you about," Axel tried to avoid Loki's eyes. "I found this diary, which seems to me to be Jacob Carl Grimm's diary, or at least, part of it."

"Who is Jacob Carl Grimm?" Fable asked.

"One of the Brothers Grimm, the two brothers who wrote the Snow White fairy tale," Axel looked irritatingly at her.

"How come such a book is in this library? Jacob Grimm's diary? You're talking about a precious one-of-a-kind-diary manuscript," Loki said.

"I'm still not sure, but it has the initials J.G. on it," Axel said. "I can't think of anyone else with the same initials."

"Wait," Fable interrupted. "So you didn't discover all of this by yourself, right? You got the information from this diary."

Axel shrugged. "What do you care? I am helping you out here."

There was a moment of silence when Loki and Fable exchanged looks again.

"Anyway," Axel said, averting their eyes. "I haven't read the whole diary, but it seems to me that whoever wrote it wasn't fond of Snow White at all. Remember when she whispered in your ear yesterday?"

Loki nodded.

"This J.G. mentioned that whenever she feels a weakness toward one of her victims, like attraction, she'd confuse them by manipulating their feelings somehow."

"Manipulate?" Loki frowned.

"Like playing victim and asking them to *save her*. She keeps doing it until her weakness toward that person subsides and she can kill him," Axel wiggled his eyebrows at Loki.

"That's what she told me, yesterday," Loki said, almost talking to himself. As much as it was all he wanted to here, he was also disappointed. Something inside him made him wish she did need his help.

You're better that way, Loki. Now you have no excuse to not let her play her games.

120

All you have to do now is kill her and get back home. She's like any other manipulative demon you've met before.

"What?" Fable sneered at Loki. "Did she really ask you to *save her*?" Fable's eyes widened. "Really? I can't believe it! What's wrong with you, Loki? She needs your help."

"She was only playing me," Loki avoided Fable's eyes. He thought that if he'd stared at her longer, he might have softened and changed his mind. Fable's admiration for the vampire princess was contagious.

"Talk to me, Loki," she pulled him by his arm. "How could she ask you to save her, and you still want to kill her?"

"Stop it, Fable," Axel said. "She is definitely playing him. Can't you see what this diary says about her manipulating those she feels soft for?"

"Yeah?" Fable snapped. "According to your diary, she has a soft spot for Loki. After all your research you still haven't asked the most important question. Why does she have a soft spot for Loki?"

"That's what's bugging me," Loki made a fist. "So please stop talking about it. I have to kill her, and you're not making it easy for me with all your theories. My life depends on it."

"Your life?" Fable and Axel said at exactly the same time.

"I don't want to talk about it," Loki brushed his shoe against the floor and watched it for distraction.

"I don't know what he means, Fable," Axel said. "But believe me; you didn't see what she's capable of."

"Say something, Loki," Fable pleaded. "I thought I liked you. Don't make me regret it."

"I don't know what to think," Loki snapped. "Axel's discovery and that diary he found says we've uncovered the mystery behind one of the greatest fairy tales of all time. If that's true, it means we're going to change history if we tell the world about it—well, at least the fictional history of fairy tales. Which should be fantastic, but I'm sorry if I don't share that feeling with you, because the truth is that I don't care. I don't belong here. I don't believe in fairy tales, and I don't want to. I came to kill her and that's what I have to do."

Loki took one last look at the siblings, and something struck him as unusual.

"I'm going back to finish her," Loki said slowly. "I advise you to stay away from me. I want to thank you for the help, but my life is nothing but trouble, and I don't want you to catch my curse."

"And our life is all pink bubbles and ice cream," Axel rolled his eyes. "I'm the most popular, un-pathetic, loved, boy in school. Can't you see that?" he mocked himself.

"And my life is great, too," Fable said. "My mother was never a lousy witch, and no one ever mentions this in school, or belittles me and reminds me that I'm nobody. I'm just walking on sunshine."

"Alright, stop mocking me. I understand," Loki said. In their zany way, they were telling him that he'd been whining this whole time and acted as though he had the weight of the world on his shoulders. In all actuality, they were no different from him, only they faced their fears and enjoyed their days.

"It's time to split. The journey ends here."

"Where are you going?" Fable asked.

"It's daylight, and I think the vampire princess should be sleeping in the coffin somewhere in the castle. It's the perfect chance for me to get the job done," Loki said. "Axel kept convincing me that we should go after midnight yesterday, but after I gave it a second thought, it makes better sense to visit her when she's asleep during the day."

Axel fell from the chair, trying to catch up with him. Fable's tender hand touched Loki's. "Wait," she paused. "I think we should come with you."

"Why?" Loki questioned.

"Why?" Axel snapped, standing up. "Because this is the great adventure I've been waiting for all my life. I feel like Tom Sawyer!"

"And you?" Loki gazed back at Fable.

"I'm actually worried about you, Loki," she said.

Axel's face blushed with anger. "Take your hands off my sister."

Fable reddened and pulled her hand away. "Stop that dirty mind of yours," she said to Axel. "Loki's a good friend. What's wrong with you?"

"I have to protect you," Axel fell over some books.

Loki and Fable laughed, and Loki knew that what she said was true. What he felt toward Fable was a brotherly feeling. It was only intensified because none of them had felt this way before. Fable never really felt safe with Axel, and Loki had never felt the magic of caring for a little sister.

As they left the library, Loki thought about it and knew why Fable was really coming with them. Unlike Axel, she wasn't just out for a great adventure, and it wasn't only because she cared for him. Fable was coming along in hopes that she'd be able to persuade him to not kill Snow White when the time was right.

13

The Glass Coffin

The sun splayed through the big windows and illuminated everything inside the Schloss; the marble floors, the painted ceilings, and century-old chandeliers. There were a number of golden-framed portraits on the wall, portraying battles where people rode unicorns instead of horses. Loki noticed one of the unicorns was ridden by a woman wearing a cloak; the unicorn was hornless. It made him grip the Alicorn in his hand tighter.

There were also a few pieces of ancient furniture scattered among the vast space of the entrance hall, and they were covered with white, clean blankets. It looked like someone was taking care of the Schloss, and Loki wondered who it could be.

Loki fidgeted at the thought. The castle made him feel uneasy, even with the dreamy sparkling morning sunlight that painted the air, hinting to a misleading sense of security. Everything looked friendly and inviting that one couldn't help but to explore further. Had it not been infested by a vampire at night, Loki would have fallen for the trap.

There was no evidence of last night's victims, no traces of blood or signs of struggle. It was just a charming, empty castle in the middle of the Black Forest. Even the Swamp of Sorrow wasn't as creepy as it was yesterday night. They'd been surprised how easily they crossed the swamp and forest before reaching the castle—which made Loki worry even more. Again, something about this whole island and the castle was wrong, but he just couldn't put his finger on it. Axel was right when he said that this place had a soul of its own.

"Wow," Axel said. "This looks nothing like the haunted castle from yesterday."

Loki gave a couple of inspecting gazes, expecting a sinister detail to hold him back from advancing. He couldn't find any.

"Awesome," Fable said, dancing in circles with her arms stretched out, like Julie Andrews in the Sound of Music. "I've always dreamed of a castle like this. Can we move in here, Axel?"

Loki couldn't help but adore her. He didn't bother telling her that it was best if she didn't dance around so she wouldn't wake up the vampire princess.

"You think she hid the bodies in the basement?" Axel asked. He stood reluctantly in front of the door leading to the basement.

"She isn't a serial killer, Axel, and she has nothing to hide," Loki said. "Relax; I always save the cellar for last."

"Um—" Axel said. "Because there are two things I hate the most, you know—"

"Not really. "

"Cellars and attics, that's where all things scary happen."

Loki took the fancy spiral staircase upward, the one the flashlight barely managed to illuminate last night with all of its blinking. "We need to get upstairs. Remember Dee saying she'd found Snow White's glass coffin up there?" he said. He could hear Fable and Axel's footsteps behind him. The staircase was wide enough a carriage could pass through it. The steps were covered with a red carpet, and potted plants were placed on one side—real plants. Who was taking care of these plants?

Loki found himself murmuring:
Snow White One, Snow White two,
Sorrow was coming out for you.

"Boy. It takes some time to climb these stairs. I should've bought a bag of Sticky Sweet Bones with me," Axel said wearily. "I bet those 19th century kings and queens rarely got anything done other than climbing up and down the stairs."

"It's a royal castle. Everything has to be large and majestic," Fable spoke her mind, fascinated with the Schloss.

Loki pulled out his phone and read the notes he'd copied from the dissolved page he'd read in his Dreamhunter notebook. "Tell me if you see any mirrors," he said. "We can't kill her without at least two mirrors."

"Stop saying kill her!" Fable reminded him.

"Slay her?" Loki teased.

"Why mirrors?" Axel wondered.

"Part of the killing ritual is laying her body in the coffin between two opposite mirrors to enter her dream," Loki said.

"If I were you, I'd worry about stabbing her first," Axel panted. "And what's that dream thing you keep talking about?"

"I'll tell you later, now just look for mirrors I can use."

"You two are just awful, talking about *Snow White* like that," Fable said.

"Honestly, I hated the Snow White tale when I was a kid," Axel said. "She was a pale girl who should've tanned more. Her father was absent and weak while her stepmother belonged to an asylum for the beautifully insane. I like Jack and the Beanstalk more. Jack was badass. He stole from giants."

"Is that why you eat so much, to fight giants?" Fable said.

On the second floor, a long hallway led to a number of rooms on the right; ten rooms or more of wooden double-doors with golden handles the shape of a crow's head. Loki started pushing the doors open then peeking into the rooms. The doors squeaked against the floor, and it took considerable strength to push them for they were very heavy. Only a hunk like Big Bad opened the doors with ease. The squeaking sound echoed in the huge, almost vacant, space. Loki heard a couple of birds flutter away somewhere.

"Those are really big doors," Fable said, pushing hard with all her might, causing her body to bend over as if she was stretching in an aerobics class.

The rooms were ridiculously large, almost empty, except for an occasional bed with a nightstand, and large wooden wardrobes.

Fable welcomed each room with a happy dance of her own, tapping on the floor with a rhythmic tempo and stretching out her arms at her sides. She was excited, looking at the high ceilings as if waiting for the rain.

Since the rooms looked safe, Axel started opening more doors, feeling brave, silencing the fear inside him with the irritating sound of squeaking doors.

Axel pushed another door open and Fable dashed into the room with her dancing routine. Axel kept two forefingers crossed in the air, arching his back and examining the rooms like a bad cop with a crucifix in a B movie, the one who usually had two scenes left before he died.

"Don't worry, Loki," Axel said. "As long as I believe in the cross, I'm safe and protected."

"It has to be made of wood or silver," Fable suggested.

"If you really think it works, why didn't you use it on her yesterday?" Loki said, walking back to the hallway.

"I was still weakened by my disbelief, but today I'm stronger," Axel said, trying to sound old and wise, like mentors do in movies. "Ever hear the saying, 'What doesn't bite you makes you stronger'?"

"I want what you had for breakfast, because it must've been some good stuff," Loki said. "Oh, wait. I forgot, the boogeyman ate your breakfast."

Fable laughed; it was a snicker, almost like a sneeze.

Loki opened another room, and it was as empty as the rest. Was it possible that Snow White didn't sleep in the castle? And why were there no mirrors anywhere? Such castles usually had mirrors, a lot of mirrors. Fairy tales were all about mirrors.

"Mirror, mirror on the wall?" Loki whispered, rubbing his fingers together as if tempting a horse with an imaginary cube of sugar in his hand. He turned back to look for a bathroom. There had to be at least one mirror in there.

"Hey," Loki said to Axel and Fable. "Did you find any bathrooms?"

Looking out in the hallway, Loki couldn't find Axel.

"Axel, where are you?" Loki wondered.

There was no answer; only Loki's echoing voice.

"Fable?" he said.

There was no sign of Fable either, no sounds of clicking feet or singing to an invisible rain.

Loki swallowed hard, and pulled out his Alicorn.

"Stop playing tricks and come out now," the loneliness of his echoing voice worried him.

What happened to them?

He hurried his pace, pushing more doors open, merely glancing inside, and looking for them.

They weren't here.

And not there.

"If you're trying to pull a prank on me, it isn't funny!" Loki said.

Three rooms away, he saw the sun bursting into the hallway which meant the room had been opened before he'd reached it. He approached it cautiously, listening to the cacophonic drumbeat of his heart. A light, too bright, was shining out of the room.

"Are you there, Axel?" Loki asked, two steps shy of the room's entrance. The sound of his footsteps approaching added creepiness to the worrying symphony in his brain.

Loki stopped before the door, raising his stake with his back to the wall. He cocked his head–which Snow White had been twisting yesterday—trying to sneak a peek into the room.

And then, something wicked this way came.

It was a black creature, beating its large wings at him, and hitting him in the head. Loki landed in the hallway.

On his back, he took a second look at it and saw a huge crow, the size of a man, rustling its large wings, crossing over the staircase to the chandeliers, then flying away through an open window on the other side.

Loki picked up his Alicorn again and stood up, wondering if the room was full of other crows. He had to face whatever else was waiting for him in the room.

"Stupid Loki," he mumbled. "Neither Axel or Fable should've come with you. This is your war. It isn't fair if something happens to them because of you," Loki noticed this was one of the longest mumbling episodes he'd ever had. He suspected that it meant he really cared about them.

Finally, Loki found Axel standing in the middle of the room, right in front of him. Then he saw the horror on Axel's face. He looked paralyzed with an inanimate stare in his eyes and an open mouth. Loki thought he looked like he was made of wax, standing with his hair as stiff as a witch's broom, his face pale as if he'd just been bitten by a vampire. Loki stayed put, watching the goose bumps on Axel's arms.

Axel was speechless, his eyes reluctantly shifting sideways; looking as if they were someone else's standing behind a statute of Axel in a celebrity museum. Loki got the message, and stared in the direction of Axel's gaze.

The room was full of mobile, stand-up mirrors. They were set against each wall, and reflected the sun back inside. Each mirror reflected the other's reflections; spooky stuff that caused the blinding brightness in the room and in the hallway. It was distracting, forcing Loki to look at everything twice to identify it. The back of his eyes hurt, as if he'd stared at the sun too long.

Still, Loki stepped inside, slowly getting used to the brightness. That was when he understood what was going on. The mirrors weren't the reason for Axel's fear. It was something else, simply laid on the floor in the middle of the room: a glass coffin.

Fable was kneeling down, hugging the glass coffin and gently brushing the back of her hand against the glass. She was watching the *sleeping beauty* of Snow White inside. Loki never imagined this scene the way he saw it right now. Aside from scared-to-death-with-chattering-teeth Axel, and hopelessly romantic Fable, Loki was emotionally touched. He thought if Snow White were the old-fashioned vampire type, he'd find her in a darkened room with a bluish-brownish vibe, full of bloody curtains. She'd be next to a wooden armoire with an old rusty lock with intimidating shadows on the wall. On the other hand, if Snow White was the glass coffin princess, he'd imagined the scene before him taking place in a forest with seven dwarves mourning over her and Prince Charming, kneeling down to kiss her.

Loki nodded at Axel, reminding himself that everyone was allowed to pee in his or her pants occasionally.

The mirrors in the room were like those at a fun house. Loki could see himself from different angles, his reflection repeated and multiplied into smaller and farther versions of him inside the mirrors. He wasn't going to complain. The mirrors were more than enough for him to bury Snow White in the Dreamworld.

He knelt down next to Fable.

"Shhh," Fable said, "she is sleeping," she caressed the coffin as if it were her baby. Loki decided he wouldn't argue with her now, because he wanted to examine the coffin instead.

The glass coffin was padlocked from the inside. It was a devious trick. To stake her, Loki had to break the glass, which would be like sending her a text message: *Hey baby, I'm coming to kill you. Wake up.* Vampire's reflexes were fast so he had to find a way around it.

"I wouldn't be that sentimental if I were you," Loki said to Fable. "If she wakes up, she'll bite you."

"Yeah," Axel mustered the courage to squeak out a useless word.

"You two are horrid," Fable whispered, which made Loki think she was also a little bit afraid of Snow White but wouldn't admit it. "She is just a young beautiful girl. You didn't tell me she was this beautiful."

"Isn't she supposed to die when exposed to sunlight?" Axel asked Loki, knowing he couldn't win the conversation with Fable. "Or burn?" he seemed to like the idea better.

"She isn't an ordinary vampire. That's if she is actually just a vampire," Loki said. "There is something different about her. Besides, not all vampires burn in the light. It might be dangerous to stay out in the sun for a long time, but dying is so Hollywood tabloid stuff. Those few vampires who burn in the light have charms and spells to protect them against it."

"Don't kill her, Loki," Fable stared at him with moistened eyes. "She is so beautiful. I can see why her evil stepmother wanted to kill her out of jealousy. Please, Loki, please."

Loki could easily cry now, burst into tears and throw himself against the floor, kicking with hands and feet like a two year old who shoots long-range tears out of his eyes into the air, and cries: *waaaaaaa!*

But instead, he took the high road and didn't reply.

Bringing Fable along was a bad idea. Too emotional.

Inside the coffin, Snow White had her arms crossed over her white dress like an ancient Pharaoh Princess in an eternal beauty sleep. She was only sixteen but exuded an aura of being ancient. Loki felt as if he was pulled by an invisible power from his chest toward her. It was a strange feeling he hadn't experienced before; a feeling of belonging. His eyes scanned every inch of her body. Her whole being screamed three colors: white, red, and black. It was as if every other color in the world disappeared when he looked at her.

Her skin was pale, the color of a peaceful dove; the color of snowflakes on beautiful winter nights, lighting up the dark. Those snowflakes that urge you to tip your head back and enjoy their tiny splashes against your face; the kind of snow that makes you want to build a snow castle or a snowman and stick a carrot in its face, gifting it with a new nose. The color of her skin was hypnotizing. Yes, it was pale, yet it flowered with blooming youth. Loki hated when he found himself thinking of her that way, knowing that her beauty was only a mask of the great darkness in her.

She had red-manicured fingernails, and Loki wondered if it was the blood of her victims. He couldn't help but notice a faint red glow on her cheeks as if there were two small red apples shining through from underneath. Then there was that red ribbon in her hair, making her look innocent. It was one of the few things that didn't change about her when she changed into a vampire.

That damn red ribbon! That damn innocent feel about her. It makes it hard to plunge the Alicorn into her heart.

She had a red apple tucked between her hand and her chest. She was gripping it tightly as if it had sentimental meaning.

Snow White's hair was smooth, tumbling down her shoulders as if it had been combed every day, handled with the finest natural oils, reminding

Loki of ocean tides in a moonlit night. It had the power of sending you to shore with a loving push or drowning you between its tangled arms.

How did she clean up all the blood? How does she look so goddess-like?

Watching her sleep was euphoric. Loki thought he'd forget about the Mona Lisa, or the Seven Wonders of the World, or even how every child pictured Sleeping Beauty in her sleep. Snow White's beauty, in normal form, was a serenely beautiful sight. She had that beauty Loki never saw on the cover of magazines. It was pure, not artificially hiding behind plastic surgeries and plastered colors on her face. She didn't need it. Loki even noticed Snow White's cheeks were a bit chubby, but her beauty wasn't something you could fully comprehend with the eyes. It was that feeling he had in his tummy. He thought that this was why the evil stepmother never asked the mirror: Who was the most beautiful of all. Instead, she asked: Who was the *fairest* of them all.

The exact word Loki thought described the girl in the coffin now: Fairest.

Loki shook his head, trying to wake himself from this trance.

What's wrong with you, Loki? She's playing you, and you should not be tempted to end your quest. Evil looks so good sometimes.

"She spared your life yesterday," Fable reminded Loki, sewing cobwebs of guilt into his being. "She must've done it for a reason. Why do you insist on killing her?"

Fable's words were cutting through Loki's half-angel soul. He stood there silently, unable to make the next move.

"You're not falling in love with her? Are you?" Axel said. "You saw what she did yesterday."

"I'm not falling in love with her, you hear me?" Loki grabbed Axel by his shirt and said with a firm voice. "I'm not falling for a demon girl again. You understand."

This time Axel didn't say anything—he didn't even understand what he meant by falling for a demon girl *again*. Loki scared him more than ever now. Even Loki noticed the anger that welled up inside of him was ridiculous, as if he suddenly had no control of his actions. He finally let go of Axel.

What's happening to me? How can I be so villainous?

"Wooh, I don't want to get you angry at me again," Axel said. "That's more like Dr. Jekyll and Mr. Hyde. Next time, please warn me before you turn into the Incredible Hulk."

Loki fidgeted a little, unable to take his eyes off Snow White. He had his fortune cookie in his grip. Again, it was the only object he trusted whenever he didn't know what to decide in this world—especially when Charmwill Glimmer wasn't nearby.

"What should I do?" he asked it, almost sweating. Then, gritting his teeth with closed eyes, he crushed the fortune cookie in his grip.

When he opened his eyes, he read the small paper with the answer. It simply said:

Kill her.

Loki let out a sigh. Something didn't feel right, killing the vampire princess, but Loki had no choice but to trust the fortune cookie. It had always helped him, and had gotten him this far.

"You're talking to a fortune cookie?" Axel asked while Fable didn't even comprehend what just happened.

"It helps me make up my mind when I can't decide where to go, or what's wrong and what's right," Loki explained.

"Who are you, Loki Blackstar?" Fable asked with big, disbelieving eyes.

"Just a boy trying to find a place I can call home," he mumbled, and it was obvious that he wasn't going to elaborate.

"Good," Axel adjusted his shirt—and prestige. "Now, I know we need to get you home before you go ballistic on us like your vampire princess did on the teens yesterday."

"The coffin is locked—" Loki explained, not commenting on Axel's remark.

"Good for us," Axel said.

"From the inside," Loki continued.

"Not good for us."

Loki rummaged through the items in his bag, and pulled out a small hammer and handed it to Axel. "You will have to break the glass with this hammer."

"Why me?" Axel backed up a little, staring at the hammer as if it were a poisonous snake.

"That, or you'll have to stake her yourself while I break the glass. Pick your poison," Loki said.

Axel shook his head, kicking the floor in frustration. "I guess cracking the glass open is like messing things up, which I'm good at," he took the hammer. "You don't happen to have some gum in that bag of yours, do you?"

Loki shot him an incredulous stare.

"What? I just need something to chew on so I can relax. Out of the way, Fable. Do you always have to stand in my way?"

"You're evil, Loki!" Fable stood up. "Why did you even come to this town? We were all happy before you came."

Loki shrugged. Fable was definitely a weak spot.

Fable ran at Loki and started hitting him in the chest. Loki didn't react to her sweet anger. The way her head ended up buried in his chest, and the smell of her pure soul on his skin, made him truly vulnerable to her. Loki and Axel had just shattered all she loved about her childhood princess in a matter of hours.

"I have to do this, Fable," Loki said. "She's a demon. Besides, I'm only staking her. I promise you that if I find a reason not to kill her when I enter her dream, I will let her live."

"As if you can kill her," Axel mumbled.

"You promise, Loki?" Fable looked up to him, literally and emotionally.

"I promise," Loki said, eyes closed, running his hand through her hair. He lied to her, only to calm her down, and he was ashamed about it. How was it possible for a half-angel to lie? Wasn't he supposed to be the good guy?

Loki wanted to tell Fable that it wasn't his fault that the world was full of vampires, or that it was his job to kill them, or that Snow White turned out to be a demon. Hell, Snow White wasn't supposed to be real in the first place. Even with all those fairy tales Charmwill had told him, Loki never believed that they were true.

"Could we get this over with?" Axel groaned. He parted his legs and stood over the coffin, holding the hammer up high with both hands, ready to break it open. He looked eager to break something. Loki thought he'd have to talk to him about the downside of repeatedly playing those Zombie games; they were causing him to be violent.

Looking at Fable and Axel, Loki still wondered why they acted like they were twelve. He felt like a sixteen-year-old who was a father and an older brother at the same time.

That's the last thing I need, to have to care for someone else.

Loki patted Fable on the shoulder, after kissing her on the forehead. He knelt down next to the coffin, ready with his Alicorn.

"Pass the Magic Dust to Fable," Loki told Axel. "In case I can't stake her, you will have to throw it all in Snow White's face," he told Fable. "It will keep her unconscious for a while. If that happens, you should escape with Axel, and run as far as you can. I will handle the rest."

"Why didn't you use it yesterday," Axel wondered.

"I was so paralyzed I couldn't even think about it," Loki said.

I'm not really telling Axel the truth, which is that I suck when it comes to demon girls.

"Are you with me, Fable?" Loki said.

Fable nodded, brushing her tears away, adding one last unnecessary sob at the end.

"Fable," Loki stressed, gazing into her eyes. "Don't do anything stupid. If you use the Magic Dust against us, we're all going to become vampires-ever-after."

She smiled with approval. "Then why don't you use the magic dust on her now instead of the stake?" she asked.

"According to the Dreamhunter's notebook, to enter her dream, I have to stake her in the heart while she is awake. If I stab her while she is asleep, I can't enter her dream."

"Why?" Axel asked.

"I don't know, but I think because the stake in the heart is the only way to infuse the Sleeping Death," Loki snapped. It felt confusing being told he was one of the greatest Dreamhunters in the world when he didn't know much about it, and had to learn about it from a notebook as if it was Chemistry.

"Are you ready?" Loki stared at Axel to make sure he was super alert. "The glass has to crack open on the first hit. It has to be big enough for me to stab her in the heart, or we'll be in trouble."

"I'm ready," Axel took a deep breath, and kept it in his chest.

Fable imitated Axel. She hoped it would help her calm down.

Loki counted, "One."

Axel was holding his breath so that his cheeks grew bubbly like small red balloons. Strangely, one was bigger than the other.

"Two."

Fable closed her eyes, let out a sigh, and parted her legs.

"And Three—"

Before Loki finished counting, Snow White opened her eyes.

14

Now I Lay Me Down to Sleep

Snow White's demonic eyes flipped open. They looked as dead as black buttons sewn to her eye sockets, like black coins that rested on the eyes of the deceased, sucking Loki's soul into darkness. With her blood red lips and sharp fangs, she snarled at him.

"Three," Loki heard Fable say enthusiastically. She still had her eyes closed and her face tightened, unlike terrified Axel.

The way Snow White became snow-bite in a flip of a switch was unbelievable. Loki wondered if this ever happened to Prince Charming when he tried to kiss her.

Everything changed in milliseconds. Axel hammered down hard. It was one effective hit, finally letting the air out of his lungs with a hysterical scream, like a mad samurai jumping out of the pages of a Manga. He acted out of fear, not courage.

The glass coffin broke open, splinters flying in every direction, and shards of glass scattering on the floor. Snow White yelped, as if her awakening was just as painful as being staked. She turned her head and growled at Axel.

"Oh my God," Fable shrieked, having opened her eyes. Loki didn't have time to comfort her, or ask her if she changed her mind about Snow White being so beautiful after she saw this. "Oh. My. God." Fable might've repeated the phrase forever, forgetting about the million other words that could express her surprise.

The reason why everyone was still alive was that the crack in the glass coffin wasn't big enough for Snow White to leap out. Axel had just cracked the part over her chest open, the rest of the coffin remained unbroken. Contrary to common belief, Loki had known from previous experiences that vampires took a few minutes to adjust to their surroundings when they woke up.

The vampire princess tried to reach her hands out and grab for Loki's arms. Loki had about one hundredth of a fraction of one tenth of a second to sink his Alicorn into her heart. Faster than a scared pussycat, he pounced down on her and staked her in the heart. His grip was so tight on the stake the knuckles of his fingers whitened. He held his grip longer than usual, staring at her, and he wasn't going to let go until she went back to sleep.

Snow White let out another yelp, wrapping her cold hands around Loki's, sending a slight shiver through his body when they touched. Her hands were too cold and again, Loki felt something strange touching her, as if she managed to pass her feelings to his soul. It bugged Loki that he felt as if she was blaming him for something.

Why do I always feel that I'm the bad one when it comes to her? I really wish this feeling would just go away.

Blood gushed out from her heart around the stake. It covered their hands, and splattered on his face. Snow White's upper body leaned forward in shock and her black eyes stared at Loki. She didn't look angry as much as betrayed. Loki could swear that he could hear Axel and Fable breathing behind him. It was an intense moment. The little Snow White princess was a fighter. She didn't give in easily.

Finally, Snow White surrendered, her eyes turning into the loveliest ocean-blue color again. She was in her Sleeping Death.

Her eyes were so beautiful that Loki couldn't let her head fall back into the coffin without assistance. He had to hold her by the shoulders, placing his other hand under head so she could rest upon it like a pillow.

"May you sleep in peace," he found himself whispering to her.

"Is she dead?" Axel asked. With his back against the mirror and a hammer in one hand, he looked like a psycho killer—so did Loki with the stake and blood on his hands.

"Temporarily," Loki said, looking at the blood on his hands.

The blood of Snow White is on my hands. If she turns out to be the real Snow White, I must be the worst person in the world. What am I doing?

"Temporarily? You mean she could wake up again?" Axel freaked out.

"Not on her own. Only if someone pulls the stake out," Loki explained, remembering that he hadn't succeeded in killing most of the vampires because of this silly fact.

Fable moaned with a double layer of hands over her mouth. Then she pointed speechlessly at the blood gushing out of Snow White's heart around the stake.

Loki wanted to kneel before her, and beg her not to hate him. "Don't worry," he said. "Her wounds will heal when she wakes up and feeds—if we let her. And don't ask me to pull the stake out now," Loki gathered the courage to talk in a slightly aggressive tone to her. She nodded obediently.

"Why would anyone want to pull the stake out?" Axel asked.

"Someone who wants her to turn back into a vampire, probably another vampire like her," Loki guessed.

"So what now?" Fable asked reluctantly.

"I'm glad you asked," Loki said, pulling out his phone with the notes from the Dreamhunter notebook. "Now, I will have to enter her dream and kill her in it once again so she stays in this Sleeping Death forever."

"It's time you explain to us how this dream-hocus-pocus works," Axel said.

"I'm going to explain this once, so please pay attention," Loki said,

"Vampires are immortal demons, which according to my notebook are called Demortals. Generally, Demortals don't die. When a vampire hunter stakes them, the Demortals enter a state called the Sleeping Death, the same as mentioned in the Brothers Grimm version of Snow White's tale. It makes the vampires look dead while they're only sleeping until someone pulls the stake out."

"So there's really no way to kill them?" Axel said.

"The one and only way to really kill a Demortal is to enter their dream after you stake them and actually kill them again in that dream. The Demortals dreams take place in a realm called the Dreamworld. If they're staked in the Dreamworld, their brains freeze and they will never wake up in our world, not even when you pull the stake out."

Fable wanted to take a peek into the Dreamhunter's notebook as she became more curious about it. "What is this Dreamworld like?"

"I haven't read much about it yet, but think of it like a rabbit hole, one that is six levels deep. The waking world, which we live in now, is the earth. The Dreamworld, where a Dreamhunter kills a demon in their sleep, is the first level down the rabbit hole."

"Six levels?" Fable snatched the notebook. "That's awesome."

"Yes," Loki nodded. "Somewhere the notebook mentioned a forbidden place called 'Six Dreams Under,' but that's of no concern to us, because I just need to kill her in the 'First Dream Under,' which is simply like the dreams we all know about."

"May I ask an annoying question?" Axel said.

"No," Fable said.

"Who wrote this notebook?" Axel questioned.

"I don't know," Loki shrugged his shoulders. "Many articles are signed by an A.V.H, though."

"I think his name is 'All Vampires go to Hell'," Axel speculated.

"So that's it? You just enter the dream, stake the vampire again and come back?" Fable said.

"That's all I know so far."

"Count me in," Axel said.

"And you?" Loki asked Fable.

She tried to avoid his gaze.

"Fable?" Loki demanded.

"Look," she said, unconsciously wiggling her nose under her glasses. "I will help you if this is a good thing for our town, so the teenage killings and disappearances stop. But you promise me, Loki, that if we find out she needs help like she told you, we help her."

Loki was hesitant. He didn't want to promise and lie to her again.

"Promise me, Loki," Fable raised a warning finger in the air. "Doesn't the fact that she asked for your help mean anything to you?"

She is only fooling me because I have a weakness for monster girls. You have no idea.

"I promise. Cross my heart," Loki said, hating himself for lying to her again.

"And, Loki?" Fable asked, gazing sensationally at him. "Come back alive."

This moment made Loki feel even worse about himself. It was a good feeling having found a small family. It felt good but also strange, because he'd always been a loner as long as he'd lived in the Ordinary World—his mom didn't really count in her ghostly condition. Having others caring for him, and him caring for them, was beautiful but also a responsibility and an attachment. He was doing all of this to go home, and not to make friends that he'd end up wanting to stay with in Sorrow.

"Now, it's time to tell you about the dream ritual that allows me to enter the Dreamworld," Loki said.

Following the instructions from the notebook, Loki placed two of the mirrors opposite to each other with Snow White's coffin in between. This way the two mirrors reflected one another as if they were staring into infinity. It was the only way to enter the Dreamworld.

"Mirror number one mirrors mirror number two, while mirror number two mirrors mirror number one mirroring mirror number two, and so on," Loki read from his phone. "Can you imagine it?"

Axel stood with wide eyes, mouth ajar, looking at one of the mirrors. "Wow. This is trippy, and so cool. Why don't they teach us this stuff in school?"

Loki pulled a piece of chalk out of his bag and drew a huge circle on the wooden floor, encompassing the mirrors and the coffin in the middle.

"That's like creating a medium to commune with the other worlds," Fable said, "In your case, the Dreamworld."

"Exactly," Loki agreed. "It's called the Epidaurus Circle, named after an ancient Greek town. A high priest used to come and heal ill people in the middle of a circle like this one. He healed them by entering their dreams."

"Except in your case, you're killing them," Axel noted with a forefinger on his lower lip.

"I understand why you have to use mirrors," Fable said. "Mirrors have been used to imprison demons, and commune with other worlds throughout history."

"Not to mention that Bloody Mary hides in one of these," Axel stepped into the circle, marking his territory.

"I'd prefer it if you get out of the circle," Loki warned him. "According to my notebook, this circle will become a monstrous gate sucking non-Dreamhunters into a nasty world beyond your imagination. Only Dreamhunters are allowed inside."

Axel jumped out awkwardly, checking his clothes and looking around as if something from the circle had stuck to them.

Loki handed a number of candles to Fable; "You know what to do with these, right?" he winked at her.

Fable smirked. "Yeah, a witch always does," Fable lit the candles one by one and placed them carefully adjacent to the circle. For a wannabe witch, this was as easy as ABC.

"Now we pull down the curtains," Loki read from the notebook. "Axel?"

Axel jumped eagerly and pulled the curtains, conjuring darkness into the room, except for the candle-lit circle in the middle.

"Perfect setting," Fable said. "Romantic, I have to say."

"And I thought I was the one who was weird," Axel mumbled, flicking her earlobe with his finger.

"Everything inside the Epidaurus Circle is called the Dream Temple. If you want to be my assistants, you'll need to learn the terminology."

"Whateva ya say, boss," Fable giggled.

Loki grabbed his bag and got into the Dream Temple. He pulled out two ancient Obol coins he'd found in the bag and placed them on Snow White's eyes. He was following the instructions from the notebook. It said that the coins prevented the dreamer, in that case Snow White, from connecting the waking world to the Dreamworld with her eyes. It was a precaution used because some evil entities in the Dreamworld might want to escape to the waking world.

Then Loki pulled out an hourglass from Charmwill's backpack, and placed it inside the circle.

"So what's that for?" Axel knotted his eyebrows.

"It's apparently an hourglass, but the notebook describes it as a 'Waker'," Loki read. "It has a switch where I can set the amount of sand, thus the time, I want to spend in the Dreamworld, and it only works inside the Dream Temple. The maximum time allowed in any dream is *two and forty* minutes."

"What does 'two and forty minutes' mean?" Axel said.

"It's a fancy word for saying 'forty-two minutes'," Fable said. "I remember I read that phrase in Shakespeare's Romeo and Juliet, which I'm sure you haven't heard of."

"Does it have zombies in it?" Axel said.

"It's a Romance. Juliet drinks a poisonous potion that puts her to sleep for 'two and forty' minutes," Fable said then suddenly stopped in the middle of her sentence, and looked at Loki. "Does that mean that Juliet's poisonous potion might have been a Sleeping Death, too?"

"Please," Loki waved his hand. "I'd rather not analyze."

"You're right; too much analyzing will cause confusion. We have to focus on Snow White's dream right now," Fable said.

"So once all the sand falls through the Waker, the Dreamhunter's connection to the Dreamworld ends and he wakes up?" Axel wondered.

"Yes, as long as nothing prevents the Dreamhunter from waking up," Loki nodded.

"What do you mean by that?" Fable frowned. "Could you stay trapped in the Dreamworld?"

"The notebook mentions that the Dreamworld could be dangerous. Previous Dreamhunters were unable to wake up from it, but it never explained how or why it happened. However, there's another tool that allows me to send you a signal if I'm in danger and need help," Loki said and pulled out a red ball of thread from the bag. "It's called an 'Ariadne Fleece.'"

"A ball of thread?" Axel scowled. "Looks like it belongs to someone's grandma."

"Watch closely," Loki took the tip of the fleece and touched one of the mirror's surfaces with it. The meeting point turned the mirror into a water-like surface, rippling as if he'd thrown a pebble in it.

"Now that's real magic," Fable said.

Slowly, the Ariadne Fleece became a part of the mirror, sticking to its surface from one side while Loki pulled the other and wrapped it around his wrist. Once he did that the length of the thread between the spot in the mirror and Loki's hand became invisible.

"Now, I have a physical connection between the waking world and the Dreamworld through this thread," Loki explained, reading from his phone. "And although this magical thread stretches for infinity, it will stay invisible to everyone, and untouchable, too."

"And how is it supposed to help you send us a signal if you're in danger?" Fable tilted her curious head.

"It's really simple; I just have to tap the thread around my wrist three consecutive times," Loki explained. "You should then see it unwrapping itself from my fingers toward the mirror, if someone is pulling it, which means you'll have to wake me up instantly."

"How are we supposed to wake you up when we're not supposed to get into the circle?" Axel said.

"You'll have to break the mirror with something, a baseball bat, an axe, or a rock, anything to break the connection between the two mirrors. Think of the two mirrors as if they are connected by an invisible electrical force. Breaking one of them is like pulling the plug from the connection between the waking world and the Dreamworld."

"Who are you, Loki? Like really, who are you?" Fable shook her head.

Loki dismissed her question. It was silly for someone to ask him this when he didn't know the answer himself. Instead, he lay on his back next to Snow White in her coffin, perpendicular to the mirrors, preparing for sleep.

"It's time for you to use the Magic Dust on me so I can enter the dream," Loki said.

Fable walked closer, still tangent to the Epidaurus Circle, with a handful of Magic Dust, her face shimmering in the candle light.

"Before you do, I will have to recite a prayer mentioned in the book," Loki said. "Just don't get mad at me. I'm following the rules," Loki closed his eyes and said:

> *Now I lay me down to sleep.*
> *Pray the lord my soul to keep.*
> *And if I die before I wake.*
> *Forbid Snow White*
> *My soul to take.*

15

Birthday Bloody Birthday

Loki opened his eyes.

It felt strange waking up in a dream *knowing* it was actually a dream—let alone someone else's dream. He hadn't seen what happened in the real world after Fable poured Magic Dust in his eyes, but he imagined the Dream Temple shimmering with light while he was lying unconscious next to the vampire princess.

Here in the Dreamworld, Loki took a second to adjust to his surroundings. He had a headache so intense he imagined there were birdies humming above his head. He wondered if this was supposed to happen, because he hadn't read about side effects of traveling the Dreamworld in the Dreamhunter's notebook.

The headache faded slowly, and he started looking for clues to his whereabouts. He found himself lying on his back, staring at the ceiling. It was engraved and painted with all kinds of ancient motifs, drawings of stories of battles that he didn't know of. It looked like he was somewhere in the 18th or 19th century like Axel had suggested.

Loki stood up and looked around. He was alone in a majestic room, a girl's room, probably in the Schloss. He could hear voices celebrating outside the room.

Suddenly, the door sprang open, and Loki took a step back.

A big woman, dressed in a maid's outfit, came through the door. She looked angrily at Loki.

Wow, this woman is a giant. Where am I?

"What are you doing here?" she shook Loki by the shoulders. "And what are these clothes you're wearing?" she asked. "Take these," she handed him a warrior outfit that looked childish. "Get dressed and follow the other children outside," she demanded.

Did she say children? Of course, to a giant woman like her, he seemed like a child, but he didn't like anyone calling him child or kid, not even in a dream. Loki examined the outfit with an open mouth. It was too small. How did she expect him to wear it? The giant had totally misjudged his size. What was going on?

"What are you waiting for?" she grunted. "I don't have time to wait for you. Get dressed. It's the princess's birthday. The little princess will meet the young prince in a moment."

Little princess and little prince? What crazy dream was Snow White having?

"But these are too small," Loki complained. They were his first words in the dream, and they felt awfully real.

The woman sighed and pushed Loki toward a mirror. Staring at his reflection, he almost laughed and cried at the same time. The woman wasn't a *giant*. Loki was just small. He'd entered the dream as a seven-year-old.

What? Is this supposed to happen?

"Hurry!" the woman urged him.

Loki got dressed, unable to take his eyes away from the mirror, thinking he looked a bit too skinny.

"What should I do now?" he asked the woman.

"Are you making fun of me? Move it," she guided him out of the room and then walked to whatever business she had to manage.

Loki was glad she was gone so he could pick up his Alicorn from the floor. He stomped out to the hallway of an enormous castle; it was the Schloss in earlier times. Everything was different but fancier. Gold and blue were two prominent colors in the decoration of the Schloss. He could hear the sounds of a celebration outside the castle. There must have been thousands of people outside gathered for the princess' birthday.

Loki wondered where Snow White was. He had already wasted time with this woman, and he couldn't wake up before he accomplished his job.

Closer to the edge of the stairs, he watched a ceremony taking place down the hall. The king and the queen were sitting on their thrones, but Loki couldn't see their faces. There were another king and queen standing opposite to the throne with a seven-year-old kid. He looked like a prince.

"God bless this meeting," the standing king announced.

"Where is the princess?" asked the standing queen.

"I'm right here, my queen," a young girl said, her voice coming from the hallway. The kings and queens downstairs turned their heads up to look at the princess talking from behind the banister. Loki retreated against the wall. Looking sideways, he saw her, Snow White, seven years old, looking down at them from the hallway.

"Good job, Loki," he mocked himself. "Now, how are you going to have the heart to kill a seven year old girl?"

"I will be right down," Snow White said. "Sorry I was late," she held the rim of her dress in her hands and strolled down the hallway to the stairs and the awaiting ceremony.

Loki stood silent, watching her walk the hallway the way elegant young princesses do. She tripped over her dress once and managed to pick herself up fast, making sure no one saw her. She sighed and mumbled something about how tight her shoes were, and that she hated being a princess, preferring to play outside with the other kids. "Silly shoes, silly etiquette. Everything in this castle is so boring," she talked to herself like Loki usually did. Loki liked the idea that he wasn't the only one who talked to himself.

The two of them actually had a couple of things in common.

On her way to the stairs, she suddenly stopped in front of him.

Snow White turned her head slowly toward him. His heart raced so fast he thought he'd wake up from the dream. He pressed tighter on his Alicorn, unable to pull it up to stake her when she approached. If a Dreamhunter had to have the heart to kill a cute seven-year-old girl then Loki was definitely the lousiest in the world.

Snow stared at him with her doe eyes as if she had seen ice cream and wondered if she should try it. Loki heard her mother summon her again. Snow White craned her neck toward Loki and stuck out her tongue. Then she smiled a teasing smile.

"What are you going to do now, Loki Blackstar?" she whispered.

"You can see me?"

"No," she shook her head. "I'm a crazy princess who sees imaginary friends. Of course, I see you. Did you think you could kill me so easily?"

"Snow White!" her mother's demanding voice was peculiar. It had a twinge of unusual authority to it. Was that her mother, or her stepmother?

"Alright, I'm coming!" Snow White said. "You can't kill me, Loki," she turned back to him. "Try it. Go on," she whispered, stepping closer to him. "I'm stronger and I know you have a weakness for monster girls. Go on; pull that stake out from behind your back."

Loki gritted his teeth. He hated that he didn't have the nerve to stake her right at this moment. How long was he going to battle his fears? He tried his best to kill her, but something held him back.

"Ora Pedora," he whispered, closing his eyes. He wondered if the Alicorn could give him strength, but it didn't. What was all that talk about the Chanta? Why isn't this Alicorn ever useful? "Ora Pedora," he repeated, but nothing happened. This Alicorn was useless.

"I thought so," Snow White laughed at him, and walked elegantly down the stairs. Loki walked to the edge to watch her from behind the banister.

Loki stood there helpless, still wondering how he was supposed to kill a seven year old, even if she were a demon.

Princess Snow White was being introduced to the prince from a neighboring kingdom. Loki couldn't hear what his name was, but he heard the maids describe him as 'Prince Charming.'

It seemed that the gathering was more of a political merge between kings and queens of both kingdoms. Loki heard them call it the Kingdom of Sorrow.

So this was the town of Sorrow centuries ago? It was a kingdom?

The two royal families were gathering to discuss the possibility of the prince and the princess getting married when they grew up. Loki understood that it was the first time Snow White met Prince Charming. He walked the hallway to its end and peeked through a huge rectangular window. There was a big celebration waiting outside with flowers and balloons and carriages. This was where the kings and the queens were going to go after they had their initial introduction. Many children outside were dressed like Loki. They were an army of children, most of them held their small swords.

So that's what the woman thought I was? One of those kids?

But why am I a child in this dream? How did that happen? Can she control her dreams?

Loki remembered he'd read in his notebook that a few Demortals had such powers, although it was said to happen rarely.

Suddenly, Loki heard a scream. He darted back to look from behind the banister.

The young prince was lying on the ground, blood seeping out of his neck. His king and queen parents were in shock and Snow White's parents were trying to persuade them that the prince was going to be all right.

What happened? The poor young prince was going to die.

Zooming in, Loki saw the seven-year-old Snow White staring at the prince with blood trickling from her mouth. Loki gulped when she tilted her head up and stared at him with that cute, scary smile of hers. She was making fun of him, licking her lips as if it was chocolate syrup. Loki held tighter to the banister bars like a scared kid. He was appalled and confused at the same time. Again, she looked so innocent, although she just bit the prince.

"What did you do?" Loki saw the queen slap Snow White on her hands. Loki still couldn't see the queen or king's faces from where he was standing, and he didn't know how to explain who he was if he was discovered.

Look guys, I just came into this dream from the waking world. I'm gonna kill your daughter because she is a badass vampire. It will only take a minute, everything will be fine, and you will live happily ever after. By the way, don't bother thinking that your life isn't real and this is just a dream. Happens all the time.

"Tabula!" the queen summoned the giant woman Loki had met before. "Come over here."

Tabula rushed down the stairs.

"Take Shew with you and clean this mess up," Loki heard the queen say. Shew? Loki thought it was a lovely nickname for a nasty princess. "Postpone the ceremony until I say so," the queen followed. "No one from the locals outside can know about this, you understand?"

Tabula nodded obediently. She took Snow White by the hand while the King of Sorrow promised the other king and queen he could save their son.

Tabula and Snow White talked in the hallway while Loki hid in one of the rooms, leaving the door slightly ajar.

"What were you thinking, Snow White?" Tabula said to her. "Didn't we speak about controlling those urges?"

"I couldn't control myself, and he's delicious," Snow White said, holding Tabula's hand. "So yummy, I want more."

"You think his blood is delicious?"

"He's handsome, too," Snow White said. "I liked biting him. I don't know why he freaked out. Is he hurt?"

Loki tried not to kick himself in the head with a school bus driving infinity-miles-per-hour when he heard this.

"We'll see about that," Tabula patted her gently. "But you can't bite boys because they look handsome and delicious, Shew."

"Why?" Snow White stomped her foot.

"One bratty little princess," Loki mumbled.

Tabula sighed, "It's not the proper way princesses should behave. You have to be more polite than that because you're not an average run of the mill street urchin."

"But I want more, and it's my birthday. I'd rather not be a princess if it means getting to bite whomever I want."

"What an awful thing to say. You can't just bite anyone you like. Do you understand? Now let's go to the bathing chamber and wash this bloody mess off of you. The whole kingdom is waiting for you to come outside and greet them. You can't go out looking like this."

"No!" Snow White said, kicking Tabula in her big leg and running away.

Outrunning the slow Tabula, Snow White came back to Loki whose head was sticking out from behind the door. He didn't know why he was still in this dream when it was obvious he didn't have the heart to kill her when she was manipulating it. He needed to get back to the waking world and check his notebook to see if there was a way to kill vampires who control their dreams.

Snow White, the young and feisty, pushed Loki inside and entered the room, then closed the door behind her.

"How do you like that, Loki?" she sneered at him. "Aren't you supposed to be the greatest Dreamhunter in the world?"

"How do you know that?" Loki frowned. "And how do you control your dreams?" he wasn't sure why Charmwill told him he was the greatest Dreamhunter in the world anymore. Apparently, Loki wasn't even strong enough to kill a chicken vampire.

"Poor you," she teased him and held his head with her hands as if he were a good puppy.

Loki kept looking around while she talked to him. He should have tapped his Fleece three times as a sign from Axel to break the mirror. He reached with his left hand to tap the fleece on his right hand three times, and prayed Axel would hurry breaking the mirror.

"Don't wake up, Loki," Snow White pleaded. "We can play together here. There are things that I need to show you. I need you here. You're the only one who can save me," Snow White whispered in his ears as if she was scared of someone again—or something.

Why does she do that to me? Why does she play me when she can just kill me? Is it that she really needs to be saved, and I am just too stubborn to admit it? I need someone to save me.

"You're just playing games with me," Loki said, wondering why Axel hadn't broken the mirror yet.

"Not now, believe me," she held Loki's head in her hands. Although she had drawn her fangs back, and her face returned to normal, he still didn't trust her. "I'm not the evil one," she whispered, glancing momentarily at the locked door behind her as if scared of what lay behind it.

"Then who is?" Loki said.

Damn it, Loki. Don't ask her that. You don't care about her. You only care about yourself.

"I can't say," she lowered her head. "I can't," she repeated, her eyes scanning the ceiling as if there were hidden monsters somewhere up there. Loki looked up and saw nothing suspicious.

Is she trying to tell me something?

"And yes, I'm controlling this dream," she said. "You keep trying to kill me when you should save me, and I won't let you in my dreams as long as you still want to kill me without knowing my real story."

Suddenly, Loki heard the cawing of crows. There were many, and increasing, circling outside the castle. They looked a lot like the crow that had knocked him down and flew out Snow White's window in the waking world. Loki didn't know what this meant. He watched the crows outside the window fluttering hysterically in the sky.

Then he heard a thud, and another.

He felt the earth shake underneath him as if there was an earthquake. He couldn't believe his eyes. The world outside was collapsing; mountains were crumbling, the earth was shattering, and the stars were falling like snowflakes from the sky.

Loki turned back to Snow white, but she was gone.

The room was falling apart. Everything was shaking violently, and it was only seconds before the castle was going to crumble to ashes.

The dream was ending.

It was healthy sign, though. It meant that he was just waking up from it, and that he wasn't going to drown in it. Loki closed his eyes, and took a deep breath, ready to wake up, and planning to have a nasty encounter with Axel for not breaking the mirror.

***

145

Loki thought that waking up from the Dreamworld would give him enough time to relax and catch his breath.

He was wrong.

When he opened his eyes, he heard Axel and Fable's screams. The curtains had been pulled open, sunlight filled the room. Loki stood up instantly, checking to see if someone had pulled the stake out of Snow White, but no one had. Axel and Fable weren't in the room. They were screaming outside.

"Run, Loki, Run!" Fable shouted.

"It's Big Bad," Axel screamed. "He's still alive!"

Before Loki could recover from his dream enough to comprehend this, he saw Big Bad in front of him. He had a big smug smile on his face, holding Axel and Fable like two sacks of potatoes, one in each hand.

"Aren't you supposed to be dead?" Loki asked Big Bad whose face was wounded badly. Loki assumed it was from yesterday's little adventure with the vampire princess.

"He's here for revenge for what you did to him in the parking lot, Loki," Fable said, hanging like a yoyo in Big Bad's hand. "Axel and I stopped him."

"Let them down, Big Bad," Loki said.

"No way," Big Bad said. "I'm going to kill them both, kill you, and then finish the sleeping vampire princess."

"Kick his ass, Loki. You can do it!" Fable kicked her legs in the air. Amazingly, she reached with her hand and slapped Big Bad on his cheek as hard as she could. It was a brave move.

"You little brat," Big Bad threw Axel rolling on the floor, and grabbed Fable with both his hands. "I'm going to kill you first, lousy witch," he grabbed her by the throat.

"I've been called worse by better!" Fable choked.

"Lousy witch, daughter of a lousier witch," Big Bad reddened with anger.

"Get away from my sister," Axel screamed, and ran into Big Bad with his head, but ended up on the floor again. Big Bad didn't even wince. He just stood there like a truck, and Axel slid down from the crash.

Axel went hysterical, looking for the Magic Dust, but he couldn't find it because Big Bad was stepping on the bag.

Loki stood firm in his place, balling up his fists. It puzzled him why he hadn't moved yet to save Fable. Deep inside, he knew he was becoming too attached to her and her brother. As repetitive and annoying as it sounded, he wasn't there to get involved. He wasn't there to make friends or fight bullies. He wasn't there to care about anyone. It all seemed trivial to the grand aspiration of being forgiven and going back home.

But he did care, with all his heart. How did he get attached to the siblings in a course of a day? How was it that they'd became more than friends to him? He hadn't felt this way about anyone during the whole year he'd spent in Snoring. And it reminded him about his mother telling him about the Chanta, that he'd only feel it when he cared for others the way he cared for himself.

What will it be, Loki?

"Bite me," Loki snapped, and charged Big Bad, bumping him with his shoulder. There was no Magic Dust now; he had to fight on his own, with bare hands.

The impact made a crunching sound, and Big Bad only winced a little while Loki ended up on the floor like Axel.

"I kill vampires and I can't hit a bully," Loki mumbled.

"Thank you, Loki," Fable pecked him on the cheek. The thud was useful after all. It had caused Big Bad to drop Fable.

Big Bad picked up Loki by his shirt, and started swinging him in the air. Loki watched Axel and Fable do nothing, his arms and legs flailing, as he tried to free himself from Big Bad.

"How do you like it now?" Big Bad said. "I don't mind killing you before I kill the Crumblewoods."

"Do something," Loki said.

Axel's lips crinkled as he stood still. "I love you Loki, but I can only save one person. I love my sister, sorry," he hugged Fable.

"You didn't save her, you coward!" Loki snapped. "I did."

"Actually, I dropped her," Big Bad laughed. "None of you losers saved the lousy witch."

"Wait, Loki," Fable said, standing at the edge of the Dream Temple. "I have an idea."

Fable knelt down, and reached for the Alicorn and pulled it from Snow White's heart.

"Are you out of your mind?" Axel screamed, staring at the vampire princess.

"Don't—"Loki managed to say from under Big Bad's arm. "She'll kill us all!"

It was too late. Fable had pulled out the Alicorn, and Snow White's red eyes fluttered open.

She took a moment to get her bearings, enough for everyone to take a step back. Then she stood up with her fangs drawn out, and anger pulsing through her veins. Loki wondered why she didn't wake up so swiftly the first time they broke the glass.

"I don't understand this," Axel said. "Vampires should die in the sunlight. Why doesn't she die?"

"Shut up," Fable said.

"No I won't," Axel said. "I want to say at least a couple more words before I die."

"She won't hurt us," Fable said, staring at the vampire princess. The dark power of Snow White when she was angry fascinated Fable. She wondered if she could be as powerful as her one day. "Don't you get it? She likes Loki. She won't hurt us."

Snow White walked barefoot, and slowly, toward Big Bad as if he was her only enemy in the room. Big Bad dropped Loki to the floor, unable to avoid Snow White's penetrating eyes.

Loki couldn't take his eyes off her, too. Fable's decision of removing the Alicorn was surprisingly the right thing to do.

"You don't want to do this," Big Bad tried to convince Snow White.

Like always, Snow White didn't say a word. She walked toward him slowly with blood dripping from her white dress. Whenever she was angry with someone, there was always blood dripping from her.

"Does she always have blood on her dress?" Axel wondered. Fable cupped his mouth, watching the vampire princess do what Fable always wanted to.

Suddenly, Big Bad's face reddened and the bones in his body started cracking. It was as if something inside him was about to burst out. It reminded Loki of the same sounds he'd heard Big Bad produce yesterday. What was going on?

Big Bad let out a painful moan, arching his back, and then he screamed with all his might:

Awooo!

Loki wondered why he did that; there was no way Big Bad was calling for the Bullyvards. He stepped over to protect Axel and Fable, preparing to run away.

"It's the call," Axel said. "He is calling the Bullyvards to help him."

"If they come, they're going to die today," Loki said, picking up his bag.

"Don't you boys get it?" Fable was still observing tentatively.

"What?" Loki said.

"Big Bad is turning into a…" Fable said.

Big Bad's eyes became slits and turned yellow. A mass of hair started growing on his face, his arms, and the rest of his body. His nails grew longer and sharper, and his hairy feet grew noticeably bigger, ripping out his shoes.

His transformation scared everyone, all but Snow White. She stopped in front of him, and snarled once more.

"So he's not Big Bad?" Axel wondered. "He's the—"

"The Big Bad Wolf!" Fable celebrated the weirdness of their town.

Big Bad dared Snow White's eyes one last time: both of them threatening each other with their fangs.

"Clash of the Titans," Fable commented.

Finally, Big Bad gave in and retreated, crashing out through the second story window and running away on all fours.

"This isn't happening, right?" Axel rubbed his eyes.

Snow White turned back to them, and snarled at them, too.

"We have to run," Axel yelled. "How many times does she have to spare our lives?"

Loki and Fable stood fixed to the floor, their faces painted with the color of confusion. This time, Snow White wasn't going to treat them nicely. She swung her hand at them, and a sudden snowy swirl hit the room and flung them out of her way. They got the point and ran as fast as their legs could carry them out of the Schloss.

16

Baby Tears

Surviving a bad day at the Schloss wasn't the worst that could happen to Loki. The surprises kept on coming.

Entering the Candy House on Seven, Breadcrumb Street, Fable rushed into her room and slammed the door behind her, cursing and crying.

On their way back, Fable had begged Loki to give up on killing Snow White. She'd told him that after seeing Big Bad turning into a wolf, it was obvious that something wasn't right in Sorrow. Loki had to tell her and Axel who he was while driving his Cadillac back to the house. He told them everything about being a half-angel banned from Heaven, about the demon girl he was banned for loving, and about his need to kill Snow White to go home and find out who he really was.

"Cheer up, Fable," Axel said on his way to the refrigerator. "We have a fallen angel in our house. It's not like it happens every day."

"Half-angel," Loki corrected him politely.

"I don't care who he is," Fable snapped. "I don't even care if he can spread his wings and fly."

"You can do that, right?" Axel said to Loki, skeptically. "Oh, I remember they gave you two black star tattoos where wings should've grown on your shoulders."

"That's right," Loki nodded, wondering what Fable was doing in her room.

"If I get Abe Von Noxious, the tattoo artist on Scrimshaw street, to draw me black star tattoos, you think they will think I am a fallen angel in school?"

"Shut up, Axel," Fable shouted. "You're both going to pay for this!"

"What did we do that was so bad? Aren't you glad we all survived the Big Bad Wolf," Axel chuckled to himself, pounding his forehead with his fist. "I can't believe I literally met the Big Bad Wolf. This is insane."

"OK, Fable," Loki said. "I'm sorry. I know how you feel toward her, but just think about all the other teens she killed."

"When are you going to understand that she is my favorite fairy tale character? She killed those who interfered and trespassed in the castle," Fable fired back. "We never heard anything about her hurting someone *outside* the castle."

"She's got a point," Axel said, licking jelly from his fingers. "Why doesn't she leave the castle and come kill everyone in town? I'd do that if I were her."

"All Snow White wants is for no one to intrude or interrupt her life in the castle," Fable continued. "It's like living in a town with other people who don't share your lifestyle, and all you ask is to be left alone."

"Vampire lifestyle, that's funny," Axel said with a mouthful. "What are you doing in there, Fable?"

Loki and Axel exchanged looks.

"Oh. No," Axel suddenly let the plate of Jelly drop to the floor. "You better not be doing what I think you're doing, Fable."

"You bet your gluttonous belly I am," she replied. "Finally, I found it!"

"What's going on, Axel?" Loki said.

Axel looked terrified, examining the place around him, searching for a hiding spot. "Not good, man. Not good. We need to leave the house, now!" Axel pulled Loki by his shirt. "Remember when you first came to the house? This is worse."

The door to Fable's room burst open. She stepped out with another giant book that she could barely hold with both hands. Only this one was called:

A Midsummer's Night Scream:
Shakespearian Enchantments to Punish the Unrighteous

Loki didn't think Shakespeare had ever written a book like that, but arguing in a town where Snow White was a vampire was pointless.

A sudden breeze combed through the house and Fable's pigtails loosened and flipped back in the wind. She stared angrily at Loki and Axel.

"I am sorry, Loki," she said, not sounding sorry at all. "I can't let you leave the house. I can't let you kill Snow White."

Fable adjusted her glasses, and started reading from her book. It was a spell, in some language Loki had never heard and went like this:

Shaka ree maka nee
Teka teti teka zee
Door re moor no tamor
Tether thether ola orr

The breeze turned into a swirling wind, escalating to a mini storm inside the house, spiraling madly as all doors and windows shut on their own. Itsy and Bitsy ran to each window, sewing their cobwebs, creating their own crossbars over them, and trapping everyone inside the house. Bitsy didn't forget to write *dork* for Axel on one of the windows.

"It's a *tethering* spell to trap people within a house. Only this one makes sure that the house itself won't let us out," Axel said. "Why can't you just say: Double, double, toil and trouble?" Axel yelled back to Fable as he ducked behind the couch, avoiding the cyclone. It hit Loki instead and he fell back. Every door, window, or shaft was closing, summoning dimness into the Candy House.

Fable continued chanting, breathing heavily, with her hair loose and flapping behind her. This side of her was really scary, but Loki knew everyone had a little bit of 'scary' in them.

When the mini-cyclone finally faded, Fable was panting. She let the thick book drop, and slumped upon the couch with a smile on her face. She was weakened from the power it took out of her to cast the spell.

"Now, I'm sure Snow white will be safe from you," she blew out a long *phew*.

Loki stood up, wanting to leave the house and forget about this crazy family. When he reached for the doorknob, it was so hot he had to pull away. The books and vases on the shelves shook nervously. Stubbornly, Loki grabbed a kitchen stool and hit it against the window but the spider web acted like a rubber band and the stool just bounced back.

"It's no use, Loki," Axel said, still hiding behind the couch. "I was held prisoner for a week in this house when I denied her request for going out on her first date."

Loki stood up again and then sat back down on a chair opposite of Fable on the couch. She sort of smirked and giggled at the same time. The problem with Fable was that whatever she did, silly or not, deadly or not, she still looked innocent enough Loki couldn't choke her or throw her out the window. No wonder she sympathized with Snow White.

Loki's real problem was that he wasn't used to caring about Minikins, let alone dealing with their quirks. He didn't yet understand that part of loving people was to accept them during their dark times as much as the times when they were shining bright.

"Ok, Fable," Loki said, resting his elbows on his knees and clasping his hands together. "Let's talk this over like two sixteen-year-old adults."

"I am fifteen…and a half."

"I know. I'm not even sixteen yet but you get the point," Loki said. "Let's just find a solution that will make everyone happy."

"I'm happy the way I am," she held her chin up. "As long as you're trapped in here, Snow White is safe."

"Believe me; I don't have a clue how to kill her. I thought that my problem was that I couldn't stake her, and then when I did by entering the castle in daylight, I found out that she controls her dreams. She is much stronger than any vampire I've seen. There is no way I can harm her now."

"But you want to, right?" Fable leaned forward, posing and giving him that look.

"I have to," Loki leaned back in his chair, almost embarrassed he said that. Sometimes, I feel I don't know what's wrong or right, what's bad or good. I don't know where I belong."

"I understand, Loki," she said, "but you need to forget about that stuff for a minute and concentrate. You should be asking why you are still alive when she could've just killed you. You know the answer Loki! It's because she needs you to save her," Fable said.

"She is right," Axel said. "The vampire princess likes you."

"Shut up, Axel," Loki snapped.

"It's like you refuse to open your eyes to the world around you, hanging onto a silly dream of going back to whatever place you think you come from. You saved Axel from the Bullyvards, saved me from Big Bad—I saved you later, but you did try to save me. Why can't you see that you can help other people and that you care about other people? Aren't you supposed to be one of the greatest Dreamhunters in the world? Do you think great Dreamhunters don't help people? Do you think your father didn't help other people?"

Suddenly, something crashed through the window behind Loki.

"Loki!" Fable shouted as she ducked down.

"Holy Moly!" Axel snapped as that something grabbed Loki by the back of his shirt. It was something with huge claws.

"It's the Crow—"Axel pointed out in horror, "the one that flew out of the room in the castle."

Loki had no time to look. The crow was already clawing at him from behind and dragging him across the sofa.

"Do something!" Loki yelled, unable to free himself.

"Like what?" Axel yelled.

"Don't yell at *me*!" Loki screamed, feeling the pain in the back of his neck. "It you're going to yell at someone, yell at the crow."

"It's huge," Axel said. "I don't want it to get mad."

"It's already pissed off," Loki said.

"Do something, Axel!" Fable screamed.

"Why don't *you* do something, Ms. Good witch," Axel bounded back at Fable. "Where is your magic recipe book?"

Axel wrapped his arms around Loki's legs, and tried to pull him away from the monstrous bird.

"Blah, Blah, Blah," Fable said with her hands on her waist.

Loki kicked his feet in the air as the crow dragged him over the couch.

If Axel and Fable didn't act quickly it was going to kidnap him.

Axel pulled one of Loki's shoes off and somersaulted back onto the couch. Fable picked up a baseball bat, darted behind Loki and started hitting the enormous crow. The creature only lost its sense of direction and flapped a couple of strides away deeper into the house. It circled like a black fan near the ceiling, not giving up on Loki who circled like a merry go round horse at an amusement park.

Afraid he'd be taken, Loki wrapped both legs around Axel's neck to add more weight to the crow. The bird struggled with the new weight while Axel's eyes almost popped out, unable to breathe. He tried pulling Loki's feet apart to save his own life. Loki didn't let him. Axel was his only hope.

An idea appeared like a light bulb hovering over Loki's head: "Fire!"

"Can you create fire, Fable?"

"I don't know a spell to make fire," she shouted, swinging away.

"Shouldn't your spell prevent it from dragging me outside?" Loki yelled from the ceiling.

"That's it, it can't get out, if you look behind you, the window it crashed through has sealed itself again with the spider webs. That's why it's so angry. And that's the problem. We have to kill it before it kills us." Fable gave her best attempt at a scream to answer Loki, but she was she was worn out.

The crow was lost in the room, moving haphazardly away from the window. The house was mad as well, turning into a horror house again.

The crow knocked Fable to the floor and she dropped the bat. Her head smacked the table where Loki's Zippo lay. She looked at them and shrieked.

"Fire!" she shrieked, as if it was her idea, and Loki hadn't been screaming it for a while. She lit up several cigarettes, coughed and cursed smokers, stood up, and began poking the crow with the cigarettes, punishing it with small but effective cigarette burns.

The crow let out a crazy high-pitched squawk from the pain.

"I'm hurting it, but it still won't let go of you," Fable said.

"I know that," Loki bellowed. He decided to let go of Axel before he fainted.

Then, a miracle happened. The crow let go of Loki who collided with the floor.

Loki whirled back and saw the crow heading to the window it came from although it knew it couldn't pass through.

Next to Loki, Fable was screaming; a long uninterrupted piercing note that hurt his ears and should have broken the windows had Fable's spell not protected them.

She held her trembling hands to her sides, showing her tiny veins, unable to stop as if she had seen a ghost. Before Loki turned to see what she was screaming at, he saw Axel finally picking himself up. But when he looked in the same direction Fable was looking in, he bent like a dying plant and fainted respectfully and silently on the couch.

The crow was so scared from whatever Fable was looking at that it kept banging its head against the window until it broke, and escaped the madhouse.

Then Fable fainted as well. Even the spiders were scared and crawled out the windows.

Loki turned to look at what caused the horror, feeling like the last man on earth to survive the apocalypse.

But Fable *had* seen a ghost. A scary ghost with its head cocked to the side, checking Loki out. It floated two inches above the floor.

The ghost smiled at him. Loki smiled back reluctantly at it, saying, "hi... mom?"

***

The fact that Loki's mom saved them by scaring the crow away made Loki gorge on food like Axel. He needed to eat and re-energize himself to handle the ridiculous amount of scare trauma he had been through in the last few hours.

All the people I like are scary, mom, Fable, and Snow White. Did I say I like Snow White? Of course not: I didn't just say Snow White. I must've imagined saying that.

Well, Loki couldn't deny there was something about Snow White that was terribly attractive, like a nagging girlfriend that he couldn't live without; but, nah, he didn't like her, no staking way.

It escaped Loki how Axel, Fable, and him had gathered around the table, eating dinner with Babushka who had cooked for them. He only remembered fainting next to Axel after he'd said 'hi' to his mom—*pile'm up mama.*

When he woke up, his mom had changed into an almost human-looking form with a few scars and slashes here and there. It was one of the few times he'd seen her look like most mothers do, almost.

Now that she looked a little more human, it felt good to have a mom he could introduce to his friends without being embarrassed—or frightening them. Axel and Fable being weirdoes who lived in a weird house in an even weirder town helped a lot, too. They adored Babushka, and she double-adored them.

As Babushka stood cooking in the kitchen, Loki noticed that she had altered her ghostly appearance to look as if she had a little chubby belly and lovely full cheeks. She was wearing an apron, and had her hair pulled back in a ponytail, only missing some locks, some parts burned out, but that was much better than when she first arrived at the Candy House. Fable had given her a pair of oversized glasses, homey rabbit flip-flops, and let Bitsy help her with the cooking—he came walking with a bowl full of spoons and a fork on his back.

Loki liked looking at his relatively new mother. She actually had a caring motherly smile—altogether she was missing one of her front teeth—and had the most beautiful grey-blue eyes.

Way to go, mom. How did you learn to change like that? And why didn't you ever cook for me?

No matter how she looked though, it still didn't make her human. She was as dead as the chicken she cooked for them; ice cold and pulse free, but at least she was here now, which reminded him to ask her about something.

"How come you appear whenever you want to, mom?" Loki said, watching Axel devour a chicken wing as if it was going to somehow teach him how to fly.

"I don't know, sweetie," she said, watching Axel and Fable, making sure everyone liked the food. "I told you. I suddenly got the feeling as if you were calling me."

"So you have no control over this?" Loki remembered she told him the same thing in the Cadillac.

"I told you I still need to learn a lot. It just happens. I'm here now. That's what matters."

"But you won't be for long. You always disappear eventually," Loki said.

"I can't help it, sweetie. I'm not a normal mother, and you should respect that. I am a—" she looked at Fable and Axel reluctantly.

"A Ghost," Axel said with a mouthful. "We know. But you cook the best chicken ever."

"You're so charming, sweet cheeks," she said to Axel. Loki didn't feel comfortable with his mom calling Axel sweet cheeks. He was sure no one had called him sweet-anything since dinosaurs roamed the earth.

Mrs. Babushka, you're an amazing cook!" Fable cheered.

"Just Babushka, no Mrs.," she said to Fable.

"You're an amazing cook Babushka! I haven't eaten such good food for some time," Fable said.

"You're such a sweet girl," Babushka blew Fable a kiss.

All the fluffy love filling the room made Loki furious. Babushka and Fable made him feel like they had found love at first sight. When Babushka cooked, Fable kept asking her how to do this and that and tried learning from her. Loki thought it made them look like mother and daughter, which also annoyed him.

"So, *mom*," Loki tried to remind her that she was *his* mom. "Why don't you stay for a while? Why do you have to go, especially now that you seem to have mastered looking normal?"

"Don't talk to your mom this way," Babushka said, slapping him on the back of his hand while sipping from the bowl of soup. Loki hated it when parents referred to themselves in third person. *'Don't talk to your mom this way?'* As if she wasn't even there, which in this case, was kind of true? Babushka wasn't really Babushka. She was Babushka's ghost.

"Yeah," Axel grinned. "Don't talk to your mom this way."

Loki was about to send two chicken wings flying across the table, hitting Axel in the face, maybe poking out his eyes and then drowning him in his bowl of soup.

"I can't stay for long," explained Babushka, addressing Fable and Axel. "I have business to attend to. Ghost business, you know."

"Of course Mrs.—I mean Babushka," Fable agreed. "Being a ghost isn't easy. I think you're doing a great job, being a ghost and raising a kid."

Loki was thinking of drowning Fable in her bowl of soup as well.

Being a ghost isn't easy? The next thing Fable is going to tell my mom is that she wants to become a ghost like her when she grows up.

"You're such a sweetheart, and you're *fabulous*, too," Babushka said. Fable giggled with rosy cheeks.

"You should've seen her evil grin when she cast the spell on the house earlier," Loki said.

"That was for your own protection," Babushka defended her. "And she broke the spell—I mean, I saved the day and broke the spell with my powers. Look around, everything is fine. After we finish eating, Fable and I will clean the house. You and Axel should fix the broken window."

Axel stopped eating as his jaw dropped, looking at the window. "Is there a possibility the crow can come back, Babushka?"

"Not a chance, dear," Babushka said. "It's scared of me."

"You're absolutely awesome, Babushka," Axel said.

"Thank you," she said, and turned to Loki. "I really wonder why you still insist on killing Snow White when you have amazing friends like Axel and Fable."

"Yes, Babushka," Fable said. "Please tell him to forget about killing Snow White. She needs our help."

"Are we really going to have this conversation again?" Loki said, and stopped eating.

"I think Fable is right," Babushka said.

"Ugh," Loki was about to leave the table. "This is unbearable."

"Sit down, Loki," Babushka demanded, losing parts of her human form to ghostly anger. "It's impolite to leave the table like that, kiddo."

"I am not a kid, mom," Loki slammed the spoon on the table. Axel hid his laughing behind the sound of the ringing spoon. Fable wondered why Loki acted so grouchy in his mother's presence.

"You're going to be sixteen soon, baby," Babushka reached to touch his face, but some of her flesh peeled off and got in the way a little. She pulled it back and covered her bones with it.

"Look mom, I don't need to have this conversation now. Not when I don't even have a clue how to enter her dream without her controlling me."

"Who said you can't?" Babushka said.

"Didn't Fable tell you?" Loki said. "She can control her dreams, and there is no way for me to kill her like that. She even told me that she won't let me enter her dreams if I don't try to save her."

"But of course you can still enter her dreams," Babushka said. "It's all written in your Dreamhunter notebook."

"No, it's not," Loki said.

"Yes, it is," Babushka insisted. "Show it to me."

"I can't. If you read the page it will dissolve into sand."

"I won't read it. I will just point out the page. Show it to me."

Loki handed her the notebook, wondering what his mother knew about the notebook. She flipped through it as if she had read it many times before. She stopped where the missing pages had once been and rubbed her chin thoughtfully. "Some of the missing pages are those that tell exactly how to enter a controlled dream. There are also other pages missing, too."

"How do you know that?" Loki said.

"I just know. And since the pages are missing I will tell you how to enter Snow White's dream, under one condition."

"And what would that be?" Loki asked worriedly.

"That when you enter her dream, you investigate her story and why she wants you to help her—"

"But, mom—"

Babushka shushed him. "That or I won't help you."

Loki said nothing, staring at Axel and Fable.

"What will it be, son?" Babushka said. "Make up your mind because I'll be leaving soon."

"And I can still kill her if I decide I need to, whatever her story is?" Loki said.

"You can do what you want. It's your life. You only need to gather the right information to make your decision," Babushka said.

"Why would you want me to do that? Don't you care if I find my way back home?"

"I care for you to be happy. Home is where the heart is," Babushka said. "So I need to hear you say that you'll investigate her story first. And remember that good people keep their promises."

"Yes, I will," Loki said, lowering his eyes. "Now how can I enter her controlled dream and defeat her if need be?"

"If a vampire controls her dream, there's actually no easy way to enter it," Babushka said. "But you could enter something we call a Dreamory. It's still her dream but it's also a memory. It's a very sophisticated medium in the Dreamworld, but it will do the job—whether you want to kill her or investigate her story. To enter a Dreamory, you need two things."

"I'm listening," Loki's eyes glittered.

"The first thing is called an Incubator."

"What's that?" Axel said.

"An Incubator is a word and date, that when whispered in the dreamer's ear while they are in the Dream Temple, triggers a certain memory so the dream takes place around the time and the 'word' of the memory."

"That's awesome," Loki said. "What is that word?"

"It's not a fixed word," Babushka said. "It differs from Dreamworld to Dreamworld. I think this is where Axel's knowledge comes in handy."

"Me? How so?" he said with a mouthful.

"You have to find a word and date from your research that would transfer Snow White's dream into that memory. It could be many words—most words describe places. You will have to search hard for it."

"Can you explain this a bit more?" he asked.

"It has to be a word like her place of birth, the real name of her father or the queen, anything that you can get from the books in the Bedtime Stoories library."

"Oh. That makes sense, but what if I don't get the word right?" Axel wondered. "Will she still control the dream?"

"If you manage to get the second thing, she won't be able to control the dream, but there will be no guarantees where her dream will take Loki, or how dangerous it will be. So finding the right word will be your job, Axel."

"I can do that," he said.

"And what's the second thing?" Fable asked.

"That's the best part, I have to say," Babushka smiled. "You'll have to go on a little adventure to obtain a liquid that when dropped into her eyes stops her from controlling her dreams…or any dreamer that has that power for that matter."

"There's such a thing?" Loki said.

"Indeed. Remember how part of the ritual was to place two Obol coins on Snow White's eyes so she couldn't connect the dream and the real world? It's almost the same, only the liquid fills her eyes in a way that she will not be able, no matter what, to control her dreams or play games with you. It blocks any powers she's obtained in the waking world from controlling the Dreamworld."

"Where is that liquid?" Loki's eyes widened. "Does it have a name?"

"It does, and it's a very rare and rather sensitive liquid," Babushka said. "It's called Baby Tears."

"Really?" Fable raised an eyebrow. "You're not trying to say that it's actually real baby tears."

"In fact, it is," Babushka said unapologetically. Loki remembered she was a ghost, and that in her job she must have made many baby's cry.

"Where can we get Baby Tears, mom?" Loki asked eagerly, remembering that Lucy had offered him a drink called Baby Tears when they were back in the Deadly Ever After party. He wondered if it was real baby tears. "I mean are they easy to obtain in Sorrow, or are we going to end up having to scare babies to make them cry?"

"I think I know where you can get Baby Tears in Sorrow," Babushka said. "It's not going to be an easy ride, though."

17

The Boogeyman

Babushka left right after lunch. It was an abrupt disappearance like usual, only this time she didn't leave him alone.

Loki was surprised to learn that Axel and Fable were preparing a room for him to stay in—finally, an actual bed. He was eager to sleep in a room he could call his own for the first time. He had to admit that Axel and Fable had become like family.

He decided he'd go out to his Cadillac and nap in it one last time. He'd been exhausted, and he needed a little relaxation—and the chance to say a small goodbye to Carmen's driver seat.

A couple of hours later, Axel came back to wake Loki up.

"Hey," Axel shook him. "Wake up. We got work to do."

"Uh—"Loki looked at Axel, right next to him in the passenger seat. "You finished my room?"

"Fable did," Axel said. "But that's not important right now. You're not going to use your room before we get the Baby Tears."

"Baby Tears!" Fable almost repeated the word a little too joyfully from her spot in the backseat.

"Yeah, I'm not deaf," Loki said. "Can you remind me again where Babushka said we'd get the Baby Tears from?"

"Your mom said we should get them from a Boogeyman," Fable said.

"Ya—my mom. Um—where is she?"

"Are you on drugs or something?" Axel asked, checking Loki's pulse. "She had business to finish."

"Ghost business," Fable giggled. Did I tell you I thought your mom was awesome?"

"Yeah, I noticed," Loki muttered. "So what was the plan again?"

"Offff. What kind of Dreamhunter are you?" Fable puffed, folding her hands. "We need to get back to the castle so you can get into Snow White's dream again, and since she has the ability to control her dreams, the only way to strip her from that power is to drop Baby Tears into her eyes—"

"Yes, I remember," Loki blinked, looking at Fable in the mirror.

"And then I have to find the Incubator," Axel said. "I just came from Bedtime Stoories. I brought all the books needed. I'm on it. You think we could use the word 'Sorrow' as an Incubator?"

"How should I know?" Loki said with a hint of contempt.

"According to what we read, the kingdom where she lived in the dream was called Sorrow. I am guessing this town is the Kingdom of Sorrow, two hundred years later. I think the word 'Sorrow' should do it." Axel speculated.

"Maybe her real name could be an Incubator," Fable said.

"How can I get her real name," Axel said. "Even Jacob Grimm's diary doesn't mention her real name. And who said she has a name other than Snow White?"

"I don't remember the Brothers Grimm fairy tales mentioning names," Loki tried to interact with the detective duo.

"That's actually true," Axel said. "I don't think I've ever read a fairy tale with names of the prince or the huntsman or even the queen. I wonder why no names were ever mentioned? Maybe that proves they were forged or played with, someone hid the names intentionally."

"Now you're reading too much into it. So how about the Baby Tears," Fable said. "We need to find a Boogeyman."

"About that," Loki said. "Don't you think this is a bit rediculous?"

"You don't believe in Boogeymen, now?" Axel said.

"I don't know," Loki shook his head. "I know we live in a town full of vampires, ghosts, haunted houses, and even werewolves, but I don't think we can just go find a Boogeyman. Do you even know what a Boogeyman looks like?"

"Ugly," Axel shrugged, remembering the one who ate his cereal when he was a kid.

"Your mom told us Boogeymen live in children's closets. Maybe we could ask around," Fable said.

"She was positive that if we ask the right person, we can hire a Boogeyman to get us the Baby Tears," Fable said.

"Right person?" Loki said.

"Someone whose an authority on specific items teen vampire hunters might need to know about," Fable said.

"I think I know someone who might be able to help," Loki picked up the phone and dialed a number.

"Who're you calling?" Fable inquired.

"Lucy Rumpelstein" Loki replied, waiting for the Beep.

"Lucy?" Axel's eyes glittered.

"Who's Lucy?" Fable asked.

"She is Professor Rumpelstein's daughter," Axel informed her.

"Kewl," Fable mused. "Who's Professor Rumpelstein?"

"You don't know the owner of the school you go to?" Loki asked with amazement.

"Oh, that one," Fable said. "You know I hate school. Don't go much unless I feel like I want to have a bad day, which is a good thing for witches. The bad energy is sometimes needed for certain spells."

Loki and Axel exchanged looks, trying not to remember the Fable who had trapped them in the house.

"Don't let her go to school again," Loki mouthed to Axel.

"So why do you care so much about Lucy, Axel?"

"Me? I don't," Axel said defensively, averting his eyes from meeting Fable's. Loki shot him the you-are-such-a-dork glance. "I don't even like her. She's weird," Axel said, leaning back in his seat and putting the hood back on to cover his lie. "Does it really show that I like her?"

"Not with the hood on," Fable said. "I can still see you, by the way. You're not wearing the cloak of invisibility, you know."

"I know. This is my cloak of *nerdidity*," Axel muttered.

"Nerdi—what? That's not even a word," Fable said. "Anyway, so this Lucy knows how to find a Boogeyman?"

Lucy finally picked up.

"Hey," Loki tried to sound cheerful.

Lucy didn't reply right away. Loki heard strange crunching sounds on the phone and the last breaths of a long moan, and Lucy laughing in the background.

"What do you want, buster?" a voice growled.

"Moonclaw," Loki acted happy to hear his voice, something that he hadn't done since he'd arrived in Sorrow. "Wussup, man?"

Axel grinned.

"Don't wussup me, buster," Ulfric said, spitting into the phone. "You made my boys look like fools, and you're gonna pay for it when I see you."

"Pay? How much?" Loki mocked him.

"Are you trying to be funny?" Ulfric lowered his voice, maybe so that Lucy couldn't hear. "My friend, Big Bad, saw you in the castle, you and the two lousy witch's kids," he grunted. "It was foolish of Big Bad to expose himself, but now that you know our secret, you'll have to die."

"Is that it?" Loki said. His heart was beating faster already. They had escaped Big Bad once and he knew that facing him again wasn't going to be easy.

"What do you mean?" Ulfric said angrily.

"Where's the 'Muahaha' part?" Loki said. "I mean you talk like an evil goblin. There's always a 'Muahaha' in the end."

"Who's on the phone, Ulfy?" Loki heard Lucy ask as she seemed to grab it from her boyfriend. Loki wondered if she knew that he and his gang were werewolves.

"*Lemme toke to ya gal*," Loki said with sleazy smile on his face. The one syllable words felt like music to him. He ended the sentence with a high note, more of a cliffhanger. "Mooonclawww," Loki said.

He heard Ulfric tell Lucy that he was going to make Loki pay for making fun of him.

"Hey," Lucy said. "What's up, Loki?"

Loki could hear Ulfric tickling her or something. "So what kind of help do you need this time?"

"How did you know I need help?"

"You always do, Loki," she said, shushing Ulfric behind her. "I take it you haven't killed the vampire princess yet. Two girls were missing from school today. So what do you want?"

"Do you happen to know a reliable, not too scary, not too expensive—did I mention not too scary—Boogeyman?" Loki said. He glanced around as if not wanting anyone to hear him.

"What?"

"Like I said," Loki shrugged. "I need a Boogeyman, tonight. And again, one who isn't that *boogey*."

"Wow," she said. "Sorrow has gotten to you, too."

"We need the Boogeyman to—"

"We?"

"Yeah," Loki said. "I'm working with a team now," he explained, looking at Fable biting her nails in excitement in the rear view mirror.

"Spare me the details. I really don't want to hear about all this nonsense. Anyway, I don't know a Boogeyman, but—" Ulfric was laughing at Loki in the background. "But I can call my dad. He surely knows about that creepy stuff. In fact, he might give me a name and address."

"Remember, I don't want the best Boogeyman in town. The worse, the better," Loki didn't want to get scared.

I'll call you in an hour," Lucy hung up.

"One hour from now and we have our Boogeyman, recommended by Professor Rumpelstein himself," Loki told Axel and fable, watching the sun about to sink.

"So, Fable," Axel said. "Since you and Loki's mom are friends like Cinderella and the Fairy Godmother, why exactly do we need a Boogeyman? I know we need him for the Baby Tears. I just don't see how they're related."

"Boogeyman, Baby Tears, Hello?" Fable said slowly as if Axel was the dumbest person in the Cadillac. "What happens when babies cry? They shed tears! Who makes babies cry—an expert in scaring babies. Duh."

***

It turned out to be true; they could actually hire a Boogeyman in Sorrow.

Loki drove his Cadillac, following the address Lucy had given him. The radio turned on by itself, and the Pumpkin Warriors played a song that went like this:

There's a big-bad-boogeyman dancing through our house.

164

He locks himself in the dark of a closet like a mouse.
And when you sleep, snore, and dream,
He'll scare you silly until you scream.

Fable giggled as she heard the Pumpkin Warriors stop playing and argue that the singer sung the wrong lyrics to the song.

"It's how Carmen works," Loki explained. "She plays the songs she wants, and this band seems to be her favorite."

"Wow," Fable leaned forward from the backseat. "Can I talk to them?"

"Yes, you can," a band player said. "So what's on your mind?"

"I know another Boogeyman song," she told the Pumpkin Warriors. *"Better run away, better run away, pretty little maiden better run away. When the woods are black as night: that's the Boogeyman's delight. Better run away, better run away, pretty little maiden run away."*

"You like this one, boys?" the band member asked his fellow players. After a little discussion, he talked back to Fable. "Here's the thing. We know you all think that this is the kind of Boogeyman everyone's told you about, but our records here tell of something else entirely, so we're going to stop playing until we get to know who the Boogeyman really is."

Loki then drove to Nifelheim, an unusually vibrant neighborhood in Sorrow that Lucy had texted him about.

"Wow!" Axel's eyes widened, wanting to reach for the fancy-looking girls walking on their way to the few clubs and bars in high heels. "I didn't know that such a place existed in Sorrow. Hell on heels, baby!" He waved at the girls, drool hanging from his chin. "The closest I've been to any girls that hot were on my computer.

"This is very strange, Loki," Fable said. "I don't think this neighborhood ever existed before."

Loki didn't comment. He knew Fable and her brother didn't get out much. How were they supposed to know about this place?

"You want to find the Boogeyman. You got to go to Boogie-town," Loki frowned in the mirror at Fable. "Lucy said we should meet her here so we can hire a Boogeyman."

"Why here?" Fable wondered. "I thought we'd find the Boogeyman in a closet."

"We're looking for a bar where Boogeymen spend their time when not working."

Loki took a left at a street called Sackman Street. According to Lucy, we should find the bar here and she should be waiting for us. Do you want to guess its name, Fable?" There was no use to start a conversation with drooling-Axel at the moment. He was too busy checking the girls out.

"Let me guess," Fable leaned forward, resting her head on Loki's shoulder. "Is it called The Scary Fairy Boogeyman Bar?"

"Noooo," Loki circled his lips into an O. "That's too long. It has two words and really makes you think of a Boogeyman."

"Boo Bar?" she tried to scare Loki in the mirror. He felt her booing breath on his neck.

"Nah," Loki drove past the curb and parked the Cadillac, pointing at a purple neon sign flickering off and on. A big, tall bouncer stood next to the sign.

Fable read the sign, "The Closet?"

"Right to the point," Loki said as he hit the brakes, giving his wheels a chance to squeak. "You want to hire a Boogeyman; you have to go talk to him in The Closet."

"So clichéd," Axel shook his head, finally giving up on the girls. "The Closet my—"

"Is there a specific Boogeyman in The Closet who will help us?" Fable asked.

"We're looking for a Georgie Porgie," Loki replied.

"Georgie Porgie?" Axel laughed. "I feel like drowning in a pool of clichéd pudding."

"That's the worst metaphor I've ever heard," Loki said. "For your information, Georgie Porgie is the most famous Boogeyman in Sorrow. In fact, he's the leader of all Boogeymen," Loki stretched his arms. "Even though I wanted the worst, Lucy said he was the only one who could help with Baby Tears."

"This can't be." Axel insisted.

"Yeah, Loki, "something is wrong here," Fable backed her brother up for the first time.

"You have no problem believing there is a Boogeyman, and then you complain about his name?"

"The thing is no one names their child Georgie Porgie," Axel said, "Because it's a famous nursery rhyme."

"Huh?" Loki had only spent a year in the Ordinary World, and he hadn't heard about the nursery rhyme.

"*Georgie Porgie, pudding and pie,*" Axel started singing.

"*Kissed the girls and made them cry,*" Fable followed, laughing at this part.

"*When the boys came out to play,*" Axel raised his questioning eyebrows at Fable.

"*Georgie Porgie ran away,*" Fable completed the rhyme. "I love it," she added.

"OK?" Loki was confused. "I still don't get what the problem is. The Boogeyman is named after a rhyme, so what?"

"Well, for one if he is a Boogeyman, he wouldn't have been described as '*Running away when the boys came out to play,*'" Axel said. "Why would he be able to scare girls and be afraid of boys?"

"What Axel is saying is that in a town where we supposedly have the real Snow White, and a Big Bad Wolf, we might have the real Georgie Porgie," Fable said.

"What are you two talking about?" Loki said.

"That all nursery rhyme characters and all characters in fables are real," Axel said. "That's what I partially understood from Jacob Carl Grimm's diary."

"Oh, come on," Loki waved. "You don't even know it's *his* diary. Give me a break—"

"And they are all living in Sorrow," Fable seemed to like the idea.

"Please," Loki said. "We have other things to take care of, and I'm exhausted. Let's just focus on how we're going to get the Baby Tears from Georgie Porgie."

"How are we going to get inside The Closet anyway?" Axel, the pessimistic, questioned. "We are minors. We aren't allowed in bars."

"Please tell me we're going to break the law," Fable said with bright eyes. "If you give me some time, I could find the right spell to make the bouncer see us as adults, or I could turn him into a troll."

"How is the bouncer turning into a troll going to get us in?" Axel wondered. "Besides, you're not going in there anyway," Axel played protective brother again.

"Yeah?" Fable fired back. "So I can't go into a bar, but you can get drunk without me knowing? Just for your information, I saw you drinking last Valentine's Day in your room."

"You got drunk on Valentine's Day?" Loki asked in amazement.

"It was Strawberry Sawdust, and don't be a smartass, Loki." Axel puffed in anger-coated embarrassment. "Not all of us are good looking and have dates on Valentine's Day like you."

"That's not the point," Fable said. "You're underage and you're not supposed to drink."

Loki didn't say anything. Playing big brother was getting annoying, but watching Axel suffering was fun.

"It's no big deal, Axel," Loki said. "Just let her in with us. They won't allow any of us to drink if we manage to get inside anyway," Loki heard the sound of boogie music being played inside the bar. Nice guitars and a lot of boogie. "It's better to have her with us than to leave her out here with the likes of Mr. Godzilla," Loki pointed at the bouncer, who seemed not to like them at all.

Someone tapped the Cadillac's window. Loki freaked out, thinking about Ogres. Fable and Axel laughed.

It was Lucy Rumpelstein, sticking her nose to the glass again. Loki rolled the window down.

"You need to get yourself together," Lucy said in her elegant voice.

"We need to stop meeting this way," Loki smiled. "Always knocking on my window?"

"Yeah, right," she handed him three fake IDs that were very weird. The IDs had their names on them, but not pictures; those were photos of crying children.

"May I ask what this is?" Fable said.

"Under normal circumstances, nerdy birds like you may not," Lucy said. "But since it's a crazy day, you should know that Boogeymen take their trophies very seriously."

"Their trophies?" Loki said.

"To a Boogeyman, the most important thing in the world is to scare a baby, get its tears, and brag about it."

"The Closet gives away VIP cards to certain visitors every now and then," Lucy explained, "so we're pretending we're those."

"So all we have to do is get in, meet this Georgie Porgie and get our Baby Tears?" Loki asked.

"Yes," Lucy nodded. "We need to look like a couple so they let us in, though, and you should lose the hood. It's not the Grim Reaper's club," Lucy told Axel.

Axel swallowed hard, losing his smile. It didn't seem like he'd be able to impress Lucy today.

"You two should play couple while we're at the door," Lucy suggested, talking to Fable and Axel.

"They can't," Loki said, handing Axel and Fable their fake IDs, hoping Mr. Godzilla didn't see them. "They're brother and sister."

Lucy laughed, pulling the door open. "Why are you still in the car, guys?"

Loki got out of the car and saw the long line of people waiting in front of the bar. Then he introduced everybody formally.

"So this is Fable," he pointed. "Lucy."

He knew Lucy met Axel before in the parking lot.

Fable said 'hi' with a big smile, even though it was obvious that she and Lucy weren't going to get along. Instead of warming at Fable's amazing smile, Lucy rolled her eyes, greeting her back. "What's with the pigtails? You look goofy."

"Oh?" Fable blushed as if she'd done something wrong and loosened her hair. "Better?"

"Take off the glasses too." Lucy folded her hands.

"I," Fable hesitated. "I'm afraid I can't see without them. I'm dyslexic, if you don't mind," Fable folded her hands in response. She seemed to want to punch Lucy in the face, but she was also intimidated by her. Loki thought that Fable wanted to make a girlfriend, instead of being friends with all the boys surrounding her, but counting on Lucy to fill that space was a great mistake.

"No wonder your mother was a lousy witch." Lucy said. "How can a dyslexic read spells?" Lucy laughed.

"I think you should stop there," Loki threw Lucy a sharp stare, which Lucy seemed to like all of a sudden. Loki knew she liked rough boys, but this time he did it for Fable. If he didn't think they still needed Lucy's help, he'd have done even more.

"I like that," Lucy said. "Didn't know you could get so…"

"So, are we going to play couple here or what?" Axel interrupted.

"Since you and this *nerdy-nerd* girl are related, we'll have to switch roles," Lucy said.

Axel stood like a vibrating fork hammered in the ground, buzzing to Lucy's insults.

"You and Loki act like a couple," Lucy pushed Fable slightly into him. "You actually look good together. Awww," then she glanced at Axel with pursed lips. "And you and I will play couple, too. If you try anything funny, I'll chop off your mouse-clicking forefinger."

Axel didn't reply. It was the luckiest day in his life, entering the club pretending to be with Lucy. Loki thought this was tremendous progress. He was really looking forward to having a picture of them on his phone together. That would drive Moonclaw crazy.

"B-But—" Axel stuttered. "I don't want Fable pretending to be Loki's girlfriend. She's never had a boyfriend before."

"How do you even know that?" Fable cried out with blushing cheeks. "Loki is going to be my third. Just for your information," she snapped.

"Edgy girl," Lucy said, impressed. "See how letting your hair down makes you feel?"

Fable smiled.

Lucy walked toward Godzilla, dragging Axel who was mouthing the word *awesome* behind her back as they held hands.

"I really hope Ulfric doesn't see that or you will be toast!" Loki mouthed back.

"Let's go, *honey*," Fable said to Loki, engaging his arm, and teasing Axel.

Lucy said something to the bouncer and he suddenly treated them like VIP's, almost puffing rosy lilies out of his ears now. Loki frowned then nodded at him as if he was the mayor of the town and the bouncer was his employee.

"Hey," Loki greeted him, chin up high.

"It's a pleasure to have you with us sir." The bouncer bowed his head at Fable too. "Ma'am."

Fable pulled Loki's arm harder. "Did he say Ma'am? That's so cool."

What was supposed to be a scary night looking for a Boogeyman was turning into an unexpectedly lovely night out with new friends. That wasn't something Loki had thought probable coming to Sorrow. Good friends, jokes, and adventure to boot. What more could he have asked for? For the first time he wondered, for only a fraction of a second, if home would be as much fun.

Spooky Woogy Boo!

The Closet buzzed with partying Boogeymen like bees looking for honey. Most of them were unusually tall, wearing strange clothes that made them look like they were dressed for a masquerade party, not a typical night out on the town. It reminded Loki of the Deadly Ever After Party, only with adults who for the most part were dressed as pirates.

The rate of clicking glasses was intense. The pirate-looking goers spilled beer from the edges of their big wooden cups, the laughter and cheering getting louder than the band performing on the stage. It was a five-man boogie band, nothing Loki had seen before. Their instruments were oversized enchanted animals. The drum set was a huge octopus that held differently sized cymbals and drum pieces in each arm. Its head was used as the enormous front bass drum. The drummer struggled when the octopus wasn't holding still and had to stretch his arms to hit the unstable drum pads. The singer's microphone was a giraffe's neck sticking out of the floor, leading Loki to assume its body was buried underneath the stage. The bass and lead guitar players held flamingos instead of guitars, strumming their stomachs and changing the chord positions on their necks. The guitar strings ran from each flamingo's beak all the way to their necks, which were longer than usual. Every time the guitar players strummed a flamingo's stomach, it got ticklish and bent its neck, causing the player to strum the wrongs notes. And last, but certainly not least, the piano was one big turtle. Its legs held it still on the floor, and its shell was open at an angle like a baby piano's lid, even though it was no baby. Where the turtles head should have been sticking out, there was a keyboard. The keys were green and black instead of white and black, and they were slimy. Whenever the piano player struck a note, a number of frogs pulled the strings inside to create the desired tunes. Loki hated frogs, so he made sure to stay as far away from it as possible. This big turtle wasn't going anywhere, and if it did, it'd be in slow motion.

Still, the customers in The Closet were unimpressed by the band. Everyone was occupied with a seemingly much more important event taking place right in the middle of the hall.

Loki and his friends couldn't see what everyone was looking at. They tried to squeeze themselves through the big crowd to get closer.

"I have a better idea," Fable said. She crawled on all fours, finding her way under the pirate's legs, but she had to stand up again when she was road-blocked by a couple of heavy boots.

The crowd cheered enthusiastically. Loki and the rest were curious to know what it was everyone was looking at. They forgot about the Baby Tears for the moment.

Stuck in the middle, Loki took another look at the crowd. None of them looked monstrous, although most of them wore eye patches, pirate hats, and too much jewelry. They also acted like pirates; loud, vulgar, and full of themselves. Most of them had bad teeth with green slime drooling from them.

"Hey you," Lucy yelled at a partygoer. "Is Georgie Porgie here?"

The man thought he heard something then looked away. Of course, they were all way shorter than he was. Lucy, in her bratty feistiness, punched him. "Hey, I'm talking to you!"

Loki noticed that Fable was pleased with the way Lucy treated people without fear or hesitation.

"Whaddya want, kiddo?" the man looked down at her.

"N-nothing," Lucy said, as she backed away from him. The man's breath was unbearable.

"Wow," Axel said. "My poop doesn't smell that bad."

"Apologies Mr—" Fable interrupted, trying to save the day.

The man's eyes lit up as if he'd seen Santa Claus.

"How does she do that?" Axel scowled.

"How can I help you, kiddo?" the man asked Fable.

"We're looking for someone," Fable yelled as she was squeezed by the crowd. "Someone called Georgie?" Fable shrugged; afraid the man would laugh at her. "Georgie Porgie?"

"You call Georgie a 'someone'?" the man laughed, bad breath fuming out. Lucy was going to faint. "You're cute." He raised his head and cheered with the rest, saying, "Georgie! Georgie! Georgie!"

It was obvious that Georgie was there by the table in the middle and was the spectacle everyone was looking at. Suddenly everyone was singing:

Georgie Porgie, puddin' and pie,
Scared the girls and made them cry.
When the boys came his way,
He scared them harder and they ran away.

"Yeah!" others called out after singing the rhyme.

"This isn't the real rhyme," Axel noted. "It's been changed."

"What do I care?" Loki said. "Stop analyzing."

"In the real one Georgie Porgie runs away when the boys come to play," Axel recited. "He's basically capable of scaring girls but fears boys."

Loki and his friends wedged themselves through until they reached the first row of the crowd, where they found something slightly different from anything they'd expected.

There was a round table with two men sitting opposite to each other. They were looking at a lot of small glasses on the table; really small glasses, enough for just one *glock*.

Each man wore the same crazy pirate outfit, only the one on the right stood out for many reasons. He was much bigger than the rest, stronger, and had a neat beard that hung like a pony-tail in a spiral dreadlocked line dangling from his chin. Each lock on the tail had something glittering in it, a small emerald, diamond or other jewel. The hair on the man's head was long and curly, and it added a certain wilderness to his persona, like a tough and rugged warrior who everyone should respect. He had faint patches of blue mascara on his one visible eyelash, and wore an eye patch on the other. His nose was straight, and he had a strong jaw. Loki thought he looked more like a twisted version of Long John Hawkins in Treasure Island. His jewelry and outfit looked more expensive than what the other people wore especially his purple coat and boots.

"That's Georgie," the man with yellow teeth told Fable, having followed them. "Everyone knows him," he called out Georgie's name one more time.

Loki noticed Georgie had a bowl of pudding pie next to him on the table. He suddenly wondered if he should paid more attention to Axel's theories.

"The man opposite to him is Cry Baby," the man with yellow teeth said, booing at Cry Baby who was chubby, with a bushy beard and bubbly cheeks. He had a pumpkin pie next to him.

Each man picked up one of the small glasses, took a long breath, and gulped the drink down. Each one did it separately, and while he did, everyone's eyes were on him, watching to see if he could finish the drink.

"So this is a drinking competition?" Axel whispered in Loki's ear.

"Looks like it," Loki said. "They've been drinking for a while because there are a lot of empty glasses," Loki saw men holding dollar bills in their hands while cheering. "It's obvious that the crowd is betting on who'll be able to drink the most without giving up."

"Or passing out," Axel suggested. "Or even better, puke it all into the other's face."

"I wonder what's in the glasses," Loki uttered.

"I think I have an idea, but you might get mad at me," Axel replied.

"Shoot," Loki said, not taking his eyes off the table.

"The other man is called Cry Baby, right? There is a nursery rhyme about him, too."

"Interesting," Loki rubbed his chin. "Tell me about it."

"It goes like this: *Cry Baby, cry, put your finger in your eye, and tell your mother it wasn't I,*" Axel said.

"What kind of a demented song is this? Why would you tell it to a baby?"

Suddenly, Axel grabbed Loki's shoulder even harder. "I got it. We're here to get Baby Tears. This man is called Cry Baby, and the nursery rhyme is about babies. It all makes sense now."

"What makes sense?"

"All these people around us are Boogeymen," Axel said. "They visit children at night and scare them, only they don't do it because they like to scare children they do it to collect Baby Tears."

Loki's eyes sprung wide open as the crowd bellowed. Georgie Porgie gulped another drink down then smirked at Cry Baby showing his yellow teeth.

"So Boogeyman scare children to collect their tears?" Fable considered. "Why do they need those Baby Tears?"

"I have no idea," Loki said. "It seems plausible, though, even if it's just plain awful to make a living from scaring children."

"Since you need the Baby Tears, I don't think you should complain," Lucy said. She couldn't take her eyes off Georgie Porgie. She was fascinated by the man, leader of the twisted pirate-looking Boogeymen, even though he was at least ten years older than her.

"Your turn," Georgie Porgie howled at Cry Baby amidst the crazy shouting crowd. He looked a bit tipsy from the drink now. His voice was gushy, and he was full of himself, laughing at everyone around him. "Who calls themselves Cry Baby?" Georgie Porgie laughed at his opponent. The crowd shared his laugh instantly.

Cry Baby's last shot made him dizzy. Georgie Porgie gave him a choice to continue and pass out eventually, or give up now. Cry Baby decided he'd give up, waving his heavy hands in the air. Georgie picked up his pudding pie and slammed it into Cry Baby's face, declaring himself a winner. The boogie band started playing louder now, the singer squeezing harder on the Giraffe's neck, spilling out his lyrics. Everyone went back to their tables or started dancing.

"All drinks are on me tonight," Georgie Porgie announced with two pirate girls in his arms.

"I'm going to tell you something that none of you will like," Axel said to the rest. "You know what they were drinking in the competition?"

"What? Whiskey?" Lucy asked.

"Nope," Axel said. "Baby Tears."

"No way," Fable said.

"Those tiny glasses were filled with Baby Tears," Axel nodded.

"I can't believe that," Fable said. "Are tears like their fuel or something?"

"We missed a great opportunity," Lucy said. "We could've just picked up a glass before they cleared the table. We'll have to go talk to Georgie Porgie now, so we can get the Baby Tears."

Georgie Porgie pushed the groupies clinging to his arms away and walked to the bar. It looked like he was about to make a speech.

"To all my fellow, creepy, ugly-looking, baby-scaring Boogies," he shouted as the music stopped again, making a toast. "I salute you for your hard work, sleepless nights, and sacrificing your time with your family all for the cause of Boogism. It's a lost art."

The crowd roared.

"Yeaaaaah!" Axel picked an empty glass and hailed with them.

"What are you doing?" Fable sneered at him.

"We have to fit in, and pretend we belong," Axel explained. "Besides, Georgie is so cool."

"People these days are only interested in vampires—" Georgie continued his speech.

"Overrated—"

"And ghosts," Georgie said.

"Stupid—"

"And the silly moon demons who call themselves werewolves," Georgie Porgie added.

"Too hairy!"

Georgie gulped down his drink and ordered another one instantly. It wasn't Baby Tears anymore, or Loki would've snatched it and ran away.

Georgie burped out loud, and the crowd burped back.

Loki and his friends clipped their noses with their fingers. It was going to be a whole lotta smelly, and they couldn't take it anymore.

Axel clipped his nose for the smell and covered his ears to mask the unbearable roar.

"We are the Boogeymen!" Georgie announced as if he were saying, 'We are the champions.' "We're the scariest, most primitive monsters on earth…and we're proud," Georgie watched the crowd nod their heads. We've been here since man invented the amazing closet and wardrobe. Thus, man invented us by his own will," the crowd agreed. "And then they started calling us names, making movies about us, and belittling us."

"But we scare the boogie woogie out of their babies," someone replied from the crowd.

"Stupid humans, stupid babies," Georgie said. "If they only knew how hard our work is…"

The crowd nodded agreeably.

"We work hard, and we work at night, the time everyone else is resting and dreaming," Georgie said. "Each Boogeyman spends the whole night trapped in a closet until the right moment comes when the child is alone in the room, so he can do his job and scare it," Georgie's eyes scanned all his fellow Boogeymen. "Obnoxious children!"

"Yeah!" someone said.

"Human children are horrible!" another said.

"I really should've caught this on camera," Axel said. "I could win the Noble Prize posting this on the forum."

"Nowadays children aren't easily scared, having watched all those gory movies. So we have to build up the suspense all night, making creepy sounds, whispering from the closet, creaking the closet doors—"

"Even those tactics hardly work anymore," a Boogeyman interrupted Georgie. "They have all closet doors oiled these days."

Everyone agreed with him.

"I feel ya," Georgie drummed on his chest with one hand. "All that hard work we go through, and for what?" Georgie said, pulling out a small glass full of Baby Tears. Loki and the rest tiptoed, looking at it, thinking they could snatch it and run away. But could they outrun a Boogeyman? If they did, revenge would follow every night for the rest of their lives, unless they lived in homes without closets.

"And why do we still do it? We do it for this!" Georgie raised his glass of Baby Tears in the air, staring at it as if it were the Holy Grail. The rest of the crowd raised other glasses of Baby Tears in the air. Georgie's eyes were teary for a moment, and the atmosphere in The Closet was intense.

"Now that's a lot of Baby Tears," Axel said.

"More than we could ask for," Loki followed.

"Wouldn't that be awful for someone who lives in children's closets?" Lucy asked. While Fable wondered why Boogeymen needed Baby Tears so much.

"But we get our tears in the end," Georgie's face changed, and his pirate attitude returned. He made a toast and everyone clicked their glasses again. "Always remember our motto," Georgie said with happy eyes. "Spooky Woogy Boo!" he said and gulped the Baby Tears.

"Spooky Woogy Boo!" the other Boogeymen cheered and gulped.

"Spooky Woogy Boo!" Fable shouted, tiptoeing, but no one heard her.

"That was so boo," Georgie said, slamming the glass against the bar.

"I guess boo means fantastic or something," Axel speculated.

"What a night! Let the music play again," Georgie ended his speech.

It was time for Loki and his friends to go talk to the Boogeyman.

"Hi, are you Georgie Porgie?" Lucy approached him. She was the tallest of them in her high heels. "I'm Lucy," she said eagerly.

"But of course, you are," Georgie flirted.

"Lucy Rumpelstein."

"Oh," Georgie said. "I didn't know Rump had a beautiful daughter like

176

you."

"Thank you," Lucy blushed. It was the first time Loki saw her like that. "I need some Baby Tears. My father said I could ask you to give me some."

"Baby Tears," Georgie muttered suspiciously. "Why would a beautiful girl like you need those? Do you want to join Boogism?"

"Me, no," Lucy talked softly.

"So why do you need Baby Tears. We work hard to get them, and we don't give them away easily."

"I was told they would help me enter someone's dream," Lucy said reluctantly, expecting Georgie to make fun of her.

"I assume it's a controlled dream then," Georgie spoke seriously, and it surprised Loki that he knew about it.

"Yes," Lucy said. "I didn't know you knew about…"

"Dreamhunting?" Georgie said. "Not so much actually, but I'd love to. The last time someone asked me for Baby Tears to enter a dream was a hundred years ago."

He gulped another drink and raised his glass, saying, 'Spooky Woogy Boo!'

"So can I get the Baby Tears?" Lucy wondered. "I think just one of the glasses here would do."

"Nah," Georgie said. "Baby Tears for dreams are different. They have to be a hundred years old at least. I have some in my room. Follow me."

They all followed him to a side room that he locked from inside when he got in. It was full of souvenirs and bottles that they assumed were filled with Baby Tears. Some bottles had dates on them—they went back as far as 1812. And some bottles were labeled 'boys' or 'girls.' Then there was a set labeled with the craziest words, 'obnoxious,' 'sad,' 'cry happy,' and 'hardest to get.'

There was also a closet set against one wall. It was open and empty.

"So what's the closet for?" Lucy was curious.

"It's where I sleep," Georgie said.

Fable inspected the room with her curious eyes until she saw something that upset her greatly. There was a toddler in a crib in the room. It was a girl and she was asleep.

"Who's that?" Fable asked.

"Someone's daughter," Georgie said. "I stole her for training purposes."

"Training purposes?" Loki frowned. "You mean—"

"Yes. Yes," Georgie said, searching for the right Baby Tears bottle for them. "A Boogeyman has to practice."

"That's so horrible—"Fable frowned.

"But of course, you have to practice," Lucy said.

Loki and Axel exchanged looks, torn between taking the child back to her parents and getting the Baby Tears.

"So you just scare the child once in a while?" Axel said. "Is that what you mean by practice?"

"You haven't seen my Georgie Porgie's scary face yet, right?" Georgie said.

"Of course we haven't, but we'd definitely like to," Lucy said.

In a flash, Georgie gripped his fists and his face turned into a monster, breathing out that awful smell of his. At first, they were all taken aback while his face was transforming, but then Fable started laughing. Georgie's monstrous face was more funny than scary. It was truly disfigured with one eye bulging out from under his eye patch and dangling like a yoyo, his nose crumbled into something like an empty ice cream cone, and his cheeks bubbled like they were balloons. But he wasn't scary at all. The only awful thing about him was the bad smell.

"Fable!" Axel yelled at her, afraid they'd upset Georgie. Even if he looked funny to them, maybe he did really scare babies—and he certainly scared Axel.

Georgie wasn't upset with Fable's reaction. He was sad and frustrated. "You don't think I'm scary?"

Fable shook her head no, her hands folded in front of her.

"Then watch this," Georgie said. "I'll show you scary."

Georgie walked over to the child's cradle and screamed into its face, transforming into that ugly monster again. The child woke up from its sleep and stared with horrified doe eyes at him for a moment. It took a while but then it broke off into a lovely laugh, wiggling its feet.

"No!" Georgie shook his head, returning to normal form. "I can't believe this."

"You're such a loser," Lucy said, disappointed that the evil man she'd liked was not as scary as he pretended. "Do the other Boogeymen know about you?"

"Please, don't tell anyone," Georgie turned into a weak, childish man, begging Lucy on his knees. "They shouldn't know about the real me. They think I'm the scariest thing on earth, and I have to keep it that way. I don't know why I'm like this. I inherited the Leader of Boogeymen title from my father, but I have always failed to scare children," he looked back at the child in the cradle. "Those damn children."

The child wiggled its feet again and smiled when Georgie stared at her.

"You shouldn't be sad," Fable patted him, happy that she could talk straight to his face since he'd knelt down. "You should be really happy. The child loves you dearly. I mean look," Fable tried to get the child's attention but it had its happy eyes focused on Georgie. "She's fond of you. You don't scare her at all."

"But that's a curse to me," Georgie complained, standing up. "I tried all I could. I read all the books on scary. I practice hard and all the children do when they see me is laugh."

Loki and Axel omitted a chuckle. In fact, Loki thought that there had been nothing worth laughing at in the past two days as much as laughing at the Boogeyman. This definitely wasn't the Boogeyman who stole Axel's cereal when he was a kid.

"You're a good man," Fable insisted and held his hand.

"Pathetic," Lucy folded her arms. The man of her dreams turned out to be goodhearted.

"Think of me what you like, but please don't expose me," Georgie said. "I have a reputation to keep."

"Don't worry," Loki said. "We won't. You'll always be Georgie Porgie who scares every child away. We just want the Baby Tears and we're gone."

"Thank you," Georgie said, and handed Loki the bottle of one hundred year old Baby Tears.

"You really fooled me, man," Axel said. "You were so close to becoming my scary idol."

Suddenly, the door sprung open and Cry Baby entered. Georgie had already stood up and dried his tears of disappointment.

"What's wrong?" Georgie faked being angry. "Didn't I tell you to knock three times and say 'Spooky Woogy Boo' before entering?"

"It's an emergency," Cry Baby lowered his eyes, respecting Georgie.

"What kind of emergency?" Georgie asked.

Cry Baby raised his head to answer, but then he saw the grinning baby, wiggling its feet. "Is this a happy baby?" he pointed at it, appalled as if he'd seen the devil.

"Yes, it is," Fabled sneered at him.

"I thought you were practicing on it, so you could make it cry," Cry Baby said to Georgie.

"No it's not laughing," Axel interrupted, doing his best not to expose Georgie. How could the leader of Boogeymen have a laughing child in his room? Axel grinned at the baby and it started crying instantly. Loki rolled his eyes, noting that not only animals hated Axel, but little babies as well. "See?" Axel said to Cry Baby. "It's your imagination."

Cry Baby scratched his head. "Must be all the Baby Tears I drank making me see things."

"So what's the emergency?" Georgie demanded.

"The Bullyvards are outside," Cry Baby said.

"What?" Georgie said. "How dare they enter The Closet?"

"They say they're looking for a Loki Blackscar," Cry Baby said.

"Blackstar," Loki corrected him.

"Why are they looking for you?" Georgie said.

"They love me," Loki said.

"They say they don't want any trouble with us," Cry Baby explained.

"They want the kid and his friends because they have some old business to finish."

"So the werewolves think they can enter Georgie Porgie's place and take whoever they want and leave?" Georgie said. "Not in a million years."

"You understand that there's going to be a massacre outside if Boogeymen and Bullyvards clash with each other?" Cry Baby said.

"I don't care," Georgie snarled. "I'm Georgie Porgie, and I hate those hairy, ugly werewolves."

Georgie pushed the door open, walked outside, and the rest followed.

The Closet was on fire. The two tribes were standing opposite to each other while Loki and the others found themselves in the middle.

"Spooky Woogy Boo!" The Boogeymen clutched their fists, showing their ugly faces to the werewolves—all except Georgie.

"Awooo!" The Bullyvards howled on the other side of the bar, led by Ulfric Moonlcaw, Big Bad, and Paw Paw.

"This isn't really happening, right?" Axel said, shielding his nose from the awful smell.

"We aren't here to make war, Georgie," Ulfric said. "We're here to get Blackstar. Hand him and his friends over to me. They don't mean anything to you."

"Ulfric, baby," Lucy jumped into her werewolf boyfriend's arms. "Kick his boogie butt. This Georgie tried to kiss me."

"Now this isn't really happening," Axel mumbled, trying to hide his face in his hands.

"No one comes into The Closet and insults me," Georgie said. "If you don't leave now, we're going to eat every one of you right now."

One of the Boogeymen pointed at Fable holding the child from Georgie's room in her arms.

"So you don't let us werewolves come take those we want, but you let that lousy witch's daughter take your children?" Big Bad mocked all the Boogeymen.

"It's not his child," Fable yelled. "It has parents and it belongs to them."

Loki watched Georgie's face go red. Fable's action made him look embarrassed in front of his peeps.

"Are you going to let her take the child?" the other Boogeymen asked Georgie.

The Bullyvards started laughing at Georgie.

"Do something, Loki," Axel said. "They are going to eat us alive."

"Fable?" Loki looked back at her.

"Loki," she furrowed her brows back. "You're the hero. You could help me get this child to its parents."

"Shouldn't we get home first?" Axel said as the two clans started closing in on them. Georgie wasn't going to do anything, or he'd be exposed.

"Loki?" Axel repeated. "You're the fallen angel. You should have some power to do something."

"I'm not a fallen angel," Loki gritted his teeth. For a moment, he couldn't understand why he was in the middle of all this. How in the world did he end up here, stuck between the Bullyvards and the Boogeymen? How did his mission become so complicated?

"Ora Pedora," Loki muttered to himself, gripping on his Alicorn again, hoping it would be of some help.

But Loki knew better: escaping never works. One has to face his troubles head on.

"Ulfric," Loki said firmly. "This is between me and you. Don't get Fable and Axel into it."

"Oh," Ulfric mocked him. "We have a hero here. Awooo!"

The Bullyvards started laughing while the Boogeymen approached as well. There was no way out.

"It's too late to play hero," Big Bad said. "If the Bullyvards don't get you, the Boogeymen will."

Loki turned around and the Boogeymen were laughing at him too, rubbing their hands, ready to eat them alive, at least to punish them for Fable's endeavor to take the baby back to its parents.

"I'm about to suffocate," Axel panicked. "I feel trapped in a room with its walls closing in."

Loki pulled Fable closer to him. "Man up, Axel," Loki said. "We're going to have to face them."

"What's your plan? You still got some Magic Dust?"

"Not here," Loki said. "We'll have to use our fists."

"So you're not a superhero after all?" Axel said.

"I'm sorry to disappoint you," Loki shook his head. "Man up, Axel," Fable said, both clans one stride away from them. "You can do it, and then I will escape and save the baby."

As the three of them got ready to face the two clans, a parrot fluttered above their heads with its beautiful green feathers and yellow body.

"I'm Pickwick," it said to Big Bad, hovering before him. "And I'm…going to kick your ass!"

Loki had a big smile on his face. The door flew open and Charmwill entered the bar, smoking his pipe. He stood in his cloak and hood as cool as ever.

"And who are you, old man?" Ulfric sneered.

"It's not who I am," Charmwill said calmly, as he took a drag from his Dragonbreath pipe. "It's what I can do."

Charmwill took one last long drag from his pipe and breathed out fire into the Bullyvards faces, causing them to step back, providing a way for

Loki and his friends to escape The Closet.

"What the holy flickering hell is that pipe?" Axel had to stop and ask Charmwill. Loki pulled him away and the three of them jumped into Carmen and drove away, Pickwick the Parrot flying over its hood. They were heading back to Candy House. Loki was hoping that Charmwill would meet them there.

19

Follow Your Bliss

Back at Candy House, Fable invited Charmwill in and offered to cook fresh Pookies for him. Charmwill thanked her, but said he wanted to talk to Loki outside on the porch. Although Fable was disappointed, she didn't argue. She would have loved to know more about Loki's guardian. She wanted to ask him questions about Loki's story and the Council of Heaven, Snow White, and about Charmwill's powers and why he didn't stay near Loki all the time.

Axel didn't get his answer about Charmwill's Dragonbreath, or how he possessed such a cool power. Instead, Loki let him try to make his Alicorn work. But no matter how many times Axel said 'Ora Pedora' nothing happened so he decided to make himself a Cinderella Mozzarella sandwich and eat a Reluctant Jelly for dessert.

Outside, Loki stood waiting for Charmwill to speak.

"I'm glad you showed up," Loki said. "I thought you'd never visit me in Sorrow."

"I don't know how many times you expect me to save you, Loki," Charmwill said, his hands behind his back.

"I know," Loki lowered his eyes, although Charmwill wasn't staring at him. Instead, he was staring at the stars. "I should have done something back in The Closet to save us, but I didn't know what to do."

"You think everyone around you knows what to do when they look trouble in the eyes?" Charmwill puffed his smoke, staring back at Loki.

"But everyone around me isn't like me," Loki explained.

"Oh, so you think you're different than everyone else?"

"Of course, I'm different," Loki said, knowing that Charmwill loved to be tough on him sometimes. "

"Why am I here?" Loki said. "I know you're going to tell me that it's my choices that led me here because I'd do anything to go home. But all the things that I've witnessed in Sorrow have messed with my mind. I feel things that I haven't felt before, and it's bugging me."

"Things like caring for friends like Axel and Fable?" Charmwill relit his pipe.

"Things like that, yes," Loki said.

"Why does it bother you to have friends?"

"I'm not bothered. In fact, what's better than to have friends to care for and to have them care for you? It's just so confusing, because I feel like I shouldn't. Until the moment I set foot in Sorrow, I hated Minikins. I have even started to feel like this is…" Loki shrugged. "Like this is—"

Charmwill bowed his head a little as if knowing the words Loki was about to say. "Home?" he asked.

Loki nodded. He couldn't even say it.

"And why is it so hard for you to say it?" Charmwill wondered. "Ah, I remember. You don't want to feel home here because I've told you about your *other* home."

"Are you more interested in knowing your past than knowing your future?" Charmwill puffed smoke proudly.

"What kind of questions is that?" Loki said.

"It's a simple question," Charmwill said. "Would it matter who you were before if you've found a home and friends who will help you become whoever you want to be in the future? What matters more, past or future?"

"Are you saying that my future is more important than my past?" Loki said.

"I'm not saying anything. I only ask, and the answers are all inside you," Charmwill said.

"Look. I have no grand answers about how things should be," Loki said. "It just drives me crazy not knowing who I was before, so crazy that sometimes I envy Axel and Fable for knowing who they are."

"What makes you think they know who they are?" Charmwill said.

"What do you mean?" Loki looked as if he had been hit with a pebble in the face. It's not like he hadn't been questioning Axel and Fable's identities before. But he figured it was none of his business since he was destined to leave Sorrow.

"Look around you, Loki," Charmwill breathed the night air in, gazing at the curving hills and streets of Sorrow. "This isn't an ordinary place; although it could fool you into thinking that it's only a small town. What's crazier than a town that is inside another town called Hell, a town that is East of the Sun West of the Moon, a town that a first-timer enters on a Train of Consequences? It has fairy tale vampires, werewolf bullies, nursery rhyme Boogeymen, and..." Charmwill gazed back at Loki with shining eyes, "the craziest food menu ever," he pulled out a bag of Sticky Sweet Bones, summoned Pickwick and fed him a bone. The parrot closed his eyes and moaned, licking the sweets from it.

Loki was speechless.

"So in a town where almost everything insane is possible, you still think people know who they are?"

"Are you saying..."

"Most of the people here don't know who they are," Charmwill explained. "They've been sent to this place just like you. They just don't remember it and unlike you, they accepted it and want to make something good out of it."

"Are you saying they have their own homes, too?

"Why?" Loki said. "Why can't you just tell me everything I want to know without being cryptic?"

"Because if I just tell you, how could you learn or make choices? I'm only your guardian. I will show you the way, or part of it, but it's up to you to walk the line, Loki. No one can choose your life for you."

"But I remember you said that no one deserves to die before they know who they are," Loki said.

"Yes, indeed," Charmwill nodded. "I said 'who they are' not 'from where they're from.' You're not your place of birth, Loki. You're not your past whether it was shameful or endearing. You're not your name, or your looks, or the way you walk. You're who you choose to be."

Loki swallowed any other questions he wanted to ask for the moment. Being told that he was what he chose to be just felt right. It was a relief in many ways.

"I understand," Loki nodded. "So this isn't just about finding my way home. This is about finding my way back to me."

Charmwill said nothing. He pointed at Carmen's plates that now clearly read, 'Home is Where the Heart is."

Loki wasn't surprised that the word 'home' had become visible now. He turned back to Charmwill to ask more questions.

"So I'm not here to kill Snow White?" Loki said.

"Do you expect me to answer that?"

"I see," Loki said. "You can't answer that because right now that is my choice. It's my decision."

"Well said," Charmwill said.

"But don't you think I need more clues to make that decision?" Loki said.

"The only clues you need are in your heart," Charmwill said.

"I'm still a bit unsure about what that means," Loki said.

"If you want me some practical advice, expect to find all the clues you need in Snow White's dream."

"So you agree that this is what I have to do," Loki said. "I'm glad I got the Baby Tears then."

"You did a good job getting those," Charmwill said. "And Fable did an amazing job taking the child back to its parents. She's a bright kid. Do you know why?"

"Not particularly, but I can't deny she is amazing," Loki said.

"She is amazing because she believes in her Chanta. She doesn't need logic to act. She only acts on what her heart tells her. She simply follows her bliss," Charmwill said. "And let me tell you about something that is preventing you from finding your Chanta."

"Really? What is it?"

"One of the items you carry with you is holding you back."

"Holding me back?"

"In order to follow your bliss, and in order to let the world conspire with you to get what you want, you need to get rid of an item that's in your possession all the time," Charmwill said.

"Item?" Loki furrowed his brows. "What item?" he started touching his pockets, thinking about what he owned.

"Again, I can't tell you," Charmwill said.

"But that's going to drive me nuts," Loki said.

"When the right time comes, it will be shown to you," Charmwill said. "But you will have to be smart enough to get rid of it then, or you will miss the chance to save yourself from a great evil."

"Great evil? Do you mean in the Dreamworld?"

"It's not going to be an easy dream, Loki," Charmwill said. "Now, I have to go."

"Not so soon," Loki took a step forward. "You haven't answered all of my questions."

"This is your destiny, Loki," Charmwill said. "Only you can write it and answer the questions. I'll see you again when you find your bliss."

"But wait," Loki said. "Am I doing everything right? I mean I got the Baby Tears. Is there anything else I have to do so I can finally enter her dreams without her controlling it?"

"Who's her?" Charmwill asked.

"Her? Snow White, the vampire princess," Loki was furious by Charmwill's question.

"Who said she's controlling her dreams?"

"Oh. Come on, Charmwill," Loki said. "What do you mean now? Of course it's her who is controlling her dreams so I can't enter them and kill her."

"Didn't she ask you to save her?" Charmwill's features revealed nothing.

"Um—yes, but it might be a trick," Loki said. "And even if it wasn't, who could she possibly want me to save her from?"

"It's not a who. It's a what," Charmwill said.

"You've totally lost me now."

"Do you have any idea of what a 'Genius Loci' is?" Charmwill said in his educational flat tone again.

"I don't think so," Loki said.

"A Genius Loci is the entity or spirit that lives in places, especially archaic places. It could be malevolent or benevolent, depending on its history and where it came from, and who summoned it. A Genius Loci is a place that has a soul. It's smart, it hears, and it can act."

Loki wondered what this had to do with Snow White asking him to save her.

"The Schloss is a Genius Loci," Charmwill said. "It's a malevolent one, bewitched by an evil entity hundreds of years ago. The Schloss has a soul, a dark one, and it could do dark things if it needs to."

"So Snow White wants me to save her from…"

"The Schloss," Charmwill said. "She's imprisoned in it by a greater force. That doesn't say much about whether Snow White is or isn't evil. It only explains what she wants to be saved from. That's why she can never leave it."

"So it has been the Schloss the whole time, sending the huge crow after us, controlling her dreams, and maybe controlling the vampire princess herself?" Loki gazed at Charmwill for more answers.

Charmwill nodded. "I believe that Snow White controlled her dreams so you didn't kill her, because she wants to show you something in her dreams. But at the same time, someone has imprisoned her in the Schloss, and she will never be able to tell you or show you everything, or what she really wants to tell you, unless you free her from it."

"And that's why she needs me to enter her dreams?" Loki asked. "Because the answer of how to save her lies in there?"

"I believe so. Now, if you'll excuse me, I have to a sail over to another town to read a fairy tale to some kids," Charmwill checked his watch, turned around and walked into the darkness.

It was hard on Loki watching him leave, but he knew it was inevitable. He had to finish this journey on his own now. There was one last thing he needed to ask him, though.

"Hey Charmwill, how about Axel and Fable; who are they?" Loki tiptoed although Charmwill had disappeared in the dark.

"Don't you get it yet?" Charmwill asked from behind the curtains of the night, his voice fading away. "Axel and Fable, their father was a woodcutter, and they live in a Candy House? Axel is always hungry, and eats too much candy, and Fable is fond of eating bread. It doesn't get easier than that to know who they really are.

20

A Prison of Pearls

The night settled its wings and caressed the Schloss. Even though it posed so beautifully with its pearl windows, Loki knew that the Schloss was looking back at them. He could feel its presence and anger like a ghost's cold breath on your cheek late at night.

There was a faint, low drone coming out of the Schloss's walls, a rumble of rejection, poisoning the air in the Black Forest. It was the same drone he'd heard when Snow White told him that she needed saving.

"Can you feel this?" Fable panted like a clairvoyant who was trying to commune with the castle. "The castle doesn't want us here tonight. It knows we're here to help Snow White this time."

"I can feel it," Loki nodded, although he hadn't made a decision as to whether he would let Snow White live. However, he made a promise to himself that he'd enter her dream to help decide.

Inside the castle, the chandeliers swayed slightly above their heads, like a pendulum or an iron maiden ready to slash them at any moment. The dangling crystals clanged together like warning bells, a last chance signal to the intruders. There were faint sounds of nails scratching against the walls, which they all dismissed as the Schloss playing with their minds.

Everything else in the prison castle vibrated slightly; the walls, the floors, and even the suffocating air they were breathing.

"This place is creepy," Lucy whispered, standing by the entrance behind Loki. Her voice was unusually thin. "I'm so not entering it."

Fable led the way, walking ahead of Loki. She was staring at the ceiling and the walls, her eyes trying hard to pierce through.

"How did we miss that this place is actually a prison? It explains why Snow White never attacked someone outside the castle," Axel said, standing as close as possible to Lucy.

"Which makes me wonder why your father and the town's council want Snow White dead?" Fable turned to face Lucy.

Lucy shot her a flat stare.

"How should I know?" Lucy said. "All I know is that he's following the town council's orders, and asked me to go search for Loki because somehow the council believed he could kill her," Lucy said.

"How about that new principal you told me was coming to Rumpelstein High?" Loki said. "You said she'd only accept the job if the vampire princess was killed."

"It's true. My father said she wanted to use the Schloss as a tourist attraction," Lucy replied.

"What kind of principal has such powers over the town's council?" Fable queried. "Who is she? What's her name?"

"I don't know her name," Lucy shrugged her shoulders. "Again, all I know is that she's a prestigious woman and will also become the town council's new chairwoman."

"I think I know," Fable rubbed her chin.

Axel and Loki turned their head to Fable while Lucy tapped an impatient foot.

"She's the Wicked Stepmother, of course," Fable announced.

"Stepmother; are you serious?" Lucy chimed incredulously.

"You know, Snow White's Wicked Stepmother who poisoned her with the apple in the story?" Fable said. "Somehow, they live among us, and now she's going to be our school's principal and town's chairwoman. She wants the princess dead so she can remain the fairest of them all."

"Wow," Axel said with an open mouth. "Your mind is more messed up than mine."

"What a happy family," Lucy commented.

"I tell you what," Axel said. "Since the Stepmother is coming to town, and we're going to have a whole lotta adventure ahead of us, why don't we go back and get us a good meal at the Belly and the Beast, then talk this over?"

"Stop being a puss in a boot," Loki said.

"You're pathetic, Axel," Lucy said with disdain as she finally entered the castle. "So where is our nasty blood-sucking princess?" Lucy looked around. "Knock, knock?" her high heels echoed on the marble floor. "Mirror, mirror?" she summoned with a grin on her face. "Who's the scariest of them all?" Lucy enjoyed mocking the vampire princess. "Coochie, coochie!"

"I don't think it's a good idea to coochie-coochie her," Axel took a step back.

"Shut up, son of a woodcutter," Lucy shushed him.

Loki was curious to see Lucy's reaction after she met badass Snow White. He doubted she'd stick with the condescending attitude.

"Shhh!" Fable hushed them, pointing at the dim lit staircase.

Loki looked up and saw Show White. She was in her white dress, floating at the top of the stairs, watching them. Everyone held their breath. When Snow White's dress waved in the usual cold breeze, Axel let out a muffled whimper.

"See? The mirror trick always works," Lucy said. She was the only one continuously capable of offending the living… and the dead.

Snow White stepped forward into the light. Her dress began dripping blood, which clutched at her small feet before she glided down, just hovering over the third step. She looked like a marionette, hung with invisible threads from her hands by a vicious puppeteer—and he finally understood why. The Schloss was Snow White's prison of pearls. It controlled her. The big question was, 'Why had she been imprisoned for a hundred years, and by whom?'

Loki gripped his stake as she glided down over the last step. Although he knew she was a prisoner, it wasn't easy to trust her when he saw her veins snaking up her arms and neck, reaching her pale face. Her eyes had turned into two holes filled with black oil, and for the first time, she had tears rolling down her cheeks—black tears.

"What a freak," Lucy blurted.

Snow White's bloody feet landed on the floor. She began walking toward Loki, leaving red footprints behind. She showed no anger or intentions of hostility. Something watery dripped onto the floor behind Loki. It was Axel; he was drooling.

Loki could almost hear Fable's heart pounding as if it was his. She watched her favorite vampire princess with appalling eyes.

"Don't you dare come near me wicked princess." Lucy grunted. "I just manicured my fingernails, and had my hair styled."

Snow White snarled at Lucy, only once. She did it over Loki's shoulder, and Lucy stumbled back into Axel's arms. Even Axel, who'd normally want to save Lucy, wasn't happy about it.

"You don't have to be rude about it," Lucy snapped back. "I know you're sweet on the champ. He's all yours," she pointed at Loki. "Just don't bite him on the first date."

Snow White was an inch away from Loki, and she uttered words for the second time.

"Are you here to kill me?" she said.

Loki wished she hadn't talked, because she did it in her innocent sixteen-year-old teenage voice, which was smooth and lively with a hint of adventure. It confused him, trying to match the voice with her gruesome look. He hesitated before replying.

Fable, although shocked, managed to wave her hands at Loki behind Snow White's back, suggesting he should tell her that he wasn't there to kill her.

"Are you here to kill me, Loki?" Snow White repeated without the slightest hint of anger. She was just a sweet girl his age. For all he knew, she could have been asking him if he liked pink or yellow cotton-candy. In another world, another lifetime, Loki would have asked her out and they would have watched a movie together, had a little popcorn, and snuck in a few kisses in the darkness of a theatre. When she spoke his name, he felt so... so close to her... as if he'd known her for a very long time.

Although Loki never believed in fairy tales, he still couldn't dismiss the importance they held in people's lives. It was hard to imagine meeting someone who hadn't heard Snow White's tale, but it was possible that some people didn't know about a certain religion, country, or food. When it came to fairy tales, everyone knew about them as if they were the one and only language uniting the world. Loki suddenly understood why Charmwill described his Book of Beautiful Lies as the most important book to mankind. If the world couldn't agree on one religion, or one nationality, or even one perspective of what is good and what is evil, they agreed on fairy tales.

"No, he isn't here to kill you," Fable finally uttered on behalf of Loki. "He wants to know how you died," Fable continued. Snow White didn't turn back. She was staring at Loki with those black eyes. "He wants to know what made you," Fable shrugged. "The way you are now—"

"Not that there is anything wrong with that," Axel drew upon flattery like a magician pulled rabbits out of his hat. "In fact, you look...you look so—" Although Axel didn't mind being a hypocrite to save his life, he couldn't bring himself to tell her that she looked beautiful. He shrugged so loud it echoed in the castle.

"So gross," Lucy spit out. "Princess my—"

"Don't listen to them," Fable broke in. "We're here to help you. We know there is something wrong..." Fable looked around her, afraid she'd offend the castle. "We know there is something wrong with this castle," she whispered. "We know that you spared our lives—Loki's life. You saved us, now let us help you. Allow Loki to get into your dream without controlling it."

Although Snow White's eyes didn't change, their golden tint shimmered momentarily when Fable mentioned helping her. Loki noticed it only happened when she was looking at him, and only when she liked something she heard or saw.

"Is that true?" Snow White asked Loki, her voice was pleading for him to say 'yes.'

Loki nodded, only once. Words couldn't escape his mouth. Part of it was that he didn't want to lie to her. Killing her was still his only hope to return home if he chose to, and it wasn't easy to shake a feeling that had ran in his veins for so long. But he still wanted to enter her dream and know what happened to her in case he changed his mind.

"Can you tell me what happened to you?" Loki managed to say.

Snow White didn't reply. She looked as if she were trying to remember. Her silence was even scarier than her rage.

"I can't say," she finally spoke. In a most mesmerizing moment, she lowered her head as if she was embarrassed she didn't remember. Her peaceful gesture made everyone sigh, all except Lucy.

"Seriously? Are you buying into her tricks?" Lucy said.

"How so?" Loki asked Snow White.

She raised her eyes to meet his, this time they were a beautiful blue. She held Loki's hands, and he found himself giving in to her, and loosening his grip on his Alicorn.

Snow White looked at him as if searching for something or someone behind his eyes. No one had ever looked at him this way before.

"There is so much I want to say but can't," Snow White whispered. Her eyes gazed to the left and then to the right as Loki narrowed his. She looked up at the ceiling and back at him. Her eyes were telling him she couldn't speak because of the castle and he needed to do something about it.

Fable slipped behind Snow White again and mouthed the following words behind her back: *I don't think the Baby Tears will be enough to enter her dream. We have to get her out of the Schloss, and—*

Loki didn't wait for Fable to finish her sentence. "I'll get you out of here," he told Snow White. He didn't care about the Schloss' anger, although he could already hear its walls vibrating louder, like a giant about to wake up.

"Not so loud. The Schloss can hear you," Fable gritted her teeth. "If you'd only listened to all I had to say," she rolled her eyes.

The castle started shaking, and Snow White's eyes changed to black again. She stared around her at the shaking interiors. She looked like a child afraid her parents would catch her doing something wrong.

"You have to go now, Loki," Snow White said. "I don't think it will let me get out."

"No," Loki stepped closer to her. "I will enter your dream. I want to know what happened to you."

"You can't as long as I'm trapped in here," Snow White screamed over the now deafening roar of the Schloss. With the castle controlling her, she was going to turn into her other self soon; they needed to hurry.

"Then I'll get you outside, and perform the ritual there," Loki insisted.

"I can only survive forty two minutes outside, or—"

"Or what?"

"Or this town will wither away," she explained. "My soul is connected to this town. As long as I'm in the castle, the town is safe. But if I play tricks on it and stay out for more than forty two minutes, the whale, which this town is settled upon, will sink into the ocean, dragging the town down with it."

"Wow," Axel said. "Better keep the princess inside the Schloss."

"How is this possible?" Loki asked.

"It's part of my curse," she said. "Can I trust you with my life?" she looked straight in his eyes as the world around them fell apart.

"And the town's life, including mine!" Axel felt the need to remind them.

It was a hard question to answer. *Can I trust you with my life?*

Snow White looked disappointed. So did Fable, glaring at Loki for his indecisiveness.

"Use the Chanta," Fable told him, pointing at her heart. "Some questions aren't answered with logic. Use the Chanta like your mother told you, and you'll be able answer her truthfully."

Loki didn't care about the Chanta. He still couldn't understand what it was. But he knew he had strong feelings for Snow White.

This demon girl had spared his life. If he had to choose between knowing who he was before and why Snow White spared his life, he was going to choose the thing he was in control of now. He wanted to know why she needed saving and why she hadn't killed him.

"You can trust me with your life outside," he nodded, his thumbs pressing on Snow White's hands. "I have to know your story!"

Fable did a secret fist pump in the air behind Snow White's shoulder. She had to duck to avoid a flying vase. The castle's anger was a million times worse than Fable's spells from her second-hand witchcraft books.

Snow White's demonic transformation was complete.

"Stake her!" Lucy shouted as a lightning bolt struck outside and the castle shook. "Or she will kill us all."

Loki raised his Alicorn and carved it into Snow White's chest, putting her to sleep again.

"Sorry," he whispered in her ear, catching her before she fell on the floor, her arms wrapping around his shoulder.

It was amazing how fast her black eyes turned back to blue. Doors slammed and windows broke on their own. The floor cracked from underneath and the banister turned into snakes gliding toward them.

Loki held Snow White in his arms, brushed her hair off her eyes with the back of his hand then looked back at Fable. "We have to get her out of here," he said. "I have to enter her dream."

"It's about time," Fable screamed.

***

Loki, Fable, Axel, and Lucy were about to pull Snow White out of the castle into the light of a thin moonbeam. They needed to prepare their Dream Temple about a hundred feet ahead in the snow. The two opposite mirrors, the Epidaurus Circle, and Loki's items all had to be prepared like an exact science. Time was tight and they had to move fast.

Axel and Loki dragged two mirrors from the angry castle to the chosen location. They fixed them opposite to each other, and propped them up with two heavy armoires they'd managed to steal from the castle in spite of the door slamming in their faces, chandeliers falling from the ceiling and swirling winds.

Fable drew the Epidaurus circle using black oil that Loki had told her to drain from his Cadillac. It wasn't exactly a girl's job, but she never ceased to amaze. She insisted on pouring the oil counter-clockwise since this should empower the spell. She had also suggested they place the mirrors facing North and South. Not something that was written in Loki's notebook, but he didn't mind the input.

Loki brought his hourglass, Alicorn, and Ariadne Fleece along while Lucy did nothing but stand back and protect her manicured fingernails.

After a while, Lucy decided to help in her own way. She made Axel fetch an ax from her four-wheeler. She suggested they'd use it if they needed to break the mirror in case Loki was stuck in the Dreamworld. It was impressive how she'd learned everything Loki explained to her about the process in no time at all—still, he was worried why she had an ax on her four-wheeler in the first place.

Loki was proud of his three assistants, learning the rules of the Dreamworld, and helping him as the Dreamhunter. The four ran back and held the glass coffin by its corners, standing at the threshold of the angry castle. Axel and Fable grabbed the two corners in front, Axel and Lucy grabbed the backsides. The ground between the castle and the Dream Temple sloped slightly upward, which made it hard to push the coffin forward. It was strange that an icy pond good enough for skating had formed over the ground. It would be dangerous if it cracked and someone fell into the freezing water underneath.

A lightning bolt struck again. The castle was huffing and puffing. It made such boiling and bubbling sounds Loki thought it was ready to explode.

"I understand that the castle is angry with us, but why is the weather getting worse?" Lucy yelled back, the wind eating at her words and taking her breath away.

"Snow White is manipulating the weather," Axel offered his expertise. "You know vampires can control the weather, right?"

"That's not her now," Fable corrected him. "It's the castle!"

"Enough with the chitchat," Loki said. "Adjust the timing of the Waker, Axel," Loki shouted. "Make it thirty five minutes. We need about five minutes to move the coffin to the Dream Temple, and hopefully five minutes when I come back from the dream."

"Done!" Axel said.

Loki's hands were ice cold. The wind was so intense he imagined he might go flying through the air like a street sign ripped from its foundation.

"Is everyone ready," Loki gazed into their faces one by one. "Let's go!" They started pulling the coffin out.

If the castle had hands and feet, it would've chased them—Loki looked behind him to make sure it wasn't. It was roaring as if it was the belly of a ferocious beast. Loki thought its huge double doors opened as wide as a whale's mouth for a second. The sounds it made were loud and deafening, and the weather was quickly nearing an intolerable state. Still, they kept going.

The little slope upward was exhausting, the ice cracking slightly underneath them.

"Don't look down," Loki advised.

They reached the Dream Temple and pulled the coffin into the middle. Loki knelt down and parted Snow White's eyelids with freezing fingers, and dropped the Baby Tears in her eyes. Her eyes took on a bluish-gold tint with tiny white spots floating around in them as if they were inside a snow globe. Then he closed her eyes and covered them with his two Obol coins.

"Why cover her eyes?" Lucy asked.

"The eyes are windows to the soul," Loki shouted, spitting out snow. "In this case, they are windows to the Dreamworld. Covering them prevents evil from crossing over from the Dreamworld to our world."

"So what's the Incubator?" Fable said, looking at Axel, praying he had found the right word.

"Don't worry, Loki, I got it," Axel said proudly. "I got it; a word and a number. It will help you enter Snow White's dream, and you'll enter it right where she wants to show you what happened to her."

"So what is it?" Fable yelled impatiently.

"The word is 'Jawigi'," Axel yelled as lightning screeched in the sky. "It's the word that is written on the library's floor."

"Does it have a meaning?" Loki asked.

"It's the key to the Dreamworld," Axel said. "It turns out the Brothers Grimm created this Dreamworld, Jawigi, for some reason."

"What?" Fable said. "I don't understand. What does Jawigi have to do with the Brothers Grimm's names?"

"The 'j' and 'a' are from Jacob's first name," Axel explained. "The 'w' and 'i' are from Wilhelm, his brother. The 'g' and 'i' are from their family name Grimm. It's a code, something like an anagram."

"So who are the Brothers Grimm again?" Lucy asked. Everyone stared incredulously at her.

"They wrote the Snow White fairy tale," Axel said.

"And what's the number?" Loki asked, the wind ruffling his hair.

"What do you think?" Axel said. "1812, the year the tale was written, about two hundred years ago."

Loki connected the Ariadne Fleece to a mirror, watching its surface rippling. This time the rippling was accompanied with a purple shimmering light. Loki wrapped the other side of the fleece around his wrist. He could still hear the castle's anger behind him, but he was undeterred. He then lay next to Snow White, and whispered the word *Jawigi* in her ear, repeating it three times. He watched her head move slightly as if nodding while staked and asleep.

"Wow, Lucy pronounced in amazement, this is so cool!"

"It isn't just cool, it's magic!" Fable said. She stood tangent to the circle, preparing to throw a good amount of Magic Dust into Loki's face. "Take care of yourself, Loki. From this moment on, there is no turning back."

"Don't forget to say the prayer," Axel reminded him as Fable blew Magic Dust from the palm of her hand into his eyes.

"Yeah," Loki said. "I will recite it silently," he gripped his Alicorn, and quietly hoped it would be useful.

"Hey," Axel and Fable shouted in one breath, staring at Loki as he was becoming more and more drowsy. "Come back," Axel said. "This world you dislike so much isn't that bad, you know," added Fable.

Loki took a deep, cold breath, and said the prayer:

Now I lay me down to sleep.
If I die before I wake.
Forbid all evil
My soul to take

He couldn't bring himself to say, 'forbid Snow White my soul to take' this time. He knew there was something evil waiting for him in the Dreamworld, but he wasn't sure it was her.

Loki sank into Snow White's Dreamory; into her memory of how she became a vampire, and what had really happened to her. Little did he know that it would change his, and the lives of the people in Sorrow, forever. The Boy Who Was Only Shadow was about to open the Dreamworld and expose the secrets of fairy tales.

21

She Who Must Be Obeyed

Loki opened his eyes in Snow White's dream. He knew that his body in the waking world looked as if he were in a coma, and that if anything went wrong in the Dreamworld, he might never wake up again.

Loki lay on his back. Although there was no headache like in the last dream, he blinked a few times to clear his blurry vision. He also preferred not to stand up until he figured out the place and made sure it was safe. Wherever he was, the place was full of hot steam.

The smell of some aromatic soap filled the air. At first, he thought he smelled ripe apples, then he also smelled flowers, followed by dozens of other alluring smells, including chocolate, milk, and...

...it was hard to recognize that last smell, although it stood out the most, but it seemed oddly out of place.

One thing was obvious; he was in a bathhouse, lying on his back in a bathtub.

When the steam thinned, Loki was able to see the paintings on the ceiling. They were like nothing he'd expected, depicting horrifying scenes of a bathhouse—probably the same one he was in. Painted in an ancient European fashion, they illustrated young beautiful girls being dragged by servants to a huge bathtub where a beautiful woman laid bathing. She had inescapably attractive features, posing like a Queen, even in the bathtub. Everyone around her bowed their heads out of respect. She wore a thin, golden crown, braided into the golden locks of her wavy hair. She was bathing in what looked like a mixture of milk and dark chocolate syrup. But that wasn't the horrific part. It was the drawings of the young girls lying slaughtered like lambs all around. Each one had been bitten on her neck. Their blood filled the curvy grooves in the bathhouse's floor, filling the bathtub where the Queen bathed.

Loki rocked back on his feet, gripping his Alicorn, inspecting his surroundings. Most of the steam had cleared, and it was obvious he was in the same bathhouse depicted in the painting, now vacant with no traces of blood. Still, Loki could smell it in the air. Now he understood what the smell was he'd thought was out of place.

This close, the curvy grooves in the floor looked like an Octopus's arms stretching from the sides of the curvy, and peculiarly big, bathtub. Loki jumped out of it and inspected the place further.

The bathhouse was built of crème-colored fancy bricks. The walls were carved with absolutely amazing scenes of battles like the ones he'd seen on the castle's walls. Blue and gold were the most dominant colors, and almost everything around him incorporated curves in one way or another. It was as if the place had been sculpted carefully by the hands of the likes of Michael Angelo.

A seven year old version of Snow White appeared out of nowhere in front of him. She was holding onto her white dress with her small hands, swaying her body slightly back and forth. Her hair was long and black, flowing down her shoulders, and pulled back in a red ribbon. Her eyes were as blue as the clear summer sky, her lips were cherry red, and her skin was blindingly pale.

"So this isn't really a dream?" Loki said. "Is this a memory of you being young again?"

"Bit of both," Snow White replied.

"Please don't tell me the Baby Tears didn't work." he said, gripping his Alicorn harder.

"Don't bother using your Alicorn," she said. "It's useless as long as you can't *see*, Loki."

"See what?"

"Believe and then you will *see*," she said.

"Can you clarify?" Loki inquired, "you aren't still controlled by the Schloss, or?"

There was a sudden rumbling outside the bathhouse, sounds of women's laughter and approaching footsteps. Snow White looked worriedly at the bathhouse's closed door.

"Come with me," she urged him, stretching out her small arm, and pulling his hand. "I can't risk her seeing you although it's unlikely."

"Who's *she*?" Loki said as Snow White dragged him, her bare feet smacking against the marble floor. She ushered him through a small-sized trap door then let go of his hand. Whoever was coming to the bathhouse scared the heck out of her. Loki crouched and followed her through the door.

He recognized the castle once more. It was no surprise they were in the Schloss again, now thronging with servants and residents. It looked like a gloriously different castle with no hints of being haunted or evil. The sunlight burst through every pearly window and lit the majestic entity.

Snow White pulled Loki's hand again. "Come on," she whispered. "I can't keep saving your life, even in my dreams."

Loki gave in and followed her as if he was a seven year old being escorted by his mother.

"Why are there so many people in the castle?" he asked, glimpsing part of the landscape outside. It was unbelievably enchanting, still covered in snow with the exception of the sun living side by side with the snowflakes falling down from the clear blue sky. The castle was on top of a hill, overlooking a vast garden, protected by swan-shaped gates preceded by calashes and carriages.

"It's the King of Sorrow's castle," Snow White said. "It's usually crowded with visitors in the day. Just wait until nighttime, and you'll see the other side of it."

"I don't have time for nighttime," Loki said, following her into a dark room.

"I know," she lit a gas lamp, and closed a door behind her. They were in a built-in closet. "That's why you have to get used to time shifting. It will happen fast and frequently."

"What time shifting?"

"You'll see," she was about to walk out when she turned back and pulled him down to her by his shirt. Loki bent over and she stamped a kiss on his cheek. "Open your heart, Loki, and cross the oceans in your mind," she whispered, turned off the lamp, and strode out the door, repeating the words again. "Only when you open your heart, will you understand everything."

Loki was stranded in the dark of the closet, feeling like a fool. A little later, he opened the door again to call for her, but suddenly it was dark and silent in the hallways. It was evening.

"So that's what she meant by time shifting," he told himself. He thought the time shifting closet was cool, and he wished the bathroom's door in his school would've served the same purpose. He'd go in, close it, open it, and school was over. Or better, the school would be gone. "That would've been the coolest built-in time machine ever. Someone should invent such a door," Loki whispered to emptiness.

After he'd stepped out of the closet, he thought that maybe he should have picked up some different clothes. It wouldn't be classy to meet the King and Queen of Sorrow in jeans and a tee shirt. Babushka wouldn't have approved of it.

No manners whatsoever. Didn't you learn any etiquette, Loki? he imagined her saying.

Loki hid behind a suit of armor then knocked on its head to make sure it wasn't occupied by an ancient huntsman. He peeked into a majestic dining room from under its metal arms, and saw Snow White having dinner alone on a ridiculously long liver-shaped table.

There were two servants standing respectfully near the window, waiting for the princess to snap her finger so they could bestow her with whatever she wished. One of them was Tabula, the giant woman from the first dream. She was a tanned woman in a black and white dress with notable white-silver hair. The other servant was a gray-haired old butler. Loki had never seen the man before.

The dining table was filled with food that Axel could've stuffed himself with for life. An enormous roasted turkey, so many colorful and different kinds of rice, salad, soup, and all kinds of meat shimmered on the candle lit table. Loki felt hungry—hunger in a dream was a bit nightmarish.

In the candle light, Snow White looked sad eating alone.

"Such cruel people," whispered Tabula to the butler. "Why don't they ever eat with their child?"

"Shut your mouth, woman." the butler hissed, keeping his pretentious pose and chin up. "We're not allowed to talk about this."

"Such a strange king and a queen to abandon their child at meal times," Tabula mumbled.

Snow White didn't hear them, playing with her fork and nudging an impenetrable olive on her plate.

"Not yummy enough, eh," Loki commented. "Not like Prince Charming."

"My dear princess!" a broad voice called happily for Snow White from outside the room.

Heavy boots thumped on the floor before the man with the voice entered the room. He was wearing an expensive warrior outfit, had shoulder-length black hair, a notable double chin, and a strong jaw. It was Snow White's father, a very masculine king.

"Where were you in the Brother Grimm's fairy tales," Loki mumbled. "No stepmother could have hurt the child in your presence."

Snow White jumped out of her chair and ran to her father, covering him with hugs and kisses. The resemblance between father and child was uncanny. She'd inherited that strong, silky, black hair from him. Even his lips were unusually red, filled with life. All but her pale skin; the king was tanned, almost burned by the sun, which made Loki wonder where he had been.

Snow White's father lifted her up with his strong hands. She wrapped her arms around his broad shoulders and leaned against the armor he was wearing on his chest.

"I missed you, father," Snow White said, brushing her cheek against his scruffy beard. "I only came back for you my little cherry snowflake," the king squeezed his daughter harder.

Snow White giggled. "Are you going to eat with me?" she asked.

The king's face knotted as he helped her down. "You know the castle's etiquettes," he said, kneeling down for her. The butler and Tabula seemed taken by the scene of such a powerful man on his knees. "The king and the queen have to eat together without their lovely daughter in order to discuss important matters regarding the kingdom."

"You said I would be able to eat with you when I turn sixteen. I want to be sixteen now. Do something about it," she demanded.

"That's true," he laughed. His laugh was majestic, echoing as if his chest was hollow. "Why would you want to grow up that fast, princess? You have the time of your life ahead of you."

Snow White tiptoed and chopped through the air with her arms as if she was a fearless warrior. "I want to grow up now so I can fight the enemy with you."

The king laughed again. "By the time you're sixteen, I promise you, my fairest, that I will have chopped their heads off one by one so you can rule the kingdom in peace and with prosperity."

"Chop their heads one by one?" Loki murmured. "No wonder your daughter went nuts later."

"I have to go and rest now," the king told Snow White. "Your mother and I will summon you after we finish our nightly discussions."

"I'm finished eating," Snow white shrugged her shoulders.

"Then go to your chamber," the king ordered her. "I will call for you soon."

Loki watched the servants ushering Snow White out of the dining room after her father had left. Hiding behind the armor, he hesitated, wishing for another time shift. He didn't know if he should follow Snow White or her father, or if he should go back to the closet. He scratched his head, thinking it was funny that scratching one's head only pulled the hair out and never brought new ideas—or hair—to it.

"Time to go," a female voice said behind him.

Loki whirled around, thinking he was caught by one of the servants. To his surprise it was Snow White again; the sixteen year old, beautiful, fangless version of her. Loki *had* to scratch his head this time.

"Have I told you lately that I missed you?" Loki smiled, pretending to be calm.

Snow White laughed. It was the first time he'd ever seen her laugh, and he was sure she didn't have any idea how magnificent and mesmerizing her laugh was.

"Too much wit will kill you, Loki," she said. "And don't look back for the younger version of me. There are two Snow Whites in this dream."

"Are there other manifestations of you I should know of, my princess?" Loki bowed his head playfully. He felt safe with her after that laugh.

"No, and it's only me and my younger self who can see you in this Dreamory," she said.

"So why are there two of you?"

"I wanted to introduce you to my younger version so you don't freak out and try to kill me before I get a chance to show you what I want you to see. I know you're fond of staking me in the heart," she threw an investigative look around her to see if someone was coming. "I also wanted to show you how closets work in the Dreamory," she grabbed his hands and started running again.

They entered another room where she opened the door of another closet filled with the finest dresses, probably the Queen's because of their bigger sizes. Snow White pushed him inside, hopped in and closed the door behind them. Although the closet was big, the plethora of dresses and shoes on the floor barely allowed enough room for the two of them. They were standing face to face, breath to breath, too close for people who wanted to kill each other.

"I once had a girl force me into a make out session with her in a broom closet," Loki said, remembering Pippi Luvbug.

He doubted Charmwill would come and save him this time, and he double-doubted he could bring himself to stake the beautiful princess.

"You better start whispering," Snow White drew a serious face. "Or the Queen will find us and she'll send you to an eternal *blackout* session."

"Are you always so serious in the Dreamory?"

"Loki," Snow White rested one palm on his chest, and suddenly he was about to forget all about the dream and the vampire killing business. He wondered why he felt at ease with her in this Dreamory. For some reason, he doubted that those she laid her eyes upon didn't live long enough to tell about it.

Those she laid her eyes upon, fell for her slowly, and forgot about her fangs and bad temper.

"You're being ridiculous," she added. "You need to learn as much as you can about me in this dream. Focus, please."

"OK," he grabbed her palm, held it to his face like a handkerchief and let it slide down again where it landed on his chest. "Back to serious face, my princess. What do you have in mind?"

"I need to show you my story in different periods and places as fast as I can, so you know how all of this started."

"Why don't you just tell me? I got a D+ in chemistry so I'm kinda smart."

"I can't, and I have my reasons why I can't," she sighed, but we need to go back in time."

"What do you have in mind; The Renaissance, Dark ages, dinosaurs and stuff?"

"Please. Please. Stop it."

"What do you want me to say? We're already in the 19th century, right? How far back in time is *back in time* from here?"

"I will take you back, five years before I was born. I was born in 1796, so we're going to 1791."

"That's interesting." a surge of seriousness hit him.

"Why?" she looked puzzled.

"It means you were exactly sixteen years old when the Brothers Grimm wrote your story in 1812," Loki thought Axel was actually useful all of a sudden.

Snow White smiled, looking satisfied, "1812," she nodded. "It's the first version they wrote. It was a bit closer to the truth, unlike the 1857 version which was filled with more lies and hidden messages."

"Lies?" Loki frowned. "Are we talking about you being the real Snow White?"

"Of course, I'm the real Snow White," she seemed insulted by the question. "How can you even doubt that?"

"I have to be honest with you," Loki said. "I don't know what I should believe.

"That's because you resist opening up to your Chanta," Snow White said.

"You know about the Chanta, too? Is that some kind of a *new cool* catch phrase?" Loki said. "I don't get it."

"Please stop being stubborn."

No one had ever mentioned to Loki that he was stubborn, but now that she'd pointed it out, he knew it was true.

"Are you alright, Loki?" Snow White said.

"Never been better," Loki pretended he was, unable to open up and show her his confusion.

"I have a question. Since you're sixteen now, I assume it's the same year you died, right?"

Snow White smiled again.

"Why are you smiling? You know I have a weakness for demon girls when they smile," he avoided her eyes, and for the first time he was sincere about his emotions.

"Yes, I know about your weakness. I'm smiling because your question shows you finally care, even if it's just a little bit. Yes, someone tried to kill me when I was sixteen years old, but I didn't die. I found a way to stay immortal."

"Immortal?" Loki frowned.

"Most of the fairy tale characters are," she said.

"Say that again? Fairy tale characters? Are you saying they're all real and alive?" he said, remembering Charmwill saying the same thing. "So who tried to kill you, your Wicked Stepmother?" Loki never thought he'd be asking such a question.

"That's a complicated subject, but I'll get to it later."

"I can't help but wonder why you just can't tell me," Loki sighed. "Why is it that no one can tell me anything I need to know?"

"I can't answer that, but we can start with going back in time to learn about my father."

"The king?"

"Yes," she bowed her head a little. "Angel von Sorrow. That's his name. Angel Night von Sorrow."

"Nice to meet you, Snow White von Sorrow," Loki said sincerely; "Von means 'from', right?"

"Yes, we're from German descendants, and my father was a very important man," Loki sensed how proud she was of her father. The way she stressed the word *very* was as if she was pleading for the innocence of someone who was wrongfully convicted.

"Of course, he was important. He was king. I don't remember him showing up in your fairy tale, though."

"I told you the tales were forged."

"So he wasn't an absentee father?"

"Stop being rude," she hit him on the chest. It was a playful gesture, and Loki liked it.

"I'm serious, that's what everyone in the Ordinary World thinks of your father."

"There is a reason why the Brothers Grimm forged his part," she said.

"Since this is turning into a friendly conversation between fairy tale characters and half-angels, why don't we get out of this closet and get some coffee. You've had coffee in the 18th century, right?"

Suddenly, Snow White winced. Someone was calling for her outside; it was the deep, mysterious, and powerful voice of a grownup woman.

"Shew, where are you?" the voice summoned her. The woman's voice was so demanding and acute that Loki felt a twinge in his body, and an uncontrollable urge to respond.

"It's her," Snow White said. Her eyes were a mix of horror and sympathy. "Don't answer her. Her voice has an effect on people. You will want to answer her. You will want to obey her, and even sacrifice your life for her. Don't let that feeling consume you."

"How can she have such an effect on me?" Loki said. "Who's she?"

"She is…She Who Must Be Obeyed," Snow White answered.

"That's a pretty long name. I'm serious. Who's she?"

Snow White nodded, grabbing the doorknob tighter. "It's time to go back before she finds me, are you ready?"

"Wait a minute. Why are you afraid of her? Isn't she your mother? Tell me about her."

"Stop talking, or she will kill you in the Dreamory and you will never wake up again," Snow White pleaded, listening to the woman's voice approaching. "We have to leave," she whispered.

"To where? How are you sure of what time and place you are taking us?"

"It's my dream, remember?" Snow White whispered. "Shut up for a second."

"But the Baby Tears—"

"The Baby Tears prevent me from controlling my dream so you can't kill me, like when I made you enter it as a seven year old. But it doesn't prevent me from showing you what I need to. When you used the word 'Jawigi', you gave me that power."

"So Axel was right, again," Loki told himself.

"Shew?" the woman's voice was already in the room. Standing in the middle of it, the woman was alerted by the noise in the closet. Loki saw her from behind the small gaps in the closet's door. "Oh there you are, darling," the woman was approaching and Loki felt that a wicked witch was closing in on them.

"I agree. Better travel back in time. Do whatever you need to do," Loki said, gripping his Alicorn. He'd never been afraid like this before. Even the creepiest demons couldn't stir such fear in his heart like this woman. "Who is that woman?" Loki pleaded as she was about to open the closet.

"You were led to believe that she is my Wicked Stepmother," Snow White said.

"And the truth is?"

The closet was already shaking. Snow White was using her magic.

"The character known as the Wicked Stepmother wasn't my stepmother," Snow White said and pushed the door open to another dimension. "She was my m—"

22

Angel & Carmilla

"—ooooooom." Snow White screamed, falling from the sky.

Loki's heart darted up into his throat. He flung his hands out, trying to hold onto anything that might slow their sudden decent. He knew that the closet was some kind of portal that would lead them to a new time and place, but he didn't expect to be falling from the sky when she opened it. He tried to grasp at the branches but leaves tore off in his grip as he hurled to the ground. His weight caused his body to sink deep in the snow. Stretching his neck out so he could breathe, he sucked the cold air into his lungs.

"I'd rather fall in love than fall like that," he mumbled, sitting up straight. As soon as the words left his mouth, Snow White landed in his lap, knocking him down, flat on his back again. Their arms and legs tangled, and Loki coughed strings of her hair out of his mouth.

"Does it have to be hair in my mouth?" he complained, trying to wriggle free from under her. "Lips would be just fine."

"Ouch!" Snow white whined, laying on top of him and staring at his face. "Couldn't you just move? This isn't the closet anymore, you know."

"Sorry I didn't bring my parachute, Miss I-control-my-dreams," Loki said, leaning up on one elbow while she regained her breath from the fall. "Actually, you're the one who should move; I'd like to breathe if you don't mind," his forehead banged into hers accidentally. Their cold noses touched slightly, infusing an electric feeling into his body. His lips felt dry so he licked them spontaneously.

"Not in your wildest dreams," Snow White banged his head with her forehead, knocking him back. Loki saw the blue sky behind the tree branches of yellow and brown leaves over Snow White's shoulder. It was autumn wherever she had teleported them.

"Oh. Come on," Loki said. She had a strong forehead, and he wondered if it represented her stubbornness. "As if I really want to kiss a vampire in a dream; I was just trying to stand up and lick my dry lips."

Snow White snarled at him, showing off her fangs. It was a much friendlier way than when she did it in the castle, the way friends *growl* at their annoying friends. She was just messing with him.

"I'm only scared of frogs," Loki wanted to stick out his brave tongue but he worried it was going to get frost bitten in the cold.

Snow White laughed, puffing cold vapor onto his eyes. "Too bad I didn't take pictures of you in the waking world," she teased him. "You were as scared as a little puppy, holding your stake in your trembling hand as if it were your magic wand. I could've posted those pictures on the internet."

Loki imitated her laugh, mocking her like a mirror, mirror on the wall.

"Besides, I had no choice but to fall on you," Snow White stood up, hands on her waist.

"Oh, really, why then do I have the feeling you did it on purpose? Are you trying to take advantage of a lonesome boy in a dream? "

"You have no idea how many boys in my father's kingdom dreamed of marrying me."

"Did you seriously just say that?"

"If you can't stand me, then why are you even here? Why haven't you killed me yet?" Snow White said. "You're dying to know about me so don't make fun of me. I'm not like any other girl you ever met. You do like me whether you want to admit it or not!"

"I should've just killed you," he said as he wiped the snow off his clothes.

"So why didn't you?" she stood on her tiptoes so she could meet him eye to eye, clenching her fists.

Loki had to admit she was a much better version of the Snow White in the fairy tale. This one was kind of kickass. He liked that, even if she was a bit bratty sometimes.

"Why do you care so much about me then? Huh?" she said.

"You were the one who asked me to save you," Loki tilted his neck since she was unapologetically pushing hers forward. One more exchange between the two of them and he imagined she'd be sticking her forefinger up his nose.

"So what?" she squinted. "Why don't you just go to the nearest closet and leave me alone? I will make sure you'll wake up in the Ordinary World again, the same pathetic, aimless boy who's always wishing he could go back to Fairy Heaven."

"How do you know so much about me?" Loki swallowed hard, wanting her to back off since he couldn't really resist her red juicy lips.

"I just know," Snow White waved her hand in the air.

"Look," Loki said. "I think we started off on the wrong foot here. Let's start all over again like nothing ever happened," he stretched out is hand for her to shake. "Hi. I'm Loki Blackstar—"

"—and I'm here to kick your ass!" Snow White interrupted.

"Really, how do you know all this about me?" he was impressed. Never had someone treated him with plain honesty.

"You're too easy to read, Loki," she walked away. "You just think you're not."

"Wait," he said, and turned around. He walked to her and placed his hands on her shoulders. "Listen. I will take care of you," he managed to say, the words heavy on his heart. "I've never said that to anyone, but I promise you that I will."

Snow White's eyes glittered, although she knew that it was him who needed her to protect him in the Dreamworld, not the other way around.

"Forever?" she asked sheepishly.

"Hell no," he brushed her nose with his hand. "Just until this dream is over."

"I'm fine with that," she smiled, satisfied. "Now, follow me before you get stuck in this dream… *forever*," she said and walked toward what looked like an 18th century school.

"Did you see that awesome look she gave you?" Loki talked to himself behind her back, following her to the school's main entrance. "Eat eggs, Prince Charming. She likes me better," Loki was about to jump in the air and click his heels together like a happy harlequin, but refrained from the embarrassment of her catching him.

"Hurry up," Snow White said.

The front iron-door of the school burst open. A horde of young boys and girls stormed out. One of them walked right through Loki as if he were invisible.

"So no one can see me in the Dreamory, right?" Loki asked.

"I'm the only one who can see you because it's my dream," Snow White said, looking for someone in the crowd. "But don't push your luck. The longer you stay in a dream, the more your presence could manifest and people will be able see you, talk to you, and also kill you."

"What do you mean by my presence manifesting itself?"

"If you get involved in something that can't be avoided, you will become visible and will have to deal with the consequences of messing with the Dreamworld. That's why you shouldn't stay too long in people's dreams."

"Get involved in something like what?"

"Like screaming or making too much noise, anything that will attract attention to you. We're like ghosts to them in the Dreamworld. Sometimes ghosts do something and get exposed."

"That's interesting," Loki rubbed his chin. He still had a lot to learn about the Dreamworld.

"Look!" she pointed at a young boy with long, curly, black hair; a handsome and strong nineteen year old. "It's my father," she said with a panting voice. "Angel Night von Sorrow."

"So this dream is before you were even born?"

"Yes. Come on," she followed Angel as he walked into an alley after saying goodbye to his friends. A black raven tailed him into the ally, fluttering above his head. "If the things around you change shapes and forms a lot, don't panic," Snow White explained. "I am trying to show you about ten years in a few minutes of dreamtime," she hurried into the alley after Angel.

"How can you dream of something you haven't experienced?" Loki asked.

"Think of it as time traveling. The Dreamworld is complicated," Snow White said, stopping cautiously as Angel slowed down in the alley.

Angel was standing alone in front of piles of garbage. He was watching a big rat, looking for food. In a flash, Angel caught the rat with his bare hands and sunk his fangs into it. He inhaled its blood into his veins as the yellowish autumn leaves fluttered in a gust of wind, circling around him.

"So your daddy king was a vampire?" Loki said. "How come he will wage a war against vampires later?"

"Nobody knew he was a vampire then," Snow White said. "You see that wind around him. It's protecting him, covering up his secrets."

"What secrets?"

"It's the 18th century," Snow White explained, "Vampires weren't as strong as they are today. They were outcasts, and they were hunted and slaughtered all over Europe. Historians call this time 'the Vampire Craze.'"

"I know about that," Loki remembered his talk with Axel in the Bedtime Stoories library.

"Sometimes, when people got sick or caught a contagious disease that forced them to cough blood, they were thought of as vampires. They were hanged, burned, and cremated. Sometimes, they were staked in the heart and buried six feet under. Whole villages were burned in Europe during the Vampire Craze. Just like witches had been hunted in Europe in the sixteenth century. Thousands of witches were burned here in Lohr; and vampires were the next to be hunted."

"What did you say? Lore?" Loki wondered.

"Lohr, with an 'h'. It's where we are now, a small town in Germany where my ancestors lived for years. My father, Angel Night von Sorrow, was born in this town. It's in Bavaria, Germany. There's even a castle here called the Schloss, the same as the castle in Sorrow. My father later built a replica as an epitaph to his hometown."

"So is the word 'lore' as in 'vampire lore' taken from the city of 'Lohr.'?"

"I have no idea. You should visit Lohr when you leave this dream. It looks like it has been cut from the fabric of fairy tales. It's where my family originated."

The colors in the world around Loki changed gradually. The wind that was protecting her father whirled and spiraled in the sky like mad paintbrushes spattering different kinds of colors into the air.

"What's going on?" Loki asked.

"Hold on," she said, pressing her fingers against her forehead like psychics sometimes do. "I'm trying to show you other things while we stand right here. The colors painted a graveyard around them. Everything that the wind painted turned into flesh, blood, stones, and it was all in 4-D. It was so real that Loki couldn't believe it was a dream, as if they were living inside an animated portrait that changed its scene on its own.

In the middle of the graveyard, Loki saw Angel talking to a man in a black cloak.

"That's my grandfather, Night Sorrow," Snow White narrated like a voiceover in a movie scene. "He was the most vicious vampire king in Transylvania, a direct descendant of the very first vampires in the world."

"Did you say the very first vampires?"

"Yes, and don't ask me who they were because I don't know. Night Sorrow, my grandfather, fled to Lohr from Transylvania after the peasants burned his castle when they discovered his true evil nature. Night Sorrow isn't his real name. It's said that the name was inspired from the fact that he brought 'sorrow' to the 'night' when he fed mercilessly on humans in Transylvania."

"Quite a resume you have here.

Snow White continued her story. "Once Night Sorrow settled in Lohr, he was ordered by the mother of vampires to create a secret vampire clan that would be strong enough to stand up against the vampire hunters who were chasing them all over Europe. She wanted to create a kingdom and rule all of Europe.

It was the only way for vampires to come out of the dark and declare the right to live among humans," Snow White said. "Night sent his son, Angel, my father, to a regular school attended by other peasants in Lohr, disguising him as a human. He wanted Angel to mingle with humans and study their lives so he could learn their weaknesses."

"I thought vampires were so powerful such maneuvers weren't needed," Loki said.

"Not during that time of history," Snow White Said. "They were weaker and they were few. They were hated and hunted everywhere. In order for my father to mingle among humans in Lohr, the mother of vampires delayed Angel's transformation into a full vampire until the age of sixteen."

"Didn't his human friends ask about Angel's family?" Loki wondered.

"My father was granted two human slaves—those who were bitten by vampires but not fully turned—to assume the role of his parents. The vampire slaves did anything they were asked to because they were neither humans nor vampires, and they needed the vampires to feed on them or they would die. They were two women, pretending to be my father's mother and aunt, claiming Angel's father had died. Their names were Jeanette and Amalie Hassenpflug."

"Why do these names sound familiar?"

210

"Because the Brothers Grimm collected the Snow White story from them; it's written in history books," she said.

"Are you saying they lied to the Brothers Grimm?"

"Or the Brothers Grimm lied to the world."

Loki saw Angel sink to his knees, begging his father for something. His father's eyes turned red with anger.

"What's going on there?" Loki said.

"Angel is asking Night to spare him from feeding on human blood to complete his transformation. As you have seen, my father only fed on animals. He was about to turn sixteen. His spying mission was about to end, and it was time that he transformed into a real vampire which he didn't want to do anymore. Raised with humans, my father was torn between two worlds. He resisted becoming a full vampire against his father's wishes. Are you ready for the next shift?"

Before Loki could say anything, the wind snaked around him. Like a sponge erasing the writing off a chalkboard, it erased the trees and the sky over the graveyard, and started drawing a new life and space in front of them.

They were transported to a beautiful summer day and stood in a vast garden with a fountain in the middle.

"Where are we now?" Loki asked.

"In Styria, under the reign of Francis II, the Emperor of Austria," Snow White replied. "It's late in the 18th century."

Loki saw a beautiful young girl running in the colorful garden under a blistering sun with her pink dress fluttering over the lilies. Loki had thought Styria was always cold and snowy but he couldn't argue with dreams.

"Who is she?" Loki said. He liked how Snow White looked, but this girl was as beautiful and lovely as she was, if not a notch lovelier. She had curly blond hair, sea blue eyes, and a smile that sucked in the air and made the lilies she ran through giggle.

Snow White didn't comment for a while, watching the girl in the lilies with caring eyes. Her eyes followed her every move, every laugh, and every breath.

"That's my mother, you're looking at," Snow White finally talked. "Her name is Carmilla Karnstein."

Angel rose like a sneaky cat from between the lilies, hugging Carmilla and kissing her from behind. He kissed her on the neck once before she slid playfully away from him, and he had to chase her all over again.

"My father was sent to Styria on a school trip," she continued. "Night Sorrow had sent him to spy on Carmilla's father in the House of Karnstein, a wealthy family known for hunting vampires. It wasn't known to the public yet that the Sorrows and the Karnsteins had one of the biggest family feuds in history. One family was vampires, the other, vampire hunters."

"So Night Sorrow and Carmilla's father were as different as night and day?" Loki said. "And your father just fell in love with the Karnstein's daughter? Nice move, Angel." Neither Carmilla nor Angel could see them, although Snow White and Loki were standing in the middle of the field of lilies.

"She was worth it," Snow White said, her eyes a bit watery, staring at her parents.

Loki was still watching. Carmilla lay in Angel's arms on the bed of lilies while he stroked her hair gently. She looked ecstatically happy while a butterfly rested on her palm. Angel, although son of one of the darkest vampires in the world, didn't look like a vampire at all, except for his almost inhuman beauty and strength. He waited until Carmilla slept and gathered a bed of purple and yellow lilies and laid her upon it, then sat watching.

Carmilla was as pure and innocent as a fairy tale princess; Angel was as tortured and beautiful as vampires depicted in novels, a perfect portrait of a beauty and a beast.

"So when was he going to tell her he was a vampire?" Loki asked.

"He already had," Snow White said. "She admired his courage, and that he wanted to be a good person in spite of the evil nature his father wanted to pass on to him."

Loki watched Carmilla waking up to Angel's kiss. She whispered something in his ear, and his face lit up as if he were an *angel*.

"What did she say to him?" Loki said.

"Why are you so curious?" Snow White wondered.

"Seriously," Loki's face knotted like an impatient child.

"What did she tell him that made him so happy? I want to know."

"Angel always saw himself as a beast," Snow White explained. "My mother told him he was a beauty to her, but that wasn't what lit up his eyes like you just saw. It was when she told him that she loved him and that she would stay with him until death do them part."

"Wasn't Angel immortal like other vampires?" Loki said, unable to take his eyes off the couple. He didn't know what it was that attracted him to them, but he thought he would have loved it if he could have seen his own parents like that within a Dreamory of his.

"Angel wasn't immortal yet because his transformation as a vampire wasn't complete," Snow White said. "He chose mortality as long as he was in my mother's arms."

"And what happened next?" Loki asked as if she were telling him an amazing bedtime story.

"Carmilla told her father about Angel. Surprisingly, he welcomed him to be with his daughter, believing Angel would be of great help to the Karnsteins in defeating the vampires—which also meant Angel had to go against his own tribe."

"So Angel stayed in Styria?"

"He wanted to, but had to save his half-human parents, Janette and Amalie, who'd raised him in the human world. He was afraid Night Sorrow would hurt them if he didn't go back," she explained. "Angel returned to Lohr and managed to help them escape, but Night caught him, aware of his son's plan to turn against the Sorrows. Night Sorrow imprisoned Angel in a towering castle called the Cachtice, and offered him all kinds of human blood to complete his transformation. He'd regretted postponing his son's transformation since it made him more human than vampire."

"Just keep going," Loki said. "Don't stop."

"My father fought the temptation and managed to escape the castle. Because he had no allies in Lohr and hadn't acquired the full powers of a vampire yet, he had to escape on foot through the forests, crossing from Transylvania through Hungary, in mid-winter, risking freezing to death, to return to Carmilla in Styria. When Night learned his son had escaped, he unleashed vampire bats and black panthers after him. Night, like his name, was fond of everything black. I heard one of his powers was being able to control almost every black animal."

"What kind of a father does this to his own son?" Loki wondered.

"He wasn't an ordinary father, he was one of the cruelest vampires known to mankind, but that wasn't all. There was another reason why he wanted Angel dead, but I will get into that in a while," she said. "Eventually, my father fed on the black animals Night had sent after him. It's still a mystery how he killed them, but feeding on the vampire bats and animals increased Angel's inherited vampire powers dramatically, although it didn't formally transform him. Night sent members of his vampire army after him. In their hunt for my father, they were looking for *black* animals, dead and bitten, in the *white* snow with *red* trails of blood," Snow White turned to face Loki. "This is how the three doomed colors came into my family's life. Remember the phrase, 'lips red as blood, skin white as snow, and hair black a…'"

"As night? As ravens? As Night Sorrow?"

"See it the way you like, but remember how the colors came into my family's life," Snow White said. "Night Sorrow spread rumors about Angel being the sadist vampire the locals were searching for, that he was the one responsible for spreading the fatal disease everyone feared in Europe. The description of my father spread all over Europe; people imagined that he could be Snow White, Red as Blood, or Black as Night. Angel was hunted by everyone. They called him names like: Black Sorrow, Snow Death, and Red Dragon. You know that the origin of the name Dracula was 'Dracul,' which means 'son of dragon', or is even sometimes interpreted as devil, right? So Red Dragon meant red vampire. My father had become this 'Red Dragon' vampire in the eyes of the world."

Loki still wondered how everyone else knew more about vampires than he did. Sometimes, he doubted he was the greatest Dreamhunter in the world.

"Angel finally reached Carmilla in Styria. They set a date with her father for a royal wedding, inviting the kingdom's noblemen to celebrate," Snow White continued.

"What happened to his vampire-slave parents?"

"Jeanette and Amalie did escape but never made it to Angel's wedding. They sent him letters from different towns across Europe throughout the years, telling him they were alright.

"Sounds like a happy ending for Angel and Carmilla so far," Loki said, still wondering what all this had to do with Snow White.

"Not really," Snow White said as the wind started to redraw their surroundings again.

"Not again," Loki huffed. "This is like 'around the world in eighty days', except it happens in one dream."

Snow White's dress fluttered in the wind. "The news of the wedding frustrated the noblemen of Styria," she raised her voice, using her hands as a feeble shield against the whirling wind. "My mother was young, beautiful, and desired by many of them. They despised her getting married to a stranger from a town plagued by the vampire disease."

"Where are we going now?" Loki said, unable to hear his own voice. To his surprise the words she spoke to him turned into smoky, readable letters, waving upon the surface of the dancing wind that whirled before his eyes. The words read:

Something unexpected happened the night before the wedding.

"Another dark and stormy night," Loki said as they were transported to what looked like a cottage in the middle of a forest.

Loki saw Carmilla holding Angel in her arms, heated waves dancing like curly guardian ghosts from a fireplace behind them.

"My craving is growing stronger," Angel whispered to Carmilla, wrapping his arms around her waist. Loki saw the veins on Angel's arms and neck throbbing. "The blood of animals isn't quenching my thirst," Angel told her.

Carmilla, with her hands tangled up in his curly long hair, pulled him closer, not knowing what to say. She pulled his chin up and kissed him, trying to help him deal with his pain. Next to Loki, Snow White fought a trail of tears seeping from her eyes. Loki wanted to hold her close in his arms—he had wanted to do that for a long time—but he was afraid she'd snap at him or burst into tears. He didn't want to stir emotions that would cause his presence to be manifested in the Dreamworld. He couldn't risk being seen.

As they were kissing, Angel smoothly moved his lips toward Carmilla's neck, and drew out his fangs.

Angel raised his head up a little, preparing for the bloody dive into Carmilla's neck.

Although this was a memory, Snow White couldn't help but shriek. Loki saw the air ripple slightly as if it was a pool of water. Carmilla's eyes were diverted momentarily as if she'd heard them. Even Angel seemed to have felt their presence. Gladly, they didn't see them. Loki understood now how easily they could be exposed.

Then the colors in Angel's eyes turned normal. He stopped himself from feeding on her, although his pain was excruciating.

"Love conquers all…" Loki said. "I mean fangs," he mumbled to himself, making sure his voice was very faint so he didn't manifest his presence.

"Why didn't you bite me?" Carmilla asked Angel. "I want to be with you forever."

Carmilla held Angel's head between her hands, and this time, he lost control. His fangs drew out again, still reluctant to feed on Carmilla, even though she'd given him permission.

"He tried his best," Snow White said. "He knew their lives would be hell after this moment."

As Angel struggled to hold back, he accidentally pricked Carmilla's finger with his sharp teeth. The image instantly reminded Loki of when the mother pricked her finger in the Snow White tale by the Brothers Grimm, except this wasn't a needle, it was Angel's fangs.

The image of her drop of blood froze the air around them. Angel stared at the human blood with blackened, demonic eyes, appalled and yet longing for it. He had never tasted human blood before that moment. It was his lover's blood, which smelled better to him than anything in the world.

Carmilla nodded with approval. "Maybe if you only take two or three drops of blood at a time, you won't fully turn into a vampire. If you manage to only take a drop or two from me every day, I believe there'll still be enough goodness in you to fight your dark side."

"Are you sure?" Angel said.

"I would do anything for you, my love," Carmilla said, and pulled his head nearer to her finger. Angel sucked the little drops of blood as if his life depended on it—which was actually true.

"My mother made a deal with my father; that she would give him two or three drops every two days for the rest of her life and he accepted it in exchange to stay a good man, and not feed on humans," Snow White said.

"She wasn't just sacrificing her youth," Loki commented. "She was practically saving the world from the potential darkness of the son of the most vicious vampire in the world."

"It was a turning point in Angel's life," Snow White said. "It helped him control his craving, and stopped him from fully turning into a vampire. The best thing about this moment was that their love grew stronger as they were bound to need each other."

"What about Carmilla?" Loki wondered. "Didn't this affect her health and beauty?"

"On the contrary," Snow white said. "Carmilla grew more beautiful and healthier. When Angel drew blood from her, his saliva healed her and kept her young. It was like magic."

Loki wanted to say that this was pretty damn gross, but he decided to stop talking and be polite for once.

"Unfortunately, her father knew about this deal on their wedding day. He didn't take it lightly and called off the wedding. Carmilla had to leave the land with Angel, against her father's wishes."

"Sacrificing her family to be with Angel," Loki bemused.

"It was a moment when they chose their own destiny and went against everyone's wishes. They were cursed by everyone, hunted by everyone for different reasons, trusting in only their love for each other," Snow White said. "Everyone in Europe was looking for them. They embarked upon a Spanish ship, sailing across the ocean, looking for a new start, away from Europe."

"Wind, please?" Loki said, looking up at the sky. He knew that this must be the right time for them to be delivered to the ocean to see the ship.

"How many times do I have to remind you that this is *my* dream?" Snow White grinned. "Only I call for the Wind of Change."

"Princess," Loki said, bowing like an 18th century nobleman—he struggled with where to place his legs in that position, but he improvised. "Would you please deliver us to the ocean?"

Snow White omitted a smile. "Come here," she signaled for him with her forefinger. Loki accepted her calling. "You don't want to find yourself smashing against the ship's deck when we fall, do you?" she wrapped her arm around his neck. "Wind," she summoned.

The wind circled around them, ready to transport them to the next scene.

"I just remembered something that happened in the closet," Loki put a finger on his chin as if thinking then raised his head a little. "In my first closet, there was a young girl with me, and, if my memory serves me right,

216

she kissed me," Loki lowered his head again, looking her in the eyes. "That was you, right?"

"Shut up," she shouted against the wind. "I kissed you as a kid. It was just a peck on the cheek."

"You like me," Loki winked.

Instead of getting a response from her, Loki got splashed with ocean water on his face.

"Hang tight," she said, pulling his hands over her waist. They were standing on the deck of a pirate ship, struggling against the tides of the ocean.

23

A Kingdom of Sorrow

"Why are we on a pirate's ship?" Loki managed to say, spitting salty water out of his mouth.

A black flag fluttered above his head as the ship swayed against the waves of an angry ocean. A white skull, crisscrossed with bones, was drawn on the flag.

"So clichéd," Loki commented.

"I'm what you call a fairy tale princess," Snow White said. "Cliché is almost my middle name."

Loki read the name engraving on the inner wood of the ship; "Jolly Roger?"

"Don't bother with too many details," Snow White said, all wet and shivering, eyes closed, and spitting out water. Her wet hair was sticking flat to her face. "Just focus on what I want to show you."

All around them, the pirates were loading cannons, speaking a language Loki didn't understand. The ocean got angrier and coughed up more salty water onto Loki's face.

"I love you, too," Loki said back to the ocean, watching lines of clear water rolling down Snow White's face. She was shivering.

Hanging tight onto a pole with one hand, Loki took off his jacket, and put it over her shoulders, pulling it tight around her. His legs stood fixed on the ground, rebelling against the swaying ship.

"Thank you," she nodded, and blushed as if no one had treated her with care for some time.

"Don't you dare lose it," Loki said, trying to escape the drama. "It's my father's. He gave it to me the last time we were sailing with my uncle Jack Sparrow in the same awful weather, looking for a patch-eyed mermaid."

Snow White looked at him with blurry but smiling eyes. "You're horrible!" she yelled.

"And you love it!" Loki's hands were about to lose grip on the pole they clung to.

Snow White rolled her eyes, and then sneezed in his face unintentionally.

"Can't say I feel sneezed at," Loki said, wiping his face with one hand. "I can't tell the difference between you sneezing and the spewing sea."

"I have never met anyone with a twisted sense of humor like yours," she said.

"Isn't that what close friends are about? Accepting each other's awful personalities?" Loki accidentally spit water onto her face. "And sometimes, each other's—"

"Spit, I get it," she said, soaked to the bone.

"The weather is so beautiful," Loki said all of a sudden.

"Where did that come from," she wondered.

"I always thought it was the worst pick up line, but in this weather, it really is amusing," Loki said. "I could also ask, 'if you come here often'," Loki laughed. "How do you like me now that I am trying to make normal, conversation?" he said as a bomb fell right behind Snow White. There was a pirate war going on here.

"If I die in my own dream I will never wake up again."

Snow White commented, a little tense because of the explosions.

"I know," Loki said, water trickling down his nose. "That was the whole point of me entering your dream, to kill you once and for all."

Both of their eyes met again. The raging war didn't stop them from clearly gazing into each other's souls. It was a long stare, a wondrous one. Loki couldn't believe that this was the vampire princess he'd come to kill two days ago. Demon or victim, Loki knew that he wasn't going to be able to kill her. Not after this dream. Not ever. It wasn't because she was a stronger demon, but because he couldn't kill someone he liked. If she had really tricked him, then she played it well.

"Who are you really, Miss Snow White?" Loki asked, actually longing for an answer.

"The real question is who are you, Loki Blackstar?"

Loki let out a big laugh, one that came from the heart. He certainly liked her in the Dreamworld better than the waking world.

"What are you laughing at?" she wondered.

"In all this mess around us, the world could end tomorrow, and I couldn't care less," he replied.

"Why?"

"Because somehow the only thing I care about right now is this moment with...you," Loki said, and this time it wasn't hard to confess it.

Not sure if she wanted to know the answer, Snow White cautiously asked "even if it's only a dream?"

"I think the worst part about this awfully big adventure is that it's only a dream," Loki said, aware that he'd previously declined wanting to be with her forever.

"So back to work, tell me what's going on? Where are your parents?"

Snow White pointed at another ship in the ocean, the one the pirates were shooting at with the intention of hijacking. "There! That's my mother and father. They're going to get hijacked by pirates as you can see. The pirates will kill everyone on board, but my parents will escape."

Loki watched the pirates shoot passengers ruthlessly on the other ship, stealing from it and sending the stolen items on smaller boats back to their ship.

Loki saw Carmilla and Angel's ship sink. Minutes later, he saw Angel lifting Carmilla onto his back like an infant onto its daddy's shoulders. Angel swam relentlessly like a shark that knew the ocean well. Carmilla wrapped her body around his body, almost choking him, but he didn't complain. Loki was starting to like Angel immensely—

"Angel was getting very strong," Snow White said. "The blood of ravens, the blood of animals, and specially my mother's blood helped him discover the strength of vampires in him, even without fully becoming one."

"You're not trying to tell me that he'll swim all the way to the shore from here,   with your mom on his back?"

"Seven days," Snow White showed Loki seven proud fingers, risking her own fall from the pole. "His powers grew scary-cool," she added. "He was strong enough to keep swimming. He never slept. He could even breathe underwater for a long time. Whenever he found a log in the ocean he would leave my mom on it for minutes as he went hunting fish for her to eat."

Loki wanted to tell her that he didn't quite believe this part. Vampire or not, he couldn't imagine someone with that kind of heroism and strength. But he didn't, because she came from a fairy tale world—that she claimed was real—and characters with the heroic powers like Angel's filled every fairy tale ever told.

"I assume we're not going to be able to see this heroic act," Loki speculated.

"No one's stopping you from jumping into the ocean," Snow White smirked.

"Nah," Loki squeezed water out of his t-shirt with his bare hands. "I didn't bring my swimsuit along."

Snow White leaned forward, while showing a curious look on her face. "May I ask if it was a one-piece or two piece swimming suit?"

"Ha, ha," Loki said, literally. He placed his palm onto her face gently and then playfully pushed her away. "Now, call your genie-in-a-bottle to sweep us away after your parents. I really want to know what happens next."

Snow White clapped her hands. Although she was soaking in salt water, looking like a homeless person, she still clapped in a majestic way. "Your wish is my command," she said playfully.

"I think she's just awesome when she doesn't have her fangs out," Loki talked to the night sky above.

This time, they were back in the 19th century Schloss, standing in Snow White's room, which was full of mirrors.

Loki fell back on her enormous bed; it was soft and comfy. He saw drawings on the ceiling, full of doves, ravens, owls, and apples.

"You're not here to take a nap," Snow White said. "That's my bed, and you didn't ask permission."

"It's your bed, your castle, and your dream. I believe we've been over that, my princess," Loki sat up, resting his elbows on the cushiony bed. He had a big smile on his face. "Speaking of naps, how long is this dream. I thought it was only supposed to last around forty two minutes?"

"Time is different between the Dreamworld and the waking world," she said. "I don't know how, but when the dream is about to end, the crows will start to gather—"

"And then the world will fall apart," Loki nodded. "I know."

She sat next to Loki on the bed, a bit too close for a boy who was afraid of demon girls up until less than half an hour ago. "What?" she narrowed her eyes, "never been with a girl alone in her room?"

"Room, yes. Bed's a bit different," Loki said, averting his eyes from her.

She said nothing, trying her best not to laugh at how polite he was trying to be.

"And also not when the girl's father is the King of Sorrow," Loki added.

Snow White moved even closer. He couldn't stop looking at her lips, red as blood. Whoever had written this about her forgot to say: lips as hot as chilies.

"Tell me," Loki said, literally pushing her away a little. "So Angel swims all the way to the shore, finds an island, and makes it his Kingdom of Sorrow. What happens next?"

"They found land after being lost in the ocean for seven days. They decided to build their own kingdom there. Years went by, and the kingdom became one of the greatest in the world."

"So far so good," Loki said. "Your parents escaped their pursuers and started a new life as king and queen."

"That was the case until Night von Sorrow found the kingdom," Snow White said.

"What?"

"Like I said, Night wasn't going to give up hunting them. My father gathered and trained an army of young and strong huntsmen and soldiers to protect the borders. It was a very special army," she explained. "And although the kingdom was safe, my father paid the price of having to fight Night's vampire army at the border forever. Each day he fought them, and people died to keep the Kingdom of Sorrow safe."

"What about your mother?"

"My father prevented her from getting involved. She was ruling the kingdom in his absence, which was enough of a burden already. Maybe he also wanted to keep her safe because he needed her blood—I'm not sure, but every two to three days, he had to travel back to her to get his drops of blood."

"Ah. I forgot about that. She was his most important source of power against the vampires."

"Exactly," she said. "So my mother, being the Queen of the Kingdom of Sorrow, was lonely and stressed most of the time. Although she was still young, she wanted to have a child to fill the void and the absence of my father."

"She begged my father repeatedly to have me, but he denied her wish at the time."

"Why?"

"He said that he needed to win the war with vampires first, that he couldn't risk what could happen to her or the baby if he lost the war."

"And what was your mother's reaction to that?" Loki asked.

"There was nothing she could do, but her lonely life and the responsibilities of the kingdom were suffocating her, and she started killing time by practicing witchcraft."

"That's an odd thing to do."

"She'd toyed with witchcraft long before that, never for evil purposes, though. She learned how to cast protecting spells on the kingdom's borders to prevent the avenging vampires from entering when she first built the kingdom with my father. Still, she always felt lonely, and she pleaded with my father repeatedly to have a child. Eventually, my father granted her wish."

"So did she really wish you'd have lips red as blood, skin pale as snow, and hair black as a window frame just as its told in the Grimm Brothers fairy tale?"

"Yes, and she had her reasons. On the night my parents decided they wanted to bring me into this world, Carmilla used a spell she'd learned, wishing for me to look like my father in every way. She loved him dearly, and she wanted me to grow to be a stronger woman than her. She hadn't seen anyone as strong as Angel in her life, and she thought if I looked as beautiful as my father, I'd be as powerful and determined as him."

"I understand totally," Loki said. "A man who can cross the ocean with his lover on his back is no ordinary man. So tell me about that spell."

"Looking like my father meant that I'd inherit the features he'd been described as having when he escaped from Transylvania to meet her in Styria. Remember the descriptions he was famous for, the ravens and everything black Night had sent after him?"

Loki nodded.

"The ravens and panthers he'd fed upon were black, the trails of blood were red, and the snow he struggled through was white," she elaborated. "In my mother's attempt to honor my father's courage, she cast a spell that would grant her a daughter with lips red as the blood of the ravens he fed on, skin as white as the snow he walked on, and hair as black as the long nights she had to wait through for his return."

"That explains it," Loki said, looking at her tenderly. "Now, prepare yourself for a horrifying sequence of

events. What you're going to witness now is very important."

Loki heard a rumble outside the room. He thought it was the sound of horses, which was illogical.

"Are you ready for the next ride?" Snow White walked to the closed door and gripped the doorknob.

"No Wind of Change this time?" Loki followed her as she opened the door.

"No," she said, and opened the door, snowflakes entering the room. This time, the door didn't lead to a hallway, but to a cold forest where snow was falling late at night.

"I wish I had that kind of shortcut from my Cadillac's door to the bathroom," Loki said, stepping out into the Black Forest.

The night outside was black, white, and blue, with golden glittering stars up in the sky. There were red glinting eyes flickering in the dark beyond the thick trees. Loki saw a calash, pulled by two unicorns, racing through the night. It was driven by Angel, whipping at the unicorns and demanding speed.

Loki and Snow White stepped outside where the calash was approaching. One of the unicorns tripped on a fallen tree branch and twisted its legs, disrupting the balance. The calash came crashing down on its side. Angel took flight into the night sky just like a loose cannon and landed on his feet in the snow. The man's strength was unimaginable. One of the unicorns stood up then ran away into the night, fearing the red eyes.

Angel headed back to the calash, calling out for Carmilla. He opened the door and she fell out into his arms as he knelt in the snow.

"That's how I was born, in the Black Forest," Snow White explained. "See how beautiful my mother looked although she was about to give birth?"

She was right about Carmilla. Her beauty was ageless. No amount of surgeries or health tips could have produced such a natural beauty—Loki couldn't help but think it was enhanced by Angel's vampire saliva.

Angel begged Carmilla to stay strong. He told her that another calash full of servants should be bright behind them, and that they should wait for it. Carmilla was breathing rapidly. It showed that she was going to bring her daughter into the world, no matter what, even if the price was her life.

The red eyes in the dark got bigger and closer, accompanied by the sound of heavy breathing and growling. A slant of moonlight exposed their forms as they approached. They were black panthers, probably sent by

Night Sorrow.

The panthers approached Angel and Carmilla, showing their wickedly sharp teeth with saliva drooling from their mouths. Angel, suddenly aware that the servant's calash was doomed, stared back at the panthers with slit eyes, holding Carmilla in his arms while on his knees.

"The panthers didn't scare Angel," Snow White said. "He knew they were sent by his father, and he had killed them before and was going to kill them again. He was only worried for my mother's safety."

Loki saw Angel growling in a low drone, disturbing the steady flow of snowflakes hanging in the air. Then he snarled back at them in a way that scared Loki. The darkness that Angel had inherited from his ancestors surfaced, but he used it to protect his family—Loki remembered when Charmwill had told him about the darkness he'd possessed inside him, too.

Angel was fighting fire with fire, and he'd become so strong that he was able to kill many of them.

"I need your father to teach me how to be badass," Loki said.

Snow White turned and looked at him when he said that. It was an undecipherable look, again, as if she wanted to tell him something but couldn't.

Why is she looking at me like that? Do I have something in common with her father?

"What?" Loki hated when she looked at him like that. "Nothing," she said, and Loki was sure she was lying, but he still trusted her nonetheless. Maybe she wasn't allowed to tell him what she wanted to. "Wait until you see what the remaining panthers did after he killed more than half of them."

While Angel killed most of them, Carmilla gave birth to their daughter.

As the infant girl's cries filled the air, the panthers sniffed the air and let out a soft moan. It made them look like pets more than panthers now— Loki saw that their bellies were striped white; with their red eyes and black skin, they still represented the three colors.

The panthers crouched and lay down onto the snow with stretched paws and chins touching the ground like obedient pets. They reminded Loki of the Egyptian Sphinx as they were bowing obediently in front of the new born pale princess.

"What's happening?" Loki asked. "How come they're suddenly welcoming you?"

"They aren't welcoming me, Loki," Snow White said. "They're *afraid* of me," she didn't seem happy about such an incredible power, though.

"Afraid of you?" Loki said. "But they were just chasing the calash wanting to kill you moments ago."

"That was before I was born," Snow White raised her head, and Loki worried she'd turn into a ruthless vampire again for a moment. "Now that I was born, my enemies feared me the most."

"I don't understand. Why? What powers do you possess? What makes Night Sorrow's messengers so afraid of you?"

"I'm Snow White von Sorrow, Loki," she said as the Wind of Change arrived and started repainting the forest back into the castle like magic brushes drawing the world. "Why do you think I was imprisoned in the Schloss for a hundred years? Why do you think that killing me is worth ninety-nine vampires? And why do you think the Town Council of Sorrow wants me dead, sending the best Dreamhunter to kill me? It's time for you to know who I really am."

24

The Pale Princess

"Didn't it occur to you why Angel was so important to the vampire clan?" Snow White continued. "Didn't you wonder why they bothered searching the whole world for him, hunting him down, wanting to breach into the Kingdom of Sorrow when all he wanted was to live peacefully away from them?"

Loki thought her questions were sound, but couldn't imagine why.

"Because Angel married my mother, Carmilla, a human, descendant of the very first vampire hunters in the world, the Karnsteins, Sorrow's oldest enemies, which meant that sooner or later he was going to have a child with her..." Snow White hesitated for a second.

"I understand that the Sorrows didn't want a descendant from their enemy's blood," Loki said. "But that doesn't explain why the panthers feared you."

"You don't get it, Loki," Snow White said. "In the vampire world, there is a prophecy that a Sorrow vampire will marry a Karnstein human and have a child with her. That child will be a girl and she will be a Dhampir—"

"A Dhampir." Loki said. "I always thought that Dhampirs were just myths."

"No, it's not a myth, Loki," Snow White said. "A Dhampir is the daughter of a vampire and human. A Dhampir is real and is absolutely prohibited in the vampire world, because the prophecy said that a Dhampir girl will have certain powers that no vampire wants to confront."

"Powers like what?" Loki knew the answer already, but couldn't say it out loud.

"The Dhampir girl will have the power to end the reign of all vampires in the world," Snow White said. "I'm that girl, Loki," she added, almost disappointed.

Loki took a moment to comprehend what she'd just said. It explained why everyone wanted her dead, but it was still hard to fathom. How is a sixteen-year-old supposed to possess this type of unsurpassed power of all vampires?

"Dhampirs, if trained well, are much stronger than any vampire in the

world,

226

world. They're sometimes compared to gods. They have a natural desire for killing vampires. If I learn to control the powers I have in me, I will be able to cause a vampire apocalypse. That's why the Sorrows wanted to kill me and waged wars against my father's kingdom."

"So you're the chosen one?" Loki said, and it wasn't really a question. He just needed to speak the words loud enough to believe them. So many questions filled his head now. He could understand that the vampires wanted the princess dead because she threatened their existence, and that Igor and Lucy's father probably worked for them, summoning him to Sorrow to kill her. But what didn't make sense was why the Council of Heaven thought that killing Snow White equaled ninety nine vampires? Shouldn't the Council of Heaven be on Snow White's side, or was it that they still considered her a vampire, and nothing else mattered to them? The biggest question of all was if Charmwill knew any of the things Snow White had told him, and if so, why didn't he tell him?

"So who imprisoned you in the Schloss? Was it Night Sorrow? Did he finally catch you?"

Snow White tried her best not to tremble. She looked away from Loki's questioning eyes, through the window in her room, overlooking the wonderful meadows and rivers outside. "It wasn't Night Sorrow who imprisoned me in the Schloss," she said with her back to Loki.

"Then who was it?"

"Will you believe me if I tell you?"

"Of course, I will," Loki stood up, wondering why she wouldn't look at him. "What kind of question is that?"

"It was Carmilla," she said, her voice was low as if she were embarrassed.

"What?" Loki stepped forward.

"Carmilla, my mother, trapped me in the Schloss," Snow White said.

Loki tried to touch her shoulders, but she didn't let him. She turned around, her eyes full of tears.

"Why would she do that? I thought she was a great woman, mother, and lover. The sacrifices she made, her love for your father. She fought the world to bring you into it. How could your *mother* end up imprisoning you? I thought the one who wanted to hurt you was the Wicked Stepmother. Did Carmilla die, and your father remarried, maybe?"

"No, my father didn't remarry," Snow White said.

"That's unbelievable," Loki said. "How could she trap you for all these years?"

"Well, in many ways, she wasn't my mother anymore. It's really hard to explain," Snow White said. "Just for the record, the Grimm's wrote the first version of my story in 1812, when I was sixteen. In this version, they mentioned the queen was my mother. This text is available to the world."

"Really?" Loki wondered how Axel missed that part.

"They rewrote most of their tales again in 1857, and they changed her from being my mother to a Wicked Stepmother, claiming they did it to tone down the tale so it'd be suitable for children. They changed it to hide the truth."

"What are you implying?"

"That the awful things she would do to me later would sound less horrifying if you think of her as my stepmother," she buried her face in her hands then turned back to the window, then she used her powers to turn it into a portal seeing into her memories…

In consecutive flashes, Loki saw Angel and Carmilla cuddling their adorable infant, Snow White. When she smiled, wiggling her small feet in the air while on her back, the world of the Sorrows was filled with joy. Angel and Carmilla hugged each other; the servants sent their blessings, the trees outside the house danced and the branches tangled with mirth. Snowflakes decorated the days, and tiny purple-glowing faeries lit up the night.

Later, Carmilla went to look into the mirror, and saw that she had aged quickly. It was if she'd grown ten years older in a day. She touched her face with the tips of her fingers, wondering what happened to her skin; it used to be smooth and baby-like, now there were many wrinkles. Avoiding an inevitable panic attack, and out of wishful thinking, Carmilla tried another mirror, hoping it would show her otherwise.

"Mirrors were made of copper or obsidian stones in those days," Snow White began. "The reflective ones people use nowadays weren't invented yet. After she'd bravely given birth to me; her years turned into sand falling unapologetically through the hourglass of time. I don't know how, but no matter how many mirrors reflected her sudden decay, she couldn't believe it was true and thought it was some kind of a curse bestowed on her. In her denial, Carmilla became addicted to mirrors, sending her messengers over to Europe to buy the latest mirrors invented by the most prestigious scientists. It was an odd thing to do, but it was as if she thought that all these mirrors were wrong, and that there was this one mirror that would show her real beauty. On the other hand, my father hated mirrors, because sometimes they reflected his darker soul when he hadn't fed enough. But he didn't stop Carmilla from buying the most expensive mirrors in the world, even if he knew they weren't going to change a thing about her unexplainable aging," Snow White spoke fast while the images flashed in the window. "My mother started to grow ill and tired, complaining of fatigue and feeling as though her bones were breaking in her body. She fainted repeatedly, became dehydrated frequently, and needed servants to take of her as if she were elderly and not a young and beautiful queen."

Loki saw images of Angel taking care of Carmilla. He sent for doctors from Europe to investigate her illness and hopefully heal her. After trials and errors, the doctors proved to be useless. Only gypsies and fortunetellers could explain Carmilla's dilemma.

"It turned out that giving birth to a Dhampir had sucked the energy and vitality from my mother," Snow White said. "As the chosen one, I was unconsciously feeding on her soul. The situation had been predicted in the prophecy, too. It said:

The chosen one will feed on her mother's beauty and energy until she grows up to become a woman of sixteen years. Only then will her powers blossom, and only then will she be capable of ending the vampire's reign. And then the human mother will die, because only one of the two women can stay alive.'"

"Didn't Angel know about the prophecy?" Loki commented.

"Yes, but since no Dhampir had been born before me, and like you were led to believe, he and all people thought Dhampirs were just a myth," Snow White said. "Angel was torn between wife and daughter, and he was eventually going to face an even greater crises; Carmilla couldn't offer him his dosage of three drops of human blood from her pricked fingers anymore. She grew so weak that it was impossible for her to give away her blood."

"What did he do then?" Loki said.

"There was nothing like Carmilla's blood that could quench his thirst so he spent much time hunting outside the kingdom for animals like before," Snow White said. "He was becoming a blood addict. He started losing his mental sharpness and was stripped of the humanity his soul once bore. He was mostly a vampire after all, and he had to face his true nature. He couldn't feed on his servants or his huntsmen, let alone the locals of his kingdom because he couldn't trust anyone with his secret. How could he explain to his own people that he was a descendant of his own enemy?"

Loki saw flashes of the events before his eyes. He saw Snow White, the child, walking now. The servants, who seemed to be taking care of her instead of her parents, brought Snow White to see Carmilla from time to time. Carmilla looked older, sick in bed, isolated in her Queen's chamber. Her face turned into sheer delight when she saw her daughter, though. They spent little time together due to the physical pain Carmilla was suffering, sacrificing herself for the growth of her daughter.

Then the window shifted to Angel, uncombed, unshaven, looking like half the man he once was. He was sitting in a cave in front of a fire with gypsies and wizards all around, trying to find a cure for his wife—and for himself. He found none. He was holding a crumpled letter in his hand, which he unfolded and read over and over again. It was from his father, Night Sorrow, advising him to let go and complete his transformation and turn his wife as well, surrendering to his destiny.

'Once Sorrow, always Sorrow,' his father had written.

Night allured him with becoming the King of Vampires, but under one condition, he had to kill his daughter. Lastly, Night mentioned that the spells Carmilla had cast on his kingdom preventing vampires from entering were soon to be broken. Angel wadded up the letter and threw it into the dancing arms of the hungry fire.

The window showed Carmilla again, barely standing in front of a large mirror in her room. She let out a cry when she saw her ill image again, and threw a silver candlestick at it, crashing it into pieces.

"When Carmilla understood that no mirror was going to lie to her and reflect a beautiful Queen, she refrained from looking into mirrors anymore. It deepened her sorrow and weakened her faith in me. *Seeing* what was happening to her, made her have some disdain for me, and she couldn't stand feeling that way, so she ordered the mirrors to be taken away from the castle."

"Is that why your room here is full of mirrors?" Loki asked.

"They sent all the mirrors to my room because I asked for them. It seems that I liked mirrors," Snow White said. "My father refused to have mirrors anywhere else in the castle."

"Even then, we managed to get by," Snow White said. "Carmilla showered me with presents and I cherished the little time we spent together, not knowing the real reason for her illness. Angel was always looking for a cure, until a doctor informed my mother of the horrible fact that she was going to die within months. Her body had suffered enough—and mine was growing fast. She was going to give in to the pain and aging eventually. Still, there was one last hope that Angel hadn't considered yet."

"To turn her into a vampire," Loki easily predicted.

Snow White nodded. "She asked Angel to turn her into a vampire, but he refused to make her into what he had resisted to become all of his life."

"I imagine he had no choice," Loki said.

"Exactly," Snow White let out a long sigh. "If Carmilla died, who was going to take care of me while he was away looking for a cure or fighting the vampires? The thought of Carmilla never getting better tortured him. He blamed himself for dragging her into his cursed life and couldn't stand the thought of being unable to feed on her blood drops again," Snow White looked at me for a second then shied away. "Eventually, he turned her into a vampire," she said in a voice I could barely hear. "Although his transformation wasn't complete, he learned from Night Sorrow that he had the power to turn her into a half-vampire like him."

"Since you didn't project an image for this, I take it you don't want me to watch it happening," Loki noted.

"Not you," she said. "I couldn't bring myself to see it."

"I understand," Loki said. "So how did it go, your dad saving your mom's life?"

"A vampire does not have their lives saved, but cursed. Trust me," Snow White said. Loki could see her chest rise and fall like an unsure tide searching for a shore to crash on. "Carmilla woke up the next morning alive and beautiful as ever. I heard stories about how her beauty was intimidating to other women in the castle, shining a darker light onto their average looks."

"And you?"

"I was no problem anymore. The life energy I sucked unconsciously out of her, she could compensate for with her new strength. I remember her becoming so acute and sharp, seeing things far away, hearing inaudible conversations and predicting the weather, and even running as fast as Angel. My father taught her how to control her cravings, and feed on sparrows, bats, and animals."

"So she was able to stay a half-vampire like Angel as long as she didn't feed on human blood," Loki said.

"But like always, there was a catch," Snow White said. "It turned out that no mirror reflected my mother's new beauty. Instead, all mirrors reflected a beast, which was what she was changing into on the inside."

"But that wasn't the case with Angel. Why was she different?"

"The Karnsteins were no ordinary vampire hunters. They were descendants of a holy bloodline, and thus, the curse of seeing a beast in the mirror when she looked into it was a righteous punishment."

"Your family is doomed, princess," Loki commented.

"Still, we managed to survive. Carmilla avoided mirrors again, fed secretly with Angel while raising me, and kept the secrets from the rest of the kingdom," Snow White said. "Things were kind of acceptable until the day we received the package," Snow White said.

"What package?"

"One day, in my father's absence, we received a package from Europe," Snow White said. "It was from a Justus von Lieblig, a German scientist who'd been gifting my mother with the finest mirrors the whole time she was collecting them, before she banned them. This time, Justus sent us his latest invention; a silvered mirror like the ones we use today. The servant accepted the gift and sent the mirror directly to my room, of course. I have to say that I was fascinated by it. I had never seen my reflection so clear in my life."

"Seems like just a regular mirror to me," Loki said.

"I wish it was, but that's not true. In my boredom, and loneliness, I started talking to the mirrors in my room. In the beginning, I was only talking to my own reflection, killing time, and substituting them for dolls and playmates. I wasn't allowed to go to school anymore—of course, I wasn't told how dangerous I was yet. The girl in the mirror was just some lonely girl imitating my moves and combing her hair at the same time I did mine, saying the same words I said. Then one day, the mirror started talking to me, and it wasn't my voice or hallucinations. There was another girl in the mirror," she said. "I couldn't see her, but could hear her. She sounded a little older than me, and she told me that she was trapped inside. To my surprise, she didn't like talking to me. She said that she was capable of healing my mother and making her reflection look beautiful, and she kept asking to meet her over and over again."

"Did you tell your mom about her?"

"Only once; she became angry with me, and threatened she'd break all the mirrors in my room if I mentioned it again. I explained to her that I was feeling lonely and needed someone to play and talk with, especially after I had been grounded when I bit the prince. Remember him?"

"Ouch," Loki pursed his lips, trying not to laugh. "I forgot you had an irresistible taste for hot, good looking young princes, yummy, yummy."

Suddenly, the door burst open, and the Snow White Queen, Carmilla, walked in.

Loki sprang up, standing with his back plastered to the wall. Snow White laughed. "Be cool," she said. "It's just a new scene that you have to observe."

"So why aren't we transported?" A lonely trickle of sweat glided down his forehead.

"Because the scene takes place in this room," she said. "Keep watching."

25

The Queen of Sorrow

Carmilla, as beautiful and glowing as ever, stood by the threshold of the room.

Her majesty was looking at the mirrors lined up in what seemed like a circle, making it harder for her to step in. She was standing in her elegant red dress and golden crown braided into her hair, golden locks hanging down her shoulders.

Carmilla took a deep breath before she stepped into the middle of the room. She avoided looking at her dark reflection in the mirrors as she walked ahead—even Loki avoided looking at her reflection; he didn't want to distort Carmilla's beautiful image in his memory.

Carmilla hadn't been in her daughter's room because of those mirrors. But this time she was here for the mirror Snow White had told her about. Her curiosity had peaked, and she couldn't help but investigate the talking mirror that promised to show her reflection as the beauty she was.

Carmilla could easily identify the mirror. It was the only one with a silvered surface, but that wasn't its greatest attribute. Of all the mirrors in the world, this one granted the Queen the illusion of a gorgeous face even though she was half-vampire.

Carmilla cocked her head, unable to comprehend such a miracle. She approached the mirror eagerly, touching her face. It didn't matter that all the other mirrors in the room showed her beastly nature. All that mattered was the one single mirror that made her look like the beautiful Queen she'd been before.

"Mirror, mirror on the wall?" Carmilla wondered slowly, her eyes investigating the mirror as if it were alive. She wasn't sure if she was talking to herself or actually expecting the mirror to respond.

"Yes, my dearest Queen?" the invisible girl in the mirror replied.

"Mirror, Mirror on the wall," Carmilla repeated, as if to make sure the mirror was really talking to her.

"I'm at your service, Queen of Sorrow," the girl in the mirror said.

It was the first time someone had ever addressed her as the Queen of Sorrow, and it made something shimmer in Carmilla's eyes. "Just ask, and I shall answer," the girl continued. "Your wish is my command."

"Mirror, Mirror on the wall," Carmilla repeated again. "Who's that I see, standing tall?" she inched closer, straightening her back, and pushing her chest forward, her voice implying power.

"It's you, Queen of Sorrow," the girl in the mirror replied. "You're the fairest of them all."

Carmilla narrowed her eyes, worried and also suspicious of a mirror that talked, but seeing her reflection blinded her judgment.

It occurred to Loki that he was watching the real version of one of the most famous scenes in the history of storytelling; the moment the Snow White Queen first talked to the mirror.

"Who's the girl in the mirror, and did Justus send it as a gift, or did he work for someone?" Loki asked.

"Of course, Justus worked for someone," Snow White told him. "The mirror was sent by Night Sorrow who had been working tirelessly to turn my parents into full vampires so they could join his forces. Night Sorrow had found a way to reach my mother without having to breach through the kingdom's barriers. A haunted mirror was just enough. As for the girl in the mirror, I assure you have heard of her."

"You're mistaken," Loki argued. "I don't recognize the girl in the mirror."

"You do, Loki," Snow White insisted. Think about nursery rhymes you've heard, and about urban legends. It's all so obvious. You only need to connect the dots."

"Think of an evil girl who escaped a mirror, her prison, a girl that when you say her name three times in the dark, comes out and hurts you."

"You don't mean:--" The name was on the tip of Loki's tongue.

"Bloody Mary," Snow White nodded. "She's real, and she's the girl who turned my mother into a beast by appearing to her in the mirror."

"That's—"Loki was at a loss for words.

"That's the truth," Snow White said. "Sometimes, I wonder why no one ever questions where the mirror in my fairy tale came from. The person in the mirror who the Snow White Queen talked to was Bloody Mary."

Carmilla's eyes glittered suddenly. She looked as if she had been awakened from the hypnotizing effect of Bloody Mary. She sensed that this was all a work of evil.

"No, I am not the fairest of them all," Carmilla resisted Bloody Mary's suggestions. "And if I am, I know that I shouldn't be seeing a beastly reflection in all of the other mirrors but this one," she said while reaching for a candlestick to do away with the mirror. "This isn't right," she said. "You're an evil mirror and you have to be destroyed," she swung the candlestick at the mirror.

But before she could break it, the mirror's surface rippled and showed her images of other vampire women who seemed to suffer from an aging condition like Carmilla—of course, none of them were a chosen one's mother, but they were all aging after giving birth. The vampire women in the mirror seemed to have no problems with their aging condition because they had a solution for it. They fed on young human girls, and consumed their youth so they themselves wouldn't age. Once they fed on them, the young girls grew older instantly and died while the vampire women grew younger and healthier.

Carmilla stopped in her tracks, her fangs drawing out. The women in the mirror were checking out their beautiful faces in their hand mirrors, enjoying their eternal youth. They were combing their nurtured hair, checking their fine skin, putting on makeup and lipstick and rubbing their lips together, putting on mascara, and slightly squeezing their cheeks into reddish patches full of life and energy.

"What good is beauty if one can't see it?" Bloody Mary said, toying with Carmilla's weakness. "You have done nothing wrong to deserve to become a beast. You deserve much better. You've sacrificed your youth, your love, and yourself for your daughter."

Loki wanted to scream into the dream to warn Carmilla of the girl in the mirror, but he couldn't risk her seeing him.

"Will your daughter ever appreciate what you've sacrificed for her?" Bloody Mary said.

The images in the mirror turned into a single image of a seven year old Snow White who looked lovely.

"All this beauty she has sucked out of you has gone to waste," Bloody Mary continued. "Your pain was never appreciated. You could have simply died young and beautiful without having to bring her into the world."

The mirror rippled into a liquid surface and showed another live scene of Snow White in the future, wearing her white dress and walking barefoot in a garden of purple and yellow poppies. Men of all ages watched her with longing eyes in the background; knights, huntsmen, and princes as one of the servants placed a crown on Snow White's head; the Queen's crown.

"Sooner or later," Bloody Mary said. "Snow White will be the fairest of them all by feeding on your pain."

The movie in the mirror showed Snow White walking into a cemetery, now wearing warrior armor stained in blood, thousands of vampires lying dead at her feet. She stomped over an abandoned grave that was left behind with no care. Snow White kneeled down and touched the tombstone. Upon it, Carmilla's name was engraved:

Carmilla Karnstein
The Queen of Sorrow
1777 - 1812

The Snow White in the mirror laughed in a tone very different from the way she laughed in real life. It was an evil tone. "I killed her," she said. "I killed them all; including my beastly mother."

Carmilla shielded her face with her hands from the mirror. "No," she said. "She wouldn't do that."

"Why wouldn't she?" Bloody Mary wondered. "She is the chosen one, the Dhampir girl. It's foretold in ancient books that she will be half human, half vampire, with extraordinary powers, royal blood, and undeniable beauty. She, your daughter, Snow White, will be the end of vampires in this world, for she will be become a deadly hunter, and a legendary savior of the world of humans. You will die when you start aging and as the prophecy says, only one of you can live."

"What do you mean age?" Carmilla's face tightened. "This can't be true. Angel turned me into a half-vampire. I'm not supposed to age anymore."

"Is that true, my dear Queen?" Bloody Mary mocked her.

The mirror then rippled again and showed Angel talking to the gypsies about her illness before transforming her into a half-vampire. The gypsies told him that Carmilla's transformation was irreversible and that sooner or later, she'd start aging again at a rapid rate until she died. There was no way Carmilla could escape her fate as long as her daughter lived. Angel had lied to her.

"I can't believe this," Carmilla buried her face in her hands, crying so hard her body shook. "I can't believe Angel lied to me."

"See?" Bloody Mary said. "You, my dear, are one of us now."

"One of you?" Carmilla frowned, lifting her head.

"One of the Sorrows, the original ones," Bloody Mary said. "You will become a vampire and you'll belong to the Sorrows. Being a half-vampire does not ensure your youth and immortality. Sooner or later, you'll need to complete your transformation in order to save yourself. Only then will you become the real Queen of Sorrow, ruler of the kingdom and ruler of your fate."

Carmilla's eyes yellowed and her cheeks were flooding with black tears. "Who are you?" she asked the mirror.

"I'm the one who can give you what you want, your majesty. You could have everything," Bloody Mary said. "If you want to stay beautiful each day of your life—and stay alive—to experience the real powers a vampire queen should enjoy, be strong enough to face your daughter when she reaches the age of sixteen all you need to do is taste human blood."

The images in the mirror turned back to the other vampire women, now swimming in the blood of their victims. Carmilla watched them. She licked her lips and ran her tongue over her fangs. The women were bathing in blood and honey, bending their bodies in total ecstasy. The mixture was healing the wounds on their skin, infusing sparkle into their eyes, and toning their smooth skin, making them look even younger than the young girls they had bitten.

Suddenly, Carmilla snapped, her face returning to normal. "No," she said, taking a step forward toward the mirror as if wanting to fight it. "If only one of us can live, it should be her. I'll die for her."

But Carmilla's words were meaningless. Bloody Mary reached her scarred hands out of the mirror and pulled the Queen inside.

"Enough," Snow White said next to Loki with tears in her eyes. "I can't take this, but I had to show you."

"What happened to Carmilla?" Loki asked. Carmilla had been sucked into the mirror and was nowhere to be found in the room. He could only see the mirror's surface turning red and hear screams behind it, as if the mirror contained a world of its own behind its glass.

"She came back as someone else," Snow White said, "someone…evil." The first thing she did was feed on the poor young peasant girls of Sorrow to complete her transformation as a vampire."

Loki stood speechless. He was overwhelmed and confused. Part of him wanted to sympathize with Carmilla, and part of him couldn't imagine the endless young girls she was about to kill. Loki imagined that she must have really tried to kill her daughter later. If only Snow White hadn't gotten so emotional, he'd have asked her about what happened next.

"It's OK." Loki told Snow White. "You don't have to show me more. I understand. Just bury your worries in my arms."

"No, you don't understand," Snow White sobbed. "You have to see the final scene of the dream."

The Wind of Change was transferring them to the final scene, which was where the dream had all started, back in Carmilla's bathhouse.

"Do I really have to see this?" Loki said, standing in the bathhouse already. Loki pulled Snow White closer and hugged her tightly, chest to chest, heart to heart, and didn't let go of her. Even if he had to see this, he didn't want Snow White to watch the horror again, so he buried her face in his chest.

"Just close your eyes as the scene passes," Loki said. It still confused him why she insisted to show him the bathhouse memory.

"Everything changed after that day," Snow White said in a muffled voice. "My mother made her full transformation into a vampire. Her craving for blood grew stronger. She bathed in blood of young peasant girls she'd lured into the Schloss. They were poor girls, orphaned, lost, looking for work and for a better life; young girls who were naively excited about meeting the enchanting Queen of Sorrow. She fed on their youth. The girls grew old instantly, and she gained their youthfulness."

Loki saw the Queen bathing in the blood of young girls. She sank her body into the apple-shaped tub full of blood, milk, and dark chocolate. She laid her head back and inhaled deep through her nostrils, and let out a long sigh of relief, staining the steamy air with circles of vapor.

Loki wondered why chocolate and milk with blood? Was this some youth preservation ritual?

He couldn't believe his eyes, seeing this new Carmilla, having turned into a monster that only looked beautiful on the outside. The way she lay in the bathtub, enjoying it, was as if she was devoid of all heart and soul. She didn't care about the girls she killed. She didn't even flinch or feel sorry for them. She loved killing them.

Loki tried to avoid staring too long at the horrible scene. He imagined there were dead girls—now old—lying on the floor somewhere and he was grateful he didn't see them or he might scream and manifest his presence.

This newly turned Queen would be more than happy to kill him and Snow White in this dream. His eyes caught silhouettes of the poor girls on the floor, and his brain refused to comprehend. It was just a dream, he told himself. He'd wake up with Snow White when the Waker's sand finished falling, and they'd both be both alright.

"My mother started breaking the spells she had created on the borders to occupy my father with the exhausting war against vampires. It diverted the locals from digging deeper into the mystery of the disappearing young women, focusing on the war instead. They thought the disappearances were caused by the few vampires sneaking into the kingdom."

The Queen stood up in the tub. The servants covered her body with a white robe with pearls sewn into it. She pulled it closer with her chin up, sniffing the scent of blood and steam, feeling the power of youth running in her veins. A servant handed her the crown and she put it on her head before the servant started braiding it into her hair again. Another servant rolled her favorite mirror back into the bathhouse. The Queen stared at herself in it. Although her lips dripped with blood and her body was covered in it the mirror deceived her with the most beautiful reflection. The Queen's mouth curved slowly into a victorious smile. "Mirror, mirror, on the wall," she said slowly.

"It's Mary, Mary, on the wall, my Queen," Bloody Mary said happily.

"Who is the fairest of them all?" the Queen of Sorrow asked again.

"Finally, she could see her reflection in the mirror and indulge in her vanity," Snow White narrated as Loki watched.

"Horrible," Loki said. "I just can't believe this is the Carmilla who sacrificed everything for you and Angel."

"She needed more blood, more girls, and another bloodbath. Like people addicted to drugs, she was addicted to her beauty and youth in the mirror. Sometimes, I think it was the only way for her to forget her evil nature. What good was immortality if it was without youth and beauty?"

"You my majesty are the fairest of them all," Bloody Mary said.

"Her cravings grew stronger and stronger," Snow White continued. "And there were side effects of bathing in blood. The more she repeated the bloodbaths the more her skin and health deteriorated in the absence of the ceremonies. One bloodbath would gift her with three days—a week at most—of prosperous health and exceptional beauty. Then it was time for another bloodbath or she would grow older, faster than before.

"Did she try to hurt you?" Loki asked, holding her tighter.

"Not then," Snow White said. "She became selfish, and her bloodbaths killed her true heart. She didn't realize she had become a killer. Black holes filled her heart day by day, a step closer to turning her into the likes of my immortal grandfather, Night Sorrow. She denied my father her blood, claiming she had become weakened by the process and being tired of it; that he had to respect her wishes and find a another way to feed himself. She wanted him weakened and hesitant of his love for her and his need for her blood. And he was so busy with the war that he didn't see the big picture or her terrible plans. And of course, she had little time for me. She grew more distant, looking at me in strange ways and avoiding conversation. I think she was trying to find a way to fight her cravings, but was worried about her sudden aging whenever she stopped the bloodbaths. And then…"

"And then what?" Loki gasped.

"And then my famous Snow White journey began," Snow White said. "She sent me to the Black Forest to collect roses and play with the wolves without me knowing what was really going on, why she suddenly hated me, why she was jealous of me, or why she wanted me dead. She sent the Huntsman after me to kill me," Snow White lifted her head and stared into Loki's eyes. She was sobbing harder, and Loki saw the air rippling around them again, the way it happened when they were close to exposing their presence to Angel and Carmilla in the cottage. "He's a vicious person, full of darkness in his heart, and she told him to stake me in the heart and bring it back to her, along with my liver as proof of my death."

Loki was amazed that Axel's theories were mostly right. But digging deeper into the mystery of all those fairy tale characters was the least of his concerns. The air around him was rippling harder with Snow White's continued sobs. He wanted to hold her even closer to his chest to muffle her cries a little. But he didn't. He decided it wouldn't be right to deprive her of expressing herself. Sometimes tears, although painful, wash the pain away, and he wanted Snow White to let it all out, even if it meant manifesting their presence in the Dreamworld.

"That's how they thought vampires—Dhampirs in my case—were killed at the time. Her plan was to rid the vampires, and herself, from the threat I was imposing as the chosen one. She also wanted to use my blood to bathe in, and gain my powers for herself. She was blinded by lust for beauty and power," Snow White continued. Then she cried out her last words, "My mother had become my own enemy."

That was when Loki saw Carmilla noticing their presence in the dream.

26

What Dreams May Come

Loki saw the air ripple like waves before his eyes. The Dreamhunter and the dreamer's identity had been exposed in the Dreamworld.

In a flash, the servants tilted their heads toward Loki and Snow White. They seemed shocked for a moment…all but Carmilla.

She turned her head toward the intruders. She did it slowly as if she had all the time in the dream on her side. It was as if she'd been expecting them. A wicked smile curved on her fine lips as she looked at Loki holding Snow White in his arms. It was as if he was protecting her from a hurricane that was about to huff and puff their lives away.

The Queen of Sorrow's confidence was intimidating. She held her chin up high, brushed her hair back behind her shoulders, and looked down upon them like a lion watches its prey. Her face oozed with vitality, shining bright and deceivingly elegant as if there was no beast living behind her blue eyes.

A trickle of blood dripping from her lips exposed her disguise, and showed her wrath. Slowly, her tongue, that of a snake, appeared from between her heart-shaped lips. It was thin and it stretched long enough that the Queen managed to lick the trickle of blood from her chin. Drawing her tongue back, a smile curved itself on her face. She closed her eyes, swallowing the blood then opened them again. It was puzzling how she looked so beautiful and yet capable of doing something so gruesome. She wiped her lips with her fingertips, showing a pearl ring around her middle finger.

Loki was speechless, almost paralyzed, and unable to shake the Queen's presence away. Carmilla was incomparable to all of the stories he had heard before. Her presence was powerful and unavoidable. Again, Loki experienced that strange feeling like he had when he was in the closet and felt the need to obey the Queen. It was a wicked feeling, as if she was able to control him in some way. It was if he had to obey her, and he needed all his strength to resist her deadly charms. No wonder they called her, 'She Who Must Be Obeyed.'

"Don't let her control you," Snow White told Loki. "Avoid her eyes."

Loki was still hypnotized. The short moment of confrontation felt like long days, struggling against his own shadow to free himself from her—or from the evil inside that inexplicably connected him to her.

"Look at me, Loki," Snow White pleaded, caressing his face.

Slowly, Loki glanced back at Snow White. It wasn't easy, though. Looking at Carmilla made him understand a little bit about the darkness inside him. He knew that whatever darkness he possessed, Carmilla knew about it and was trying to use it against him. How much did she know about his past?

The only thing that saved him from Carmilla's effect was looking back into Snow White's eyes. It brought him back to his senses.

It brought back…home…

Freed from her trance, Loki looked back at the Queen, a little blurry now behind the steam. He held Snow White's hand for assurance. He needed it while he thought about how to escape this dream. This or the Queen would devour them both like the young girls she'd killed before.

"The Fleece," Loki remembered. He reached to tap it three times on his wrist, sending an emergency call to Axel and Fable. It was time they break the mirror with Lucy's axe to save them from this horrible, never ending dream.

As he tapped his wrist, he carefully observed the Queen of Sorrow. To his surprise, he couldn't feel the Fleece on his hand. Loki's eyes widened and his heart pounded against his chest. Looking at his wrist, it was impossible to believe what he saw.

The Fleece was gone.

The Queen of Sorrow laughed in a high pitch that sent a chill through their spines. Loki knew she was laughing at him. He looked back at her and saw her wrapping his Fleece around the fingers of her right hand. She was biting into an apple with the left. He had no idea how he lost his Fleece, or how the Queen had possession of it. It didn't matter. The Queen wasn't going to give it back, and now he was trapped in this dream until the Waker's sand passed through the hourglass in the waking world.

Loki's instant reflex was to step forward to protect Snow White who stood behind him, as if he was ready to take a bullet for her.

"What are you doing?" Snow White snapped.

"I will try to distract her," Loki said. "You should escape, and then wait until the dream is over and wake up in the real world. I'm sure Axel and Fable will pull you back to the castle safely."

"And you?"

"I lost my Fleece, which means I'm trapped here. I can only wake up when the dream ends, or—"Loki shrugged, and didn't know what to say. All that came to his mind was to flash his Alicorn at the silently observing Queen. Her silence and confidence were scarier than her wrath. It was as if she'd known they couldn't escape so she was in no rush to finish them off.

Carmilla smirked at Loki's heroic reaction. It was a belittling gesture, and Loki wished his Alicorn would finally provide some usefulness. He'd taken the long journey to Sorrow wanting to kill Snow White, only to realize that the Queen was the evil one behind all of this. All this talk about going back home didn't matter now. He remembered when his mother had told him that he'd come to Sorrow to discover who he really was, and that there was a difference between who he was and where he came from. Right now, Loki was where he wanted to be; in love with a girl he came to kill. Snow White was his home.

Carmilla handed one of her servants the bitten apple, which had a small worm climbing out of it. She wiped her mouth with the tip of one of the dead girls' dresses. Loki assumed she had that eerie power over him because of the Fleece. He wondered if owning a Dreamhunter's Fleece was the same as owning his soul. Flashing his Alicorn, he wanted to step forward to fight like a man, but the Queen was faster.

Carmilla showed her snake tongue again, curling from between her lips toward them. Reciting an indecipherable incantation she rippled her tongue in the air, spraying some kind of invisible force at Loki. It wasn't poison. Instead, Loki found himself elevated off the floor. She pushed him with her tongue without laying a hand on him, the same way Snow White had manhandled Big Bad in the castle in the waking world.

Against his will, Loki flew in the air, his arms stretched sideways as if he were a man floating in space. Carmilla pushed her hand a little further and Loki flipped back in the air. He was prepared to hit the wall with his back and then land on his tailbone. Instead, he ended up plummeting downward, splashing into the bathtub he'd came through when he first entered the dream, only the tub was full this time.

Loki made sure he still gripped his Alicorn as he slipped underneath the blood, milk, and chocolate. He doubted he'd make it out alive. He was dizzy from the Queen's *push* and imagined he'd lose consciousness under water.

Is this the way it's going to end? In a bathtub? That's some fairy tale.

Lying on his back with eyes closed at the bottom of the tub, he wished there was something he could do to energize himself and go back to fight the Queen and save Snow White. He was fighting the urge to pass out.

No one's supposed to die before they know who they are. He remembered Charmwill had told him once. *This can't be the end.*

Where were the Godmothers, the Godfathers, and Mother Goose when you needed them?

But Loki wasn't used to believing in fairy tales and he doubted such a person would appear to save his life and his head hurt too much to give 'Ora Pedora' one last try. How could he even speak underwater if he had the strength to?

Pick yourself up, Loki. You can do it.

His inner voice gave him a momentary burst of strength, and he tried to lift up his hand.

But he was too late. The tub grew arms, like an octopus, and wrapped them around his hand, pulling it back down. He tried to move his legs but the octopus' arms chained them as well. The octopus seemed to only move when Loki resisted drowning.

Loki decided he wouldn't move his free arm for now, or it would chain it, too.

What did my mother say about the Chanta? Didn't she say that I should follow my bliss and then the whole world would conspire to help me? I need to use that Chanta right now. It has to be true.

He knew his longing for Snow White, and the journey he'd taken, must have changed him in a better way. He wasn't the Minikin-hating half-angel anymore. A week ago, if he would have been this close to death, he might not have cared about living, because all the things he loved and longed for had been wiped from his memory. But now, he had friends; he had a girl he liked, and ironically, he had a new home. Even if it was called Sorrow, even it was in a town called Hell, he still wanted to live in it. Maybe all Loki had to do was decide to make this Hell town his own Heaven, his home. Home was where the heart was, where we bled, where we laughed, met those we love, where we built, and what we fought for. Home was the dry soil we nurtured unconditionally, the place we took care of, faithfully believing that one day the rain would fall and quench the earth's thirst. Only then, the cracks in the earth would heal and green dreams would grow from the ground.

Loki wanted to survive this moment, more than ever. He wanted to enjoy his life with his friends, the girl he loved, and maybe devote his life to helping others when he could.

But *maybe* Loki was too late.

He was out of the breath, and out of answers.

If he had any chance left, it was his free hand that the octopus hadn't wrapped its curvy arms around yet. How could he use this one last chance appropriately?

His only free hand was closest to the pocket where he kept Sesame, the fortune cookie. Was Sesame going to be able to tell him what to do now? He knew that it wasn't necessary to vocalize the question he wanted to ask. He could simply use his mind and it would understand and answer him.

Loki pulled Sesame out slowly from his pocket, not to alert the octopus arms, and held it to his side.

All he had to do was ask it a question and crush it open with his hand. He'd always believed in Sesame, and now, it was his last hope.

Wait. Don't do it. Remember when Charmwill said that one of the things you keep hanging onto is useless, that you will only be able to use the Chanta when you let it go?

Almost fainting, Loki remembered that he couldn't figure out what that item was. But it seemed clear now. It was Sesame he had to get rid of. It was a useless fortune cookie. He'd used it in the past and relied on it without questioning or thinking for himself.

Loki crushed Sesame open this time, but without asking it questions or awaiting answers. He crushed it to get rid of it, not wanting to own it or use it again. He had no use for a fortune cookie in his life anymore. He'd become who he chose to be as long as he breathed. He was the sum of the choices he made. Everything that happened to him was part of his previous decisions, and even if it was sometimes hard to make his own decision, he was old enough to face it, and young enough to correct his mistakes.

I'm young enough to do it, and old enough to do it right.

Loki chose to fight the Queen to save the princess. Ironically, he'd never thought he'd say that because before this moment he'd always mocked fairy tales. He'd never believed in fairy tales, but now he had to.

Once Sesame was crushed open, Loki experienced an unusual strength in his soul. It was like a burden on his shoulders had been lifted and he felt lighter and freed from the chains of the unknown. He'd found his potion after all. His Chanta was his belief in himself, only himself, that he was the only one that could decide his future.

Amazingly, the octopus let go of Loki after he'd crushed Sesame. Loki rocked up to his feet, inhaling all the air his lungs permitted him. Dripping with blood, milk, and chocolate, he continued inhaling as he embraced the miracle of life like a long lost lover.

Letting the air fill his veins and adjusting to his surroundings, Loki saw he still had another problem.

Neither Carmilla nor Snow White was there, not even the Queen's servants. Instead, Loki saw someone else through the bathhouse's stream.

Charmwill Glimmer.

"Charmwill?" Loki wiped his wet face clean. "I didn't know you could enter dreams."

"I was once a Dreamhunter myself," Charmwill said, dressed in his cloak and walking with his cane. "But that was a long time ago, before I devoted my life to protecting the Book of Beautiful Lies."

"But how did you enter this Dreamory?" Loki said. "Are you lying next to me and Snow White in the Dream Temple now?"

"No," Charmwill chuckled, hiding all the secrets Loki wanted to know behind his smile. "Does it matter how I got here?"

"You're right," Loki said, stepping out of the bathtub. "Snow White matters."

Charmwill nodded sneakily as if it was what he'd always wanted to hear Loki say.

"Where is she?" Loki said.

"Carmilla took her, and she has no intention of giving her back to you," Charmwill explained.

"But the Dreamory might end any moment now," Loki said. "I can't wake up without her."

"Is that what you want to do?" Charmwill asked, his eyes piercing through Loki.

"Of course, it's what I want to do," Loki said impatiently. He hated when Charmwill needed confirmation of his words. "I thought you were here to help me save her."

"I don't need this kind of talk right now. Time is tight Charmwill," Loki pleaded. "It doesn't matter if I go home now," he hesitated for a moment then said, "I know it's strange and I have no rational explanation for it, but Snow White is now my home."

"Why didn't you say that all along?" Charmwill smiled from ear to ear. "Let's go save the princess like they do in fairy tales," he waved his cane at Loki, too enthusiastic for a man his age. "Follow me."

"Where are we going?"

"Carmilla has Snow White in her carriage," Charmwill said. "She wants to imprison Snow White in a tower. If you stop talking, we could save your princess."

"Why imprison her in a tower if all she wants is to kill her?" Loki asked. "That doesn't make sense."

"I really need you to stop talking now," Charmwill said as he hurried through a side door out of the bathhouse and into the Black Forest. A set of horses were lined up in front of them, ready and able.

"I hope you know how to ride horses," Charmwill said. Pickwick landed on his shoulder.

"You never taught me that. I only know how to drive a car," Loki said. "I suppose you don't have any of those in the 19th century."

"Of course, not," Charmwill replied. "A princess has to be saved the old fashioned way, on a horse, in a forest or castle, right after you slay the dragon."

"That's so text book fairy tale," Loki said. "I thought this world was all messed-up fairy tales."

"The characters are messed up indeed, but the heart and soul of love and transcendence never change," Charmwill said. "Faces change, hearts remain," he winked at Loki, and Pickwick nodded with approval. "But no worries; get on the horse, and give it a chance. It should be like riding a bicycle. We're in a dream anyways. Use your Chanta."

Reluctantly, Loki got on a horse. Once he did, Charmwill tapped it gently. The horse took off and was at full speed within moments.

Loki screamed, hanging onto its neck, unable to control it, doing his best not to fall off.

"This Chanta isn't working," Loki yelled, the horse sprinting away into the dark forest.

"That's because you still don't believe enough in yourself," Charmwill said from behind. "Keep trying. Use your imagination."

"But I crushed Sesame! I got rid of the one thing that was holding me back, and it saved me from drowning. What else should I do?" Loki shouted as he struggled with the speeding horse, arching his back and hugging it like a rodeo cowboy.

"You need to believe in things that you haven't seen with your own eyes yet," Charmwill yelled, his sound faint and far away. "Believe it and you will see it."

"I can't think straight while I'm on this horse," Loki said, knowing that Charmwill wouldn't hear him. He felt exactly like he had in the Candy House when the crow had grabbed him. This wasn't good. He needed to control the horse to save Snow White. He was wasting precious time. He didn't even know where he was going, but he assumed the horse was following Carmilla's carriage. The moon above was the only light guiding his way into the forest while he looked like a clown on the back of a reckless horse. "Loki do this. Loki do that. Loki go kill the princess. Loki don't kill the princess," he kept mumbling to himself, almost falling off the horse. "Loki ride the horse. Loki save the princess. Loki use the Chanta. Loki believe in yourself. I'm Loki's all confused and fed up conscious. I hate this dream."

"For someone who should be saving a princess, you look embarrassingly amateur," Charmwill shouted, riding next to him on a unicorn. It was an unusually fast unicorn, so beautiful it had a glittering aura surrounding its curvy body. Loki was glad Charmwill was at his side.

"Why do you get the unicorn and I get the horse?" Loki's face reddened.

"I'm Charmwill Glimmer," he said proudly, riding his unicorn as if he were as young as Loki. "I deserve it. I did many amazing things in my life."

"Do you think this is really the right time to brag?" Loki puffed.

"I'll tell you what," Charmwill drew nearer to the side of Loki's horse. "Jump behind me, but this is the last time I will save you, understood?"

Jumping off the horse was as hard as riding it, but Loki thought it was the lesser of two evils. He grabbed Charmwill's cloak with one hand and managed to jump on the unicorn behind him.

"Yeeha!" Charmwill said and the unicorn sped up. Loki had never seen this side of Charmwill before. He wondered why he'd never been fun like this in the past, and wondered if it was because they were in a dream.

Suddenly, Loki heard growling sounds approaching from behind. Fear surged into his soul. Someone or something evil was after them.

"Who's chasing us?" Loki asked, holding onto Charmwill.

"Whatever happens, don't look back!" Charmwill's tone changed back into having a serious edge. "You hear me? Don't look back!"

"Who are they?" Loki asked.

"The Queen's huntsmen," Charmwill sped up. "Led by *the* Huntsman.

Whatever happens, fight the urge to look into his face, or all will be lost. You understand?"

Being Loki, he couldn't help it and looked behind to get a glimpse of his pursuers. Behind him, leading all other huntsmen, a black-cloaked Huntsman rode a hornless unicorn like nothing Loki had ever seen. This wasn't the white, good looking unicorn like Charmwill's. It was a black one with scars all over its body, and it had a third eye where its horn had been cut off. It sped up once it saw Loki looking back. It was hungry for him, and bared its lion-like canines.

But the black unicorn was the lesser of Loki's horrors. It was the Huntsman riding it that gave him goose bumps. Loki felt a sudden headache, a needle sharp pain in his head. He stared at the cloaked Huntsman against Charmwill's advice, but couldn't see his face. The Huntsman's cloak showed only hollow darkness underneath it. But Loki could sense the amount of evil in him just like when he looked into the eyes of the Queen of Sorrow. Loki's eyes were glued to the hunter. He regretted looking back at him, but he was too stiff with fear to turn back around. The Huntsman let out a dark laugh and was about to lower his cloak and show his face.

"What are you doing?" Charmwill pulled Loki back from the Huntsman's spellbinding trance, and turned him around. "Didn't I tell you not to look at him? He is evil and full of darkness like you've never, and will never, see again in your life!"

"I don't know what happened to me," Loki shook his head. "This Huntsman and Carmilla have the same effect on me."

"That's because you're still not strong enough," Charmwill still rode the unicorn skilfully as Carmilla's carriage was coming into view. "Did you look into the Huntsman's eyes?" Charmwill asked Loki worriedly.

"No. You turned me around before I could see what was under the cloak," Loki said.

"That's good," Charmwill let out a sigh. "I will take care of him and his hunters, once we get closer to the carriage."

Loki and Charmwill quickly caught up to the golden-framed carriage. Like everything else having to do with Carmilla, the carriage looked majestic and expensive. It was the shape of a pumpkin. Nothing hinted to the evil Queen who rode inside it. From this angle, Loki couldn't see the wolves pulling it, nor could he see Snow White inside. The back and side windows were barred with rods made of pearls.

It was a dire situation. They had to save Snow White and escape their evil pursuers.

"We're close enough, now," Charmwill said, right behind the carriage. The Huntsman's heavy breathing was so close Loki knew he wasn't just behind them. He was riding right next to them. "You'll have to ride the unicorn from here and save the princess. I can't help you anymore."

"Whatever happens don't look at him," Charmwill said, focusing his eyes on the carriage. It was as if he couldn't bear looking at the Huntsman himself. "Ride the unicorn and stop the carriage, Loki. Let me take care of the Huntsman."

In a flash, Charmwill jumped through the air and onto the Huntsman's unicorn. Loki was worried about the man who taught him everything, but managed to control his urge to look at the Huntsman while he fought Charmwill. He rode the unicorn and followed the carriage, listening to the sounds of struggle between the Huntsman and his guardian behind him.

Someone pulled the curtain behind the window open. It was Carmilla, showing her fingers wrapped in rings of pearls. She stared at Loki as if she were amused that he'd made it his far. Then she bestowed an infuriating look upon him from the top of his head to the bottom of the unicorn's legs. Like usual, she didn't speak.

The Queen mocked Loki without saying a word. She mouthed, "Peekaboo," as she pointed her forefinger and middle finger at her eyes and back to Loki. "I see you."

The words sent a shiver into Loki. The Queen loved to play games. Killing her enemies abruptly seemed not to be her thing; she loved to see them suffer slowly; she loved to watch them decay as she sat and slowly devoured her precious apples.

Loki saw her gripping Snow White tightly with her other hand. Although he knew that Snow White wasn't a damsel in distress, and that she was badass, he wondered why she didn't fight the Queen.

"Run, Loki," Snow White screamed as the Queen pulled her hair. "Save yourself. She won't let go of me. I tried to get your Fleece from her, but now it's too late. Run!"

"No, I won't," Loki said, gripping his Alicorn. "I won't wake up without you! We're going to wake up from this dream together, and then I'll never leave you again."

"She's mine now, Dreamhunter," the Queen of Sorrow yelled from behind the pearl bars. "As mother and daughter—or shall I say once-mother and daughter—she's bonded to me. That's why as long as I hold onto her, she is trapped in this dream and won't be able to wake up," she turned her head back and called for the one of the wolves pulling the carriage in the front, "Managarm!"

Loki assumed this was the wolf's name, but he was oblivious of what she'd ordered him to do. Seconds later, the unexpected started happening. Loki tried to calm himself as he saw the carriage slowly start to rise into the air, pulled by the wolves. It was a slow lift off; they were pulling the carriage towards the moon.

"No!" Loki screamed, trying to grab the window's bars with his hands.

"Peekaboo," Carmilla mouthed again from a higher angle behind the bars. "Goodbye to you."

Loki sped after them, wrapping his hands around the unicorn, wondering if it could fly. Spontaneously, he raised his Alicorn in the air and shouted, 'Ora Pedora.'

"This should work," he said to himself. "I've had a long journey, and I've changed a lot. I believe that I can do the impossible now. He closed his eyes, trying to concentrate on the sincerity of his emotions. He imagined Snow White back in his arms again. He imagined he could save her. He'd spent a whole year trying to be forgiven for falling in love, and he wasn't going to do make that mistake again. He wasn't going to resist his feelings this time, or apologize for having them. To hell with his memory, the hell with going back home, and the hell with the boundaries that chained him and prevented him from transcending and becoming what he wanted to be.

With eyes closed, he could feel the spiral surface of his Alicorn changing. It was moving, gliding as if it was becoming…alive.

Loki opened his eyes and saw the spirals around the Alicorn were circling around it like a snake. The truth was that this *was* a snake. He whipped it in the air and it let out a scream and got thicker, spiralling higher toward the flying carriage. Loki soon discovered it would stretch as long as he needed it.

What he was holding in his hand was partially an evil weapon. He wasn't that fond of snakes, especially after seeing the Queen's forked tongue. But he knew this was what Charmwill repeatedly told him, that Loki had darkness inside him, darkness that had to do with whoever he'd been in the past. Only he could use this darkness and control it to use it against the likes of the Queen of Sorrow. It was like fighting fire with fire.

Loki whipped the snake one more time until it reached the carriage. He saw the Queen snarling with her fangs at the Alicorn's snake. It was like a clash of titans, the same species eye to eye with each other.

Loki whipped his Alicorn for a third time. His snake slithered through the Queen's hair and sprayed poison into her eyes. Carmilla screamed and backed away from the bars as Loki's snake curled itself around them and started pulling the carriage down.

The struggle disrupted Loki's balance on the unicorn but he gripped it harder with his free hand. Then he tightened his other hand around the Alicorn to help the snake pull the carriage back to land.

"I deserve an Oscar for this acrobatic performance," Loki said, still struggling with both hands.

But his snake was amazingly powerful. It grew smaller snakes from its sides that stretched even further and sprayed poison into the wolves' eyes. The wolves dizzied and dropped back toward land, pulling the carriage down with them.

The scene from Loki's eyes was epic. A golden carriage in the air pulled by poisoned wolves and strapped to the snakes from his Alicorn, all of this with the full moon in the background. Loki thought it was so crazy that he must have been dreaming. But hell, he was in a dream and this was what dreams may come.

The carriage came crashing down in front of him. Loki jumped off the unicorn as the snake pulled itself back curling around the Alicorn's surface. He ran toward the carriage's remains and saw Snow White sprawled on the floor. Carmilla was gone.

He pulled the demolished parts of the carriage away and knelt down next to Snow White. He patted her lightly on the cheek but she wasn't responding. She was also paler than she'd been throughout the entire dream.

"Wake up, Shew," he pleaded. "Wake up. I'm here beside you," he rested her head on his arms but her hands fell loosely to her sides. He didn't know what to do, wondering what happened to her. She didn't look like her unconscious condition was caused by the crash of the carriage. Something else happened to her while she was in mid-air.

Crows started cawing and gathering around the trees all around him. Loki raised his head, assuming that this meant the dream was about to end. Soon there'd be earthquakes and mountains falling and they'd wake up.

Laying her back on the ground, he saw her lips were dripping blood. It didn't make sense. He wondered if she had bitten the Queen while struggling in the air.

But that wasn't the case. Next to Snow White's paralyzed body, Loki saw a bitten apple. It was a blood apple, the juice that seeped from it was red, and he assumed Snow White had taken a bite off it. Carmilla must have forced her to bite on it while they were in the carriage.

Behind him, Loki heard Charmwill screaming. Loki stood to his feet and saw Charmwill in the distance. He was on his knees, his hands bound behind his back, and surrounded by the huntsmen. They were half-circling him with their swords to their sides. Each of them wore that same black cloak that didn't show their faces. The wind puffed through their hollow heads and stirred the cloak as if they were black ghosts. They had caught Charmwill and were about to execute him. Loki wanted to run to him.

"Don't come for me, Loki," Charmwill pleaded. "I'm not as important as her."

Loki stood stranded, looking back and forth between Snow White and Charmwill. The dream was about to end and he could only save one. The earth underneath him rumbled. The earthquake was nearing.

"Save the princess," Charmwill screamed, sounding afraid. Never had Loki heard such a shiver in his guardian's voice before.

Loki expected the Huntsman to appear from the dark to kill Charmwill. He needed to think fast. Was he going to face the Huntsman against Charmwill's advice or save Snow White? It was like choosing between past and future, old and young, and it was going to break Loki's heart either way.

Slowly, someone appeared from between the huntsmen circling his guardian. But it wasn't the Huntsman. It was Carmilla.

She walked slowly among her huntsmen, approaching Charmwill. A number of goblins next to her were pulling the Queen's favorite mirror behind her. They stopped in front of Charmwill and Carmilla tilted her head, meeting Loki's eyes in the distance.

"I swear if you say that Peekaboo-I-see-u thing one more time I'm going to kick your majesty's royal ass," Loki snapped.

Carmilla let out a short laugh then turned her shoulder towards him, as if ignoring him. She reached her hand into the mirror and pulled a sword made of sharply edged glass. She walked closer to Charmwill and patted him on the cheek like a puppy.

"You know how long I've wanted to kill you, Charmwill?" she asked the old man who lowered his eyes silently with shame. "So long that I'm willing to let your prodigal Dreamhunter get away with the princess."

It wasn't surprising that Charmwill knew Carmilla. Loki hadn't figured out most of the truth about this fairy tale world after all. He just knew that he wasn't going to kill the princess, and that he had chosen to stay in Sorrow and forget about finding out who he really was. But it killed him inside him to see Charmwill like this. He'd known how proud the man was.

Even if he were immortal, killing Charmwill in the dream was putting him into sleep forever in the real world. The rules that applied to the Demortals also applied to Dreamhunters in the matters of life and death.

"Stay where you are, Loki," Charmwill pleaded again, his head still low, ready for the Queen to chop it off. "The dream is ending. You'll be safe if you have patience."

"But I can't leave you," Loki felt a tear roll down his cheek. He was about to take a step toward him. The only thing that stopped him was that it was a step away from Snow White as well. "You don't want to kill him," Loki diverted his eyes toward the Queen. "You want Snow White," the words ached in his heart when he said them, because he didn't really mean them.

"I don't need her," Carmilla said nonchalantly, raising her glass sword in the air, "at least not now."

"What do you mean you don't need her?" Loki grimaced.

"I forced her to bite on the apple. It's a blood apple. She's cursed now and she'll stay cursed until someone finds the cure, which I'm sure you will never find, foolish Dreamhunter."

"You can take her along with you to the real world. She's no threat to me at the moment. The apple will turn her into a dark vampire. She'll probably kill you once you pull the stake out," Carmilla took a deep breath, preparing to bring the sword down on Charmwill.

"Don't worry, you'll know how to save her if you open your heart," Charmwill said to Loki. "Just wake up with her and you'll be alright. And Loki," Charmwill turned his head to face him. "Take care of Pickwick."

Pickwick fluttered through the air and rested on Loki's shoulder. Charmwill's request might have sounded ordinary to the Queen, but Loki understood its many meanings. For one, Pickwick held all the true fairy tales that Charmwill collected and protected all his life. Now, it had become Loki's responsibility to do so. Two, Loki felt it was an honour; Charmwill handed him the flag to continue his quest with his blessing. Loki decided he'd close his eyes so he'd not see his guardian die.

"I'm afraid you're going to have to kill me while facing me," Charmwill told the Queen, raising his head proudly up.

Loki heard the glass sword slice through something and Carmilla letting out a sigh of relief. It was as if she'd always wanted to kill him, and Loki wondered about the many secrets he'd unravel within time about this world.

Charmwill's death came with a hysterical fluttering of crows. When Loki opened his eyes, the Queen was gone. He saw mountains falling in the distance, crumbling to dust. A river flooded nearby and the stars fell like snowflakes from the skies.

He walked back to Snow White, lifted her up with both his hands, and stood in front of the mess. A flood was approaching as he stood still in front of it. He knew whatever it was going to do him, it didn't matter as long as he had saved the girl he'd come here to kill.

27

Blood Apples

When Loki woke up, Axel was pounding his chest with his fist.

"Get off me," Loki pushed Axel away and sat up, still feeling a bit dazed. "What the heck is wrong with you?"

"I'm giving you CPR." Axel said.

"Why? I'm not dead!"

"A second ago he was almost kissing you," Lucy murmured in the background. She was texting someone, like usual.

"You looked very dead to me," Axel explained himself, ignoring Lucy. "I didn't really mean to kiss you. I meant to breathe in your mouth."

"Where did you even learn CPR?" Loki said, rubbing his wrist, feeling stripped without his Fleece.

"I took a course," Axel said proudly.

"God bless me for tolerating you," Loki rolled his eyes. It had been a rhetorical question.

"It was a course on how to rescue your pet," Axel felt the need to elaborate.

"Do I look like a pet to you?" Loki stood up, brushing the snow away. The weather was still cold and a bit crazy. "And don't answer that," Loki warned him.

"What's with you waking up so grouchy from the dream?"

"You have no idea what happened down there," Loki said impatiently. "And didn't I warn you about stepping into the Dream Temple?"

"I'm sorry," Axel said. "You looked like you were dying, and I had to save you. Am I in danger now?"

"I don't think so," Loki said. "The dream is over anyways," Loki was still in shock from his encounter with Carmilla. Charmwill's image flashed before his eyes again, and he tried his best not to cry, at least not in front of his friends. He looked at Snow White sleeping in the glass coffin inside the Dream Temple. She looked alright. He had to bring her back safely into the castle. He'd already lost Charmwill and he was in no way going to lose Snow White. Looking at the Waker, he saw they still had enough time.

"Why are you being nice to Axel?" Lucy said to Loki. "Why can't you just tell him he's useless and can't do anything right?"

Axel's face reddened. This time, he looked angry. He'd taken his share of humiliation from Lucy already. Loki knew that whatever Axel did, he did it with a good heart because he was a true friend, and he had no time to stand up for him against Lucy now.

Thinking about Axel, reminded Loki of Fable. He wondered why she hadn't said a word since he woke up. Turning back, he saw Fable staring at him as if she'd seen a ghost. She was definitely worried about Loki, but there was something else in her eyes that worried Loki.

"What?" Loki snapped at her, feeling uncomfortable with her silent stare.

"Did you lose your Fleece, Loki?" Fable asked as if she was his mother taunting him for losing something precious. He had a gut feeling that losing the Fleece wasn't good at all, and he knew Fable felt the same way.

"Don't worry, I don't think it's that dangerous," he lied again to her so she wouldn't panic.

"What happened in the Dreamory, Loki?" Fable was curious. "We were so worried about you two."

Loki took a deep breath, glad to be alive. "You won't believe it when I tell you, Fable," he dropped his head as Pickwick landed on his shoulder.

"And why is Pickwick here?" Fable squinted. "Where is Charmwill?"

"I will explain everything later," Loki wasn't going to elaborate right now. If he did, she'd get emotional and then he'd probably burst into tears as well. "We need to get Snow White back to the castle and we need to hurry."

"You don't need to do that," Lucy blew on her fingernails then pointed behind Loki.

Axel was already pushing Snow White's coffin across the thin ice toward the castle.

"Axel," Loki hurried after him, and Fable followed, "what are you doing?"

Axel wasn't responding. He was pushing the coffin with all his might, running as fast as he could before the ice broke underneath him. Cracks spread behind him as if chasing him, but he was surprisingly faster.

Lucy didn't bother risking her way back to the castle over the ice. Loki and Fable tiptoed on the ice carefully and slowly after Axel. They held hands and chose different routes than the one taken by Axel because it was unsafe. When they arrived, Axel had already pushed the coffin into the castle. The Schloss was calm and showed no anger.

"I. AM. NOT. USELESS," Axel shouted back at Lucy across the ice.

Fable let out a laugh. She actually liked how he stood up for himself for once and actually did something heroic by crossing the treacherous ice. It was the way he said that he wasn't useless that sounded funny to her.

"You definitely aren't useless," Fable kissed him on the cheek.

Loki had never seen Axel smile so much. Fable's kiss made him feel like he was her hero.

After Axel succeeded in pushing the coffin to the castle, they pulled the coffin back up to Snow White's room. Before pulling the stake out, Loki told them about Carmilla's curse and how she forced Snow White to take a bite of the apple. He explained that Snow White might be under its influence, and that none of them might be safe with her. They decided to postpone pulling the stake out, and that Loki would do it by himself. Besides, they were tired and needed to go home to clean before their foster mom arrived in the mornig.

Sitting outside the castle, Loki told them all that happened. Even Lucy couldn't resist. She sat next to them listening to Loki tell about his adventure in the Dreamworld.

"I knew I was right," Axel said. "Didn't I tell you about the liver theory, and the heart, and that the Queen wanted to eat them? And didn't I tell you about the Huntsman? I also remember reading the part about the Brothers Grimm changing Snow White's mother into being a stepmother in the later versions. I just didn't tell you because I thought it was irrelevant."

Fable didn't comment that Axel didn't discover any of this by himself and that he had read it in the diary entitled J.G. he'd found in the secret library. She decided she'd keep treating her brother as an *un-useless* hero for the night.

"I know you've been right about many things," Loki laced his hands together. "But what does all of this mean, Axel? There are so many missing pieces."

"Loki is right," Lucy commented. "Knowing Snow White's story doesn't fully explain what is going on. It seems like there's something much bigger about this fairy tale world—and I totally sympathize with Carmilla by the way."

"And we're going to find out," Axel said enthusiastically. "We're a team now, and this is our adventure. We've just started it."

"Don't think too much about it, Loki," Fable patted him. "What all of this means is that you didn't kill Snow White and that's what matters," Fable hugged him. Axel scratched his back, a little uncomfortable with her touching Loki. "Didn't I tell you from the beginning that she needed your help, Loki?" she said.

"You did," Loki nodded. He wondered if he should have listened to Fable from the start, but he knew that he had to take this journey to find out what he really wanted.

"No more thinking about going back home?" Axel wondered.

"Don't worry," Loki said. "I'll stay here for a while."

"You see it's not so bad here," Axel looked around. "I understand the town's name is creepy—who wants to live in Sorrow? And I understand that the town is a part of a place called Hell. But what the *hell*? Who cares about names and labels? If you stay here with us, we could make this Heaven. Our Heaven. We'll make the rules, and keep saving lives. You don't need to be immortal or a half-angel to be cool, right."

"Right," Loki nodded, pleased with Axel's spirit.

Loki heard Carmen's radio buzzing faintly in the distance. The Pumpkin Warriors were back. They were singing:

You don't have to be an angel to be my friend.

You don't need to be immortal to rock my world.

Fable giggled.

"I think we should go now," Axel said. "We have a lot of cleaning to do before our foster mom arrives."

"You're right," Fable said. "The house is a mess. We should also leave Loki with the princess," Fable winked at Axel.

"Yeah," Axel said. "Just don't kiss on the first night—ah; I forgot you don't believe in a true love's kiss."

"Don't blame me if she eats you alive," Lucy stood up, pulling out her 4-wheeler keys. "And you Crumblewoods; today is your lucky day because I'm going to give you a ride home. Only you have to sit on the fender wells or rack. I only allow boyfriends to ride behind me on the seat.."

They all waved goodbye to Loki who watched them walk away. Fable was reminding Axel that she'd clean the house but not the places where he ate, and Axel started whining about stopping at the Belly and the Beast to get a bite.

"Lucy," Loki summoned her, and she turned around. "Aren't you mad that I didn't kill the vampire princess?"

"Me?" she said over her shoulder. "I don't really care. But I think my dad will be mad. You'll have to deal with him later. By the way, you should know something, too."

"What is it?"

"I know this will upset all of you but I am entitled to my own opinion," Lucy said. "From what you've just told us, I totally sympathize with the Queen of Sorrow."

"I can understand why," Loki said. "But you just said that a minute ago."

"No, you don't understand," Lucy gazed at the castle. "I don't believe Snow White's story," she said and walked away.

After they left, Loki walked back into the castle and entered Snow White's room. He knelt down beside her and didn't hesitate to pull the stake.

It took her a moment to adjust to her surroundings before she snarled with her black eyes at him. Loki kept still and didn't move. He was counting on her remembering him and appreciating what they'd been through together.

Although her monstrous nature didn't change, she recognized him. Her love for him inside surpassed any curse caused by Carmilla's apple. She lay back in the coffin and placed her hands on her chest.

"You should go," she said. "I won't be able to stop myself from hurting you forever."

"If I had a dollar for every time you asked me to leave you, I'd have around three dollars in my pocket," Loki said.

Sadly, she didn't laugh. Snow White felt weary and tired. Loki knew she wasn't going to hurt him, but what if anyone else entered the castle? It was best that he stayed with her until the morning. Then he'd start a new journey to find a cure for her curse.

"Scooch over," Loki said playfully.

Snow White's face knotted.

"I said scooch over," Loki said, squeezing himself next to her in the coffin. "There's room for both of us."

"You really want to sleep with me in a coffin?" she said.

"Wow," he waved his hand. "Sleep with you, no. That's too soon to talk about in our relationship. But sleep in a coffin *next* to you, yes. It's not like I have ever slept in a bed before."

Snow White laughed. Her blue eyes struggled shining from behind the blackness. Loki didn't mind. Her laughter was enough.

"You've never slept in a bed?" she wondered as he embraced her from behind, his arms caressing her, his knees bending to fit in the coffin.

"It's on my bucket list," Loki said.

"What's a bucket list?" she wrapped her hands around his.

"Oh, I forgot you're immortal. You don't need a bucket list. It's a list mortals like *me*—now that I'm officially a Minikin—have of the things they want to do before they die."

"What else do you have on your bucket list?"

"Saving a princess," Loki teased her.

"And sleeping in a coffin with her?" she joked.

"If she'll let me grow old with her, then it doesn't matter where I sleep next to her—of course, I know you'll never grow old."

"Even if she's a monster," Snow White sounded as if in pain. She was resisting hurting him and submitting to the darkness inside her. It made Loki remember when Carmilla looked at him in the dream, provoking the same unexplainable darkness inside him. "They say that all monsters have to die, you know," she continued.

"Except the beautiful ones," Loki held her tighter and closed his eyes. He knew that he'd sleep well tonight. As eerie as it seemed sleeping in the coffin, he didn't care. He was next to her, and her cold body gave him the warmest feeling he'd ever experienced.

As he slept he saw the two black sheep he'd been dreaming about. This time it was clear to him. One was Snow White and the other was him. They were the two outcasts who were going to make it through this world as long as they were together.

Hours later, Loki woke up to a screaming in the castle. He let out a sigh, wondering when he'd be able to wake up peacefully like ordinary people do. He wiped his eyes and noticed Snow White wasn't in the coffin anymore.

The screaming got louder downstairs.

"She's mad," Loki heard someone tell him. It was Nine, the cat. "Really mad," Nine bit his nails, his tail standing upright.

"What are you doing here?" Loki snapped.

"We like to follow you, in case you need our help," the squirrel said, standing behind the cat. It was looking with wide eyes toward the door leading downstairs where the screams came from. "She's really mad, and she's going to kill everyone downstairs."

"Who is mad?"

"Snow White," Nine said, trying to get the squirrel off his back.

"Move away," Loki was worried he'd step on them and ran to the door.

He stopped midway when the Schloss started shaking heavily all of a sudden. It wasn't the Schloss's anger this time, but the whales. It was shaking the whole island. Loki looked back at Nine and Mr. Squirrel for an explanation. They'd always seemed to know more than him.

"Part of the curse of eating a piece of the apple is that the whale will keep shaking the island madly until she feeds her darkness," Nine said.

"It's Carmilla's way of making sure Snow White stays cursed," Mr. Squirrel explained.

Loki didn't care much about the island or the curse. He was only worried about Snow White, knowing the kind of pain she was suffering.

"Loki," Nine and squirrel said in one breath as Loki rushed down the stairs. "Only you can save her. Do you understand? Only you can save her!" Mr. Squirrel stood up on Nine's shoulder in case Loki couldn't hear him.

Loki dashed downstairs, skipping steps as everything in the Schloss shook violently. Lamps flickered here and there as he caught a glimpse of the forest outside falling apart slowly through the vibrating windows.

As Loki came down the stairs he noticed someone fall from the second floor and land on the couch. It was a teenager. He was bleeding, but wasn't dead.

"What's going on?" Loki quickly reached the teenager and shook him by the shoulders.

"It's her, the vampire princess. She's got my girlfriend," the boy shrieked. "I didn't mean for this to happen. We were only curious and wanted to visit the Schloss. Please, I don't want to die."

"So you're a trespasser like all the other stupid teens?"

"I didn't believe the vampire princess existed. I'm a fool," the boy said. "My girlfriend came up with the idea after she met with Genius Goblin in the forum."

"You're an idiot, you know that?" Loki shook the boy harder, listening to his girlfriend's screams upstairs. He let go of the boy, wondering how he was going to stop Snow White from hurting her. "I swear I'm going to kick the Genius Goblin's ass one day."

Out of nowhere the boy's girlfriend fell from the second floor onto the couch as well.

"She's mad," the girl screamed hysterically. "We have to get out of here," she punched her boyfriend in her panic.

"Shhh," Loki shushed them both. "Don't you two dare move. If she sees you again she'll kill you. Let me take care of this. Did she bite you?"

"No," the girl sobbed. "It's like… it's like she wanted to but held back for some reason. But I'm sure she'll kill me if she sees me again," the girl started screaming again, shaking with her boyfriend on the rumbling couch.

"Get a hold of your girlfriend," Loki ordered the boy and turned around to go look for Snow White.

Loki found her gliding over the famous stairs again, looking as monstrous as when he'd first met her. Except that she was struggling in pain this time; she was struggling between giving in to Carmilla's curse and feeding on everyone around her or fighting back. She must have sensed the nosy teenagers sneak into the Schloss when he was asleep, and couldn't control her hunger. Then after catching them, she did her best not to bite them. Loki had to find a way to deal with her anger. He couldn't think of a greater pain than that which she was suffering.

The notable difference about her this time was that she was holding her apple-shaped necklace, which she usually wore. It was hanging at the end of a thin string dangling from her hand, wrapped smoothly around her fingers. The necklace looked like it had some kind of liquid inside it.

"Why don't you ever leave me be, Loki," she said with black eyes.

"I can't," Loki said. "It's not like I have control of it. Besides, you asked me to save you the first time we met, remember?" he climbed a step higher, gripping the banister tightly so he wouldn't lose balance.

"I'm cursed and I need to feed. If I don't feed now, the whale is going to sink Sorrow into the water and all will be lost," she said.

"I know," Loki nodded, taking another step. "You told me that your soul is bound to the island in some way."

"But I don't want to feed. I want to resist it," she said. "If I resist, the island will sink and everyone on it will die. If I feed, I will fully become one of them. I'll be letting the darkness inside surface, and I also don't want to do that."

"I understand. If you just let me up there, we can work this out together," Loki said.

"No, we can't," she growled. "You missed a lot of things you were supposed to understand in the dream. This is why I can't. I have to die so everyone else lives."

"I did my best in the dream. I don't think I missed anything. And you don't have to die," Loki shook his head. "You can't die, unless in a dream, and we're not in a dream right now."

"You're wrong," Snow White said, swinging the apple necklace like a pendulum in the air. "There is a potion inside this necklace, and if I take it willingly, I can kill myself. It was given to me centuries ago in case I became stuck in a situation like this."

"Wait," Loki stretched out his hand and stepped up. He had to stop though when she drew the potion closer to her mouth. "You survived two centuries against all of this and want to kill yourself now?"

"Is he talking to the vampire?" Loki heard the boy on the couch asking his girlfriend. "He's freakin' talking to the vampire."

"I guess it's my destiny, Loki, to eventually succumb to the poisonous apple. I'm Snow White after all."

"Did she say she's Snow White?" the girl said to her boyfriend on the couch. "Has she gone cuckoo in the head?"

"Don't do anything stupid," Loki said, the stairs shaking wilder. He had no idea what to do to save her. All he knew was that he wanted to be near her.

"I've waited for you so long, Loki," Snow White said. "I guess we're not meant to be. Who was I fooling? Our love is forbidden. Dhampir or not, I'm still a vampire, and you're a vampire hunter."

"No, it's not like that," Loki said. "I don't want to be a vampire hunter anymore. I want to be with you."

"I'm sorry but I have to die now," she said. "It's the only way you, the town and its people, will live, and ease my pain."

Snow White lifted the potion up, ready to drink it.

With a sudden surge of power, Loki jumped the steps, trying to pull the potion away. Instinctually, Snow White scratched her fingernails across the left side of Loki's neck. It was a deep scratch, and he bled instantly. He still didn't care. He grabbed Snow White by her shoulders as she screamed and flashed her fangs at him. She was cold as ice. Loki didn't know if he could hold her any longer. She was like an angry child who needed a big dose of tough love to calm her down.

Snow White snapped and sent Loki flying through the air like she had with Big Bad. Loki soared high into the air, lucky to grab the diamond chandelier before he dropped two floors and crashed onto the furniture below.

"Loki in the sky with diamonds," he mumbled to himself as he swung like a monkey from a tree.

"Leave me alone, Loki," Snow White used her powers and swung the chandelier harder. Loki lost his grip and fell onto the couch with the boy and his girlfriend.

"She's mad," the girl held Loki by his shirt, shaking him out of panic. "She will kill us all."

"Seriously," Loki grinned at her boyfriend. "When are you going to get a grip on your girlfriend?"

Loki stepped off the couch, walking back wanting another go at Snow White. He flashed his Alicorn at her, saying, 'Ora Pedora.'

The Alicorn's snake spiraled in the air as he was about to whip it at Snow White. "You know I like you and all," Loki said to Snow White. "But I think you need a little spanking."

Snow White snarled at him and pulled her potion closer. With a crack of the whip, the snake curled up in the air, and pulled the potion away from Snow White.

Snow White glided through the air and tried to grasp the potion, but the snake caught up to her, grabbed it with its mouth and clamped down on it, careful not to break the bottle. Snow White couldn't take it back. She became so enraged and screamed in such a high-pitched voice that windows crashed down from their frames.

"Gotcha!" Loki said with a big smile on his face.

Snow White spread her hands again, using her powers. Loki found himself losing his Alicorn to her invisible power, which caused another cut on his hand.

"You know this love-hate relationship isn't going to work, right?" Loki said.

"I'm going to kill you," she said, darkness filling her eyes. Her reaction scared Loki this time, but he decided to fight her—and for her—until the end. He didn't have a strong enough grip on her and she slipped through his hands.

The next time he wasn't going to let go of her. He gathered himself again and ran up the stairs one more time. Loki did it fast, without thinking. He slapped her hard on the face. It was out of fear. He was hoping she'd turn back to the normal girl he loved. As her head recoiled he saw the marks his fingers left on her pale cheek. "I'm sorry," he said.

Tangled and struggling together, it was obvious that only one of them was going to live. Either the princess was going to kill him and feed on him or he'd stake her and put her to sleep again. But Loki didn't want to stake her. He wanted to find a solution. He wanted a cure for her curse. The cure Carmilla dared him to find.

They both rolled down the stairs, Loki refusing to give up on her. He didn't know what he was going to do. It was like hanging onto a tiger who was about to slash him into pieces.

Finally, they hit the floor, Snow White landing on top of Loki.

She craned her head up, ready to sink her teeth into his neck. With all his might, Loki rolled her over. Even then, he knew he only had a fraction of a second before she used her powers and rolled him back again and killed him. She was angrier than he'd ever seen her. She wasn't in control of herself, and the whale was about to sink the island.

Loki felt electricity shoot through his body. It was a shocking chill running through his veins.

On impulse, he pushed her head back to the floor and forced his lips onto her hers and kissed her.

Time stopped.

Amazingly, Loki felt her body ease and soften. It even got warmer, miraculously buzzing back to life. Loki pressed his lips harder against hers, his eyes closed. He felt like she was sucking his life energy out of him. He didn't mind, even if he'd be a hundred years older when he opened his eyes again.

It was an enchanting feeling, very different from kissing Pippi Luvbug. Every breath Snow White took was Loki's now. Who'd have thought that the boy who didn't believe in a true love's kiss would find the cure in a *true love's kiss*?

He'd saved her, and saved the town, too.

Loki felt her chest rise up to his like two tides in the ocean meeting up, wrapping their waves around each other and finally finding the way back to shore. He pulled back, out of breath, and opened his eyes.

Snow White's blue eyes came back, shining with a ray of gold connecting their souls.

"I like a girl who knows when to kiss and when to kill," Loki told her.

She smiled, and he leaned down to kiss her again. No more forcing now. It was smooth like destiny, because it was meant to be.

"He's kissing the vampire," the boy said to the girl. "Gross."

"Shut up," the girl said. "She's so gorgeous. It's a true love's kiss. You wouldn't understand," the girl captured the moment with her phone's camera.

"Buzz off," Loki told them, annoyed by them spoiling the moment.

"Is that it, the cure for Carmilla's curse?" Snow White said with glittering stars filling her eyes. "A kiss? All my suffering ends with a single kiss?"

"Not any kiss," Loki mused. "A Loki Blackstar kiss."

"I don't feel like I need to feed anymore. Can you believe this? All I needed was a kiss?" she sighed. "You're really slow, Loki. You know that, right?"

"I know," he nodded. "I should've kissed you the first night I saw you."

Mr. Squirrel and Nine came running up to them. Mr. Squirrel wiggled his nose and clapped his hands. Loki knew they weren't going to talk in front of Snow White. They only talked to him when he was alone.

He looked back at Snow White and brushed a lock of her hair back. "It's always the kiss," he said. "Charmwill tried to tell that to me many times, but I was too blind to see. I can't believe I've wasted sixteen years of my life without you."

28

The Dreamhunter

When the daylight laid its caring eyes gently upon the Schloss, Loki's phone beeped. It was a message from Lucy:

Comin' for breakfast? Axel and Fable want to introduce you to their foster mother. She's really cool.

Loki messaged back with a 'yes.'

He asked Snow White to join him but she didn't feel like going. She was tired from all that had happened, and Loki discovered she didn't feel like she was going to be able to meet people easily. It turned out that spending one hundred years in a castle made her a little introverted. Now that she was cured, she didn't know how to face the world. Regular people and real life was sometimes tougher and scarier than demons and monsters.

Loki tried to explain to her that she'd love Axel and Fable—especially Fable—but she seemed to prefer being alone for a while. She didn't mind him visiting his friends who'd helped him save her. She had also wanted to search the Schloss for lost manuscripts, pictures, or anything that could help her begin her journey as a Dhampir. She hadn't been cured to live a normal life. She was the chosen one, and soon she'd be battling the Queen of Sorrow's demons and vampires.

"I won't be long," Loki kissed her. "I might bring them back with me, and then I think you have a lot to explain to me. We both know that saving you is only the start of something bigger."

Snow White nodded agreeably, but reluctantly. She still had that look in her eyes that said she couldn't tell him everything for some reason.

"Loki," Snow White summoned him back, standing at the castle's threshold.

"Yes?" he turned around.

"I'm afraid this is all a dream," she said as a morning breeze passed through her hair.

"It's not," Loki said licking his lips. "If you don't believe me, ask your lips."

"But we fell in love in a dream," she laughed as Pickwick landed on her shoulder. Loki had ordered him to stay with her until he came back.

"And it came true," he spread his arms. "What more can I ask for?"

Loki walked back through the forest and then drove his car to the Candy House. He bought flowers on the way so he'd make an impression. Now that Charmwill had died, Loki thought a woman like Mircalla, Axel and Fable's foster mother, would hopefully be someone they could all look up to and reply on for help. The Crumblewoods had been telling him great things about the woman who took care of them.

On his way, The Pumpkin Warriors played 'Eye of the Tiger' on the radio. Loki tried convincing them that it wasn't the appropriate song for the occasion, but they didn't listen. His phone rang before he reached the Candy House. It was Lucy.

"I'm on my way," Loki said after picking up.

"That's not why I'm calling you," she said. "I've been thinking about the story you told us all last night."

"And?"

"I don't buy that Carmilla is evil. Something's wrong," she explained. "I mean after all she did, running away with the man she loved, giving him her blood, sacrificing everything for her daughter, how could she turn into this evil monster so easily? It just doesn't make sense."

"You don't understand, Lucy," Loki said. "You haven't seen the Queen of Sorrow. You wouldn't stand a minute before her. She'll kill you, cook you, and eat you alive. She killed Charmwill and I'm going to avenge him one day, so don't go on trying to make me think she's not evil. Talking about her right now already makes me uncomfortable—why do you even care?"

"Because she's the only one that interests me in your story," Lucy said.

Knowing Lucy, Loki could understand why Lucy was infatuated with the powerful Queen. He didn't expect her to sympathize with Snow White at all. To Lucy, the Queen was an idol who controlled her own life, took what she wanted and did it her way.

"Lucy," Loki said. "I've been through a lot. Let's talk about this later. I'm almost home."

"You better be here soon. Axel says that he found something about Carmilla in history books from Bedtime Stoories."

"How so?" Loki's eyes twitched.

"It turns out that the oldest female vampire mentioned in those so called vampire novels is named Carmilla."

"Did Axel say that?" Loki said. Most of Axel's research turned out to be right before so Loki had no reason to doubt him.

"Yes. Carmilla Karnstein," Lucy empathized.

Loki almost lost the wheel for a moment.

"Her tale is called, 'Carmilla', part of an anthology called 'In a Glass Darkly.' "It was written in 1872," Lucy said. "It's partially a novel, but with a lot of history references."

"What does that mean?"

"How should I know," Lucy said. She sounded in love with Carmilla. "I haven't understood most of the things you said about fairy tale characters being real, but if they are, why wouldn't Carmilla be this woman mentioned in the book. Maybe the author of this book was trying to tell the world something about her."

Loki's head ached again. Now that Charmwill was dead, he had no one to ask about such things. But he remembered that he had Pickwick. Maybe that's why Charmwill asked him to take care of the invaluable bird. Was it the right decision to leave the parrot with Snow White? Loki didn't know. But no worries, he was only having breakfast with his friends and their foster mother, and then he'd drive back to Snow White and get Pickwick. Maybe Snow White knew something about the novel.

"Listen, Lucy," Loki said. "We're not going to talk about any of this in front of Axel and Fable's foster mom. Once we have our little introduction, we'll all head back to the Schloss and find out what's going on."

"Deal," Lucy said. "I am so fascinated with the Queen. I can't wait to find out more about her story."

Loki hung up and drove to Candy House. When he arrived, he parked his car in front of Axel's house. The smell of food baking in the morning was enchanting. Mircalla must have been a great cook; he doubted Fable cooked this good.

"Loki," Fable came running out of the house and jumped in his arms. Loki held her up with her feet in the air. "Tell me all about it," she whispered in his ear. "Was it romantic?"

"In spite of a little blood, poison, and a whale about sinking Sorrow, I'd say it was romantic."

"So the whale shaking the island yesterday, that was you and Snow White?" she said. "You have to tell me everything."

"Easy with my sis, dude," Axel barked at Loki, standing with folded hands, leaning against the doorframe. His mouth formed into an unsure smile.

"What's with the squirrel?" Lucy pushed Axel away as she came out to the front porch.

Loki looked at the squirrel following him, this time without Nine, the cat. "He's nuts," Loki waved his hand. He was teasing it.

The squirrel ran directly at Lucy and climbed her leg up to her neck, then sat on her shoulder. Lucy fidgeted and cursed and tried to push it away.

"Someone's in love at first sight," Loki said, entering the house with Axel and Fable.

Fable showed Loki the way to the dining table, which looked so lovely and family-like. The house had been cleaned and filled with roses. This Mircalla was such a neat woman. Loki thought she should stay with the Crumblewoods all year.

"Mircalla did all of this," Fable said, enthusiastically ushering Loki to the head of the table. "You'll love her. We told her about all the adventures. She believed us and promised to help."

"I shouldn't sit at the head of the table," Loki said. "What about Mircalla?"

"She'll sit opposite to you," Fable explained, sitting down, trying her best to act like an elegant princess at an expensive dining table.

Lucy sat on Loki's right, opposite to Fable, and Axel sat next to Lucy, of course.

There was a red placemat next to each plate on the table. They were fancy and made of red cloth.

"Pretty fancy," Loki remarked.

"Loki, Loki, Loki," Lucy said, as she spread a napkin on his lap. "It's called etiquette. You need to use your manners when you eat with your family. Get used to it."

Fable covered a laugh with her tiny hands.

"If you say so," Loki said.

"Kids," a voice called from inside. Everyone sat straight in their chairs, making sure they had the napkins placed on their laps. "Are we ready?" the lovely voice asked, making Loki eager to meet her.

The smell of roasted turkey was approaching.

"Yep," Axel mumbled, not happy with all of this tidiness. "Do we really have to use these napkins?"

"Shut up," Lucy hit him on the leg slightly. Axel looked happy, almost buzzing. "You're such a Barbarian," she said with disgust. He looked even happier now.

"We're ready, Mircalla," Fable said. "Loki's here, too."

Loki saw the silhouette of a woman with long hair coming from the kitchen. She was wearing an apron, and holding a roasted turkey in her hands, reminding him of when his mother was there.

She came into the room smiling. But the glaring sun prevented Loki from making out her other features. He saw her silhouette sitting down, the sun still too bright for him to see her.

"Hello, Loki," she said.

A cloud blocked the glaring sunrays outside for a moment, and Loki was finally able to see Mircalla's face.

It took him some time to understand who he was looking at, and then a shriek almost burst his lungs open.

The muscles in Loki's face drooped from the unpleasant surprise. His features changed from cheerful to terrified. His heart raced and he felt a chilling tingle in his spine. He was choking. He wanted to scream but couldn't. His fear took over.

Dazed and confused, Loki rested his hands on the table. Then the placemat frayed by itself into long red threads, looking exactly like his Fleece, the one he'd lost in the dream. With his eyes still glued to Mircalla, the threads crawled like thin, mad snakes all over his body, tying him to the chair then weaving a spider's web on his lips, zipping his mouth shut.

The snaky thread started growing needle-like tips, piercing through his flesh, and entering his veins.

Loki couldn't utter a word. He couldn't think straight. He could only hear his friends screaming. Shifting his eyes, he saw they were tied to their chairs too. But their mouths hadn't been sealed.

"Oh. My. God." Fable screamed, pointing at Mircalla, finally realizing who she really was. "It's you?"

"All this time, how didn't we know?" Axel said, as his jaw dropped. *Mircalla!* Loki thought to himself. How did he miss that? Mircalla was another name for the scariest person he'd ever met; only the letters were scrambled. It was an anagram for Carmilla, the Queen of Sorrow's real name. She'd planned this all along, fooling Axel and Fable into thinking she was a good foster parent, and that she cared for them. If Axel and Fable were Hansel and Gretel like Charmwill had hinted, then why did Carmilla raise them? Did she kill their parents? What were her plans in all of this?

Loki watched the deceivingly beautiful Queen sit down in her chair, dressed in a modern day outfit, capable of fooling the world. She was the epitome of calmness, intending to eat her meal like nothing happened.

"Now that Charmwill Glimmer is dead, I'd like to tell you a little fairy tale," she said to Loki. Her words came out smoothly and slowly, taking all the time she needed to stress on every syllable. She was in no hurry. She'd fooled them all and knew she had the upper hand. "This one is a true fairy tale," she added, watching each one carefully.

Loki tried to talk, but his mouth was still sewn shut.

The Queen unfolded a napkin and rested it on her lap then grabbed a knife and fork. She checked to make sure they were clean and glinting, and then she started slicing the meat in front of her with delicate and accurate precision. She did it as if she were sculpting a masterpiece of meat then she started telling her tale.

"Once upon a time, about two centuries ago, a king called Angel Night von Sorrow was at war with evil vampires threatening to take his daughter from him in an attempt to make her one of them," Carmilla started, her eyes focused on cutting the food. "In his quest for recruiting the best warriors, and because he was loved by the Council of Fairy Heaven for rivaling his own kind, the Council sent him young warriors from Fairy Heaven; powerful warriors who had the gift of killing vampires in their dreams. They were called Dreamhunters, and they helped the king a great deal. He'd even ordered a few of them to protect the castle and the princess in his absence. Who better than angels to watch over his little chosen princess?" the Queen smirked at her own sentence, and then sank her knife into the meat again. "Only one of the Dreamhunters was different; he wasn't pure like the rest. He had great darkness buried in him. The kind of beautiful darkness only the Queen was able to detect. She'd recently transformed into a vampire and killed young girls to preserve her beauty—she was horrid," Carmilla rolled her eyes. "It turned out the boy's father, a pure angel, had fallen in love with a demon woman who'd given birth to the boy about fifteen years earlier. The Queen liked that. She taught the boy the ways of darkness and let him lead an evil army for her own purposes. Although young, the boy became her most formidable and scariest weapon."

Loki moaned, wanting to talk. In his frustration, he kicked the table to get Carmilla's attention. He wanted to dare her to look him in the eyes.

Carmilla raised her head and looked at him. "Ah, you want to talk?" she said. "Not unless I say so," she poured herself a drink and cleaned the rim of the glass with the tips of her fingers. "One day, the Queen sent the Dreamhunter to kill her own daughter—she was a big threat to the Queen. To prove that he'd killed the princess, the Dreamhunter had to bring the Queen her daughter's heart, which the Queen planned on eating," Carmilla picked a ripe, heart shaped, piece of meat and placed it slowly on her tongue. Loki thought she'd show her forked tongue now, but she didn't. She closed her eyes and moaned briefly as she chewed on the meat. "Disappointingly," she opened her eyes slowly the way a theatre pulls its curtains open for the final act, "the Dreamhunter fell in love with the princess, although she was partially a demon herself. He refused to kill her, defying me and the Council of Fairy Heaven."

Loki's face was getting redder with every passing moment. He was about to explode, trying to destroy the spider web sealing his mouth.

"You know what else the Dreamhunter did?" Carmilla wiped her lips with the tip of the napkin, then folded it and placed it carefully back on the table. "Not only did he disobey the Queen's orders, but he continued helping the runaway princess. Together, they were able to find the annoying Charmwill Glimmer to help them with an enchantment that split the princess' heart into seven tiny hearts. She gave seven of her friends she met in the cottage in the Dark Forest, each a piece of her heart. A nifty trick. This way the Queen not only had to find her escaping daughter, but she also had to find her daughter's friends, whom she called the Lost Seven. Without finding the Lost Seven and collecting the pieces of Snow White's heart from them, she couldn't kill the princess—The Queen desperately wanted her daughter's heart, because it had been foretold that only one of them could live."

Loki's eyes moistened as his memories slowly returned to him.

"Although the Queen was never able to catch her daughter or the Dreamhunter, the Council of Heaven, was fooled into believing that the princess was the bad seed and shadowed the Dreamhunter as punishment for falling in love with her," Carmilla loved every word coming out of her lips, and loved her voice. "Until that annoying Charmwill unshadowed the Dreamhunter. You know the story from there, right Loki?"

Loki felt like fainting as the shocking news sunk into his brain and he began having visions of the past. This time, the vision was extremely vivid. He saw Snow White running scared from her pursuer, hiking up the bottom of her dress as she ran, so not to fall, trying to find a place to hide in. He saw her come upon a cottage and stop in front of it reluctantly, before she opened the door and walked in.

"It's a well-known fairy tale, if you ask me, only some versions might differ a little," Carmilla said, leaning forward toward Loki, "because some would call the Dreamhunter a Huntsman."

"No!" Fable screamed, trying to free her tied hands. She knew where this conversation was going, but couldn't believe it. "You're lying. Loki is a good guy."

The Queen shushed her by snapping two fingers together. Fable's mouth was sewn shut instantly. Axel and Lucy exchanged looks; they weren't going to utter a word no matter what.

"You wanted to know who you really are, Loki. You wanted to know why you were banned, and who the girl was. More importantly, you wanted to know about the darkness you had inside of you," Carmilla leaned back now, crossing her legs. "Here are all the answers you wanted. You're simply *the* Huntsman. Always were, always will be."

As for Loki, he longed to scream. But he didn't need to. His moist eyes, filled with horror, showed how shocked he was.

The dizziness hit him again, and the flashes returned. This time he recognized that he was the one chasing Snow White, and that she'd been running scared from *him*. Loki was the Huntsman, the dark warrior Charmwill had warned him not to look at in the Dreamworld. Loki had been running away from himself in the dream; running away from the evil inside him. That was why Snow White had that look in her eyes as if she wanted to tell him something but couldn't. That was why she'd always asked him to cross the oceans in his mind and read between the lines in the dream.

Now, he knew where the darkness in him came from, why Charmwill had preferred Loki live with the Minikins and never revert to who he was before. It was like he was two people; one evil, one good, and he had to find a way to make the good one prevail against the dark one.

What exactly happened two centuries ago, Loki wondered. Did falling in love with Snow White change him into a better person? How did he change from a dark Huntsman to the boy he is now? It drove Loki mad.

"Why do you think I let you get away with my daughter in the Dreamworld?" the Queen of Sorrow said. "Yes, it's true that I was occupied with killing Charmwill Glimmer and that I forced her to bite the

270

apple. But I let you go because no matter where you go, you can't run away from me," she pulled out the Fleece and rolled it slowly over her fingers, one by one.

When Loki tried to resist, she pulled the Fleece tight around her finger, causing him to choke. When she pulled the Fleece through her fingers, the thin threads that had entered his body pinched him from inside.

"I own you now, Loki Blackstar. You know why? Because I have your Fleece, which is similar to a Dreamhunter's soul," Carmilla said, toying with the Fleece. "Now you're working for me again. You're my Huntsman and you will do whatever I say. I've got a lot of work to do in this town so I can find the Lost Seven before my daughter finds them. And you will help me enter each one's dream," she shifted her eyes towards the others. "I'd appreciate it if all of you'd cooperate and welcome your new school principal and the town's Chairwoman," she pointed at herself, and then looked back at Loki.

In Loki's mind, he'd decided whose side he was on. It didn't matter if he were the Huntsman. It didn't matter if he had great evil inside him. He was going to fight the Queen of Sorrow no matter what.

Carmilla stood up and turned around to cut up fruit on the counter. While she had her back to them, they thought they heard her mumble something, but couldn't decipher it. It seemed like she was talking to herself in a much calmer and softer voice. Lucy thought she'd heard Carmilla sob briefly as if she held a great secret she couldn't expose, and wondered if this was another side of the Queen they hadn't seen. Everyone else thought it was one of the Queen's tricks.

"Evil is nothing but a point of view," Lucy heard the Queen say to herself quietly while she was cutting the apples.

Although he could see her slightly shaking, Loki didn't buy into the Queen's solitary emotional moment. He thought it was the perfect time to free himself while her back was turned. He kicked the chair harder, trying to stand up, reach for his Alicorn and kill her.

"Tsk Tsk," Carmilla said, wiggling her warning forefinger as if she had eyes in the back of her head. She continued slicing the apples she was about to bring to the table. Her voice had changed back to the demanding Queen who must be obeyed.

Loki and his friends exchanged clueless looks.

The Queen of Sorrow picked up the dissected apples and other fruits from a basket and turned around, staring intently at Loki with her yellow snake eyes. Then she said her favorite words to Loki, "Peekaboo," she pointed her forefinger and middle finger at Loki's eyes and then back at her own, "I see you."

End of Snow White Sorrow
The Grimm Diaries book one

271

Next book will be
Cinderella Dressed in Ashes

For further reading in the series until book two comes out, you could read the prequels, (that's if you haven't read them yet). The Grimm Diaries prequels are short diaries written by each character about this world. It will give you more insight into the story, but they aren't necessary for reading Cinderella Dressed in Ashes. Links for the prequels are provided in the next pages after the glossary and afterword.

Don't forget to check the glossary and the Author's notes

Snow White Sorrow's
Glossary

Loki Blackstar: a sixteen year old Dreamhunter, presumably the best, is part good and part evil, and is one of the few in the world who can kill Demortals in their dreams.

Snow White (Shew): the Dhampir chosen girl, prophesized to rid the world of all fairy tale vampires and Demortals. Escaping the Queen two centuries ago, she used an enchantment and split her heart between her seven friends so the queen can never consume it.

Fabulous Crumblewood (Fable): Axel's sister, lives in Candy House, and is trying to prove she isn't a lousy witch like her mom. She is very sweet and loves people passionately, but should be avoided when she gets mad. She is a wanna-be witch and it's presumed she is Gretel.

Axel Crumblewood: presumably Hansel. Loves to eat, and believes Loki is his best friend. Has a crush on Lucy. He would only die for his sister, though.

Carmilla Karnstein (The Queen of Sorrow): Snow White's mother, Queen of the Kingdom of Sorrow. She has a lot of secrets of her own, but she mainly wants to find the Lost Seven so she can consume her daughter's heart.

Charmwill Glimmer: Loki's guardian who unshadowed him for mysterious reasons. He loves his pipe and has many powers, one of them being a Dreamhunter himself. He protects his Book of Beautiful Lies for life. He also has a big secret of his own.

Lucette Rumpelstein (Lucy): Rumpelstein's daughter. Spoiled, rich, and obnoxious. She changes boyfriends about every week, and doesn't hold back telling you if you suck. Loki suspects her true intentions. Fable doesn't like her although she admires how 'in your face' she is. Lucy admires the

Queen of Sorrow greatly.

Babushka: Loki's Russian mother. She's a ghost, and was the reason Loki's father was banned from Fairy Heaven after falling in love with her. No one knows what her real story is. Loki suspects she only appears when someone lights a cigarette around him. She's trying her best to be a good scary ghost.

Angel Night Sorrow: Snow White's father, and King of Sorrow. Escaped his own father and vampire clan to stay a half-vampire. He fell in love with Carmilla and would die to protect his daughter. No one knows what really happened to him two centuries ago.

Pickwick the Parrot: Charmwill's mute parrot, enchanted as the Book of Beautiful Lies, holding the true and untold fairy tales within him. He opens up to a knock on his beak: *tic-to-tic-tac-toc*.

Nine: a cat, one of Loki's talking animal friends. He usually just wants to sleep somewhere warm.

Mr. Squirrel: apparently a squirrel; he was saved by Loki repeatedly, and he loves him dearly and usually follows him for no reason. He'd shown some interest in Lucy lately.

Igor the Magnificent: a shadowy hunchback who asked Loki to come to Sorrow to kill the vampire princess. Usually annoying, has three eyes, and they're all blind.

Georgie Porgie: leader of Boogeymen. Looks evil but has a heart of a child, and can't scare babies, which is his job. Although Loki and his friends liked him, he didn't help him or stand up for them. Georgie can't help them so he wouldn't expose his weakness to his Boogeymen peeps.

Cry Baby: another boogeyman led by Georgie, always loses at the Baby Tears drinking competition.

Ulfric Moonclaw: leader of the Bullyvards, Lucy's boyfriend, hates Loki's guts. Oh, and he is a werewolf.

Big Bad: literally the Big Bad Wolf, huge, has a big chest to help him puff and huff, hated Loki and his friends, has an Elvis haircut and long sideburns, and loves to play 'Pig or Sheep'

Paw Paw: just as bad as Big Bad, only he has tattoos and earrings.

Managarm: a wolf who pulls the Queen of Sorrow's Pumpkin-shaped carriage. He hates the moon and loves chasing it in the sky.

Night Sorrow: the King of Vampires, kills ruthlessly, and would do anything to kill the Dhampir girl.

Bloody Mary: a mysterious girl in a mirror who terrorizes young people. She works for the Queen of Sorrow. In many ways, she messes with her majesty's mind.

Train of Consequences: a spooky train that you have to ride when it's your first time entering Sorrow. You don't pay for a ticket to ride it. You pay in consequences.

Carmen: Loki's devoted car. She's a red 1955 Coupe Deville. She plays music by dead bands that might have never existed according to the atmosphere and what's going on around her.

The Pumpkin Warriors: one of Loki's favorite bands. They like to talk to him and give him a hard time when he cops out. Oh, and you can hear them snoring in the radio when they're asleep.

Pippi Luvbug: she liked Loki a lot in Snoring, but turned out to be a demon. Charmwill killed her but it's not guaranteed she won't come back.

Donnie Cricketkiller, Beebully, and Beetlebuster: Loki calls them The Three Blind Mice. They're vampire hunter rivals who used to bully him in Snoring. Snow White did Loki a favor and killed Donnie in the cellar.

The Tweedle Girls. Dee and Dum, according to Axel, were friends of Big Bad. They lived a very short life.

Itsy and Bitsy: Fable's favorite spiders. One is depressed because he was in love, and he hates Axel, the other is too small to be depressed, he helped Babushka with cooking.

Godmother Justina: blind mother of justice in the Fairyworld. She has troubles with her scale. Snakes always outweigh apples, but she's still trying. Her intentions are that everyone sees justice, although she is blind herself.

The Brothers Grimm: for some reason, they forged the fairy tales and cursed the fairy tale characters into a Sleeping Death. Their names are Jacob and Wilhelm, and they will appear soon.

The Mermaids: they like to welcome everyone in the Missing Mile, giggle, and splash water. They thought Loki was really cute.

The Whale: is practically the island of Sorrow. No one knows how long he'll stay put before he rolls over.

Genius Goblin: creator of the Harum Scarum forum, dedicated to tracking the vampire princess. Loki swears he's going to kick his ass one day.

J.G.: writer of the diary Axel found in the library.

V.H.: wrote most of the articles in the Dreamhunter's notebook.

Belly and Beast Menu:

Although they have a huge menu, so far we saw Axel and Fable eat the following:

Sticky Sweet Bones: you have to lick the sweets before you eat the bones.

Tragic Beans: they will eventually make you cry and laugh in the same time.

Coffinmuffins: don't eat the carrot in the muffin.

Poisoned Apples: kinda gets you high. Because they're so delicious, you pass out for a minute and then you wake alright. You can grab yourself another one then.

Cinderella Mozzarella: Axel likes these but he hasn't talked about them yet.

Reluctant Jelly: hard to get a grip on.

Places and other things

Snoring: a very boring town in the Ordinary World that has vampires. Loki used to live there. Locals like to call it the Great Snoring. Founder: Snoring von Boring the II.

Hell: a number of towns in America that probably all serve as a portal to Sorrow. There are no towns called Heaven.

Sorrow: an island on the back of a whale where many fairy tale characters live. Very few know that it's surrounded by the Missing Mile on all sides. Two hundred years ago, it used to be the Kingdom of Sorrow.

The Missing Mile: an endless sea surrounding Sorrow. It's only visible to a few people, and it holds many secrets of the Fairy World.

Dragonbreath: what Charmwill smokes in his pipe. Smoking it isn't easy. It lets him breathe out fire sometimes.

Alicorn: Loki's special weapon given to him by his mother. It's a unicorn's horn. Someday, Loki intends to find the unicorn and give it back.

Sesame: a fortune cookie that Loki used to make his decisions for him.

Wondersack: given to Loki by Charmwill. It holds a lot of useful instruments in it.

Waker: an hourglass that can be adjusted to the Dreamhunter's liking. It times how long one stays in the Dreamworld. Once the sand falls through, the dream ends.

Incubator: a word that if whispered into the dreamer's ear, lets them remember a certain dream or memory where the dream should take place.

Ariadne Fleece: a ball of red thread that connects the Dreamhunter with the real world while in the Dreamworld. It's almost considered the Dreamhunter's soul. Owning it is owning him.

Magic Dust: makes you sleep. Some people are allergic to it, and it makes them laugh. It is very useful with bullies.

Books of Sands: books that dissolve into dust one page at a time once you read them.

Dreamhunter's notebook: a notebook used to learn Dreamhunting, most of the pages are written by a V.H.

J.G.'s diary: a diary Axel found in the library. It probably belongs to Jacob Carl Grimm.

Sleeping Death: a condition where someone is cursed to sleep forever, it's also used as a term meaning when someone is in a dream and their body is inanimate as if in a coma.

Dreamory: a dream that is based on the dreamer's memory

The Dreamworld: the place where all Fairy Tale characters live and fairy tales take place.

Jawigi: the Brothers Grimm secret word to enter the Dreamworld.

Epidaurus Circle: the circle that encompasses the two mirrors, the dreamer and the Dreamhunter inside.

Dream Temple: everything inside the Epidaurus Circle.

Enchanta (Chanta for short): only Loki's mom and Charmwill know what it really is. But Loki was sort of able to use it.

Obol coins: used on the eyes of the dreamer so they can't connect the Dream World with the waking world.

Ora Pedora: an incantation Loki uses to make his Alicorn work

Swamp of Sorrow: a swamp in Sorrow that you have to cross to get to the Black Forest. Skeliman used to be the ferryman there. If you don't like frogs, don't go there.

The Belly and the Beast: best place to eat in Sorrow. Sticky Sweet Bones and Tragic Beans are said to be the best. The menu is much bigger though.

Buried Moon Cemetery: myth has it that the real moon is buried there.

The Schloss: the castle where Snow White was imprisoned. It was also the Sorrow's royal family's residence two centuries ago. It appears when it wants to. It also has a bad temper. You don't want to go there, at least not with Axel.

Juniper Trees: spying trees that have eyes.

Rumpelstein High: the only high school in Sorrow, owned by the mysterious Mr. Rumpelstein. It's at 1812, in the neighborhood of Nefilheim.

Bedtime Stoories: you'd say it's misspelled but the school thinks it's a unique name for a library that has dark corridors that lead to another library where you can find un-forged books.

Candy House: where Axel and Fable live. It's an awesome house. In case you would like to visit, it's at Seven Breadcrumb Street.

The Black Forest: a dark forest where Snow White was born and nothing is as it seems.

The Children of Hamlin: the kids Charmwill was reading to in the beginning. There's a lisping girl, a gapped-tooth girl, and adventurous boy. Don't make fun of them. They're going to be badass at some point.

Santa Claus: Charmwill doesn't think it's cool that he enters houses without permission, but they seem to be good friends, too.

The Vampire in Forks: the vampire Loki killed and was resurrected. People say he appears in the twilights.

Dork Dracula: he's not a dork at all.

The students dressed as The Wicked Witch of the West, Robin Hood, Prince Charming, Cinderella, and the Bunny Girl: they're all dead now.

Don't bother

Murder house at 112 Ocean View: It's the Amityville Horror house's addressed. Loki didn't know that, but everyone died in that party, so forget about it.

Jeanette and Amalie Hassenpflug: Angel's fake parents. They were vampire slaves but they managed to escape and never be seen again. They are the true tellers of Snow White's fairy tale. The Brothers Grimm collected the story from them.

The Closet: a hangout for Boogeymen

Baby Tears: what Boogeymen live for

Spooky Woogy Boo: the proper way to salute a Boogeyman. You can say, 'that's so boo' if you see something cool as well.

Awooo: the annoying way to summon the Bullyvards/werewolf friends.

The Bullyvards: bad dudes who hurt other students, mostly werewolves. Loki loves to kick their asses, but then he has to run.

Jolly Roger: the pirate ship that attacked Angel and Carmilla. Some say it's led by a man called Captain Hook.

Styria: the home of the Karnsteins.

Dhampir: in Slavic folklore, it's a vampire who is born of one human and one vampire parent. It has the power to kill all vampires in the world and is stronger than a regular vampire.

Abe Noxious: Sorrow's most famous tattoo artist.

Lohr: a town in Germany that seems to be the family's origin. It has a caste called the Schloss, and a mysterious history. It's a true town, like almost everything above. Some people just don't know it.

Minikins: every one who is not a fairy tale character.

Skeliman the Ferryman (sometimes the Libraryman): although he's not a place, we decided to mention him here, because we're not sure if he's even real. No one knows if he's a myth, but he scared the skeletons out of Axel, and seems to appear every in the Harum Scarum forum. Hopefully, Loki and his friends will meet him someday.

Author's Notes:

For the lovely readers who have read The Grimm Diaries Prequels, you might expect to read a lot of notes in this book. Although Snow White Sorrow is full of allusions and secrets, I'd prefer they'd be revealed slowly through the rest of the series. I didn't want to add a lot of notes and spoil the fun of rereading or discovering them by the readers themselves. So I am only going to mention some facts that don't spoil anything for the fun of it. I hope you like them:

- The Vampire Craze did happen. People were killed and tortured when they were only ill but thought of as vampires.
- Towns called 'Hell' exist everywhere in the world.
- The Great Snoring is the name of a real town, too.
- Lohr is the name of a real town in Germany. If you visit it one day, you'll see how it's related to Snow White. It feels like a small fairy tale location. It's real fun.
- The Schloss is a real castle. It's located in Lohr, but it's not that evil in real life—or is it?
- There is no such thing as Sticky Sweet Bones—unless you live in Sorrow, of course.
- The disease that people mistook for vampirism in ancient times was cured by ingesting blood into the liver. This is a true fact. When it was discovered, people thought it was a way of resurrecting those they thought of as vampires so they decided to destroy the liver with the heart to make sure the 'vampire' wouldn't get resurrected.
- Jeanette and Amalie Hassenpflug are the original tellers of the Snow White fairy tale.
- Jacob and Wilhelm Grimm did release the original story of Snow White with the Evil Queen being her mother. They changed it fifty years later, in 1857, to a stepmother. No one knows why for sure.
- In one of Cinderella's original versions, the pigeons did pick out her evil stepsister's eyes. Actually, more horrible things happened to their mother.
- Almost all original fairy tales were filled with gore and blood.
- Prince Charming never kissed Snow White in any original version. This is also, a fact.
- Snow White woke up when the piece of apple was pulled out of her throat in the original version.
- The Sleeping Death is true, and it was mentioned by the Brothers Grimm in the Snow White story.
-The 'Follow Your Bliss' phrase is dedicated to the memory of Joseph Campbell, a great mythologist, and a greater inspiration to me.

Afterword

I hope you did enjoy reading Snow White Sorrow as much as I enjoyed researching and writing it. If you have the time and could kindly review the novel, that'd be awesome. You have no idea how much this means to me.

An honest review helps me learn and improve as an Indie storyteller. I also answer all emails sent to me if there is something you want to ask me.

And if you're interested to know the latest news about the series, explanations, discussion, and want to be the first to know about Cinderella Dressed in Ashes' release date, please join my Facebook page http://www.facebook.com/camjace.
Thanks again and wish you all a new and awesome year. You can contact me at
Goodreads
or
Facebook
or
my blog
or
Twitter
@cameronjace
or send me an email
camjace@hotmail.com
(I answer all emails personally)

List of Cameron Jace other books in
the Grimm Diaries:

The Grimm Diaries Prequels 1- 6

The Grimm Diaries Prequels 7- 10

The Grimm Diaries Prequels 11- 14

Other books by Cameron Jace in the
I AM ALIVE series:
The I Am Alive series:

I Am Alive volume 1-3: Nice Day to Die, Wheel of Fortune, Through Your Eyes (Ya Dystopian series)

Oh, One More Thing…
When you turn the page, Kindle will give you the opportunity to express your thoughts on Facebook and Twitter automatically. If you enjoyed my book, would you take a second to click that button and let your

friends know about it? If they get something out of the book, they'll be grateful to you. As I will!